**"Secure the area," T'Pol ordered the MACOs via
her suit's transceiver.**

Sergeant Guitierrez and Corporal O'Malley were already
in motion, their helmet lights illuminating the crippled
vessel's interior. They moved in opposite directions down
an extensively battle-damaged corridor. As T'Pol's sensitive
Vulcan eyes began to adjust to the low light levels, she
noticed a number of blackened rents in the exterior walls.

Stars and the damaged exterior were discernible
through the breaches. She shuddered slightly, chilled by
the knowledge of the fate that had befallen anyone in this
corridor when the hull had torn open. As T'Pol trained
her helmet lamp toward her feet, she saw that she was
standing on the remnants of a leg. Lifting her foot, she
saw a humanoid form. Its eyes, or at least the four of them
she could see arranged about its bulbous head, were easily
five times the size of those of a Vulcan, and the distal
appendages of its four upper limbs were entwined with the
gridwork of the bent, twisted deck plates beneath it.

— STAR TREK —
ENTERPRISE®
THE ROMULAN WAR
TO BRAVE THE STORM

MICHAEL A. MARTIN

Based upon *Star Trek*®
created by Gene Roddenberry
and *Star Trek: Enterprise*
created by Rick Berman & Brannon Braga

POCKET BOOKS
New York London Toronto Sydney New Delhi ShiKahr

Pocket Books
A Division of Simon & Schuster, Inc.
1230 Avenue of the Americas
New York, NY 10020

This book is a work of fiction. Names, characters, places, and incidents either are products of the author's imagination or are used fictitiously. Any resemblance to actual events or locales or persons, living or dead, is entirely coincidental.

First Pocket Books paperback edition November 2011

POCKET and colophon are registered trademarks of Simon & Schuster, Inc.

For information about special discounts for bulk purchases, please contact Simon & Schuster Special Sales at 1-866-506-1949 or business@simonandschuster.com.

The Simon & Schuster Speakers Bureau can bring authors to your live event. For more information or to book an event, contact the Simon & Schuster Speakers Bureau at 1-866-248-3049 or visit our website at www.simonspeakers.com.

Cover art by Doug Drexler

Manufactured in the United States of America

10 9 8 7 6 5 4 3

ISBN 978-1-4516-0715-4
ISBN 978-1-4516-0724-6 (ebook)

For my wife, Jenny, and my sons, James and William.

We are about to brave the storm in a skiff made of paper.
—John Hancock (1737–1793)

War is not the best way of settling differences; it is the only way of preventing their being settled for you.
—G. K. Chesterton (1874–1936)

HISTORIAN'S NOTE

The bulk of this story takes place during the period spanning June 22, 2156 (ACE), the aftermath of the terror attack on Vulcan (*Star Trek: Enterprise—The Romulan War: Beneath the Raptor's Wing*) through August 12, 2161, the day of the signing of the United Federation of Planets Charter.

PART I
2156

Prologue

Early in the Month of *ta'Krat*, Year of Shikahr 8765
Tuesday, June 22, 2156
Government District, Central ShiKahr, Vulcan

IT WAS THE MORNING after the commission of the most hei-
nous crime in Vulcan's recorded history. T'Pau, administrator of the Confederacy of Vulcan, stood looking out at the
stone and glass expanse of Vulcan's ancient capital city from
one of its highest spires.

The sense of loss she was experiencing threatened to
undermine her emotional controls. She sensed that the rest
of Vulcan felt the same way. Her entire being vibrated in
sympathy with the mood of her people. Her mind, her
heart, her *katra* sang out in mournful wails.

I grieve with thee, she thought, recalling Surak's compas-
sionate yet eminently logical words of solace. Words spoken
throughout the ages.

I grieve with all of thee, she thought and ignored the single
tear that rolled down her cheek. *And* for *all of thee as well.*

The words were hollow. Her grief had begun to
metamorphose into something uglier: blame.

T'Pau knew that blame was futile, illogical. She was Vulcan, she was in control of her emotions. Yet why did she
still seek out someone to blame? The architects of yesterday's foul act of assassination remained unidentified. No
one other than the guilty parties knew who had bombed
the Mount Seleya shrine, slaughtering the keeper of
Surak's *katra*. Whoever had done this vile deed might have

even escaped the planet. Or they might be taking refuge in one of Vulcan's major cities or smaller settlements. T'Pau wanted to lead the search of the desert bazaars of Han-shir, scour every corner of ancient ShiKahr.

Control.

Taking a moment to center herself, T'Pau achieved stillness.

Have I made the right choices? By keeping Vulcan out of the war with the Romulans, I was trying to preserve what Surak made us, she thought. *But what of Vulcan's other actions? Was it right to persuade both Andoria and Tellar to leave the conflict? Earth now stands alone.*

Alone. The sorrow started to overwhelm her controls.

Have we lost Surak, the Father of All We Became and Might Yet Become, once again and forever? No, his children may never touch his katra, but they shall know him.

"Administrator." T'Pau suppressed her startled reaction.

"T'Rama," T'Pau said without turning away from the cold tableau of the city. "My staff was supposed to go home for the day. Why are you still here?"

"When you directed me to dismiss the staff this morning, I was not aware that your order included the head of your security detail as well," T'Rama said evenly.

"At the moment, my own safety is the least of my concerns," T'Pau said. Using the back of her hand, she wiped at the moisture that clung to her cheek before she turned and faced her chief bodyguard.

"Excellency," T'Rama said. The young woman's face was swollen, her eyes moist. "After what happened yesterday, your personal safety is my *only* concern."

T'Pau nodded. "And I am gratified by your vigilance, T'Rama. But it is unnecessary."

"Unnecessary?"

"Go home, T'Rama.

"Tomorrow we shall see to the needs of the many."

ONE

Thursday, July 22, 2156
Late in the Month of *Soo'jen*, Year of Kahless 782
Qam-Chee, the First City, Qo'noS

Too PREOCCUPIED by his own glum musings to speak, Captain Jonathan Archer stood silently in the empty corridor just outside the High Council Chamber. Watching his first officer crossing her arms before her, Archer knew her outer layer of Vulcan calm was a façade; T'Pol was as tense and taut as a snare drum.

"Do you believe the Klingons will decide to enter the conflict?" T'Pol asked, her words echoing off the polished stone walls despite the quiet tone of her voice.

Archer cast his gaze about the broad hallway, searching in vain for a place to sit as he considered that all-important question. Turning to face his executive officer, he shrugged.

"Regardless of what Shran or Krell might tell you," he said at length, "I'm no warrior. When I took command of *Enterprise*, I was an explorer. What the hell happened to those days anyway?"

T'Pol's protracted silence only made him wonder if he had wasted the last few years of his life pursuing the vain hope of bringing peace and security to this mostly lawless jungle of a galaxy.

And now it may all come down to whether or not the Klingons will agree to help us beat back the Romulans, Archer thought. *Before they set up forward operating bases on even more of our colony worlds, the way they did on Calder II.*

Before they overrun Earth itself.

The moment stretched until T'Pol surprised him by actually trying to answer his rhetorical question. "As a noted philosopher once said, 'Life is that which occurs fortuitously while one pursues alternative options.'"

Archer thought the words sounded vaguely familiar, though he couldn't quite place them.

"Surak?"

"No, Captain," she said with a small shake of her head. "A Terran musician to whose work Trip—Commander Tucker—introduced me."

"So you're saying I'm a soldier, whether I want to be or not."

"We do not always have the luxury of choosing our destinies, Captain. Sometimes they choose us."

Despite his gray mood, he felt a mischievous grin tugging gently at his face. "Please don't take this the wrong way, T'Pol, but that sounds more emotional than logical."

"Jonathan, I speak from the logic of personal experience," she said quietly. Since Trip Tucker's departure from *Enterprise*'s crew, T'Pol was the only subordinate who seemed comfortable addressing Archer by his first name.

"I guess it would be pointless to argue with Vulcan empiricism," he said.

She nodded. "Indeed."

"I just don't have to like it."

"The universe has never been obliged to shape itself to comport with our likes or dislikes." She fell silent again but continued gazing at him in a manner he could only describe as expectant, if not downright anxious.

"Was there something else?" he asked.

"You never answered my question. Do you think the Klingons will assist us against the Romulans?"

It occurred to him then that her interest in this question was intensely personal—perhaps as intensely personal as his own. Though Romulus posed a far greater danger to Earth at the moment than it did to Vulcan, T'Pol obviously felt responsible for her homeworld's decision—perhaps at the cost of Earth's very existence—to sit out the conflict.

Will the Klingons help us push the Romulans back? Archer thought. He knew the idea wasn't absurd on its face. After all, the Klingon Empire had been at loggerheads, or worse, with the Romulan Star Empire for about as long as anyone with knowledge of either society could remember. The mutual antipathy might even have gone all the way back to the time of Klingon-Romulan first contact. *Or will M'Rek decide his empire would be better off just letting Earth and Romulus wear each other down for the next few bloody years? At that point, both would be easy pickings—*

The council chamber's massive wooden door opened with surprising suddenness and rapidity, interrupting Archer's train of thought. A sweat-and-lilac-tinged draft from the chamber briefly bent the flames in the ceremonial sconces in the cold rock walls. The captain could hear the deep guttural-but-clear cry of the Klingon equivalent of a sergeant at arms, mixed with the distant clatter of heavy boots against time-polished stone. The members of the High Council were filing back into the official chamber far sooner than Archer had expected.

Not good, he thought. As he led the way toward the open doorway, he said, "T'Pol, I think the Klingons may be about to settle your question definitively."

A moment later Archer and his first officer stood at attention once again in the High Council Chamber's audience area, a broad, flat stretch of stone overlooked by the raised, tiered dais upon which several dozen of the heads of the Klingon Empire's most influential houses were taking their seats and coming to order.

As the low growls of conversation faded away into silence, Chancellor M'Rek, the council's leader, strode to the central dais, where he stopped and faced Archer. Waving away the guards who flanked him and the Chancellor, Fleet Admiral Krell followed M'Rek and came to a stop to the immediate right of the gray-maned eminence. Despite his incongruously smooth forehead, Krell was a portrait of power and barely contained Klingon rage—all of which was clearly directed, like a battery of phase cannons, straight at Archer. The braids of Krell's long and narrow white beard almost seemed to vibrate with tension.

The captain had faced the admiral in personal combat a year ago, in this very room. Apparently the successful reattachment of the admiral's left arm had done little to assuage his resentment toward Archer for having wielded the *bat'leth* that had sliced off the limb in the first place.

Does he really intend to take his rage out on the entire human race? Archer wondered, even as he immediately answered his own question. *If he advised M'Rek to stay out of the fight, then that's exactly what he's done.*

"Jonathan Archer." Chancellor M'Rek intoned each syllable in a sonorous, ceremonial manner obviously intended to be heard clearly even in the vast hall's farthest corners. "The High Council has reached a decision with regard to your government's official request."

Archer felt a peculiar sensation of motion deep in his belly, as though his guts were trying to burrow past each other in search of someplace safer than their present locations.

"Thank you, Chancellor," he said, mainly to fill the maddening silence.

"You do not have reason to thank me, Archer," M'Rek said. "The High Council hereby formally declines to assist your world in its war against the *RomuluSngan*."

Archer thought he was prepared to hear the worst; he thought he could assimilate the bad news with some equanimity and grace.

His face and neck felt flushed as he realized he had read himself entirely wrong.

"So that's *it*, then?" he said, raising his voice to a near shout that had to be clearly audible even in the gallery's cheapest seats. "Your High Council 'formally declines' to engage with a common enemy?"

Krell favored Archer with a malicious grin. "I will presume your translation device is in need of maintenance. Until you can attend to that, allow me to remove any remaining ambiguity for you: Seek help elsewhere. You will find none from the Klingon High Council, and the Chancellor owes you no explanation beyond that. Have I made matters sufficiently clear to you?"

Archer ignored Krell, concentrating instead on the Chancellor. "What's it going to take for us lowly Earthers to prove ourselves worthy of your help, Chancellor?"

"Captain," T'Pol said, her hand on his shoulder, gentle yet insistent.

He shrugged her off and pointed at the fleet admiral. "Would it help if I sliced this guy's *other* arm off?"

"Captain!" T'Pol said, more sharply this time.

Krell snarled and advanced toward Archer, until M'Rek stopped him by raising his mailed fist and shouting, *"Mevyap!"*

"Mind your place, Captain," said M'Rek into the ensuing anxious silence. "You are a visitor here. Do not presume upon the High Council's patience by making vainglorious displays."

With a strenuous effort of will, Archer reined his emotions in. He tried to recapture some of the calm and peace he had experienced two years earlier when his brain had served as a temporary storage vessel for the living spirit of the Vulcan philosopher Surak. Though Surak's influence was now little more than a distant whisper, the effort was sufficient to prevent him from committing any further breaches of protocol.

But he felt no less incensed that the Klingons had

decided to throw Earth to the wolves—or to the raptors—just as Vulcan had already done.

Continuing to ignore Krell, Archer addressed the Chancellor. "Please forgive me, Chancellor. I allowed my emotions to get the better of me."

"Perhaps you should have allowed your Vulcan *SoS* to speak for you, Archer," Krell said with a chortle.

Resigned to his universal translator's occasional glitches, Archer could only wonder what a *SoS* was. Ignoring what was almost certainly an entirely intentional insult, he finally allowed his gaze to light upon the admiral. "You're fortunate I didn't, Krell. You might have wound up losing *both* your arms."

The Chancellor chuckled quietly, but not so quietly that the rank-and-file council members couldn't hear it. Fleet Admiral Krell fumed silently as the laughter spread through the chamber, very briefly dispelling the room's usual air of martial taciturnity.

In response to Chancellor M'Rek's none-too-subtle hand gesture, a quartet of armed guards approached Archer and T'Pol, making it obvious that the audience had concluded—and that the rejected supplicants had better leave *now*, while some semblance of conviviality remained in the room.

Guess I'd better leave the "vainglorious displays" to the real experts, Archer thought as he allowed the glowering troopers to usher him and his exec back out into the corridor and through the outer vestibule that led to the landing pad where they had parked Shuttlepod One.

Archer approached the small spacecraft, but before he reached the portside hatchway, a gaunt, white-haired figure stepped into his path, blocking his way.

"Captain Archer," the man said, his sonorous voice freighted with authority.

Archer nodded toward the elderly yet vital-looking Klingon and extended his right hand. "Kolos. It's good to see you. You look well."

Kolos's lips drew back, his snow-white mustachios framing an ironic, snaggletoothed grin as he grasped Archer's arm with almost painful firmness. "You are a poor liar, my friend."

"And an even worse advocate," Archer said, taking a step backward after Kolos relinquished his arm. This man, an accomplished Klingon defense attorney, had saved him from a Klingon criminal court's death sentence—and had been rewarded for his efforts with a year of doing hard labor on a prison world.

"Fleet Admiral Krell has ordered your immediate departure, Earther," said a rough voice behind Archer, who turned in time to see an armored soldier shove T'Pol forward. Archer's rage rose once again as he helped his exec recover her balance.

Before Archer could protest, Kolos barked something in Klingon that the universal translator apparently couldn't render in intelligible English. The guards spent a few moments regarding one another quizzically. One of them, doubtless the most senior member of the small squad, nodded curtly at Kolos. Then all four soldiers turned on their heels and strode away.

Impressed, Archer turned back to face Kolos. "What did you say to them?"

"I told them I would see to your departure myself. And I suggested that they might find something more constructive to do than to bully a helpless woman."

"Indeed," T'Pol said acidly. Kolos showed no awareness of having given offense, though his smile disappeared beneath a wave of solemnity.

"Evidently bad news travels fast around here," Archer said, taking care not to allow any of his frustration with the High Council to spill over onto Kolos.

"I was informed earlier of the High Council's decision, Captain," said the Klingon attorney. "It appears it was a foregone conclusion. You have my sympathies, for whatever they are worth."

That M'rek's decision was a fait accompli didn't surprise Archer in the least. "I wish my people had sent *you* to argue

Earth's case to M'Rek," he said. "You'd have been a lot more persuasive than I was."

Kolos waved a large hand through the air in a gesture of dismissal. "*Targ* droppings, Captain. The decision of M'Rek and his supporters was already etched in granite before your world asked to petition the High Council. It was as inevitable as it is unalterable."

"If that is true," T'Pol said, "then why did M'Rek make the pretense of having to subject the question to a parliamentary debate?"

The Klingon chuckled quietly, the way a patient adult might before answering a question from a precocious yet naïve child. "To obscure the unpleasant fact that the Klingon Empire faces certain intractable internal problems," he said.

"Such as?" Archer asked, genuinely curious.

Clasping his hands behind his back, Kolos began pacing slowly along the length of the shuttlepod, his tone that of a peripatetic college professor. "Like any empire that can thrive only while expanding its boundaries, the Klingon state faces many chronic difficulties. These issues must be addressed to the High Council's satisfaction before M'Rek can see his way clear to dealing with any problem that lies *beyond* our present borders."

"You seem to be saying that the Klingon Empire has entered a period of consolidation," T'Pol said, "as opposed to one of conquest. Alternation between phases of conquest and consolidation is a common historical pattern, particularly for long-lived empires."

Kolos raised one of his bushy white eyebrows at T'Pol; he appeared nettled but maintained an even tone when he replied. "Take care never to speak that way in the presence of the High Council. M'Rek would have you gutted for even *suggesting* that conquest could ever be anything other than the Empire's highest priority."

Archer put up a hand in an attempt to get the discussion

back on topic. "All right, so M'Rek is a politician who is trying to hang on to power," Archer said, paradoxically reassured for a moment to discover that such a quintessential human foible motivated the leadership of such a decidedly nonhuman species. "So let's set Klingon domestic politics to one side for the moment."

"With pleasure," Kolos said with a scowl of distaste.

"Granted that M'Rek has his own home-grown priorities to deal with, what kind of 'intractable internal problem' could be a bigger potential threat to the Klingon Empire than the Romulans? The last time I checked, they were every bit as expansion oriented as you Klingons are. M'Rek *has* to know that the Romulan fleet will be flying right up his ass someday in the not-too-distant future."

"Indeed," said T'Pol. "And if M'Rek sits back and allows Earth to fall, that eventuality is certain to arrive sooner rather than later."

Kolos nodded. "M'Rek knows all of this. But he is still contending with the aftermath of that mutant viral outbreak that afflicted the Qu'Vat colony nearly two years ago. That plague has since swept out to N'Vak and beyond, dispersing itself across the length and breadth of the Empire."

"You speak of the modified Levodian flu virus," T'Pol said.

"Yes," Kolos said. "The very same pathogen that your own Doctor Phlox manipulated at the genetic level!"

"The Klingon military *forced* him to do that!" Archer said, his anger threatening to boil over yet again.

"With *your* participation, Captain," said Kolos.

Archer felt as though he was being cross-examined by a clever attorney—which, he realized, was exactly the case. "What Phlox and I did ended up saving millions of your people from what would otherwise have been a lethal epidemic."

"I do not dispute that, Captain. However, your remedy

turned the vast majority of the afflicted Klingon populations from *HemQuch* to *QuchHa'* even as it cured them."

Have to get Hoshi to refine these damned translator units, Archer thought. He said, "Come again, Kolos?"

"*HemQuch* translates roughly to 'proud forehead,' Captain," said T'Pol.

Kolos grinned as he pointed toward the highly textured topography of his own cranium, bringing to mind a male deer displaying his antlers during mating season. "*QuchHa'*, by contrast, means 'unhappy ones,'" he said.

"Sounds like Krell," Archer said. "He's usually pretty damned unhappy."

Kolos nodded. "And he, along with countless others who received this so-called cure, now believe death would have been far preferable."

Archer was incredulous. "Why?"

"Don't you see, Archer? They now bear a stronger resemblance to *your* species than they do to any Klingon who ever lived."

"Klingons are pretty tough people," Archer said. "They'll get over it."

"Eventually," said Kolos. "But in the meantime, the social upheaval associated with this . . . change is enough to preoccupy any chancellor. It will no doubt prove troublesome to the High Council for generations to come. Which is why the council can furnish you with no help against the *RomuluSngan.*"

Archer stepped toward the shuttlepod and placed his hand against the external control pad. The portside hatch beside him hissed open in response, and T'Pol quietly entered the craft.

"Great," Archer said, still half facing Kolos as he stepped up onto the hatchway's threshold. "Earth gets invaded and burned, all because Phlox and I made the mistake of doing a good deed for the Klingons. Thanks for everything, Kolos.

Now if you'll excuse me, I've got to get back to *Enterprise* and deliver the bad news."

Before Archer could pass over the threshold, Kolos reached forward and placed a restraining hand on the captain's shoulder. "I believe you misunderstand what has happened today."

Archer released a mirthless laugh. "What have I missed? M'Rek has just signed Earth's death warrant. And you've been kind enough to drop in a little bit early to pay us your last respects."

"My coming here has nothing whatsoever to do with kindness, Captain. In fact, I am here at M'Rek's behest."

"To warn us not to expect any Klingon help against the Romulans," Archer said, no longer trying to hold back a bilious wave of sarcasm. "I think M'Rek might have said a little something along those lines already. I get it."

Despite the intensity of his gaze, Kolos's voice was quiet, as though he wanted only Archer to hear it. "No, Captain. I came here to tell you not to expect any *official* Klingon help."

Releasing his grip on Archer's shoulder, the Klingon advocate abruptly turned and strode back toward the High Council Chamber.

Emotionally exhausted, Archer let T'Pol take the cockpit's left chair, contenting himself with the simpler duties that fell upon the occupant of the copilot's seat. After running through the prelaunch checklist and initiating the shuttlepod's liftoff, Archer and T'Pol passed the brief return flight to *Enterprise* in silence.

Despite Kolos's sub rosa revelation, Archer still felt he was returning from Qo'noS utterly empty-handed. He wondered how things could have gone so badly awry so quickly.

And if the die had already been cast nearly a year ago, after his failure to prevent the destruction of the Earth Cargo Service fuel carrier *Kobayashi Maru*.

TWO

CHARLES ANTHONY "TRIP" TUCKER III was dreaming, and he knew it.

He was aware of his present dream state because of what he saw as his dream self stepped through the doorway of T'Pol's house—a dwelling he now shared with his espionage-cum-business partners Tevik, Ych'a, and Ych'a's husband, Denak. Though Trip's body told him to a certainty that the actual time could be no later than perhaps an hour past midnight, he looked out across the courtyard into the waxing ruddy light of another late-summer morning on Vulcan's northern hemisphere. Though the dream sky was still transitioning from dawn's deep vermilion toward the salmon tones of morning and the fiery reds and oranges of midday, he could see clearly enough into the backyard garden he'd been tending faithfully ever since T'Pol's departure. Despite the omnipresent crescent-shaped shadow of Vulcan's co-orbiting neighbor world T'Khut, the brilliance of the still rising yellow-orange dwarf star 40 Eridani A—Nevasa, as the locals called it—put his labors, such as they were, on brilliant display. The rows of *hla-meth* herbs were mere stubble extruded from the ruddy ground, overshadowed by the ranks of heavy, swollen *rillan* gourds that looked nearly ready to pick. The *favinit* and *plomeek* plants beyond were as bereft of flowers as the *alem-vedik* desert salt weeds that bordered them, and the *i'su'ke* and *g'teth* berry bushes were likewise bare. Only the towering *gespar* fruit trees, the *nar'ru* vines that climbed them, and the *ic'tan* conifers clustered in the middle of the courtyard had escaped the austerity of the incoming season.

When T'Pol gets back here, I wonder if she'll notice what I've done with the place, he thought as he strode through the courtyard. He was almost one hundred percent certain he'd have to point it out to her before she would think to offer him one of her customary curt *thank-you*s. Of course, he also had to concede the possibility that the *real* garden might not live up to the image created by its dream counterpart.

Dream or not, it felt good to be outside. Trip inhaled slowly, drawing the dry desert air deeply into his lungs. He was thankful that mornings here were never nippy. It was already comfortably warm out, T-shirt weather, in fact. Of course, by midday this place would become a veritable oven. Romulus had been a far easier world to get used to. He walked on, trying not to dwell on that unpleasant fact any more than necessary. There, in the morning shadows . . . T'Pol.

THUMP. THUMP. THUMP.

Trip heard a steady pounding, distant yet urgent. The garden vanished at once into a miasma of darkness. Trip closed his eyes as a sensation of vertigo momentarily overcame him. His equilibrium fled as he opened his eyes again, allowing the night to come flooding back.

Slowly shrugging off the amnesia that sometimes accompanies interrupted sleep, he realized he was lying on the bed in the main sleeping quarters—the room he had shared with T'Pol before she had returned to *Enterprise*.

THUMP. THUMP. THUMP.

The pounding was closer this time, more insistent. Now he could hear a deep, authoritative voice demanding immediate entry in clear, ShiKahr-accented Vulcan.

The front door, Trip thought as he threw back the blankets and stepped onto the chill stone floor. Not stopping to find his phase pistol, he raced barefoot through the main living area and toward the front-door vestibule.

He got there just in time to see the door fall swiftly inward, as though propelled by a great force.

"Lights!" Trip shouted to the household computer, which obediently brought the house's internal illumination up to evening levels. Though the abrupt change in the lighting momentarily dazzled Trip, he saw several large humanoid shapes race across the threshold and into the house.

Before he could react, someone—or perhaps several someones—had gotten behind him and pinned his arms behind him, placing them in an unbreakable viselike hold.

"What the hell?" Trip shouted at the half dozen or so individuals who had just invaded the house. The rough hands released him and he fell painfully to his knees on the stone floor as he realized that his wrists had been bound behind him.

Vulcan Security, Trip thought, his heart sinking. *Cops.* Had Administrator T'Pau or Minister Kuvak somehow sussed out the fact that he was a disguised human spy rather than the Vulcan businessman he appeared to be? Or maybe Silok, the head of the Vulcan intel bureau, the V'Shar, had found him out. Trip wondered if he'd inadvertently tipped his hand when T'Pol was having him added to the ownership registry of this house.

Trip heard the sounds of a struggle to his left and turned to see a trio of security officers dragging Denak to the floor. Beside him lay Ych'a, prone and hogtied with slim cables; she appeared to be unconscious, and Denak appeared to be actively protesting that fact until a well-placed neck pinch made him go limp.

Trip watched, stunned, as the officers half carried and half dragged both Ych'a and Denak outside.

"What do you people think you're doing?" Trip growled toward the nearest officer, a female. Trip had to crane his neck painfully to look her in the eye. "Denak and Ych'a are former members of Vulcan's intelligence service."

"They are," said the woman, who seemed to be in overall charge of this raid. "And they are now formally under suspicion of having taken part in the destruction of the *katra* of Surak."

Trip's jaw fell open. He closed it with an act of pure will after he considered how terribly un-Vulcan he must have looked.

"This is the last one," said a tall, thickset uniformed Vulcan male who had come to a stop beside the woman. This officer was pointing directly at Trip. "Other than him and the two suspects, the house was empty."

"Very good, Subaltern," the woman said. "Now please unshackle this man."

A moment later, Trip was rubbing his tingling wrists and once more getting to his feet. He noticed the woman eyeing him with evident patience and equally evident suspicion.

"So I take it I'm not a suspect in the Mount Seleya bombing," Trip said.

"Not at present, Mister Sodok. However, we would advise you to keep yourself available for questioning should the need arise."

Trip nodded, doing his best to look like an emotionally detached Vulcan rather than an outraged and put-upon human with artificially pointed ears. "Of course."

Now that he was free to move about, Trip stepped slowly through the doorway that once held the now-horizontal front door, and walked into the house's austere front yard. Several security officers were loading the unconscious forms of Ych'a and Denak into the back of a small antigrav transport vessel displaying the triangular logo of Vulcan Security.

There's no way they could have had anything to do with the Mount Seleya bombing, Trip thought as the Vulcan security personnel secured the rear door of their vehicle. *Denak and Ych'a are two of T'Pol's oldest friends. They've put their lives on the line for Vulcan's sake probably more times than either of them can count. How could they have betrayed everything Vulcan is supposed to stand for?*

As Trip flogged his still sleep-muzzy brain for ways to extricate T'Pol's old friends—*his* friends—from this situation, another thought occurred to him: *That cop said the house was empty except for the three of us.*

Four people had once resided in this house, a situation that had abruptly changed several weeks ago. It appeared that Tevik remained unaccounted for. Had he slipped the psionic leash that Ych'a had formerly used to control him? Had the man's artificially suppressed real identity—Centurion Terix of the Romulan Star Empire—fully reasserted itself at last and taken over?

A chill desert wind blew across the front yard, raising goose bumps on Trip's arms. *If anybody I know is responsible for destroying Surak's katra,* he thought, *then Tevik—I mean Terix—has got to be the guy.*

Trip still felt an overwhelming urge to sprint across the yard toward the transport into which Ych'a and Denak had been placed. Instead, he stood motionless as the transport's antigravs carried it slowly into a sky illuminated by only a narrow slice of bleak and pockmarked T'Rukh, whose name meant "the Watcher."

Terix has to be the key to freeing Ych'a and Denak, Trip thought as he watched the transport quickly dwindle away and vanish. *A way of killing two* lanka-gar *with a single stone.* He walked back to the house, shaking his head to dispel an unexpected wave of homesickness.

Damn. Now I'm even starting to think in Vulcan.

THREE

UNITED EARTH'S PRIME MINISTER, Nathan Samuels, slammed his fist down on the podium hard enough to send a spike of pain shooting up through his elbow. He concealed his discomfiture as the impact echoed like a small thunderclap through the high-ceilinged debating chamber of the Coalition of Planets Council.

"There is only one decision possible for my planet's government," he said, raising his voice in oratory. Wherever his small but significant audience—a collection of civilian and military leaders that included flag officers from both MACO and Starfleet, as well as senior diplomatic representatives from Alpha Centauri, Draylax, Vulcan, Andoria, and Tellar—stood on this afternoon's debate, Samuels felt confident that he at least had their full attention. "Both houses of the United Earth Parliament have voted with me on this issue, by overwhelming majorities."

Even if he were to have a sudden change of heart regarding a decision for which he himself had pushed, Samuels knew he would be powerless to defy the planetary legislature's decision; he lacked both the political clout and the constitutional authority to oppose its collective will.

"The United Earth Parliament has voted to place the force of law behind an executive order I issued back in June," he continued. "Earth now has no choice other than to employ the vast majority of its Starfleet and Military Assault Command Operations resources on the critical task of defending the Sol system. We must be prepared to bring all available force to bear immediately whenever the Romulans succeed in breaching the home system's warp-field detection grid. We can no longer afford to make the space beyond our home system the subject of regular patrols."

MACO General George Casey rose from his front-row seat, glowering at the podium from behind a forest of medals and ribbons. Samuels knew he was about to receive an earful from the iron-haired military officer, whether or not he tried to preemptively gavel the general back into his seat, as required by protocol.

"Yes, George," Samuels said with his most disarming smile. He hoped that his manner, as well as his casual use of the general's first name, would put the old warhorse off balance, at least for a moment. "You have a question?"

No such luck. Casey had clearly had a change of heart after initially supporting Samuels's now two-month-old executive order. Although the general was clearly angry, he was, at least, respectful. "I do, Prime Minister. Sir, may I assume you're aware that this decision will greatly limit Earth's ability to mount effective offensive operations against the Romulans?"

Samuels nodded, doubling down on the smile. "Contrary to what you may have heard on the newsnets, General, I didn't nod off during any of the military briefing sessions." Low chuckles echoed briefly through the chamber, providing an undercurrent of gallows humor in which all the nonhumans present were ostentatiously refusing to participate. Samuels wondered if this was because they failed to understand the danger their governments were creating through their collective inaction.

Or perhaps they understood it all too well and were ashamed.

Casey appeared unmoved by any of it. "Prime Minister, the parliament's action has committed us to maintaining a purely defensive posture. It has turned this conflict into a war of slow attrition that will ultimately trap us."

Slow attrition is better than quick conquest, Samuels thought, though he wasn't sure he really believed it anymore. If death was both inevitable and imminent, might it not be better to get it over with quickly?

"I'm not unsympathetic to your viewpoint," he said.

The general scowled. "Sir, if the MACO and Starfleet are to have any serious chance of containing the Romulan fleet—much less driving it back where it came from—then we're going to need a lot more than sympathy."

Although today's session was closed to the public—and therefore to the press—Samuels was already having visions of how weak-kneed the planetary newsnets could make him look by lunchtime. Never mind that this decision was the work of a parliamentary majority. *If that goddamned Keisha Naquase from* Newstime *somehow gets a recording of this,* he thought, *at least half of humanity will see me as a political eunuch.*

"True enough, General," Samuels said, "but we also have to think practically. We can't expect to win on the offensive while going it essentially alone." He paused, fixing his gaze firmly upon the section of the gallery where the delegations from Vulcan, Andoria, Tellar, and Draylax were seated. He squared his shoulders and turned to make it clear that his next words were intended for Earth's allies.

"We are receiving essentially *no* support from our nonhuman Coalition of Planets partners," he continued, gratified to see the usually unflappable Vulcan Foreign Minister Soval appear to squirm slightly in his padded chair, while his Tellarite and Andorian counterparts—Ambassador Gora bim Gral and Foreign Minister Anlenthoris ch'Vhendreni—absorbed the rebuke without any discernible reaction. The thoughts of Grethe Zhor of

Draylax were impossible to divine from behind her calm, still countenance.

General Casey returned quietly to his seat, now evidently content to stay out of Samuels's way.

Samuels stepped into the silence that had enfolded the room, using it to his best rhetorical advantage. "Therefore any all-out offensive on our part would be tantamount to simply casting all the military resources of both the United Earth and the Alpha Centauri settlements to the solar winds, leaving the worlds of the Sol system unable to beat the Romulans back.

"Once the Romulans are through with us, will you decide only *then* to fight shoulder to shoulder against them? Only after it's far too late for us, and therefore perhaps for your own planets as well? Or will your governments continue to sit back, each looking the other way while an aggressive empire annexes your homeworlds one by one, enslaving and murdering your people?"

A low, dismayed murmur began to pass through the extraterrestrial assemblage, but Samuels ignored it. Raising his voice a notch, he said, "A human named Martin Niemöller once thought as your leaders do. More than two centuries ago, he witnessed a great evil sweeping through his country and came to regret having made no serious attempt to oppose it, or even to speak out against it—until *after* it was far too late to stop it. Many of you have probably read his words, so I apologize in advance for repeating a familiar sad refrain:

> *They came first for the communists,*
> *And I didn't speak out because I was not a communist.*

> *Then they came for the trade unionists,*
> *And I didn't speak out because I was not a trade unionist.*

> *Then they came for the Jews,*
> *And I didn't speak out because I was not a Jew.*

Then they came for me
And there was no one left to speak out for me.

"Good day," Samuels said sharply when the last reverberations of his recitation had been swallowed up by the hush that had scattered all murmurs and now ruled the chamber.

Uniformly stony-faced, the nonhuman contingent rose and began moving toward the exits, silent except for the muted, echoing clatter of their footfalls. Samuels could only stand and wonder whether he had done either too much or not enough today to prevent the Romulans from devastating the Coalition.

Once the alien exodus was well under way, General Casey rose as well.

And began, very slowly, to applaud.

Maybe letting the holo-cameras in here today wouldn't have been such a bad thing after all, Samuels thought.

"You shamed them, Prime Minister," the staid, gray-suited humanoid woman said when she was safely behind the closed door of the prime minister's private office at the Coalition Council building.

"Goddamned right," Samuels said as he gestured toward the low sofa near his desk, offering Ambassador Grethe Zhor of Draylax a place to sit. "They had it coming. Vulcan, Andoria, and Tellar are all charter signatories to the Coalition Compact. Their decision to allow Sol and the Centauri planets to twist in the wind is a clear violation of the agreement's mutual-defense provisions."

Grethe Zhor shook her head and declined to sit. "Vulcan, at least, has provided the Sol system with an automated proximity alarm system to warn you of impending Romulan attacks."

"That's nowhere near good enough, and the Vulcans

know it. Just as everybody knows how easily the Romulans can game the Vulcans' defense grid."

The Draylaxian crossed her arms over her chest, prompting Samuels to wonder if this was a new habit she had developed after she'd noticed many human males staring during encounters with Draylaxian females. He hoped he hadn't done it himself, though he had to admit that her tailored gray suit served only to emphasize her upper body's three-breasted topography.

"You humans are living with a terrible vulnerability," she said, sounding sincerely sympathetic rather than patronizing. "I presume that is why you have asked to meet with me."

Samuels smiled, though he wasn't at all sure how Draylaxians interpreted such nonverbal cues. "Thank you for coming. I'm grateful for any opportunity to do a little gentle arm-twisting."

"Arm-twisting, Prime Minister?" She tipped her head slightly to the right, a maneuver that caused the downy coat of feathery orange-brown "hair" on her head to move as though by its own volition.

Samuels chuckled. "Polite persuasion. To do something about humanity's 'terrible vulnerability,' as you call it. And call me Nathan, please."

"Nathan, Draylax is not yet a full signatory to the Coalition Compact."

Samuels's smile faltered as his patience began to fray. "It's been over an Earth year since your world applied for membership, and nearly that long since you signed the official induction documents on behalf of your government. Your superiors got around to officially upgrading you from observer status to a full ambassadorship only a few weeks ago."

"The wheels of Draylax's government grind forward but slowly, I must admit," she said with a slight bow of apparent deference. "Unfortunately, such thoroughness is the hallmark of Draylaxian legal protocol."

"But from the viewpoint of the United Earth government," Samuels said, "Draylax is *already* a full signatory to the treaty. And that status carries certain responsibilities—prime of which are the mutual-defense provisions."

"But Draylax cannot regard its Coalition of Planets membership as active until our own internal treaty-ratification process is completed. Protocol must be observed."

Samuels held up a hand. "All right. But Draylax already had mutual-defense arrangements with both Earth and Alpha Centauri that predated the Coalition Compact," he said, conscious that a tone of pleading had entered his voice. "Why aren't you fulfilling your preexisting obligation to contribute ships, personnel, and matériel to the front lines?"

"Because the Coalition Compact has superseded those earlier arrangements," Zhor said. "Such is Draylaxian law and protocol."

Samuels bit back a scathing retort as he collapsed into the big padded chair behind his desk. He fumed in silence and slowly wrestled his frustration to the ground, pinning it there only after expending a considerable amount of effort. All the while he kept telling himself that there was nothing to be gained by offending—and possibly forever alienating—a powerful ally that apparently perceived itself as still legally able to walk away from the Coalition.

The ambassador spoke up again before Samuels could recover his train of thought. "In previous times of danger, Earth and Alpha Centauri have never hesitated to come to Draylax's aid."

Samuels nodded. "Thanks for noticing," he said curtly. He'd been about to argue that very point.

"I shall do whatever I can to . . . *hasten* law and protocol as pertains to this matter," Zhor whispered, as though she had dared to raise a taboo subject and feared being overheard by her leaders. "The Draylaxian fleet could conceivably be deployed to the Romulan front lines in fairly short order after that."

Samuels reminded himself that to a Draylaxian—the product of a culture that seemed more than content to run freighters that weren't capable of making warp two—the definition of "fairly short order" was really anyone's guess.

"Thank you, Ambassador," Samuels said, matching Grethe Zhor's whisper. He studiously avoided the contours of her chest, keeping his gaze focused instead upon her unreadable black eyes. "Because unless you can do something to expedite the paperwork back at the home office, Draylaxian law and protocol just might turn out to be the death of us all."

After Grethe Zhor had made her farewells and exited the office, Samuels reached for the bottle he kept in his desk's bottom drawer. The goosenecked flagon contained brandy from a faraway place known as Sauria.

Let's hope, he thought as he poured a single small glass nearly full, *that Captain Archer's diplomatic initiatives are all going at least this well.*

FOUR

THOUGH SHE WAS GARBED in a fully functional Starfleet environmental suit, Commander T'Pol realized that she had been holding her breath as she stepped onto the transporter platform. She exhaled quietly, took a deep breath as the sparkling blue curtain of light intensified, then faded and vanished. She was standing on a disconcertingly uneven surface, under the influence of a noticeably more intense gravitational field than the Earth-normal default setting aboard *Enterprise*.

"Secure the area," she ordered the MACOs via her suit's transceiver.

Sergeant Guitierrez and Corporal O'Malley were already in motion, their helmet lights illuminating the crippled vessel's interior. They moved in opposite directions down an extensively battle-damaged corridor. As T'Pol's sensitive Vulcan eyes began to adjust to the low light levels, she noticed a number of blackened rents in the exterior walls.

Stars and the damaged exterior were discernible through the breaches. She shuddered slightly, chilled by the knowledge of the fate that had befallen anyone in this corridor when the hull had torn open. As T'Pol trained her helmet lamp toward her feet, she saw that she was standing on the remnants of a leg. Lifting her foot, she saw a humanoid form. Its eyes, or at least the four of them she could see arranged about its bulbous head, were easily five times the size of those of a Vulcan, and the distal appendages of its four upper limbs were entwined with the gridwork of the bent, twisted deck plates beneath it.

After receiving an all-clear from both Guitierrez and O'Malley, T'Pol stepped away from the beam-in spot, moving the body aside with her foot. She activated her helmet's communicator and gave *Enterprise* the "go" signal to transport the rest of the boarding party over. Seconds later, the device's energetic shimmer returned and a trio of environmental-suited figures appeared: *Enterprise*'s armory officer, Lieutenant Commander Malcolm Reed; Chief Engineer Mike Burch; and the Denobulan chief medical officer, Dr. Phlox.

"*Damn. Can't say I enjoyed that,*" Burch said, his voice slightly distorted by his suit's comm system.

"*Welcome to the $E=mc^2$ club,*" Reed said as the Starfleet members of the boarding team began to deploy their scanners. "*Don't worry, Commander. You'll get used to it.*"

"*No, thanks,*" Burch said as he brandished his own scanner at arm's length and began turning slowly in a circle. "*Great haunted house vibe.*"

The engineer recoiled when he noticed the alien corpse on the deck.

"*I don't know. More of a* Flying Dutchman," Reed said as the group moved past the dead body.

Whistling past the graveyard. T'Pol pushed aside the intrusive human thought. "This vessel has sustained a great deal of damage. It may not remain intact much longer without considerable intervention on our part. Therefore we'll need to confirm the sensor scans as quickly as possible."

From a distance of more than fifty thousand kilometers, T'Pol had identified this vessel as M'klexa. Vulcan-M'klexa first contact was less than a year old. Relations between Vulcan and the M'klexa had been peaceful; unlike the

Klingons, the M'klexa were unlikely to misinterpret a good-faith attempt to rescue one of their vessels in distress as an act of belligerency.

Therefore, T'Pol's primary concern was to make this a quick sortie. Life signs hadn't been apparent to *Enterprise*'s sensors, even at her present distance of a mere ten kilometers. Her mission was to discover what had just succeeded in ripping open a vessel that seemed technologically comparable to *Enterprise*. Judging from the extensive pattern of damage, anything from Nausicaan pirates to an unfortunate brush with a cloaked field of Romulan gravitic mines could have been responsible.

And if the Romulans *were* in any way responsible, then their warbirds could appear at any time, intent on finishing off the M'klexa. She did not want to add *Enterprise* to their rapidly expanding list of kills.

"*Commander,*" Reed said, "*I'm picking up very weak life signs scattered all over the ship. Apparently, some sections of this vessel haven't yet lost their atmospheric integrity.*"

"*I'm picking up bio readings as well,*" Phlox said. Turning toward T'Pol, he added, "*Forty distinct life signs. Commander, we have to get them off this ship immediately.*"

"*That's not going to be easy,*" Reed said, tapping his scanner hard with a gloved index finger. "*Something's making it hard to pinpoint the exact location of each life sign.*"

"*It could be the same thing that's tearing up this ship,*" Burch said as he studied his own scanner. "*This vessel's experiencing a lot of gravitational shear.*"

T'Pol frowned. "*What's the source?*"

Despite the bulk of his environmental suit, Burch made a fully intelligible shrug. "*There could be a hidden Romulan minefield out here. Or it might be that the ship isn't far enough away from the Mu Arae magnetar to escape its effects.*"

T'Pol quietly took it all in. A relatively new phenomenon—it had come into existence less than a century ago—the extremely dense and massive Mu Arae magnetar was an extraordinarily active celestial body. Over the next billion years or more it would probably settle down and become an ordinary, relatively quiescent neutron star for the remainder of its existence. In the meantime, it would give off youthful bursts of multiple forms of energetic radiation, including colossal gravity waves—phenomena that could cause serious damage, even many light-years away.

"So all we really know for certain," Reed said, *"is that* Enterprise *is in serious danger of falling into whatever trap snared the M'klexa."*

T'Pol began to notice a vibration rattling up from beneath the deck, into her boots, and through her environmental suit. Thanks to the vibration's strength and her suit's sound conductivity, she could actually hear its reverberations in her helmet.

The vibration became an audible groan, immediately calling to mind some of the Earth horror movies she had viewed with Trip, as well as Mister Burch's unfortunate "haunted house" reference.

"Whatever we're going to do, we'd better get it done quickly." Burch gestured toward the jagged rips in the hull metal and the hard vacuum beyond. *"This ship's entire skin is going to look like that in under an hour. The cumulative damage will probably blow out a lot of the internal bulkheads as well as whatever's left of her life-support system and antimatter containment safeguards."*

T'Pol's helmet communicator chirped, and she touched its external controls.

"Enterprise to boarding party," said Lieutenant Commander Donna "D.O." O'Neill.

"T'Pol here. Go ahead."

"We're having a pretty rough ride here, Commander T'Pol. We may have to move beyond the transporter's range."

"Noted." T'Pol considered her options.

"Commander?" O'Neill's voice was tinged with apprehension.

"Get the grappler ready, Commander O'Neill," T'Pol

said with her typical crisp, confident Vulcan authority. "We're going to tow the M'klexa vessel to a safe distance from this region of gravimetric shear. Let me know when you're ready."

"*Aye, Commander,*" O'Neill said.

"*It's a risky plan,*" Burch said. "*If this ship's inertial dampers fail during a high-acceleration tow, then she could shatter like an eggshell.*"

"*It could kill anyone who survived,*" Phlox added.

"Mister Burch, I want you and Mister Reed to find and access all critical systems. Make certain this vessel is safe for towing as soon as possible."

"*That could take a fair amount of time, Commander,*" Burch said.

"Noted. I will assist Doctor Phlox, Sergeant Guitierrez, and Corporal O'Malley in establishing a transport point inside this ship's nearest pressurized compartment. While this vessel is being rigged for towing, we will begin transporting every survivor we can find to *Enterprise*."

T'Pol's communicator chirped again, heralding the return of O'Neill's voice. "*Grappler is aimed and ready, Commander. Firing Grappler One. Firing Grappler Two.*"

Several seconds later, the M'klexa vessel shuddered slightly, and O'Neill confirmed a successful contact with both of *Enterprise*'s hypertensile towing cables.

Before any of the boarding party members could begin their assignments, the deck plating beneath T'Pol's feet shuddered and groaned again. She felt all sensation of weight abruptly vanish, and she reacted by willing her voluntary muscles to a state of utter stillness. With a touch of a switch near her suit's neck ring, she activated the small magnetic field generators in her boots.

"The gravity plating is failing," she said. "I advise all of you to refrain from moving until after you've activated your magnetic boots."

Unlike T'Pol and the two MACOs, who stood immobile, their boots affixed firmly to the deck plates, the

abrupt departure of the M'klexa vessel's artificial gravity
had evidently caught Burch, Reed, and Phlox sufficiently
by surprise to send them all tumbling clumsily toward what
moments before had been the "upward" direction.

"Urgh," Reed said as he yawed and rolled, his arms and
legs pinwheeling wildly despite the mobility limitations im-
posed by his environmental suit. His complexion appeared
to have changed abruptly to a healthy Vulcan green. T'Pol
doubted this was a trick of the dim light. *"Bollocks! I bloody
hate microgravity."*

An abrupt failure of a ship's artificial gravity—particularly
a temporary or intermittent one—was one of the most perni-
cious hazards a boarding team might encounter; if the gravity
returned suddenly, the unwary could suffer grave injuries from
falls, or even die because of critical damage sustained by their
environmental suits.

"Commander T'Pol," Burch said as he grabbed an overhead
conduit, thereby arresting his own inadvertent motion.
*"About that time estimate I just gave you—I think it might be prudent
to cut it in half. In fact, it might be a good idea to quit while we're
ahead. Get the boarding team back to* Enterprise *while we still can.
And remember, this all still might have been caused by Romulans. They
might be back any second to land the killing blow."*

T'Pol looked at the MACOs. Their faces were expressionless masks of grim determination. She turned toward Phlox,
who had just pushed himself back to the deck, his equilibrium
and dignity both evidently restored. She saw twin fires of defi-
ance burning in the Denobulan's icy blue eyes.

"I'm not leaving the survivors behind, Commander," he said.

She decided right then not to waste what little time
remained in some pointless argument.

"Then I suggest, Mister Burch," T'Pol said as she began
moving down the corridor toward the nearest M'klexa life
sign, "that you work at least twice as quickly as you had
originally planned."

Tuesday, August 17, 2156
Enterprise NX-01, near Mu Arae (outbound)

Ever since the start of her tenure as *Enterprise*'s first officer, T'Pol had hoped that she would outgrow the need for the nasal numbing agents that had made life bearable in some of the ship's more . . . fragrant areas. Learning to live among humans, after all, meant developing a tolerance for their sometimes rather powerful aromas—if not achieving a Syrrannite's celebratory regard for all life. T'Pol found that she no longer needed to use chemicals to blunt the sensitivity of her olfactory system when she was with Charles Tucker, *Enterprise*'s former chief engineer.

But she still faced significant aroma-related challenges.

For one, Porthos, the captain's canine, smelled no more pleasant these days. Fortunately, the animal was padding quietly along the corridor several meters ahead of her at the moment, wagging its tail and sniffing but keeping its distance. And Captain Archer himself still tended to exude an uncomfortably powerful musk, particularly on those thankfully rare occasions when he neglected to shower following his morning workout routine.

As T'Pol walked beside Archer along the empty E Deck corridor that gently wound along *Enterprise*'s starboard side, it quickly became evident that the captain had not assigned a particularly high priority this morning to hygiene. Instead of his customary crisp blue duty uniform, Archer was clad in the baggy, dull gray garments that humans, appropriately enough, called "sweats." His short brown hair was in disarray, alternately flattened and spiked by perspiration. A Starfleet-issue padd was tucked under his left arm.

"I ran a little late this morning talking to Admiral Gardner at Starfleet Command," Archer said as he paused to adjust the white gym towel that was draped across his shoulders before resuming his brisk walk toward the captain's mess. "Had to skip the shower before our breakfast briefing. Hope it doesn't bother you, Commander."

"Of course not, Captain," T'Pol lied, willing her nostrils not to flare with distaste.

"I heard you had a little excitement last night."

Carefully keeping her face impassive, T'Pol said, "I wouldn't describe the encounter in such grandiose terms."

"Maybe not," he said with a shrug. "But *however* you describe it, you found an unknown vessel that easily could have been another Romulan trap. In spite of that, you approached and investigated—and verified that the ship was a local civilian freighter in distress."

T'Pol nodded. "I was merely following your standing orders, Captain."

"Oh, I'm not criticizing, Commander. You did everything by the numbers."

"Thank you, sir. I will file a more thorough report on the M'klexa vessel and its crew later today."

"M'klexa. I don't think Earth has ever made contact with them."

"Vulcan has, but only very recently," she said.

"What sort of damage had they taken?" Archer asked. "Did the Romulans attack them?"

"No, sir. They appear to have encountered extreme shearing forces caused by some of the very gravimetric anomalies and subspace distortions we've been mapping throughout this sector and beyond."

Archer came to a stop outside the sealed hatch of the captain's mess and depressed a button on the wall panel as he took out his padd. The hatch slid open obediently and he moved across the threshold, a moment after Porthos did. Glancing down at his padd's display, the captain said, "Mister Burch tells me that his repair team had the radiation leaks sealed and the engines back online in under four hours."

T'Pol followed him inside, and the gamy smell of thermopolymerized avian embryos nearly caused her nose to wrinkle involuntarily. A junior crewman, a human male named Stephens, was still present, evidently having just set the table and delivered the breakfast Chef had made. Once both T'Pol and Archer had assured him that they had no further needs, Stephens nodded and exited through the hatchway.

"Again, my actions regarding the freighter were per your standing orders," she said, returning her full attention to the captain. "The M'klexa are fortunate that you took the precaution of carrying additional supplies of platinumcobalt alloy." Not to mention all the extra food, medicine, and other stores *Enterprise* had taken on at Delta Pavonis. Some of those provisions had gone to the M'klexa as well.

"You never know when we might need to rebuild our antimatter relays with a fresh supply of platinum-cobalt," he said. "Besides, the stuff came in pretty handy a few years back when we discovered we had to trade a lot of it for the trellium-D shielding we needed to carry out our Xindi hunt in the Delphic Expanse."

Archer took his customary seat at the head of the dining table and gestured toward the chair opposite. She sat and lifted the tureen Chef had left beside the water pitcher and drinking glasses, trying all the while to avoid seeing or even contemplating the horrors that lay on the captain's platter; she concentrated instead on her own breakfast plate, upon which lay a fair approximation of a sliced *gespar* fruit and a pair of small Amonak flatcakes, just as she had expected. In the corner, Porthos was already busy consuming something meaty. T'Pol averted her gaze, hoping that the captain hadn't given the animal anything containing cheese, which caused canine flatulence.

"The M'klexa seemed to be in an awful hurry to get under way once their repairs were done," Archer said, speaking around a mouthful of bird blastula, Terran tuber, and what appeared to be some other type of seared animal flesh.

"The M'klexa captain said that his engines had been down for too long. He needed to make up for lost time and went to warp as soon as our repair crews had departed."

"Well, as much I would have enjoyed meeting the M'klexa, I hope they don't get taken by surprise by any more shearing forces."

"I tried to lower the likelihood of that eventuality as much as possible by giving their captain the latest maps we've compiled of this sector's gravimetric anomalies and subspace distortions."

"Good. Good."

Something in Archer's tone made T'Pol's right eyebrow rise. "I was merely acting on your standing orders, Captain. Yet you sound . . . disappointed."

A wry smile crossed his face. "You're getting better all the time at reading human emotion, T'Pol. Maybe I am a little disappointed."

Now her left eyebrow rose. "In how I have carried out my duties during your sleep intervals?"

"No, T'Pol. It's just that it would have been nice to have been included in some of the fun."

"Fun?"

"You know. Assisting the other ship. Doing some hands-on exploration and cultural exchange. I'm *Enterprise*'s *captain*, for crying out loud. I ought to at least put in an appearance whenever we encounter a new and potentially friendly warp-capable civilization out here."

"Not if they're in a hurry to depart," T'Pol said. "And *certainly* not if said encounter occurs in the midst of the captain's scheduled sleep interval. I'm sure Admiral Gardner would agree."

Archer chuckled as he took another bite of his breakfast, washing it down with black coffee. "He wrote the regulation. 'An exhausted CO is a damned worthless CO,' he'd always say. It's probably his revenge for Starfleet Command giving *Enterprise* to me instead of him."

After finishing half of her *gespar* and one flatcake, T'Pol folded her hands in her lap. "That seems unworthy of a Starfleet flag officer. Not to mention highly unlikely."

Archer pushed his empty plate toward the table's center. "You're right, T'Pol. It's this . . . picket duty we've been assigned to. This endless patrolling of the same three sectors of space, while the actual Romulan combat front is just out of our reach. *That's* Sam Gardner's revenge."

"You said you spoke with Admiral Gardner earlier today," T'Pol said. "May I presume you raised these issues with him?"

"I did. And he's not changing his mind. *Enterprise* is not to get directly into harm's way until further notice. And Starfleet Command evidently still agrees with his assessment that it's just too risky to send Earth's NX-class flagship into a situation that might end with the Romulans capturing her by remote control. So we effectively sit out the war and keep ourselves nominally busy running overlapping, redundant scans of the same region of space for God only knows how long."

T'Pol finished eating and took a long swallow of cold water as she silently contemplated the captain's words. Finally, she pushed her plate aside and said, "There is a certain logic to Starfleet's actions."

"Sure," he said. "The logic of playing it safe. How does it make sense to use my crew to scan for gravimetric anomalies and subspace distortions? Automated probes can handle that."

"Permission to speak freely, Captain?" she said.

He grinned. "I've never had much luck trying to stop you in the past. Go right ahead."

"Perhaps you should also consider the logic of patience. I will concede that automated probes might be adequate for handling the more prosaic aspects of this mission, such as charting gravimetric anomalies. However, machines can never supply nuanced judgment when it is called for. Nor can they be perspicacious enough to recognize and exploit any Romulan-pertinent intelligence we might find out here among the trade routes of dozens of heretofore unknown starfaring cultures."

The captain stood, appearing at least mildly encouraged. "You might have trouble believing this, T'Pol, but sometimes your pep talks make all the difference." He moved toward the hatch. Porthos jumped up and hastened to follow.

T'Pol rose, paused to smooth a wrinkle from her otherwise immaculate blue Starfleet uniform, and followed the captain out into the corridor. Moments later, they reached the central turbolift together. After the doors hissed open, she stepped inside, following Porthos. When Archer tried to follow her, she extended a restraining arm across the hatchway, which made him take a reflexive step backward.

"My shift on the bridge is about to start, Commander," he said.

"You have more urgent business here on E Deck, Captain," she said.

"More urgent?" He grabbed at the sweaty towel around his neck. "I don't think so."

"In your quarters, sir," she said as the hatch began to close on his confused countenance. "The *shower*."

Archer sighed, then stopped the moving hatch with his hand; he called to Porthos, who ran out. The door then closed, granting T'Pol a precious moment of solitude as she pressed the activation button and directed the lift toward the upper decks. The lingering scent of human perspiration and beagle dander made her think that it might be a good idea to stop off briefly at her quarters on B Deck before taking her post on the bridge.

Perhaps there was a vial of olfactory-numbing compound there that she had overlooked.

FIVE

"THANK YOU FOR COMING to my office, Mister Sodok," Security Minister Silok offered from behind a sleek, ultramodern desk that appeared out of place in the high stone tower that looked out over the ancient sprawl of Vulcan's capital city.

"You do not need to thank me," said Trip, who sat on the low couch that fronted the desk and maintained a Vulcan's appearance of emotionlessness only with the greatest expenditure of effort. After all, he had asked Silok, Vulcan's top-ranking law enforcement officer, for this meeting, and had received nothing in response for weeks but an extended bureaucratic runaround. "But I could use information about the whereabouts and condition of my missing business associate, Tevik. As well as that of our colleagues, Ych'a and Denak."

Silok steepled his fingers before his face, apparently gathering his thoughts and deciding just how much to reveal. "Tevik's precise location is unknown to me. However, I can state one thing about him with near certainty."

Trip leaned forward expectantly. *I'm all ears,* he thought. On their way to his lips, he amended those words to, "I suppose that means you know where he's *not.*"

Silok nodded. "We can find no trace of Tevik on Vulcan. In addition, my investigators discovered that he chartered a private transport to take him offworld."

"When did he leave?" Trip wanted to know.

"He appears to have departed during the confusion immediately following the . . . attack . . ." Silok said before trailing off into silence.

"The attack on Mount Seleya," Trip said.

Silok nodded.

Before he'd taken up residence on Vulcan, Trip had never considered himself very good at reading the emotional states of most of the planet's inhabitants. He remembered T'Pol describing one of the priests of P'Jem as "agitated," even though Trip had found the man about as expressive as a corpse. Unlike that priest, Silok wore his heart on his sleeve. He looked pale, even for a Vulcan, and he wore an expression of grief that Trip remembered having seen in the mirror many times during the aftermath of the Xindi attack on Earth.

He looks the way I did after I found out Lizzie was dead, Trip thought. It finally hit him how deeply the callous destruction of Surak's *katra* must have affected the entire population of this world.

"Tevik appears to have left no word of his final destination," Silok said with a slight stammer.

"So he could be literally nearly anywhere."

"Unfortunately so, Mister Sodok. We would like you to find him. Bring him back to Vulcan as a person of interest with respect to the Mount Seleya bombing. Administrator T'Pau herself has personally requested your assistance in this matter."

Despite his best attempt to maintain a façade of Vulcan equanimity, Trip's forehead crumpled slightly. "I might have had a better chance of finding him if your bureau had let me go after him right after the Mount Seleya attack. Why have you stopped me until now?"

"Because until very recently I believed that Ych'a and Denak were responsible for the atrocity at Seleya."

Trip's eyebrows rose at this surprising but welcome revelation; after all, Ych'a and Denak were among T'Pol's oldest friends. "Does that mean they're free to go?"

Silok's answer was free of both stammer and hesitation. "No."

Trip's eyebrows rose again, this time borne aloft on an updraft of incredulity. "No? Why not?"

"They are still being somewhat . . . less than candid concerning their knowledge of the Mount Seleya attack— and about your mutual friend, Tevik."

Of course *they're not sharing,* Trip thought. *Their operations in the Romulan Star Empire might not have been authorized entirely according to Hoyle.* It was possible that Silok had no knowledge of those ops, even though he was Vulcan's security minister and thus nominally in charge of everything the V'Shar did.

"And how did you determine this?" Trip asked, keeping his voice quiet. "Telepathic interrogations?"

The look of disgust on Silok's face replied more eloquently than any words could have done. "I am as Syrannite as Administrator T'Pau, Mister Sodok. I will countenance no such abuses in my bureau."

Trip spread his hands before him in a peacemaker's gesture. "Sorry. I did not mean to offend you."

"Does your trading company have access to a ship?" Silok said, suddenly all business.

Does a le-matya *crap in the desert?* Trip thought as he nodded. Several small scout vessels were registered to Sodok's trading company, Ych'a, Sodok, and Tevik, a business entity that Trip still referred to privately as "Dewey, Cheatham & Howe." Trip had gone out of his way to ensure that one of those vessels would always be available to him and ready to get on Tevik's trail at a moment's notice.

Silok rose from behind his desk, signaling that the meeting had come to an end. "Will you assist us in finding Mister Tevik? And in assessing and neutralizing certain Romulan technological capabilities?"

"Of course," Trip said as he, too, rose. "But I'd like to see Ych'a and Denak first. If you don't mind."

"That is a reasonable request." Silok wasted no time summoning a pair of dour-faced, uniformed Vulcan males, either of whom would have been convincing in the role of museum docent or bodyguard. Trip's guides conducted him efficiently through a maze of bureaucratic office buildings and finally into a surprisingly spacious collection of mostly empty holding cells.

There was little that either Ych'a or Denak could convey to Trip—or vice versa—without also sharing it with the guards. Nevertheless, he told them that he was going after Tevik, and at Minister Silok's official request. Trip went away from the brief meeting reassured at least that T'Pol's friends weren't being overtly mistreated.

Once he was out of sight of his Vulcan handlers, Trip took a public hovercar to the large commercial spaceport located just beyond ShiKahr's western limits, where a fully fueled and equipped vessel awaited him.

The spaceport's central control spire grew ever larger in the hovercar's windows. *Contrary to folklore,* he thought, *Vulcans can and do lie.* He wondered whether Silok's sudden decision to ask for his help was the consequence of one such lie having finally worn out its usefulness.

Or was he merely out chasing down yet another lie?

SIX

PHLOX WASN'T COMFORTABLE with the idea of intentionally spreading gossip. But despite his unique position as chief medical officer, he was a member of Jonathan Archer's crew, and orders were orders. And he wasn't putting any of his patients in jeopardy by obeying those orders, however distasteful he might find them. Archer himself had tried to assuage Phlox's initial misgivings by asking him to think of his task—a task to which the captain referred, confusingly, as "Operation Hotspur"—as a primitive exercise in mass persuasion that had been known on Earth in past centuries as an advertising campaign. Finding that the last reference raised more questions than it settled, Phlox instead tried to regard what he was doing as a kind of intelligence op, even though such matters usually lay far outside his sphere of professional experience and expertise.

"It's fortunate we found you when we did," Phlox said as he slowly moved his scanner over the apparently genderless alien—a Tenebian engineering specialist called Crenq—who lay before him on the sickbay biobed. Each of the biobeds that flanked Crenq supported an unconscious Tenebian, the last of the other aliens Phlox had yet to release and return to the Tenebian vessel.

"Indeed," the creature said, its singsong natural speaking voice apparently being converted instantly to Denobulan by a small electronic device attached to the choker it wore about its neck. Because the being before Phlox was quadrupedal, it lay on its side as it displayed an epidermis that consisted of thousands upon thousands of iridescent green-and-brown scales, many of which seemed to have been painfully charred. "Had your vessel not come upon ours when it did, I would no doubt be dead by now," the alien said in its sexless, synthetic voice. "Along with everyone else on our ship."

"I only wish we had detected you earlier than we did," Phlox said. "Nearly half of your crew had already succumbed to radiation poisoning and general life-support failure before we even knew you were out here."

"Detecting us any earlier than you did wouldn't have been likely," said Crenq as it scratched at its heavily scaled neck with one of four surprisingly nimble, double-thumbed hands. "With our sensors damaged, we had to assume that any approaching vessels were more Raptor ships, intent upon finishing us off."

"Raptor ships," Phlox said. "Interesting."

"Your vessel has encountered them before?" the Tenebian asked, its two wide-set yellow eyes large and alert.

"If their hulls are painted with the bright red feathers of a predatory bird, then, yes, we have already had our share of . . . trouble from them." *More than our share,* Phlox added silently. *And no one can guess how much more might be to come.*

"I am sorry to hear that," Crenq said. "I wish now that I was in a position to help *you.*"

Phlox set the scanner down on the tray beside the biobed. "Perhaps you *can* help us. Would you mind sharing any data you've collected concerning the . . . Raptor ships' recent movements throughout this sector?"

The Tenebian answered with no discernible hesitation. "Certainly. I will direct the underchief in my department to present that data to your repair team before it leaves my vessel. It is but a small token of the thanks we owe you—not only for rescuing us but also for making our vessel operable again for its homebound voyage. Your people have even offered to restock our food stores to replace what had been irradiated after our shielding and life-support safeguards began to fail."

"There's no need to mention it," Phlox said.

Crenq moved awkwardly on the biobed, pulling its two equine forelimbs forward in an apparent effort to sit up. "But I must. Your captain's generosity is extraordinary. It must be reciprocated. Or, failing that, it must be sung to the stars."

Phlox could feel the color rising in his cheeks. He shook his head. "There's no need," he repeated.

"There is," Crenq insisted as it perched itself on the edge of the biobed, which was sagging slightly beneath its weight. "My colleagues and I already owe your people more than we can ever repay—and we do not know the name of the captain who made it possible. Or even the name of this ship, for that matter."

Based on multiple experiences over the past year or more, Phlox was reasonably sure that the Tenebian had already heard a great deal, both about *Enterprise* and her captain. Ever since the cargo vessel *Kobayashi Maru* met her unlucky end, it seemed that one would have to venture to another galaxy to find anyone without an etched-in-stone opinion about the culpability of NX-01's commanding officer in that disaster.

"Crenq, you are aboard the *Starship Enterprise*, from Earth," Phlox said. "Under the command of Captain Jonathan Archer."

Crenq lapsed into contemplative silence for a lengthy moment, then lay back on the biobed, on its side. "Archer's reputation precedes him. His actions spring not merely from generosity but also from a need to perform a penance."

"Perhaps," Phlox said quietly. While he could never fault the captain for the difficult decision circumstances had forced upon him on the day of the *Maru*'s demise, the doctor knew that Archer was considerably harder on himself.

"When you said you were fortunate for having come upon us when you did," Crenq said, "I see now that your words carried more than one meaning."

Phlox lofted an eyebrow. "How so?"

"The good fortune was not ours alone. Some of it also belongs to your captain." Crenq raised its long skull. A knowing look crossed the alien's otherwise inscrutable features. "Archer. The Earth commander who has so much for which to atone. I may not receive my underchief's cooperation once Archer's involvement becomes known to my colleagues."

Phlox sighed as he realized it was probably not in the nature of Tenebians to simply order compliance with the wishes of a superior officer. "I suppose there are times when we can only hope."

"Perhaps," Crenq said.

A few minutes after the shuttlepod containing the last of Chief Engineer Burch's repair team had returned to the launch bay, Malcolm Reed watched from the bridge as the Tenebian vessel's impulse drive began glowing a dull red. Moments later the alien vessel was under way, dwindling in size quickly as the distance between it and *Enterprise* multiplied exponentially.

Reed checked his tactical display for incoming messages. Still nothing.

Looks like the Tenebians never intended to give our repair team the data Phlox requested from their chief engineer, he thought. *All because the rumor mill out here has decided that the one Starfleet captain who happened to be anywhere near the* Kobayashi Maru *when she exploded is the bloody angel of death.* He was beginning to question the wisdom of Captain Archer's policy of displaying absolute generosity to ships in need during this period of extended picket duty. Even given the fact that Starfleet had laid in extra stores of virtually any raw material *Enterprise* might need for the next several months, what was the point of all this mostly unreciprocated largesse, demonstrated to virtually every little ship *Enterprise* encountered, during a time of desperate struggle against an intransigent enemy? What, after all, was *Enterprise*—and by extension Earth—getting in return for such excessive unselfishness?

A glissading bosun's-whistle alarm from the tactical console grabbed Reed's attention. *"Sickbay to Commander Reed,"* came the familiar voice of *Enterprise*'s chief surgeon.

Trying to keep his voice free of annoyance, Reed said, "What can I do for you, Doctor?"

"I'm not completely certain, Commander," Phlox said. *"I just received a private data transmission from the departing Tenebian ship. However, I can't make any sense of it. I'm uploading it to your console now."*

"Yes, I have it," Reed said. "Thank you, Doctor. Tactical out."

He refused to allow his hopes to rise until he started scrolling through the data itself. The formatting was alien, as were the time referents, but he was sure that Hoshi could help him sort out those wrinkles within a day or so. What remained might well be what he had hoped to receive hours earlier—a detailed record of the movements of Romulan ships throughout this sector.

Reed grinned as he uploaded the data to Hoshi's station. *Maybe the captain's new generosity-to-a-fault policy isn't such a bad idea after all.*

SEVEN

Early in the Romulan Month of *Khuti*, Year of D'Era 1181
Wednesday, September 29, 2156
Romulan *Transport Pod Eireth*, outbound from the Eisn
   (Romulus) system

THE LITTLE VESSEL RUMBLED and shook to exclamations of
surprise and dismay from the handful of junior functionaries who occupied the compact passenger compartment
amidships.

No sooner had the *Eireth* crossed the theoretical
boundary between the heliopause of Romulus's home star
and the near reaches of the Glintara sector than the pilot, a
smartly uniformed uhlan, began shouting urgently from the
forward section.

"We're under attack!"

Seated in the most forward passenger seat, Nijil, chief
technologist to Admiral Valdore i'Kaleh tr'Irrhaimehn,
supreme commander of all the fleets of the Romulan
Star Empire, smiled as a sensation of relief flooded him.
The attack had come slightly later than his timetable had
called for, but soon enough not to pose any insuperable
problems to his overall plan. It was the eve of the fleet's
biggest offensive into Coalition space, and thus a good time
for Nijil to flee while Valdore was preoccupied by matters
strategic and tactical. Nevertheless, Nijil planned to have a
word with his *Ejhoi Ormiin* confederates once their "pirate
raid"—the cover Nijil hoped would account for his quiet
escape from Valdore's watchful eye—was completed.

"We're losing power," the pilot said as he continued

frantically flipping switches in an effort to maintain control of the dying transport pod. The *Eireth* rocked and shuddered again, apparently having just absorbed more weapons fire. A conduit that ran across the ceiling before Nijil chose that moment to rupture, spraying cold, high-pressure vapor toward the aft portion of the cabin. The shouts and screams Nijil heard behind him accentuated the escalating chaos.

Let's don't overdo it out there, gentlemen, Nijil thought. He scowled as he rose and moved toward the cockpit section, steadying himself against the deck's heaving motions by grabbing the back of the empty copilot's chair.

"Who's attacking us?" Nijil asked the pilot, as if he didn't already know.

The young uhlan in the cockpit shook his head. "I'm not sure. Sensors are blinded now, and I can't fire either of our torpedoes without risking us being blown apart. Whoever's attacking us came out of warp almost directly on top of our heads. They opened fire before we even knew they were there."

Nijil was impressed despite the annoyance this surprise departure from the plan was causing him. He knew that some of his fellow anti-Praetorate *Ejhoi Ormiin* radicals were accomplished engineers and pilots—many had served in the Romulan military—but he hadn't expected such near-surgical precision from his rescuers. Nijil had hoped to make it appear that he and his staff had been in the wrong place at the wrong time, mere targets of opportunity during their otherwise quiet passage from Romulus to the Empire's newest secret offworld tech lab and shipbuilding facility in the Glintara system.

"Try to hail them," Nijil told the pilot. "It might buy us some time."

The pilot hastened to comply. But as he began working the console, a weird orange glow engulfed him, accompanied by an otherworldly hum. Within a space of three or four heartbeats, the pilot had vanished, leaving his seat conspicuously empty.

What in the name of Erebus? Behind him, Nijil heard the hum again, repeating and overlapping. He turned to face the passenger compartment and moved cautiously back into it. Though the fog emitted by the ruptured ceiling conduit interferred with visibility, he could see plainly enough that all of his junior functionaries had vanished, just as the pilot had.

Transporter beam, Nijil thought as his momentary confusion gave way to anger. He had ordered the *Ejhoi Ormiin* crew in charge of effecting his "kidnapping" to leave the others behind, aboard a crippled *Eireth*. The faux raiders were to have taken Valdore's loyal chief technologist against his will—and alone—to cover the fact that Nijil was willingly joining a band of political revolutionaries in order to rescue one of their own from the clutches of a Romulan military commander whom Nijil had come to fear might turn on him at any moment.

As Nijil moved back to the cockpit, intent on raising his errant colleagues on the *Eireth*'s comm system, he heard the hum once again. This time it was accompanied by a vague itching sensation, as though a hundred newly pupated *kllhe* grubs were crawling on his skin.

A sheet of orange light suddenly overwhelmed Nijil's vision, momentarily dazzling him before falling off quickly into impenetrable darkness. As his eyes adjusted to a much dimmer level of illumination, he saw that he was standing on a narrow, raised metal dais inside a small gray room.

A familiar deep voice sounded almost directly behind him. "Hello, Nijil."

The chief technologist turned and faced the voice's source. "Admiral Valdore. Why have you attacked my transport? Where are my people?"

Though his expression remained humorless, the admiral chuckled. After dismissing the junior officer who had doubtless been present only to run the transporter console, Valdore strode toward the edge of the stage.

"Which people are you most concerned about, Nijil?" the admiral said. "Those who accompanied you on the *Eireth*? Or the fellow traitors with whom you were expecting to rendezvous on your way to Glintara? We'll have to relocate the Glintara facility, incidentally, since your radical friends no doubt know all about it now. The last thing we need is to lose another cutting-edge research complex to an unfortunate 'accident.'"

Nijil became conscious of the fact that his mouth was opening and closing but not emitting any sound. Doing his best to master his shock, he said, "I'm sure I don't know what you're talking about, Admiral."

Valdore sighed, a look of disgust etched deeply into his craggy, battle-hardened features. "You insult us both by pleading ignorance, Nijil. I've been keeping you under close surveillance for more than a *fvheisn* now."

All at once, Nijil's insides seemed to go into freefall. A *fvheisn*. The time it took the gravitationally entangled sibling worlds Romulus and Remus to complete a single revolution about Eisn, their mutual fatherstar.

"I know all about your affiliation with the *Ejhoi Ormiin*," Valdore continued as he approached Nijil with slow, stalking footfalls. The chief technologist was becoming hyperaware of the admiral's considerable height and breadth at the shoulders. "You've been the principal reason all along that the *Ejhoi Ormiin* have succeeded in staying one step ahead of the military for such a long time. Not to mention the reason the fleet has yet to succeed in developing high-warp capability through the late Doctor Ehrehin's *avaihh lli vastam* program."

"Admiral, that simply isn't true," Nijil said, knowing that

his words sounded lame even as he uttered them. He took a step backward as Valdore continued his relentless advance.

Glancing down at the admiral's belt, Nijil saw the pommel of the razor-sharp *dathe'anofv-sen*—the Honor Blade—that dangled from it.

"We shall see, Nijil. Those we captured from the *Ejhoi Ormiin* team that appeared to be on its way to meet you are being interrogated as we speak. Who knows, if they turn out to be innocent of any conspiracy or wrongdoing, then maybe you will, too. In that event, I will owe you a profound apology. Perhaps even a promotion." Valdore smiled as he mounted the dais, forcing Nijil to shrink against the transporter stage's unyielding back wall. "But somehow I doubt that."

"I look forward to clearing my name, Admiral," Nijil said. He tried to project as much confidence as possible, but he knew that it was doing him precious little good; his back was up against the wall, both literally and figuratively. He tried to steady himself by placing his palms against the cold metal behind him as faintness and vertigo fought over which would sweep his feet out from beneath him first. Beads of sweat gathered on his brow as he contemplated how much the admiral might already know about his covert efforts to change the Romulan Star Empire's expansionist paradigm. Was Valdore aware that he had conspired with First Consul T'Leikha in a failed attempt to assassinate him?

"You will no doubt demand the Right of Statement," Valdore said with a nod.

A small runnel of sweat broke loose from Nijil's deeply ridged forehead, stinging his right eye. "Of course, Admiral."

Valdore unsheathed his *dathe'anofv-sen* without breaking eye contact with Nijil. He was sorely tempted to look at the bright metal, but Nijil felt he couldn't afford to look away from the admiral's dark, penetrating stare.

"You'll be allowed to make your statement, Nijil."

"Thank you, Admiral."

"You may not have any reason to thank me. You will give your statement not once, but twice."

Nijil's eyebrows both went aloft. "Twice?"

"You will deliver your first statement in the traditional manner. You will then reiterate it while connected to a bank of mind probes."

Nijil's guts turned to frozen slush at the mention of mind probes. He'd seen the damage they could do, especially at their highest settings. He'd participated in the interrogation of Vulcan's erstwhile administrator, V'Las, after he'd fled his own planet in the hope of building a new life for himself on Romulus.

V'Las was still alive on his adopted homeworld, but what remained of the ousted official's mind was scarcely enough to keep a sessile, tubelike *caotai'hhui* alive and able to filter-feed at the bottom of the Apnex Sea.

"Please, Admiral," Nijil said, conscious of the quaver in his voice. "I've been nothing but loyal to you."

"Don't worry, Nijil," Valdore said, raising his blade so that the chief technologist could no longer avoid looking at it. "I won't inflict anything on you that I'd withhold from your compatriots. You may consider this an opportunity to regain my trust. If, however, the mind probes reveal you to be in possession of special, hitherto concealed knowledge of, say, a previously unknown facility where your *Ejhoi Ormiin* colleagues are attempting to turn Doctor Erhehin's theoretical work into a functioning high-warp stardrive—"

Valdore paused, emphasizing his brief silence by placing his blade's keen edge tightly against Nijil's throat. Nijil felt something warm on his throat that he knew wasn't sweat.

"In that event," Valdore said, resuming at a volume scarcely above a whisper, "let's just say that things will go very *badly* for you."

And not necessarily quickly, Nijil thought as vertigo finally got the better of him.

EIGHT

Tuesday, October 19, 2156
Enterprise NX-01
Near Vissia

HOSHI SATO THOUGHT THAT the decontamination chamber on D Deck was the closest thing *Enterprise* had to a sensory deprivation tank—a place where a person might find near-perfect solitude. Clad only in her blue Starfleet-issue undershirt and briefs, her eyes closed beneath the plastic shield that covered them, Sato stretched back across the padded bench and let the combination of radiation and cleansing dermal gel work their subtle magic of destroying whatever alien biomaterial still lingered on her skin. As on any other occasion when circumstance brought her here, she reveled in the sterilization field's warm azure glow.

Doing her best to ignore the residual burning of the tiny, still-healing bite wounds that crisscrossed her torso, she imagined herself floating. The gentle pressure of her back against the cushions faded and she became a thing of pure thought, singular and alone—and certainly immune to the predations of alien parasites of the kind that had made her presence here necessary in the first place.

Then Major Takashi Kimura, the officer currently in charge of *Enterprise*'s detachment of Military Assault Command Organization troopers, ruined her illusion of perfect solitude by speaking.

"It's been twenty minutes, Lieutenant Sato," he said. "Phlox said we'd both be done to a turn in fifteen."

Sato waited until the MACO commander was done chuckling at his own crude joke—he always seemed to think that drawing a comparison between the decon chamber's radiocleansing function and Chef's approach to grilling spare ribs was wildly funny and original—before replying.

With a shake of her head that made the eye shields fall from her face, she said, "I'm fine right where I am, Major."

She opened her eyes in time to see his hulking form rise from a nearby bench. He was clothed much as she was, though his MACO-issue undergarments differed in that they bore a gray camouflage pattern.

"I'm surprised you want to stay in such a confined space," Kimura said as he draped a white towel across his shoulders and lingered beside the sealed exit hatch.

This room would seem a whole lot less "confined" if I didn't have to share it with a side of beef like you, Sato thought. She said, "Don't worry about me, Major."

A crooked grin split his face. "I never 'worry,' Lieutenant. I just couldn't help but notice that you were having a full-on panic attack before we got you off that wrecked Neethian ship."

"I wasn't panicking," she said with a tart scowl.

He held up both hands in a placating gesture. "Sorry, Lieutenant. I must have jumped to conclusions prematurely because of all the screaming. Not to mention the master class on claustrophobia you'd given the entire boarding team by the time we got you back to the shuttlepod."

She pushed herself up onto her elbows and glared at him. "I think I'm entitled to a scream or two, Major. My environmental suit was losing pressure because thousands of microscopic alien creepy-crawlies had bitten all the way through it. And I was trapped inside my suit with those things when they started digging into *me.*"

Kimura pointed at the angry red welt that ran diagonally across his lower belly. "I was on the lunch menu, too, remember? That's why I knew there was more than a flare-up of neurosis going on."

Sato allowed her glare to soften, at least a little. "Thanks, Major. I think."

He shrugged. "I never said I thought you *weren't* neurotic. Just that I understand why you felt you had to scream."

She looked around the room for something to throw at him; other than the flip-flops on her feet, she could find no convenient projectile anywhere within reach.

"Well, you can stay in if you like. I'm getting out." He turned his attention to the hatch mechanism. Then he pulled his hands back from the latch, making a show of hesitating as turned his face back toward her. "Unless, of course, you'd like me to stay long enough to rub a second coat of Phlox's Flea-Killer Compound into your, um, back."

Sato grimaced. Any prolonged thought about the critters that had made her presence here necessary came close to prolapsing her entire gastrointestinal tract—perhaps even as much as would accepting any additional help from Major Kimura in applying dermal gel.

"Thanks for the offer, Major. I can take care of it myself."

Kimura moved back toward the hatch. "Suit yourself, Lieutenant."

"And they're not 'fleas,' Major," she said as the past several hours of her suppressed ire came bubbling upward in spite of herself. "At least, not exactly."

He faced her again, then shrugged. "The word 'flea' describes these little bastards well enough for me." He began ticking off points on his large fingers. "Whatever else Crewman Cutler might have to say about 'em, they're tiny parasites. Evolution has not only specially adapted them for drinking mammalian blood, it has also optimized them for biting through any clothing that stands between them and a meal, environmental suits included. Hell, the little buggers might have chewed right through the polarized hull plating to get at us if Commander Reed hadn't found a way to use the pulse cannons to sterilize the ship's exterior. That qualifies them for an honorary membership in the order Siphonaptera. Which makes 'em fleas in my book."

Sato was impressed to discover that the MACO had evidently read a book or two in his time. It was a somewhat dismaying discovery, however, because she knew she wasn't half the amateur zoologist that Kimura seemed to believe he was. But she also felt confident that her etymological expertise would more than make up for whatever entomological deficits she might possess.

Besides, she had always intensely disliked imprecise language.

"They're *not* fleas, Major." Shedding her flip-flops as she got to her feet, she began ticking off her own points. "No terrestrial flea species I'm aware of can live independently from an atmosphere the way these things can. Or chew through a space suit, or a ship's hull. An Earth flea would freeze solid after a few seconds in a hard vacuum, and that would be that. If you have to compare these little critters to anything from Earth, you'd be better off thinking of tardigrades—those microscopic, eight-legged animals that schoolkids call 'water bears' or 'moss piglets.'"

"Except that *these* 'moss piglets' are superaggressive parasites in addition to being able to survive prolonged hard-vacuum exposure and lethal radiation levels," he said as the hatch opened. "Maybe Phlox will name the little buggers after you. *Exoaphaniptera sato.*"

"Don't you deserve some credit, too? I wasn't the only one they tried to eat."

He shrugged again. "I know. But you were the first to scream."

Kimura disappeared through the hatchway before she

could reach for one of her flip-flops and aim it properly. Once the hatchway had sealed itself again, she lay back down on the bench and covered her eyes.

She recalled that not terribly long ago she had petitioned Captain Archer for an Earthside transfer. At the time, she had felt that she had little to contribute to the success of *Enterprise*'s mission. But Archer had convinced her instead that her linguistic expertise would become increasingly crucial as the war against the Romulans escalated, and that he desperately needed to keep on her on his senior staff, a team that had already been much diminished by the death of Charles Tucker and the departure of Travis Mayweather.

She resumed "floating" in the soothing blue radiance. *"Exoaphaniptera sato,"* she said, and contemplated the irony of achieving immortality not for solving a baffling linguistic puzzle, but because a swarm of space bugs had tried to eat her.

She knew that what her senses reported was contrary as much to logic as to the laws of physics. However, T'Pol observed the walls and bulkheads of the captain's mess as they spun very slowly around her. With an act of willpower, she brought the unwelcome, illusory motion to a halt. Discomfort, after all, was merely an artifact of the mind. A mind as trained as hers could be controlled by means of discipline, focus, and mental effort.

No sooner had the room's unsettling appearance of movement subsided than she noticed that both of *Enterprise*'s Neethian guests were watching her with quiet intensity.

As was Captain Archer, whose brow had furrowed with concern. "Are you all right, Commander?"

Silently cursing herself for her weakness, T'Pol straightened in her chair. How could she have allowed herself to run out of her olfactory-numbing compound? She had mostly adapted to the odors of the eighty-some humans who lived and worked aboard *Enterprise.* The scent of the Neethians, however, was another matter entirely.

Squaring her shoulders as though she were responding to a surprise inspection from the Vulcan High Command, T'Pol said, "There is no need for concern, Captain. It has merely been a long day."

"Indeed it has," said the nearer of the two Neethians, both of whom were seated opposite T'Pol and Archer. Their inflexible, almost crystalline features made their moods more difficult to interpret than those of most other humanoid species she encountered. "It has been a long and eventful day."

The other Neethian continued. "You have accomplished much on our behalf, Captain Archer."

Archer drank from his water glass, then set it beside what little remained of the meal he had just shared with their visitors. "Don't mention it, Captain Thenir. We're just happy we were able to provide what little help we could."

"Oh, you've done a good deal more than help us," said the other Neethian, Cerebrar, Thenir's exec.

"I wish we could have done more," Archer said. "But by the time we reached that derelict Neethian passenger transport, it was too late for everyone aboard."

"Unfortunately, we did not discover that the vessel's distress signal was automated until after we dispatched our boarding team," T'Pol said as she unobtrusively steadied herself by placing her palms on the smooth tabletop.

"It was unfortunate indeed that your team was exposed to the voreborers, however," said Thenir.

"Voreborers," Archer said. "The microparasites that attacked our boarding party."

Thenir moved his head in a manner that T'Pol could only interpret as a nod. "The voreborers are a most persistent pest, Captain. They have plagued us since the earliest epoch of Neethian star travel. I hope they have inflicted no permanent harm upon your people."

"Doctor Phlox has assured me that everyone who was exposed to them has already been treated. They're all expected to recover completely," Archer said. "We've even managed to get rid of the parasites we discovered chewing on our hull."

"This gratifies us," Cerebrar said. "As does your discovery of a thing we have sought in vain for centuries—the voreborers' main breeding ground."

"Breeding ground?" Archer said, looking perplexed.

"The region where you found the derelict vessel is evidently where the voreborers gather to mate and reproduce," Thenir said. "Some of the spatial anomalies you have charted in this sector may be the very places where the voreborers evolved in the first place."

"But I thought the voreborers came from your homeworld," Archer said. "And that they followed you into deep space."

"No, Captain," said Cerebrar. "The voreborers can live only in deep space. They are uniquely adapted to it."

"Life evolving independently of any planet?" Archer said, stunned. "Forgive me, Cerebrar, but that sounds unlikely."

"The phenomenon is merely outside Starfleet's present realm of experience," T'Pol observed. "Doctor Phlox has documented several such species, as has the Vulcan High Command. The term Phlox has applied collectively to these life-forms is 'cosmozoa'—creatures capable of carrying out all their life functions in deep space, independent of a planetary environment."

"The voreborers appear to have spread themselves from their breeding ground to points throughout Neethian and Vissian space, using the local gravimetric anomalies and subspace distortions that run through this sector," Cerebrar said. "Regions that *Enterprise* has mapped in detail."

"Now that we have located the source of the voreborers," Thenir said, "we may find ways to avoid encounters with them. Perhaps we can even find a means of eradicating them."

"I would advise against any eradication campaign, if merely quarantining this region of space would suffice," T'Pol said.

Archer coughed quietly, looking uncomfortable. "I'm forced to agree with my science officer."

"But why?" Thenir said, his facial features remaining immutable and unreadable. "The voreborers are mere pests. Not to mention potentially deadly, as you have seen yourself."

"Agreed," Archer said. "But as *you've* pointed out, they're creatures of space. Which means they must also be part of some larger, spaceborne ecosystem. Who knows what might happen to that ecosystem if you wipe out a piece of it?"

"Captain Archer is correct," T'Pol said. "Perhaps the anomalous phenomena we have mapped throughout this sector—the very features that seem to nurture the voreborers—might become more widespread. Such a development would make interstellar navigation in this sector more dangerous than the voreborers ever could."

"That is purely speculative," Thenir said.

"True enough," Archer said. "But if I've learned one thing since *Enterprise* left Earth, it's never to disregard the law of unintended consequences."

The two Neethians lapsed into a protracted silence, apparently digesting Archer's words.

Thenir was the first to speak. "Your reputation fails to do justice to your wisdom. As does your name."

Archer was smiling at Thenir, but the expression struck T'Pol as forced. "I'm afraid I don't know what you mean."

"Please understand," Thenir said, "I merely report the observations of others."

Archer nodded. "Feel free to be honest."

"Very well. It is widely believed among my people that you do not take care in making decisions."

T'Pol didn't doubt that was because the story of the final moments of the *Kobayashi Maru* was circulating through Neethian space, probably in a progressively degenerating form.

Archer's smile faded, prompting T'Pol to wonder if he was reliving the *Maru*'s unavoidable demise.

"I understand," he said. "At least the part about my reputation. But what was it you said about my name?"

"Again, I mean no offense, Captain," Thenir said.

"None taken, Captain," Archer said, though T'Pol could hear an edge in his voice. "What about my name?"

The Neethians looked at each other as though fearful of saying the wrong thing. At length, Thenir faced Archer. "You have demonstrated yourself to be something entirely different from what your own language defines as 'one who wields a weapon that slays at a distance.'"

Archer tossed the padd he had been reading onto his desk, then stormed over to his ready room port. Standing alone in the soothing semidarkness, he watched the Neethian vessel pull away from *Enterprise*'s main starboard docking port and drop into the limitless chasm of interstellar space. Within a few minutes, the immutable distant stars changed from fixed points of light to bright, distorted streaks as his ship returned to warp, headed for the next stop on her seemingly endless—and endlessly banal—itinerary.

The door chime sounded.

"Come," Archer said as he turned. T'Pol stepped across the threshold.

"The Neethian vessel left fully stocked with both food and Earth alcohol, per your orders, Captain," she said.

"Thank you, Commander. I trust you're a little more comfortable now that our guests are back under way."

"I found the Neethians to be a good deal more . . . fragrant than humans . . . or beagles. I hope no one noticed the . . . intensity of my discomfort."

Archer chuckled as T'Pol cautiously looked around the ready room. "Don't worry, T'Pol. Porthos is in my quarters."

She nodded. "I have a question, Captain."

"About Porthos? Or the Neethians?"

Unfortunately, T'Pol did not appear to be in the mood for banter. "About *Enterprise,* Captain."

With a sigh, he walked to his desk and sat down heavily on his chair. Taking up a position on the nearby couch, T'Pol did likewise.

"All right. Shoot."

"Why are we being so generous, Captain? The Neethians very likely had no pressing need for the extra consumables we furnished. In all probability, they merely took advantage of us. Just as many of the other species we have taken such pains to assist out here over the past few months have no doubt done."

Archer couldn't help but agree that it felt strange to dig so deeply into *Enterprise*'s stores for the needy and the greedy alike. "Letting the locals think they're taking advantage of us is central to *Enterprise*'s current mission."

"Hence the extra supplies we keep taking on from Starfleet's matériel convoys," T'Pol said. "Still, it seems a profligate use of resources."

Archer grinned. "It isn't as though we haven't always made it a priority to render aid to other vessels."

"But Captain, with Earth in peril, why are we not on the front lines?"

"Until we can ensure that the Romulans can't seize control of *Enterprise,* we are a liability . . . *I'm* a liability." The captain sighed. "So now we map to the Planck length everything in these sectors of space. We have one true mission priority. You could call it 'ground-level' diplomacy. Or maybe 'sea-level' is a better adjective."

The slope of her eyebrows suddenly grew more acute. "I do not understand."

He reached for his padd. "I have a piece of ancient Earth literature that may do a better job than I can of explaining why I keep spending our *sous*." He touched a button on the padd's display and tossed the device to T'Pol, who caught it expertly.

"*Sous*, Captain?"

"Gold coins, French currency during the time of the Napoleonic Wars."

T'Pol turned her eyes to the padd's display screen. "*Hornblower and the 'Hotspur'* by C. S. Forester," she said, her dark eyes intent on the archaically constructed text.

"One of Admiral Gardner's favorites."

"I gather it's a historical record of the Napoleonic Wars."

Archer hesitated. "No. It's a historical novel about a British naval commander who quietly gained the upper hand against the French by gathering information— everything from charts of the tides and sand bars to enemy ship movements, even the local gossip from the fishermen who worked all along the French coastline."

A look of dawning comprehension crossed her face. "Information that had to be purchased." T'Pol began scrolling through Forester's nautical narrative. "It seems illogical to use a work of fiction as the basis for a strategic plan."

"Perhaps—"

The boatswain's whistle of an incoming intercom signal interrupted Archer's reply. He leaned forward and punched the ACCEPT button. "Archer here. Go ahead."

"*Ensign Leydon here, sir. You asked to be informed when we got to within four hours of the Vissian system, sir.*"

"Very good, Ensign. Archer out."

Archer hoped that word of *Enterprise*'s generosity thus far had softened the hearts of those from whom he hoped to obtain some help against the ever-advancing Romulan threat.

NINE

As HE WALKED BESIDE his science officer past the Palace of
Technology and through the Hall of Deliberation's ornate
grand entryway, Jonathan Archer realized he had begun to
believe that this day might never come—the day he would
at long last be permitted to address the Grand Moot, the
greatest political deliberative body on all of Vissia Prime.

T'Pol had evidently been thinking along very much the
same lines. "I am gratified that the Vissians have finally
deigned to give our request a formal hearing," she said,
pitching her voice low so she would not be overheard by
the quartet of white-uniformed minders that guided them
toward the main auditorium.

Archer nodded, keeping his gaze straight ahead at the
broad, high wooden doors that had begun to part several
meters ahead of the group. "Let's hope all the stalling
they've done so far has satisfied whatever grudge the
Vissians might still be carrying against us."

It had taken weeks to cut through all the official red tape
that had stood between Archer's request—made on behalf
of the Coalition of Planets Security Council, the United
Earth government, and Starfleet—and landing an *Enterprise*
shuttlepod on Vissia Prime. During that time, word of *Enterprise*'s ongoing generosity could have filtered far and wide
throughout Vissian society. But he had no idea if *Enterprise*'s

recent actions had persuaded this world's foremost decision makers not to punish Earth for Trip Tucker's admittedly ill-advised interference with their cultural practices three years earlier. Indeed, the Vissian government's official rejection of multiple diplomatic requests from Starfleet, the United Earth government, and the Coalition Security Council that Vissia share its technology—their photonic weapons, warp-drive technology, and trinesium starship hulls were more advanced than their Earth counterparts—augured badly for the outcome of today's vote.

As Archer and T'Pol made their way to the main auditorium's central dais, the captain clung to the hope that these people would see that helping Earth fight the Romulan Star Empire was in both their interests. Whatever hard feelings remained on Vissia because of *Enterprise*'s botched first contact, they had to be able to see that the Romulans were as dangerous to Vissia as they were to Earth. The Vissians, particularly their Captain Drennik, had struck him as reasonable people, if perhaps somewhat blind to the shortcomings of their society. Archer couldn't think of anybody who wasn't tainted by that very same blindness, at least to some extent.

There's one thing I can say for sure about these people, though, he thought. *They've never gone out of their way to take offense. Not like the Kreetassans, who go ballistic if an alien eats in front of them—or if Porthos happens to pick the wrong tree to pee on.* And even *they* had accepted his apology—at least once the offending party had satisfied the Kreetassans' perverse need to have them jump through various hoops.

But the captain's hopes began to recede when he saw the hard glares on the faces of many of the lawmakers who were filing into the chamber to take their seats. A slender, white-garbed woman of apparent early middle age—an elderly male whom Archer took to be a sergeant at arms identified her as Grand Moot Moderator Fraddok—took the podium and brought the meeting to order with a minimum of ceremony. Although Archer wasn't encouraged by the expressions he saw on so many of the Vissian legislators' faces, he had to admire their efficiency; they made the Klingon High Council look positively indolent.

At the direction of their minders, Archer and T'Pol took seats in the gallery, which a long, curved railing separated from the seats of the Vissian lawmakers. After about fifteen minutes passed during which the Grand Moot tended to several pieces of tedious and all but indecipherable institutional housekeeping business, Moderator Fraddok raised her voice to a volume that must have been clearly audible to the very back of the vast chamber.

"Today the Grand Moot of Vissia Prime receives a visiting delegation from the Coalition of Planets. We will vote upon the delegation's formal request that Vissia Prime assist the Coalition—specifically the planet known as Earth—in its war against the Romulan Star Empire."

Fraddok's gaze dropped from where it had been focused—the back of the hall—until her eyes locked tightly upon Archer's. "Do I relay the essence of your request accurately, Captain Jonathan Archer?"

Archer slowly rose to his feet, and T'Pol followed suit. "It's accurate, Moderator Fraddok. But maybe a little bit incomplete."

She looked both irritated and intrigued. "Incomplete, Captain? How?"

It's showtime, Archer thought. Summoning a smile, he said, "There are some fundamental things that you and your colleagues need to understand about the Romulans."

"We already know a great deal about them, Captain. Thanks to our own interstellar space service, and our listening posts in the sector known on your star charts as Gamma Hydra, we understand that the Romulans are both aggressive and territorial."

Mention of the Gamma Hydra sector evoked painful

memories of the demise of the *Kobayashi Maru*. Archer put them aside, concentrating instead on his relief that these people weren't burying their heads in the sand the way Vulcan, Andoria, and Tellar had. But if that wasn't their strategy, then why did the Vissians still seem like such a tough sell?

"The Romulans are indeed both of those things, Moderator Fraddok," he said. "In addition, they are expansionists. If you've been watching them over the past few years, then you don't need to take my word on that. Therefore, joining in the Coalition's fight will benefit Vissia as much as it does us."

Fraddok shook her head, which caused a few strands of her short, neatly coifed hair to fall before her eyes. "Frankly, Captain, your Coalition appears to have little value at the moment. Haven't its nonhuman members essentially left Earth to its own devices as the Romulans continue to advance?"

"I'd call that an oversimplification of what's really going on, Moderator Fraddok." Archer gestured to his right, where T'Pol stood. "You'll notice that my second-in-command is not human. She's from Vulcan—a core member of the Coalition."

To Archer's chagrin, Fraddok didn't miss a beat. "But Vulcan is a member world that has refused to enter the fray. Isn't that true, Commander T'Pol?"

"Moderator Fraddok, that isn't fair—" Archer said.

"Captain, I was addressing Commander T'Pol," Fraddok said, cutting Archer off. "Commander, isn't that true?"

T'Pol exchanged a significant look with Archer before turning back toward the dais. "For the moment, Vulcan's government has opted out of the war."

"As have Andoria and Tellar," Fraddok continued. "That leaves us with an invitation to join a theoretical Co-alition of Planets that consists, in actual practice, of but one world, plus a few scattered human holdings in two adjacent star systems. And the one world in question is the very planet whose clumsy, arrogant, and ill-prepared explorers precipitated the completely avoidable death of a Vissian cogenitor—a death that not only robbed an innocent, hardworking Vissian couple of the prospect of becoming parents but also strained Vissia Prime's already small cogenitor population."

The room was immediately awash in a low buzz of hostile noise. *Not good*, Archer thought.

Moderator Fraddok called sharply for silence. Addressing Archer once again, she said, "Do you deny any of this?"

Shaking his head, Archer said, "No, you haven't said anything that isn't true, Moderator Fraddok. But this information is *also* incomplete."

"Again, incomplete?" Anger pulled her face taut. "How so?"

"You're not taking into account humanity's capacity to learn. I'd be the last to deny that we have made mistakes. I've made a few myself and probably will again. But whenever humans stumble, we pick ourselves back up. We learn to do better next time."

"Nevertheless, the damage remains done, Captain. Your words do very little to encourage me."

"All I can offer you is the truth, Moderator Fraddok. The truth about Earth and the Coalition to which it belongs. The truth about the Romulans. And the truth about the difference between us and them."

"And what is that difference?"

"The Coalition's priorities are exploration and peaceful coexistence," Archer said. "The Romulans are interested in fear and conquest, pure and simple."

The room fell silent again. Archer could only dare to hope. Then Moderator Fraddok, her face a mask of nonemotion that must have impressed even T'Pol, called for an immediate vote.

*   *   *

The minders conducted Archer and T'Pol to the sprawling plaza in a courtyard adjacent to the spaceport from which they were expected to depart shortly in Shuttlepod One.

"These people digested the complete works of Shakespeare and Sophocles within a day," Archer said when he was certain that they were alone. He leaned on his elbows across a railing and watched streams of Vissian civilians going about their various errands as the bloated Vissian sun slowly sank into the western horizon.

T'Pol nodded soberly. "There is no question that the Vissians have developed an extremely refined and intellectually rich culture."

"That's what I thought, too," Archer said. "So what the hell is wrong with them?"

T'Pol raised a quizzical eyebrow. "Captain?"

"I mean, for such a brainy bunch they can be damned pigheaded."

"The Vissians aren't human, Captain," T'Pol said quietly as she stepped up to the railing. "Therefore, applying human cultural standards to them can be problematic. I tried to remind Commander Tucker of that while we were making first contact with the Vissians. I can see that I need to do the same with you."

Archer shrugged. "I *know* the Vissians aren't human. I guess I just expected them to be more sympathetic toward us than the Klingons were, Trip's . . . indiscretion notwithstanding. I must have screwed the grint hound today in the speechmaking department."

"No, Captain. I found your words persuasive."

"That's flattering, T'Pol, but you're not the one I needed to persuade. What do you suppose I did wrong?"

"Perhaps nothing. Moderator Fraddok evidently believes Vissia is advanced enough, at least in a technological sense, to neutralize any Romulan attempt to annex their homeworld. Therefore she may believe that any alliance against the Romulans would be superfluous."

Archer sighed and shook his head. "Well, I hope for her sake that the Romulans don't put that belief to the test. Advanced as the Vissians are, she has no idea what her people would be up against."

"I agree," T'Pol said. "Should that occur, then I would hope that the moderator will not be too proud to ask Earth for assistance."

The captain chuckled. "I don't care what anybody says. Vulcans *do* have a sense of humor."

She lifted an eyebrow. "I am completely serious, Captain. Word has already spread—across this sector and beyond— that the *Starship Enterprise* from Earth will provide assistance to anyone who requires it. Whatever ill will Fraddok may still harbor regarding the unfortunate circumstances surrounding humanity's first contact with Vissia, even she must be well aware of the reputation you have forged for *Enterprise*—and, by extension, for the Coalition and Earth."

He shrugged again. "I'll have to help a hell of a lot more old ladies across the street to drown out all the chatter about how I handled the *Kobayashi Maru*."

"It may not be logical for the Vissians to blame you for the cogenitor's death," T'Pol said. "It is, however, understandable, given the paramount importance that any civilization must place upon reproduction."

"It's a lot more understandable than Starfleet's decision to send *me* to negotiate with the Vissians. Admiral Gardner should have sent somebody else here to plead our case. Captain Ramirez, maybe. Or Narsu. Even Duvall would have done better."

T'Pol stepped away from the railing, approaching Archer. "I believe that would have been a mistake."

"A *mistake*? Compared to what? They turned us down flat, T'Pol. Exactly the way the Klingons did. Worse, in fact—even the Klingons spent a few minutes pretending to think about it before they told us 'no' and sent us packing."

"The Vissians might not have agreed even to hear Earth's request had it come from anyone else, Captain. Your own personal willingness to come here to plead on behalf of Earth and the Coalition could be regarded as a willingness to face the consequences of your—of *our*—past mistakes."

Archer gazed at the setting sun. Thanks to the distorting effects of the thickest portions of Vissia's atmosphere, he could look directly into the swollen orange disk without even having to squint. "I guess there's no point grousing about it now. It's done. I just wonder whom Starfleet will want me to charm next. For all I know, Admiral Gardner will send me to try to win over the new first monarch of Krios Prime."

"Unfortunately, the Vulcan Diplomatic Service reports that the head of state the Kriosians installed last year is far less amenable to entering interstellar mutual defense pacts than was her predecessor," T'Pol said.

Kaitaama. He recalled the beautiful young woman whom he and Trip had freed from her Retellian kidnappers some four years ago. Surely First Monarch Kaitaama would have felt an obligation to assist the Coalition, and thereby the homeworld of her rescuers. She no doubt would have thrown her full support behind Earth against the Romulans—had her government not fallen nearly two years ago to a military coup.

The captain shook his head. "I still wonder why Starfleet keeps sending *me* out to make Earth's sales pitch."

"Why should they send anyone else, Captain? You're Jonathan Archer, the man who persuaded three Xindi species to abandon their plan to destroy Earth."

"My batting average seems to have slumped a bit since those days, T'Pol. Maybe I should try the Arkonians next," Archer deadpanned, though he was well aware that Vulcans generally considered this aggressive, reptilian starfaring race to be dangerous and irrational—even in comparison to humans. "Or maybe the Orion Syndicate, or the Kreetassans."

T'Pol's head tilted slightly in evident bewilderment. "You must be joking."

"Of *course* I'm joking." He closed his eyes and let the transitory warmth of the waning sun wash over him. "But I suppose the joke is on us. I shouldn't be surprised that Earth still has to stand more or less alone against the Romulans—with the paper that the Coalition Compact is written on as our only armor."

"That isn't precisely true, Captain."

He turned away from the sun and faced her. "Oh? Did Andoria and/or Tellar suddenly decide to get off the sidelines?"

Her lips pursed in evident irritation, and the intensity of T'Pol's gaze nearly scorched him. "Not to my knowledge, Captain. But perhaps a reminder is in order that a number of influential individuals from both societies have pledged to aid Earth's war effort by raising as much private assistance as possible."

Archer nodded, recalling a recent subspace communication during which the former Andorian Imperial Guard general officer Shran had confessed to finding his government's decision to abrogate its mutual defense responsibilities under the Coalition Compact completely unacceptable, even to the point of being dishonorable. The Tellarite freighter pilots, Skalaar and his brother Gaavrin, had echoed Shran's sentiments a few days later, after *Enterprise* had responded to their request for the tungsten, cobalt, and magnesium alloy they needed to rebuild their warp coils, which had been overtaxed by some of the very same gravimetric anomalies and subspace distortions that *Enterprise* had been so carefully mapping. Archer felt extremely grateful for these gestures, though he couldn't help wondering if they would prove any more credible or effective than the yet-to-be-realized aid that Kolos had promised at the end of the captain's last visit to Qo'noS.

"It's nice to know we might be able to count on a little help from *somebody*," he said at length.

"All across Vulcan today," T'Pol said, "my people are observing the annual rite of *Kal Rekk*."

The apparent non sequitur nearly gave Archer whiplash. "Cal Wreck?"

"*Kal Rekk*. All ordinary business stops on this day. It is a time of silence and solitary meditation."

He frowned. "You Vulcans seem to do a lot of that sort of thing anyway without having to declare a special bank holiday for it."

"Unlike other Vulcan rites, the contemplations of *Kal Rekk* have a particular purpose that requires our full attention as a people—atonement for our mistakes."

Archer took a silent moment to digest that. It occurred to him almost immediately that Administrator T'Pau would have much for which to atone. Her effective abandonment of Earth in the face of the Romulan threat made his failure to rescue the *Kobayashi Maru* seem almost petty in comparison.

"Why are you telling me this, T'Pol?" he said.

"Because you may find it useful to consider the fact that you are not the only one who feels the need to atone for the mistakes of the past."

A flare of anger rose in Archer's chest, though he wasn't certain whether it was in response to her words or her damnably calm tone. "You think this mission is about atonement? About my somehow making up for the *Maru* disaster? Or for the cogenitor's death?"

"Perhaps both, Captain. But it is not for me to say." Her cadence abruptly downshifted, transitioning instantly from that of a Vulcan lecturer to the confidential tone of a close friend and confidante. "Regardless, it's clear to me that those events still weigh heavily upon you. When I begin my own *Kal Rekk* observance tonight aboard *Enterprise*, I shall spend addition time in meditation to atone for whatever role *I* may have played in allowing you to carry such terrible burdens alone."

Archer didn't quite know what to say. *I think this may be as close as any human has ever come to getting a Vulcan to promise to pray for him.*

"Captain," T'Pol said. She was looking directly at him. *No*, he realized a moment later. She was looking just *past* him.

A voice sounded from behind, startling him. "Captain Jonathan Archer."

Archer turned quickly, not at all sure what to expect. His name had been spoken by a Vissian male, dressed in the white robe of a high governmental official. "I am Bote J'Ref, Vissia's minister of science, Captain," the old man said in a voice both strong and reedy.

"I'm sorry," Archer said. "We were about to continue to the spaceport. I just thought I'd stop for a moment on the way to enjoy the sunset."

The old man appeared confused by Archer's preemptive apology. "I haven't come to hurry your departure from Vissia, Captain. In fact, I am delighted to discover that you haven't yet left."

Archer wondered if he dared hope that the Vissian legislature had changed its mind about helping Earth beat back the Romulans.

Archer asked, "What can I do for you?"

"I have no request to make of you, Captain," the old man said.

"Then I hope you've come to announce that your government has reconsidered its decision not to share Vissian technology with us. The information sharing wouldn't have to be extensive. If, say, we could start building our hull plating out of trinesium, that alone would set the Romulans' invasion plans back quite a bit."

The Vissian shook his head sadly. "The Grand Moot passed the Permanent Embargo on Technology Transfers to Immature Civilizations Act by a significant margin. It is unlikely that the body will reconsider the measure anytime soon."

Immature civilizations, Archer thought, suppressing a wince. *Ouch.*

"Then what can I do for you?" he repeated.

"Nothing, Captain. But I do wish to discuss with you something you have *already* done."

Although the Vissian's manner remained pleasant enough, a feeling of dread seized Archer. He braced himself, waiting to take the blame for some other well-intentioned fubar.

"And what's that?" Archer said.

"Your vessel—*Enterprise*—recently responded to a distress call. My son's vessel had suffered damage from an unmapped gravitational shear phenomenon. Your crew subsequently provided us with maps of such detail that no one else has run afoul of it."

"I remember the ship," Archer said. "And your son?"

"He is fine, Captain," the old man said. Archer noticed only then that tears were standing in the Vissian's eyes. "Your people even performed significant repairs on his ship before you parted company. For coming to my son's aid, Captain, you have my gratitude. *Earth* has my gratitude."

Despite his earlier dour mood, a smile escaped onto Archer's face. "Thank you for that, Minister J'Ref," he said in a gentle tone. "But it wasn't just me or my crew that helped your son.

"It was the Coalition. . . ."

PART II
2157–2159

TEN

THE VOICE THAT REVERBERATED across the semicircular bridge module was laced with characteristic impatience. *"What's the holdup, gentlemen? Let's get the candle lit and fly this bird out of spacedock."*

"Everything reads as ready now, Captain Jefferies," Tobin Dax said, turning toward his colleague S'chn T'gai Skon. The Vulcan was on "temporary loan" from the Vulcan Science Academy to the Cochrane Institute and was due to return to his homeworld shortly. Dax hoped his nervousness about today's simulation wasn't audible in the timbre of his voice, though he suspected that Vulcans were far more sensitive to emotional cues than they let on. *They can smell a flop sweat,* Dax thought.

The Vulcan nodded in Dax's direction, apparently absorbed in the readings on the console before him. "Confirmed," he said. "Initiate the simulation." The taciturn mathematician then nodded to Dr. Pell Underhill.

The sole human on the technical team, Underhill was seated in the center of the bridge module. To reach him, one had to negotiate a railing, a couple of steps down into what the team had come to call the "command well," and then take as many steps back upward to reach the central dais—a riser that supported the bizarrely thronelike chair on which a nominal ship commander would have sat, were this an actual ship of the line rather than a mere test model.

The team had labored for more than a local year on the gray, aesthetically unappealing technological kludge that now enclosed them. All the while they had endured with as much grace as possible the constant inquiries into their progress by their overseers, Captains Matthew Jefferies and Eric Stillwell. Despite Starfleet's seeming omnipresence— and the team's apparently endless difficulties in getting the various new systems integrated, calibrated, and synchronized—Dax felt satisfied that the three specialists had finally turned out a working prototype of the starship bridge of the future.

All that remained to be seen was whether it would prove resistant to one of the Romulan Star Empire's most effective weapons.

Underhill pushed a button on the arm of his chair. "Simulation initiated."

Dax was seated at an angular computer console located near the rear of the bridge module's starboard side. A quick glance at his displays confirmed that the simulation was up and running. He turned his chair toward the bridge's center, where the two-person helm and navigational consoles blinked, whirred, and bleeped as though they were being manipulated by flesh-and-blood personnel instead of commands being relayed through the powerful central computer core of the starflight lab at the Cochrane Institute's Henry Archer Hall.

Dax noticed that Underhill was wearing a faint smile, which had to be a positive sign, an indicator that everything was proceeding well. Having been preoccupied with building and installing the bridge module's hardware and firmware, Dax knew less than did the Terran physics specialist about every specific circumstance of the test that was now under way.

"So what happens now, Pell?"

Underhill turned the big chair toward Dax and shrugged

dramatically. "Skon and I deliberately introduced an element of randomness to the tests. After all, this test would be useless if our tactical systems could anticipate every possible attack permutation in advance. You know that."

Dax reddened; of course he knew that. But with so many months of work at stake—time that might have been better applied to Starfleet's goal of building the long-sought-after warp-seven-capable stardrive—he was feeling nervous. And he knew that led to his babbling incoherently.

"The only thing we know with any certainty," Skon added, "is that—"

The bridge module's sudden violent shaking interrupted all conversation in the chamber, which now reverberated like a colossal bell that had just been struck.

"—the Romulans are going to attack," Dax said, anticipating Skon while grabbing at the sides of his console to keep his chair from being upended.

"Tactical Alert!" the Trill said reflexively in response to the flashing of his console. His neck and face flushed as he realized he had stated the blindingly obvious. Silence reigned for a few uncomfortable moments, and Dax found himself wishing that the team hadn't voted down his desire to equip the simulator with a loud alert klaxon.

"The hull plating seems to be holding, at least so far," Underhill said at length, sounding slightly winded. Dax realized only then that the human had been thrown forward out of his chair, prompting the Trill to wonder why he hadn't thought of installing some sort of inertial damper failsafe or restraint system.

Oblivious of the simulated danger, Underhill stood where he had landed, behind the helm console, as he busied himself reading the indicators from the integrated ops controls. Curiously, Underhill looked just as happy and confident as when he'd been in the captain's chair. "Programmed counterattack is now in progress," he said.

A gentle shuddering of the bridge, which repeated twice in as many seconds, confirmed the launch of a virtual return-fire volley. Photonic torpedoes, Dax guessed from the vibration patterns. The bridge's central viewer displayed the weapons as intersecting, foreshortened strings of light that vanished into the infinitude of blackness.

"How come I'm not seeing any simulated Romulan ships out there?" Dax said, frowning.

"Many documented Romulan attacks have been conducted from ambush," Skon said.

"I know, but it's not as though they're completely invisible, is it?" Dax said. "The simulation seems to be giving them a pretty big advantage over us."

"A simulation that goes easy on us does us no good," Underhill said. "If we can beat the Romulans in simulation under these conditions, we could develop a distinct tactical advantage over them."

Dax suppressed a grin; a playful part of his brain paraphrased a favorite bit of Terran musical theater that Underhill had introduced him to a few months ago: *If we can beat 'em there, we can beat 'em anywhere.*

"Let's hope," Dax said quietly as he settled in to wait for the rest of the simulated battle to unfold.

Underhill was grinning triumphantly. "Sensors have detected considerable debris from the enemy ship. We've hurt them. Helm is laying in a close approach course."

"Weapons systems are locking on the hostile vessel," Skon said, a faint edge of distaste in his voice. Or was Dax imagining it?

"Be careful, computer," Dax muttered as he gently patted the console before him. "You don't want to get cocky with these Romulans. They're tricky bastards."

But the virtual starship soldiered on, as the main viewer quickly confirmed, with a wireframe rendering of one of the Romulan Star Empire's nearly flat, semicircular warships.

Dax felt a momentary sensation of regret that Skon, who had been in charge of creating the tactical displays, had not seen fit to create a more detailed representation of the hostile vessel's hull, complete with hull-plating joins and the fiery mass of sharp talons and angry red feathers that usually covered the bellies of such ships.

Dax's console flashed. "They're hailing us," he said.

"Ignore it," Skon said. "We cannot risk any Romulan malware entering our main computer core."

"Firewall is up and functioning," Dax said. He felt uncomfortable with the notion of ignoring a hail under circumstances such as these, even in a simulation. Suppose a shipload of *real* Romulans were to make a sincere surrender attempt at some point?

"Our weapons systems are opening fire again," Underhill said as he took a seat behind the helm.

Dax expected the deck beneath his feet to shimmy slightly in response to the virtual weapons fire, just as it had during the previous salvo. He waited for a good five-count before he noticed that no such thing had happened—and that the once-grinning Dr. Underhill now looked as dour as Skon.

"The weapons haven't fired, Doctor Underhill," Skon said.

"Fire control *did* transmit the appropriate signal," Underhill said. "It appears not to have traveled past the bridge."

Another alarm flashed right in front of Dax's surprised eyes. "Comm system's just gone down. This ship's virtual crew can't get in touch with its virtual Starfleet—or anybody else."

"Weapons control systems have stopped accepting commands," Underhill said, punctuating his statement by pounding his right fist once against the top of the helm console. "Helm's gone, too. Along with our hull-plating system and propulsion." He smacked the console again.

All that percussive input can't be helping matters any, Dax thought.

The Trill turned away from Underhill to consult his console. "The Romulans are approaching."

"Confirmed," said Skon. "Internal sensors detect intense incoming directed-energy transmissions."

"Transporters," Dax said. "Romulan boarding parties. They'll take the ship."

Underhill muttered a curse. "Not if we blow it up around them."

"The crew escape pods are frozen solid," Dax said. "Autodestruct is dead as well."

With a loud pneumatic hiss, the ceiling and forward section of the bridge module began to open. Dax blinked in the late-afternoon light of Alpha Centauri III's two primary stars as a silhouette of a human male stormed into the middle of the bridge.

"*This* is all you have to show for the past year's work?" Captain Jefferies said, plainly annoyed. "*This* is how we're supposed to overcome the Romulans' remote-hijack weapon?"

"There appears to be some work still ahead of us," Underhill said, evidently unimpressed by Jefferies's military thunderbolts.

"Indeed," said Skon. "A complete failure analysis should prove illuminating."

Jefferies came to a stop just across the railing from Dax's station. "And what observation would *you* like to make about this afternoon's debacle, Mister Dax?"

Other than "uh-oh," Dax could think of little of any real relevance to say to the captain. Almost without conscious volition, he found himself beginning to stammer out what he hoped would quickly evolve into a coherent sentence.

"D-d-do you think you can talk the, um, Vulcan Science Academy," he said, "into loaning Skon out to us for a little bit longer?"

*   *   *

Immediately after his dinner break, Dax returned to the lab, eager to delve into what had gone wrong with the afternoon's simulation. He was surprised to see only Pell Underhill, who looked tired and drawn, studying the data that scrolled across his padd.

"Where's Skon?"

"Gone," said a voice directly behind Dax, making him jump slightly.

Turning, Dax found himself face to face with Captain Eric Stillwell, one of the project's main Starfleet designers. "When's he coming back? And where's Captain Jefferies?"

Stillwell shook his head. "Skon probably won't be back for a good while. The *Nyran* picked him up an hour ago to take him back to Vulcan. As for Captain Jefferies, I'm just taking the helm until he finishes running a failure analysis of the previous simulation."

Dax couldn't prevent his eyes from narrowing with suspicion. "Funny that Skon didn't mention anything about having to leave today." It was also strange that Jefferies had failed to speak up about the subject. Had he been caught by surprise as well?

"Must have slipped Skon's mind," said Stillwell. "You know how focused on their work Vulcans can get. And they don't always excel at the social niceties."

"I hadn't noticed," Dax said, though he understood that he wasn't particularly socially adept himself. "But Skon would have said *something*. Why would he suddenly—"

Stillwell cut him off, obviously irritated. "How should *I* know? Maybe he had a family emergency back home. Maybe the Vulcan Science Directorate needs him to translate some more ancient documents out of Old High Vulcan."

That second point struck Dax as unlikely. Certainly, everybody knew that Skon had created the English translation of *The Teachings of Surak*, ostensibly to encourage humanity to think in a more Vulcanlike manner. He hoped that Skon would create a Trill edition of Surak's writings—updated to include the new stuff that had been discovered stored in an unearthed archaeological artifact. However, Dax couldn't believe that his friend and colleague would have suddenly dropped out of the Romulan Countermeasure Development Team to pursue a new literary project.

That left Stillwell's first point—the possibility that Skon had left in response to some emergency back home. Turning toward Pell, Dax said, "Doctor Underhill, have you heard anything about why Skon left?"

Underhill put aside his scanner and shook his head glumly. "You know as much as I do."

Dax shook his head, concerned. "I certainly hope nothing happened to T'Rama." He turned to face Stillwell. "That's his wife. Skon told me they were planning to start a family in a few years, once he'd—"

"Could we *please* stay focused on the business at hand, Mister Dax?" Stillwell said, cutting him off. "We need to set the simulator up for a second run."

Dax could scarcely contain his incredulity. "Tonight?"

"Immediately, Mister Dax," Stillwell said with a stern nod.

"But we haven't had a chance to analyze the failure of the *last* simulation," Dax said.

"I told you, Captain Jefferies will handle that." Stillwell's tone contained enough tritanium that Dax took a step backward. "Now, *forget* about the last simulation."

Underhill stepped forward, his brow furrowed. "Tobin's right, Captain. We need to know exactly why the last run failed before we can proceed with another. To do so would be a waste of time and resources. Not to mention bad science."

As Underhill and Stillwell stood regarding each other silently, Dax tried to brainstorm possible causes of the simulation's failure but came up with nothing. It should have worked, and worked outstandingly, and yet it hadn't. After everything the team had learned from Starfleet's recent victories in the Orion sector and the previous year's costly yet surprisingly successful First and Second Battles of Altair VI—information confirmed via the back channels in Vulcan's intelligence service—the simulation should have ended with the Starfleet vessel triumphing over its Romulan opponent. The anti-hijacking countermeasure's newest analog design features looked to have been all but infallible, from the non-networked bridge computers that incorporated archaic tape drives instead of redundant memory modules, to the new system of prearranged prefix codes. They had even used decidedly nondigital data displays that resembled the mechanical mileage readouts that Dax's first host, Lela, remembered seeing on the control panels of century-old Trill ground cars.

"This isn't about science, Doctor," Stillwell was telling Underhill, his words freighted with impatience. "It's about doing whatever's necessary to defeat the Romulans before they plant their flag here, and on Earth. Or isn't that a priority for you?"

The slight to his patriotism seemed to break Underhill. His shoulders slumping in defeat, he moved toward the faux bridge's engineering console, where the simulator's main controls, including the RESET function, could be found.

"Thy will be done, Captain," Underhill said as he began flipping toggles and pressing large and colorful translucent buttons that looked like the glowing candies young children received during *syn lara* concert festivals on Trill.

Stillwell moved purposefully across the bridge and took the center seat. He pressed a button on the right arm of the captain's chair. "Game on!"

Minutes passed. Finally, a spacecraft shaped like one of the symbionts that dwelled in the underground pools beneath the Caves of Mak'ala appeared on the main bridge viewer and made a swift approach.

"Incoming!" Stillwell shouted. "Tactical Alert!"

Once again, the bridge module shook violently. *Here we go again*, Dax thought as he checked the status of the hull plating and the weapons.

A few minutes later, every system aboard the simulated Starfleet vessel was running at near optimal status. And little was left of the hostile Romulan ship other than a slowly expanding cloud of metal fragments, frozen atmosphere, and other debris.

"I don't get it," Dax said. "We won that round. So what went wrong the first time?"

Grinning triumphantly, Stillwell rose from the command chair. "What happened the first time," he said, "was that we had personnel present who represented an unacceptable security risk."

Dax realized only belatedly that his jaw had fallen open. "What are you talking about?"

His smile folding quickly into a scowl that seemed intended specifically for Dax, Stillwell said, "We finally have demonstrable proof that our countermeasure against the Romulan remote-hijacking weapon will work in the field."

"Do we?" Dax said. "We've only tested it twice, and we got radically different results on each occasion."

Stillwell shook his head. "No. The results of the first test showed you what we wanted you to see. Or, to be more specific, what we wanted Doctor *Skon* to see."

Underhill's bushy brows looked as though they were challenging each other to a duel. "Captain, you *wanted* the first test to appear to have failed? That doesn't make any sense."

Suddenly it was all becoming clear to Dax. "It makes perfect sense," he said, "if you don't want Vulcan to know what we've just developed here." Pushing aside the sense of intimidation he felt in the captain's presence, he took a step toward Stillwell. "You cheated."

Stillwell faced him down confidently. "I changed the apparent result of today's first test because I refuse to risk compromising what may turn out to be our greatest asset in this war."

That struck Dax as enormously unfair, especially when he considered Skon's contribution. He had worked as hard as anyone else on this project. "Vulcan's space force is a lot more vulnerable to the Romulan hijack tactic than Starfleet is, all our countermeasures notwithstanding. Vulcan has as big a stake in this thing as Earth does. As does my own homeworld."

Stillwell nodded. "As long as the Vulcans and the Trill don't have any skin in the game, then they have no need to know that this project was anything other than the failure it appeared to be this afternoon."

Skin in the game, Dax thought. It was a curious phrase, but its meaning was intuitively obvious to him. It made him shiver.

Though Stillwell's actions horrified him, they also piqued his curiosity. "You sent Skon away to keep Vulcan in the dark about Earth's ability to cope with the Romulan remote-hijacking weapon."

"That's right," Stillwell said. "I don't particularly trust Vulcans, especially since they've abandoned their Coalition Compact responsibilities."

"But you didn't send *me* home," Dax said. "Do you trust the Trill more than you do the Vulcans?"

Stillwell chuckled. "Mister Dax, I don't know enough about your species to know whether I ought to trust you or not. But I've spent enough time doing intel work to know that the more I know about anybody, the less I'm likely to trust him."

Dax felt more confused now than before he'd asked the question. He considered the symbiont in his belly and the pains his government had taken to conceal the fact of

Trill symbiosis from all other sentient species. Given the practices of his own society, he could hardly fault this human for keeping his guard up.

"So you're saying you *do* trust me, Captain?" Dax asked. "At least, more than you do Skon?"

Stillwell laughed again. "No, Mister Dax. I'm saying because I still have a warp-seven stardrive project that needs to move forward, I can't afford to do without both you *and* Doctor Skon. That warp-seven work should keep both you and Doctor Underhill busy for the foreseeable future. Maybe even for the entire duration of the war."

"Oh," Dax said. It wasn't the answer he'd hoped for. But at least it was good to know precisely where one stood.

"Remember, both of you," Stillwell said, "everything we've learned via today's Romulan countermeasure tests is now classified at the highest level. The fact that it exists—and that it *works*—is now one of the most closely guarded secrets of Starfleet and the United Earth government. And I am charged with keeping it that way, at least until all our ships of the line are equipped with it, and possibly for some time afterward. It is therefore a secret I will expect both of you to guard carefully." His eyes widened, and his tone took on a perfervid intensity. "With your very lives, if it comes to that."

The implied threat was not lost on Dax, and he was sure that Underhill had heard it clearly as well. That threat made the Trill engineer realize that Stillwell was flat-out wrong about something he had said a little earlier: Unlike Vulcan, Trill did indeed have "skin in the game." Trouble was, he found the stakes of the game to be far too high, even for a card-game aficionado like himself.

And all the "skin" belonged to one Tobin Dax.

ELEVEN

"ANY SIGN of the Romulans yet, Malcolm?" Archer said as he leaned forward in his captain's chair toward the weird vista displayed on the bridge's central viewscreen.

Like the periphery of the viewer's image area, the screen's center depicted a region of infinite black. This was encircled by a bright, flat orange annulus, vaguely reminiscent of the ring system of Saturn. Fountains of brilliance taller and more intense than any volcano Archer had ever seen streamed from the top and bottom of the interior space, jets of superheated matter that was being ejected from the vicinity of the black hole's accretion disk at nearly the speed of light. On either side of the brilliant ring lay an image of the yellow star known as Gamma Hydra, which lay less than two light-years distant. Although the star and its system of planets lay far enough from the singularity not to be endangered by the black hole's ravening event horizon, the object's intense gravity had lensed Gamma Hydra's light enough to make it appear to be two distinct objects rather than one.

"Not yet, sir," said Malcolm. "So far none of the other ships in the flotilla report making enemy contact. Apart from all the electromagnetic and subspace noise being generated by the singularity and its polar jets, it's still as quiet as a mausoleum out there."

Archer frowned as he considered all the deaths the

Romulans had caused since the war had begun—as well as the fact that *Enterprise* had very nearly become a flying tomb the last time she'd made such a close approach to such a highly energetic singularity. "That's an unfortunate metaphor, Malcolm," he said.

"Sorry, sir."

"Continue coordinating sensor sweeps with the rest of the flotilla," Archer said.

"Aye, Commodore."

Archer winced at the archaic naval title, though he couldn't fault Malcolm—the product of a family with a long, proud tradition of service to Britain's Royal Navy— for using it. "Commodore" actually was the correct term, because for the current mission, Starfleet Command had placed Archer in charge of several vessels drawn from the less-advanced *Daedalus*-class fleet: the *William Clark*, the *Cowpens*, the *Gettysburg*, the *Jein*, the *Lovell*, the *Nez Perce*, and the *Okuda*.

"Hoshi, any word from the Vissian government?" Operating on the assumption that the best place to look for invading Romulans would be wherever the Vissians had hidden their listening post, Archer had formally requested that the Vissian government provide *Enterprise* with the facility's exact coordinates.

"Still nothing, sir," Lieutenant Sato said after taking a moment to check the communications queue at her portside station.

Archer leaned forward in his chair, as though getting a few additional centimeters closer to the viewscreen would enable him to glimpse the Romulan attack force, which a grateful local merchant captain had warned him of several weeks earlier.

"I still must question the logic of trusting the word of an alien freight hauler, Captain," said T'Pol, who had momentarily turned away from her scanner at the port science station to face the center of the bridge. "We have no guarantee that Starfleet hasn't set eight vessels in pursuit of amphibious avian fauna."

Recognizing one of T'Pol's deadpan bids to lighten his mood despite the seriousness of the point she was raising, Archer smiled. "Nothing except my intuition that the man was sincerely grateful to us after Phlox saved his crew from that outbreak of Rigelian fever."

"That's one of the benefits of conducting a lengthy 'generosity offensive,' sir," Malcolm said. "We can cultivate goodwill and gratitude with every local commercial starfarer we encounter out here. But what we *can't* do is know whether we can trust that what they tell us about the Romulans is anything other than disinformation deliberately created *by* the Romulans."

"I concur," said T'Pol.

Archer nodded. "I can't disagree with anything either of you are saying. But there's one other piece of the puzzle you haven't taken into account—the fact that the Vissians have set up a listening post in this sector."

"So they say," Malcolm said. "So far I haven't been able to find any evidence of it."

"Probably because the Vissians are using the EM noise from that singularity to cover their tracks." Archer gestured toward the never-ending twin eruptions at either end of the enigmatic body on the main viewer. "Just as the Romulans will."

The captain noticed a look of dawning comprehension on his tactical officer's face. "You think the Romulans know about the listening post," Malcolm said.

"They're not idiots, Malcolm," Archer said. "I think their attack force will want to knock it out before they try to plunge into Coalition space."

"So if we find the listening post, we may find the Romulan attack force nearby," Malcolm said.

Archer nodded. "Assuming we find it sooner rather than later."

"It's unfortunate that the Vissians chose not to disclose to us the precise coordinates of their listening post," T'Pol said.

Archer shrugged and leaned back in his chair. "Agreed. So let's keep our eyes open."

An alarm klaxon began to shriek, leaving Archer neither the time nor the energy for second guessing.

Romulan *Bird-of-Prey Terrh'Dhael*

"It is *there*, Commander!" Centurion R'Tal said, his voice tinged with something that reminded Commander T'Met of both excitement and fear.

Hoping to set an example that would calm the excitable science specialist, T'Met remained seated and spoke in a loud but unemotional voice. "What precisely have you found, Centurion?"

Apparently realizing he'd become overwrought, R'Tal ratcheted back his intensity as he turned from his console to face his commanding officer. "The *Vis'amnaisu* spy facility now stands revealed by our sensors." Though partially obscured by his silver helmet, the young man's countenance took on an almost apologetic cast. "But for the singularity, Commander, we might have discovered it much sooner."

T'Met flashed her carefully cultivated raptor smile. "Good work, Centurion." The centurion had done far better than she had hoped. The commander had resigned herself to the possibility that the attack group would not only fail to find the alien listening post but would also cause it to activate and warn the so-called Coalition of Planets in time to allow the *hevam* to mount a successful defense against what should have been a swift and utterly devastating surprise attack.

The commander turned her chair toward the tactical console that currently absorbed most of her executive officer's attention. "Subcommander Genorex, alert the rest of the attack group. Dispatch the *Grukhai* and the *Khuea* to destroy the *Vis'amnaisu* espionage station."

"At once, Commander," Genorex said, his large fingers almost a blur as they moved across the surface of the touch-sensitive console.

The distinctive rising wail of a proximity alarm split the air. "Sensors have just picked up another set of signatures, Commander. Seven warp signatures. No, eight."

T'Met's eyes narrowed. "What kind of ships?"

"I read *hevam* vessels," said Genorex, who was still staring intently down at his console displays.

Humans, T'Met thought, astonished. *What are humans doing so far from the homeworld where they should now be cowering and awaiting the end?*

"Perhaps the *hevam* have somehow received advance word of our offensive, Commander," Genorex said. "They are nothing if not treacherous."

"Perhaps this is merely happenstance," said Decurion Tomal, the young officer who was running the communications bank through which the attack fleet coordinated its complex web of activity. "Those ships may represent simply a patrol that happened to blunder into our path at precisely the wrong time."

"A *patrol*?" Genorex said, his words painting a vivid picture of disgust at the younger man's apparent naïveté. "Consisting of at least eight ships? During a time of increasingly scarce *hevam* war matériel?" Dismissing Tomal with a sneer, Genorex fixed his gaze upon that of T'Met, his body language conveying an air of expectancy.

Because of the hard lessons she had learned on the Haakonan front, T'Met was sorely tempted to abort the current mission, to withdraw and make another attempt to carry it out at a more opportune time. But she knew that tactical matters could not be her only consideration here. *His family is a powerful one,* she reminded herself. More prominent than her own, even considering her modest consanguinity with the Current Occupant of the Romulan Star Empire's ever-volatile Praetorate.

Taking everything into account, only one survivable course of action was available to her. "Continue the operation as planned, Genorex," T'Met said. "Destroy the *Vis'amnaisu* listening post.

"And take down the *hevam* vessels as well."

Enterprise NX-01

Captain Archer watched helplessly as the spherical primary hulls of both the *Okuda* and the *Jein* erupted with the harsh pyrotechnics of molecular fire, then splintered into expanding clouds of fragments. A pair of the horseshoe crab–shaped Romulan vessels, the red raptor feathers painted across their bellies burned and scarred, met a similar fate moments later, but Archer could draw no comfort from it.

The ferocity of the multivessel Romulan surprise attack made Archer wonder if they had known that his Starfleet flotilla was coming. Whether or not that was so, they'd been prepared—the Romulan attack group outnumbered Archer's Starfleet contingent by more than two to one.

"Hull plating is down to sixty-eight percent!" Malcolm cried as the bridge groaned and shuddered beneath the ceaseless Romulan onslaught.

"Continue with evasive maneuvers!" Archer bellowed. "And keep firing the forward phase cannons on the lead ship. Plus a full spread of torpedoes, forward dorsal and ventral launchers!"

"Aye, sir," Malcolm said as he set about carrying out Archer's orders.

"The *Gettysburg* reports that the *Nez Perce* and the *Cowpens* have both been destroyed," said Hoshi, who shouted to be heard above the din and clatter of klaxons and incoming fire. Overhead, a conduit split and its contents sprayed a foglike mist across the bridge. Almost simultaneously, a rain of sparks, smoke, and fire issued from the main engineering console.

The bridge bucked, and the hull resonated with a distant, menacing whine. "Starboard nacelle's venting plasma," said Ensign Leydon, who was frantically working the helm console to compensate. She continued trying to evade the Romulan fleet's fire, keeping the starship's still robust ventral hull plating angled toward the hostile vessels. The effect of *Enterprise*'s injuries had her wallowing, sluggish as a delirious and punch-drunk boxer who could barely remain vertical on the canvas.

The ship rocked again. "Sorry, sir," Leydon said.

"Forward dorsal hull plating is down," Malcolm reported in his gratingly matter-of-fact fashion. "The *Gettysburg* is crippled, and the *Clark* has just suffered a reactor breach. The *Lovell* has given as good as she's gotten, but she's still taking the beating of her life. We've taken down as many of their ships as they have of ours, but they still have a good half dozen left that haven't yet suffered so much as a scratch."

Damn, Archer thought, *this isn't how things were supposed to go.*

"Keep firing, Malcolm," Archer heard himself shouting. "Hoshi, prepare to launch the log buoy, and—"

"More incoming ships," Malcolm shouted.

"Confirmed," said T'Pol. "I read nine—correction, ten—vessels, all dropping out of warp simultaneously, close enough to us to pose a possible danger of collision."

Perfect, Archer thought. "Romulan reinforcements?"

Malcolm paused, a guarded expression on his normally taciturn face as he manipulated his console for several seconds.

The tactical officer's eyes suddenly grew wide, as though he'd just received an unexpected but thoroughly welcome gift.

"Well?" Archer demanded.

On the main viewer, a handful of shapes began to resolve themselves into alien ships. They were long and roughly rectangular, their amber-colored hulls forming a mass of compound curves on what seemed to be their dorsal sides. Their sterns and ventral hulls appeared flattened, while the section that Archer identified as the bow gently tapered into a narrow forward area. On the nearest of the alien ships, a recessed oval that looked very much like a weapons tube was beginning to glow an angry red.

The captain realized that he had seen these ships before.

An unaccustomed grin split Malcolm's craggy features. "They're *Vissians,* sir! And they're opening fire on the Romulans!"

Archer returned his armory officer's grin. "Then let's help 'em out as much as we can."

Bird-of-Prey Terrh'Dhael

T'Met watched in both horror and disbelief as the *Grukhai* and the *Khuea,* both freshly returned from the task of eradicating the *Vis'amnaisu* espionage station, were rent and shattered by weapons fire from without and explosive emissions of burning, escaping atmosphere from within.

In the fleeting span of two *siure,* the fleet's numerical advantage had vanished. "We are outnumbered," T'Met said as the grim realization set in.

"Commander!" Genorex shouted in a fashion T'Met found insubordinate. "If we do not press the attack immediately, these new hostiles may overwhelm us."

T'Met felt the weight of certainty settle upon her bones. *They will overwhelm us,* she thought. *No matter the tactics we bring to bear against them.*

"Decurion Tomal, inform the fleet that we are withdrawing," T'Met said.

"Commander?" Genorex took a menacing step toward her. "We can still beat them!"

T'Met dropped her hand to the handle of her *dathe'anofv-sen* and favored her XO with a hard glare. Genorex's family might be more powerful than hers, but that would count for nothing if the *Terrh'Dhael* were captured or destroyed out in this savage, *hevam*-infested wilderness.

Genorex backed away, allowing her to turn her full attention to the helm. "Decurion Makar, bring us about. Return us to Romulan space, maximum warp."

Enterprise NX-01

"I think it might be fair to say they've had enough," Archer said as he watched the scarred, scorched remnants of the Romulan attack group shift into the red portion of the visual spectrum before vanishing entirely from the main viewer. Only a pair of apparently spotless bargelike Vissian vessels and a single battered *Daedalus*-class ship now lay in *Enterprise*'s forward line of sight.

"Apparently, so have we," Malcolm said. "I hope you're not expecting to chase them, sir."

"I'm content to leave that task to the Vissians for the moment, if they're up for it." Archer shook his head. "First things first. Damage report."

"Our weapons stores are badly depleted. The hull plating has taken a serious pounding virtually everywhere, but particularly in the forward dorsal areas. The starboard nacelle has sustained serious damage, and the warp drive is down. All other systems are on secondary or tertiary backups, including life support."

Archer looked to T'Pol. "Is *anything* aboard still working right?"

She nodded. "We have partial impulse power, and the batteries are keeping all basic systems operating. Obviously, the situation is not sustainable for more than, perhaps, a week."

"A week might even be a touch optimistic," Malcolm said. "I'm no engineer, but it seems clear that *Enterprise* will need to spend a good deal of time in drydock before we can put everything right. Several weeks at least, unless Mister Burch can discover some extremely clever workarounds.

"Without an operational warp drive, however, reaching an appropriate repair facility will be effectively impossible."

Damn, Archer thought, though he wasn't surprised. The captain tried to remind himself that things would have been worse had the Vissians not arrived when they did.

"What's the condition of the flotilla?" he said, though he was reasonably certain he wouldn't like the answer.

Malcolm's complexion seemed to go several shades lighter than usual, and his mien was grim. "The *Gettysburg* and the *Lovell* are in worse shape than we are, sir. And it appears that Captain Duvall and three of his senior officers were blown out into space when a Romulan torpedo breached the *Gettysburg's* bridge."

Archer gripped the arms of his command chair, but otherwise suppressed his gut-punched reaction. Duvall had been a good captain, well respected by his crew and his superiors alike. His most serious flaw had always been his tendency to introduce too many last-minute changes to already well-rehearsed tactical plans.

"And the other vessels?" Archer asked.

Malcolm slowly shook his head.

Archer struggled to grasp the cost of today's engagement but failed to get his mind completely around it. He wondered if some historian would someday describe it in overly grandiose terms, like the Battle of Gamma Hydra. Or the Triumph at Gamma Hydra, or maybe even Victory at Gamma Hydra.

With victories like this one, who needs defeats?

Hoshi interrupted Archer's unpleasant reverie. "Captain, one of the Vissian vessels has just hailed us."

"On the screen."

A moment later an unexpectedly familiar face appeared before him. "Captain Drennik," Archer said. "It's good to see you again." After the acrimony that had arisen because of the circumstances surrounding their first meeting three years earlier, the captain was surprised.

"Archer," Drennik said, his demeanor cool, his expression neutral. *"Once we confirmed the Romulan presence here, we came as quickly as we could."*

"We're grateful for that, Captain," Archer said. "Thank you."

"We didn't come specifically to rescue you, Captain. We came to protect our listening post in this sector."

"I assume the listening post was what allowed you to discover the Romulan incursion here and react to it so quickly."

Drennik nodded. *"Of course."*

"We'd hoped to surprise the Romulans before they had the opportunity to attack your facility."

Drennik's countenance grew glum, his tone regretful. *"Unfortunately, we arrived too late to prevent that very occurrence."*

"They destroyed it?"

"Utterly. We may be deaf and blind in this sector for upwards of a year until we can replace it. Of course, the personnel who operated the facility can never be replaced."

"No, they can't," Archer said, molten sorrow welling up from within. "Neither can five Starfleet crews. Perhaps if your government had given us your listening post's precise location, we might have kept the Romulans distracted long enough to prevent some of what happened here today."

Drennik's eyes blazed with restrained fury. *"Perhaps you are right, Captain Archer. Neither of us can recover what has been lost today. But, together, we can undo a small portion of the damage."*

"How?" Archer said, not yet daring to raise his hopes.

"By allowing us to tow Enterprise *to a repair station in Vissian space. To return some of the kindness you have shown during your many passages through this region of space."*

It took Archer a moment to decide that he'd heard Drennik correctly. "Thank you, Captain."

"You should reserve some of your thanks for the Vissia's Grand Moot."

Archer was downright perplexed. "The Grand Moot? When I was on your homeworld, your government's ministers weren't exactly clamoring to join the Jonathan Archer fan club." After Drennik answered with a blank stare, Archer appended, "They weren't very sympathetic toward me, my planet, or the Coalition's struggle against the Romulans."

"Ah," Drennik said, apparently understanding more clearly after Archer's explanation. *"You're right. However, Science Minister Bote J'Ref is highly influential."*

Archer nodded. "I met J'Ref. He seemed like a good man."

"J'Ref believes he is in your debt. And I certainly don't mind putting him in my *debt by assisting you—my personal feelings notwithstanding."* Drennik's manner suddenly grew distant and cool, suggesting to Archer that Vissia wasn't about to reverse its formal decision not to enter the war, despite the Romulans' actions today.

Drennik signed off without another word, his image abruptly replaced by the field of distant, lonely fires that illuminated tiny portions of the infinite darkness that surrounded them.

I suppose it counts as a victory, Archer thought, *if you get to live to fight another day.*

TWELVE

Wednesday, May 18, 2157
Romulan *Scout Ship Kilhra'en*
83 Leonis B V

PROTECTED FROM THE VACUUM of space and the hard radiation of the system's orange-dwarf primary star only by the thin polyplas skin of his environmental suit and the upper reaches of a planetary magnetic field, Charles Tucker III dangled from his tether and cursed his lack of options. A dizzying blue-brown planetary expanse turned vertiginously some three hundred klicks below, making the Romulan military base no more visible than the tumbledown, burned-out cityscapes of this world's long-extinct civilization. Trip tried to put those distracting images out of his mind as he wrestled with the unaccustomed sensation of weightlessness; he couldn't allow it to distract him from his present task—even though he would have far preferred to be undertaking it on solid ground.

But the damage recently taken by this small Romulan military vessel—a ship that had, courtesy of Minister Silok, head of the Vulcan Security Directorate, been his home for the past nine months—would not let him reach the ground in one piece.

Trip used his suit's tiny thrusters to achieve a narrow, parabolic path around his vessel, *Kilhra'en*. In spite of the ship's alienness, the scout's speedy, aggressive lines appealed to his engineering aesthetics. The *Kilhra'en* measured just shy of thirteen meters long from her narrow, gently rounded bow to the exhaust nozzles of the twin impulse engines recessed into her broad delta-winged stern section. The scout's swooping wings terminated in a pair of cylindrical nacelles, each of which curled slightly downward past the aft portion of the little ship's ventral hull—the section that bore an elaborate rendering of a scarlet-feathered predatory bird, claws extended as if in the act of pouncing upon unsuspecting prey.

Trip began a visual inspection of the hull's ventral and dorsal sections, carefully studying the externally accessible portions of the warp and impulse engines as well.

Though he wanted to do as thorough a job as possible, Trip was the only soul aboard the *Kilhra'en*. It wouldn't do for an incoming hostile to arrive and challenge him while he was in the midst of extravehicular activity, effectively catching him with his figurative pants down. And since 83 Leonis B V—a remote world that the Romulans called Cheron—was this sector's home to the Romulan Star Empire's *Rhi Rei'Karan*, or Fifth Legion, such an eventuality was an ever-present possibility.

"Damn," Trip said a few quiet, sober minutes later. Thanks to the Takret pirates that had tried to board the *Kilhra'en* nearly two weeks ago, the port plasma vent bore noticeable damage—a ten-centimeter-long, larger-than-hairline crack. Surviving a landing, or even a high-speed passage through a substantial planetary atmosphere, would be a distinctly risky proposition. *If the valves behind that vent let go when the hull's getting bombarded by ionized gases during atmospheric entry,* he thought, *then getting discovered by the Romulans dirtside will be the very least of my problems.*

Hoping he'd be able to make do with the tools and spare parts the *Kilhra'en* carried—he would cannibalize nonessential pieces from the cockpit and crew compartments, but only if he had to—Trip activated his suit's thrusters again, propelling himself back toward the scout ship's starboard airlock. The back of the suit pressed against his spine as his weightless body began to accelerate forward.

Only halfway back, Trip saw a dark, menacing shape rising up from behind the *Kilhra'en* on a steeply rising parabolic approach vector. His blood froze in his veins at the sight of it, as though his suit had suddenly failed. The size of whatever was approaching from Cheron's surface was indeterminate, as was the thing's distance. All he could tell was that it was closing on the little scout ship, and quickly. He tapped his thrusters again, forgetting to decelerate in his haste to reach the relative safety of the *Kilhra'en*'s interior. Though his gauntleted hands grabbed at the outer edges of the open airlock hatch, his body struck the sides forcefully enough to make his teeth rattle.

Before he could haul himself fully inside the lock, Trip experienced an unpleasantly familiar sensation—a tingling almost-itch, as though thousands of ants were crawling over his bare skin. A wash of orange light swept across his helmet's field of vision, and his view of the *Kilhra'en* faded, then vanished.

Trip nearly stumbled when the sensations of gravity and solidity abruptly returned, along with his vision. Below the raised dais that now supported his boots stood a trio of armed men dressed in Romulan military uniforms, their gleaming silver helmets doing little to conceal their unvaryingly hostile glares. Two of the soldiers already had their extremely dangerous-looking sidearms drawn and trained on him. The remaining man seemed to be speaking into the narrow console that stood before him; he was leaning forward, which made his face difficult to see and therefore unreadable.

Trip couldn't hear anything the man was saying.

Moving very slowly, Trip unscrewed his helmet from his suit's neck ring. The pressure differential between the suit and its new surroundings equalized with a brief serpentine hiss, and the warning voices of the uniformed Romulans suddenly became almost too audible as the two armed men stepped menacingly forward, their weapons leveled and ready.

Trip tucked his helmet under his left arm while raising his right in what he hoped was a clear gesture of surrender. With a slightly crooked smile, he said, "Permission to come aboard?"

The man behind the console approached the transporter dais, doffing his helmet as he allowed Trip to get his first close look at his face.

With a start, Trip realized that his nine-month search had finally panned out, if not quite in the way he'd hoped. "Tevik," he said in a near whisper.

"Terix," the other man corrected, his face a mask of barely contained fury. "You will address me as Centurion Terix. Do we understand one another, Cunaehr of Iuruth City?

"Or should I say, Sodok of Vulcan?"

Romulan *Attack Raptor Ra'kholh*

After nearly a full duty shift of fruitless interrogation of the prisoner, Terix Val'Danadex Trel t'Llweii felt extremely vexed at his inability simply to kill the interloper on sight. Erebus only knew how badly he'd *wanted* to do the deed—almost from the moment the man had materialized aboard the *Ra'kholh*—but the old conflicting memories had intervened. Along with the bedrock conviction that his prisoner—the man who had been instrumental in helping a treacherous nest of *thaessu* spies telepathically steal his identity—was also a close colleague, and perhaps even a friend.

Had Terix simply acted immediately and without hesitation, at least the deed would have been done. Sodok of

Vulcan would now be dead, and Terix would have presented the spy's demise to Admiral Valdore as an unfortunate fait accompli.

Instead, Terix had balked. With his initial interrogation report filed, Valdore's flagship, the *Imperial Warbird Dabhae*, was on its way to take possession of the prisoner. Terix's moment of opportunity had forever passed.

Now Terix was obliged by Valdore's explicit orders to see to it that the faux-Romulan once known as Cunaehr, a man who had insinuated himself into the Romulan military's warp-seven stardrive program, remained uninjured by the grueling questioning process. This precluded the use of mind probes. However, the admiral had not placed any limitations on either the duration or number of interrogations to which the spy could be subjected.

As he traversed the attack raptor's long corridors on his way back to the detention area, Terix considered the *eolh iarr'voi*—a roughly palm-sized musical instrument played by drawing and expelling breath along a long but narrow reed—he had confiscated from the quarters of the scout ship. He wondered whether the guards had left it with the prisoner, or if they'd taken the precaution of removing it from his cell. With his engineering background, the wily Vulcan spy might fashion a crude weapon out of almost anything.

The din that met Terix's sensitive ears definitely settled the matter of the *eolh iarr'voi*'s whereabouts the moment the detention area's outer door hissed open.

"What in the name Akraana's divine teat is *that*?" he said, addressing the pair of helpless-looking uhlan guards who stood outside the prisoner's cell.

"He's, ah, playing the *'voi*, Centurion," one of them said, unnecessarily.

"And neither of you cared to stop him?"

Both uhlanu flushed a deep Apnex Sea green. "Centurion,

he told us that we could pry the 'woi out of his 'cold, dead fingers,'" said the uhlan who hadn't spoken previously.

"You ordered us to refrain from harming him, Centurion," said the other.

Terix angrily shouldered past the guards, banged on the keypad, and entered the cell.

Seated on one of the cell's two chairs, his eyes closed tightly, the Vulcan played a rapid-fire fusillade of alien motifs, from arpeggiating giant steps to unpleasant yet almost-recognizable scalar runs to unsonorous sequences of chords that might have dragged the classical Romulan composer Frenchotte back from the surcease of death.

"Enough!" Terix shouted.

The prisoner abruptly stopped, opened his eyes, and favored his visitor with an infuriating raised eyebrow. "Terix. Nice of you to drop in on me again. And thanks for leaving this with me." He waved the small musical instrument in the air between them. "It's been a big help in whiling away the time between these interrogation sessions."

His anger getting the better him, Terix lashed out with his left hand, sending the *eolh iarr'woi* flying. He didn't see where it ended up, but he heard the very satisfying crunch it made against at least one of the walls before it struck the deck plates in multiple pieces.

The prisoner did not appear pleased, but at least he had the apparent good sense to remain seated. "Great. That was the closest thing to a harmonica I've been able to find since I left Vulcan."

"When Admiral Valdore is finished with you, you will no longer have any need of such things," Terix said. "That damnable noise sounded even worse than the monks' chanting at the T'Panit monastery."

Sodok leaned back in his chair and gave off an air of insouciance that seemed uncharacteristic for a Vulcan. "The ancient Vulcans called that piece 'Crossroad Blues.' According to legend, the composer sold his soul to Shariel, the death god." He rubbed an index finger over one of his ears. "Sometimes I wonder if I haven't done exactly the same thing."

Not for the first time, Terix wondered if the Vulcan spy might not be going mad. Since he had no idea what the man was talking about, he allowed his remark to pass unacknowledged as he seated himself in the cell's other chair.

"Why did you come back into Romulan space, Mister Sodok?" Terix asked, schooling his voice into a fair approximation of the authoritative equanimity of a professional interrogator.

"We've already been through this a dozen times," the spy said, frowning heavily. "I came to help carry out a Vulcan intelligence operation."

"And you insist you're operating alone?"

Sodok nodded. "This time, yes."

"And this . . . operation's goal?"

"Two main things, just like I told you before."

"Tell me again," Terix said, suppressing a scowl.

"I'll try to go a little slower this time, so you can keep up."

Terix's rage swiftly escalated toward the boiling point. Fists clenched in spite of himself, he rose from his chair. In the space of a heartbeat, he grabbed the front of the prisoner's shirt with both hands, and hoisted him into the air as though he weighed no more than a medium-sized Apnex longfish.

The Vulcan returned Terix's hard gaze without any evident fear. "There's an old saying," the prisoner said. "'You can't kid a kidder.'"

"What?" Terix asked, flummoxed by yet another non sequitur.

"Something tells me you're not going to go beyond putting on a show."

Despite the orders he'd received to the contrary, Terix felt an all but irresistible urge to punch the prisoner squarely in the face. He suppressed it, willing his hands not to shake. "Why do you say that, *thaessu?*"

"Because your guards didn't punish my little harmonica jam with anything stronger than gripes and complaints. When I realized that somebody must have *ordered* 'em not to rough me up, I just turned the volume higher."

"Don't make the mistake of believing I will treat you with the same deference, Vulcan," Terix said, shaking the man slightly. "I am no mere uhlan to be trifled with."

The prisoner acted as though he hadn't heard Terix's warning. "No offense, but those two outside the door seem to be more afraid of somebody a little higher up in the pecking order than a lowly centurion like yourself."

To avoid being blamed for an underling's possible indiscretion, Terix had indeed made the guards aware of Admiral Valdore's orders. While both of the uhlanu understood that Terix would bear primary responsibility if anything happened to their prisoner, they were also aware that Terix would not face Admiral Valdore's Honor Blade alone if Sodok died or became injured while in their care.

Unceremoniously dropping the *thaessu* back into his chair, Terix said, "Tell me about the goals of the reformist regime on Vulcan."

Quickly shaking off the shock of his abrupt hard landing, the prisoner sighed and shook his head. "All right. You won't get anything out of me that I haven't already told you. One of my mission's goals was to find and neutralize a secret shipbuilding and research facility being run by a faction that opposes the Romulan government. They have a special disdain for the military. You know them as the *Ejhoi Ormiin.* Their leader was a man named Sopek—at least until the Tal Shiar vaporized him."

"Ch'uivh," Terix corrected, using Sopek's Romulan name. Not having seen the man's body, he wasn't about to take it on anyone's word that the wily Ch'uivh was, indeed, dead. He was, however, impressed by the level of knowledge the Vulcans evidently had about the Romulan Star Empire's internal dissident problems.

Infuriatingly, Sodok just sat there, waiting.

Although Terix had yet to discover any discrepancies in Sodok's story from telling to telling, he nevertheless continued to find it difficult to accept. "And why would the Vulcans want to do us the service of bringing down the *Ejhoi Ormiin*?"

"I don't think the V'Shar ever intended to do you any favors, Tevik."

Terix growled. "*Terix*. Tevik was a construct of artificial memories created by your treacherous Vulcan friend Ych'a."

"Terix. Sorry. The *Ejhoi Ormiin* radicals have stolen advanced Vulcan technology. Either they'll use it to destabilize the Romulan Empire and start a civil war that will spill out across Coalition space, or the technology will be confiscated by the Romulan government—and enable you to intensify your war against the Coalition worlds."

"Logical," Terix said with a nod. "You mentioned having two goals, Vulcan. You've explained the first one. What is the second?"

The *thaessu* spy regarded him with a quizzical expression. "You ran from Vulcan during the confusion that followed the terror attack on Mount Seleya."

Terix's voice deepened to a near growl. "I've never run away from anything in my life, Vulcan."

Sodok shrugged. "You disappeared from Vulcan right after the attack. That made you into a major loose end in need of tying up."

"Why?"

"Are you serious? We were business partners, Tev—Terix. Friends."

Terix's eyes narrowed almost to slits. "Friends don't sit idly by while others force their way into your mind to alter your memories."

The Vulcan surprised him by appearing to be sincerely regretful. His eyes downcast, he said, "Maybe not. Maybe no reason can be good enough to excuse what was done to you. Not even the security of the entire Coalition." He looked up and met Terix's gaze directly. "But I couldn't just sit around after you suddenly 'went Romulan' on me and disappeared. Especially not with the whole planet grieving the destruction of the immortal soul of Vulcan's most revered ancient philosopher."

Terix nodded. "Surak." Though he was a Romulan, how could he *not* know of Surak? Terix had been thoroughly exposed to Vulcan culture, perhaps more so than any other living Romulan. Ych'a's intricate telepathic ministrations— which included a complex webwork of altered, embellished, and wholly synthetic memories—had misled him into believing himself to be a Vulcan intelligence agent rather than a loyal member of the Romulan Star Empire's proud military hierarchy.

Speaking into the silence that followed, Terix said, "Continue."

The *thaessu* nodded. "Since I knew you were actually a disguised Romulan soldier, I had to assume that you had something to do with the Seleya bombing. You have to admit, in my place you'd probably do the math the same way I did. So I kept my ear to the ground until I found out you were stationed at the Cheron garrison."

Terix nodded again slowly as he suppressed the anguished grimace that always threatened to surface whenever he thought about the Seleya attack. Although he carried no conscious recollection of the incident, he couldn't deny the distinct possibility that he'd either carried out the bombing himself or had abetted it in some manner. Given the terrible expertise Ych'a had demonstrated in altering the fabric of both mind and memory, he had to cope with the painful knowledge that the truth of the matter lay beyond his grasp, perhaps forever.

"So your mission's other goal," Terix said, "was to find *me?*"

Sodok flashed an impertinent grin that Terix—to his great annoyance—remembered almost fondly. "Mission accomplished," the prisoner said.

As though acting of its own volition, Terix's right hand fell to his holster. He drew his disruptor and took aim straight at the Vulcan's forehead. How simple it would be to resolve all the conflicting emotions he was experiencing now, the hatred, the friendship, the fear, and the camaraderie, just by squeezing the trigger.

Maddeningly, the smile on the other man's face wavered only slightly.

Terix's finger tightened on the firing stud, which he noted had become slick with perspiration. What was *wrong* with him?

He had wanted to kill this man ever since his suppressed Romulan memories and loyalties had burst free from their long confinement. But it wasn't quite that easy. *Maybe I owe this man some measure of gratitude,* he thought, recalling the long hours both he and Sodok had put into sabotaging the illicit ordnance shipments the Vulcan government had been covertly sending deep into Romulan territory. Rather than accomplishing their intended goal of crippling the Romulan war effort, those guerrilla interdictions had weakened the aggressive capacity of Haakona, an old enemy that had long threatened Romulus from the Empire's opposite flank.

Thank you for doing so much of our work for us, Mister Sodok, Terix thought as he struggled to quell the slight tremor in his pistol hand. *Whether you intended it or not.*

A shrill rising-and-falling whistle interrupted Terix's ruminations. An incoming communication. Without lowering his weapon, Terix raised the comm device from his belt and spoke into it.

"Centurion Terix," he said, trying without complete success to keep his voice free of irritation. "Go ahead."

"Uhlan Shianek, Centurion."

Terix put his pique fully on display. "Why are you interrupting my interrogation session, Uhlan?"

"Apologies, Centurion. You asked to be informed when the Warbird Dabhae *arrived. She has just come out of warp and is making her docking approach at Airlock Kre. Admiral Valdore demands immediate access to the prisoner."*

"Whew," said the prisoner. "Looks like the cavalry still arrives in the proverbial nick sometimes."

"Be silent, *thaessu*," Terix snapped, keeping his disruptor leveled at the other man's head.

"Centurion?"

Terix holstered his weapon and spoke into his comm unit with exaggerated distinctness. "Inform Captain S'Ten that I will greet the admiral at Airlock Kre. Terix out."

Returning the comm device to his belt, he addressed the prisoner again. "Place your hands behind your back, Mister Sodok. You will come with me."

Standing silently beside Terix, Trip watched the imposing form of Admiral Valdore emerge from the *Ra'kholh*'s airlock and step into the corridor. Accompanying the admiral was a striking black-garbed Romulan woman who looked no older than T'Pol, a fact that rendered her actual age effectively unguessable.

It suddenly came to Trip that he'd seen her before, nearly two years earlier, the last time he and Terix had visited the planet the Romulans called Cheron. Her manner was subtly different today, however; instead of an ambiguously flirtatious spy, her manner was somber, like that of a Valkyrie.

Or an executioner, Trip thought, all at once hyperaware of the fact that he may finally have reached the end of his tether—not to mention his life. Reminding himself that he was already dead, at least officially, provided no comfort whatsoever. He pulled unconsciously at the shackles that bound his wrists securely behind him but succeeded only in emphasizing how helpless he truly was.

"Centurion Terix, at your service," Terix said, bowing slightly toward the admiral while performing a crisp Romulan military salute, right fist over left lung and elbow over the lower abdominal cavity, where the Romulan heart was located.

It seemed to Trip that Terix was pretending that the woman wasn't even there.

"Centurion, where is Captain S'Ten?" Valdore said after taking a moment to look his welcoming committee up and down.

"The captain has remained on the command deck," Terix said in a neutral military monotone. "He wishes to remain on high alert for any accomplices of the prisoner that may be lingering nearby."

Valdore nodded. "Have you found any evidence of such accomplices?"

"Not yet," Terix said, maintaining his ramrod-straight posture. "I will summon the captain, should you wish it."

"Not necessary, Centurion. I cannot fault your commander for his diligence." Valdore turned and began studying Trip. "Mister Cunaehr. Or would you prefer to be called Sodok?"

Bastard's gonna have me killed no matter how I answer, Trip thought bleakly. He said only, "Sodok will do. You're looking good these days, Admiral. Have you been working out?"

Moving with a grace that belied his considerable size, Valdore approached Trip, fixing him in place with a hard stare that would have made a mongoose flinch. He shook his head, apparently disgusted by Trip's impertinence, while the woman in the black paramilitary clothing rushed Trip from behind and pulled roughly on the restraints that bound his hands behind his back. He resisted the urge to cry out.

"You Vulcans must truly enjoy the sound of your own voices," Valdore said.

Apparently satisfied that Trip posed no threat, the admiral approached Terix. "I have read your initial interrogation report, Centurion. Good work."

"Thank you, Admiral."

"Have you anything significant to add to it?"

Terix hesitated. Although Trip hadn't read the report, he doubted it mentioned the ambiguous friend-foe conflict that Terix seemed to be experiencing. Might Terix be weighing the possible consequences of keeping this embarrassing truth concealed?

"No, Admiral," Terix said at length. "But may I make a request?"

If Terix's slight lapse had roused Valdore's suspicions, the admiral was revealing no outward sign. "Of course, Centurion."

"Will you permit me to carry out the prisoner's execution?" The question sent a chill down Trip's spine.

Valdore answered with no hesitation. "Request denied, Centurion."

"I understand," Terix said, stiffening his shoulders. "I should have anticipated that you would already have planned the prisoner's descent into the embrace of Erebus."

With a dispassion that surprised him, Trip began to wonder exactly how they would do it. One quick, merciful sweep of Valdore's Honor Blade? Or would they convene a disruptor-rifle firing squad after he'd finished delivering an exhausting, rambling testimonial monologue for the record, per the Romulan Star Empire's revered Right of Statement?

Or maybe Valdore goes in for plain vanilla hangings, Trip thought. He worked hard to suppress an absurd surge of laughter.

"See y'all in hell, I guess," he said, chuckling slightly.

The woman reached behind him again, pulling his restraints tighter. The sharp pain in his wrists was all that prevented him from slipping into an apathetic fugue state. He noticed that Valdore was regarding him quizzically for a seeming eternity. Then he lifted an eyebrow in Terix's direction.

"Both you and the prisoner appear to misunderstand, Centurion," the admiral said. "Allow me to clarify. There will *be* no execution."

Valdore now had Trip's complete attention.

Terix stared at Valdore as though the other man had just sprouted two-meter-wide pink fairy wings and was now levitating above the deck plating.

"Admiral?"

"Your report indicated that one of Mister Sodok's espionage specialties is the *Ejhoi Ormiin* and their illicit technologies," Valdore said. "Because finding and destroying the radicals is one of my primary goals, I see no reason to allow his talents to go to waste. Therefore, Mister Sodok will discover the location of the hidden *Ejhoi Ormiin* shipbuilding facility and research complex. You will instruct Captain S'Ten to prepare and provision the captured scout ship for that mission and to make whatever repairs are necessary. I want Mister Sodok on his way as soon as possible."

"But this *thaessu* has no loyalty either to you or the praetor!" Terix said, his eyes wide as dinner plates. "With respect, he cannot be trusted!"

"Which is why I will assign him a minder, Centurion. An experienced supervisor whose loyalty cannot be questioned."

Terix calmed himself quickly, smoothing his ruffled military bearing. "I have acted in that capacity before."

"I know, Centurion."

"I hereby volunteer to do so again, Admiral."

Valdore shook his head. "Your involvement with this *thaessu* has become far too personal and emotional, Centurion. I have selected another minder for the assignment that awaits this prisoner—Special Agent T'Luadh of the Tal Shiar." He gestured toward the black-clad woman, who now stood at Trip's side.

"Nice to see you again," Trip said, making a partial bow in the woman's direction. "I like what you've done with your hair." T'Luadh's only response was to step silently behind him once more and yank painfully on his restraints.

Trip considered asking Valdore to reconsider his choice for the chaperone job in favor of Terix but decided it would be more prudent to simply hold his tongue.

And hope for the best.

Terix's offer to serve as Trip's executioner was beginning to look downright gracious.

THIRTEEN

Monday, August 22, 2157
Enterprise NX-01
Quebec sector, near Galorndon Core

JONATHAN ARCHER FELT palpably relieved that Starfleet Command had finally decided to expand *Enterprise*'s participation in Earth's defense to encompass more than her ongoing "generosity offensive." Even on the front lines, encounters between Starfleet's fastest ships of the line and their Romulan counterparts were often separated by long uneventful intervals. But thanks to Malcolm Reed's diligent insistence on continual tactical upgrades and his ever-changing menu of battle drills, Archer felt confident that his crew would remain busy enough to avoid succumbing to the ennui and frustration that sometimes surfaced when the "business" of war was slow.

As the span between Romulan encounters extended from days to weeks, however, Archer always began feeling less confident about his *own* morale. Having to endure Phlox riding him about his poor eating and sleeping habits wasn't helping. The battles that punctuated the beginnings and endings of those lengthy periods of mounting tension felt almost cathartic.

Today's battle was no different. The second-guessing, the questioning of the loss of life that seemed inevitably woven into each encounter, would come later, probably in the dark, during the dead of the ship's night.

On the bridge's main viewer, a single large, menacing

shape hung suspended. Barely visible along the viewer's bottom edge was a portion of the blue-green world over which both vessels contended.

Archer didn't doubt that *Enterprise* might have been a little worse for wear after the last exchange of fire between the two vessels. However, he noted with grim satisfaction that much of the Romulan's port side was visibly singed.

Unlike *Enterprise*, the Romulan vessel's weapons tubes were dark and cold. Archer maintained a fervent hope that this condition would not change anytime soon.

"Still no response to our hails, Captain," Lieutenant Sato reported from the comm station.

"Why am I not surprised?" Archer said. "Can you ID this particular warbird, Lieutenant?"

"The vessel's exterior markings identify her as the *Imperial Warbird Raon*. Good name. It's Romulan for 'accomplishment.'"

"Let's hope we don't give them the chance to live up to it," Archer said.

"So far there's no sign that our systems have been compromised by any remotely launched malware," said Malcolm Reed from behind his tactical console. "Apparently the Romulans have yet to counter our countermeasures to their remote-hijacking weapon."

Either that or we took that system down before they had the chance to use it on us, Archer thought. Instead, he said, "Contact the personnel at the Galorndon Core science station, Hoshi, and make sure the Romulans can't listen in on us."

"Yes, sir. Opening a secure channel and scrambling it."

At least a minute passed while Hoshi worked. Then the image of the *Warbird Raon* rippled momentarily, as though projected onto the surface of a pond, then vanished. In its place were a pair of humans, a man and a woman, both of whom wore light-hued civilian clothing and appeared to be in their early fifties. Behind them was a comfortable-looking farrago of well-filled bookcases and what appeared to be local potted ferns.

Archer rose from his chair. "I'm Captain Jonathan Archer of the *Starship Enterprise.*"

"*Archer,*" the woman said, apparently distracted by whatever task *Enterprise*'s hail had interrupted. "*I believe I've heard of you.*"

Archer wondered whether she was thinking of the humanitarian renown *Enterprise* had earned lately, or of the last minutes of the *Kobayashi Maru.* It took him all of two seconds to decide that it didn't matter.

"Everyone on the surface of Galorndon Core is in grave danger, Doctor . . ." Archer said before trailing off.

"*Jensen,*" said the woman, apprehending Archer's meaning. "*I'm Doctor Emily Jensen.*" Indicating the bemused-looking man who stood beside her, she said, "*This is Doctor Hans Ruden.*"

"*Exactly how are we in danger, Captain?*" Ruden said, his brow wrinkling in evident skepticism.

"*Enterprise* has just immobilized a Romulan warship, which is right now about nine hundred kilometers directly above your heads."

Dr. Jensen shook her head, scowling. "*Romulans? I fail to see why the Romulans would take any interest in us, Captain.*"

"They're interested in this *planet,* Doctor," Archer said as T'Pol left her science console and approached the bridge's center. "It's located in a sector of space they're trying to lay claim to as they expand outward and into Coalition territory. Believe me, when the Romulans remove aliens from the worlds they annex, they're rarely gentle about it."

"*But we're no threat to them, Captain,*" Ruden said. "*We're xenobiologists, not spies.*"

Jensen nodded. "*What's more, we're all alone here on Galorndon Core, just the two of us. This world is a treasure trove of biodiversity that could keep an army of scientists in a dozen disciplines busy for lifetimes. We're interested in the local biosphere, not in galactic politics.*"

Standing behind the empty command chair, T'Pol faced

the main viewer. "According to Vulcan's planetary database, Galorndon Core possesses resources useful to disciplines other than the biosciences."

"What do you mean?" Ruden said, his frown deepening.

"Like Coridan, this world contains substantial quantities of high-grade dilithium ore," T'Pol said. "The Romulans may very well believe that you have come to Galorndon Core merely to exploit that resource for Earth's war effort."

"What would you know about Earth's war effort, Vulcan?" Jensen said with unconcealed resentment. *"I thought your people didn't want to dirty your hands with such things."*

Archer put up his hands, like a referee in a boxing match. "Stand down, Doctor. Trust me, even if the Romulans didn't have a clue about the dilithium deposits on Galorndon Core, they'd be way too territorial to give a damn *why* you're there. That's why I'm under orders to get you out of harm's way, at least until the shooting's over up here. A squad of MACOs is preparing to land and evacuate you."

"But I thought you said you'd 'immobilized' the Romulan ship, Captain," Ruden said.

"Yes, I *did* say that." Archer smiled, though he was gritting his teeth in frustration. "I just can't guarantee how long they'll stay that way."

"But sending a squad of soldiers down—isn't that overkill?" Jensen asked.

"Not if the Romulans start sending down ground troops of their own," T'Pol said.

"You'll stop them. Won't you?" Ruden said.

"We'll do everything we can. In the meantime, I'd encourage you to archive all of your data. Be ready for evacuation within the hour. Archer out."

Without waiting for either of the xenobiologists to reply, the captain leaned on his chair's right-hand comm button, closing off the channel. The image of the *Warbird*

Raon, juxtaposed against Galorndon Core's eastern limb and the eternal stars beyond, returned a moment later.

"Captain, I'm receiving an audio transmission from the Romulan vessel," Hoshi said, her voice tense with tightly bridled excitement.

"Let's hear it, Hoshi," Archer said as he retook his seat.

After a momentary delay caused by the activation of the universal translator matrix, a stern, authoritarian voice reverberated across the bridge. *"Earth vessel, this is Commander Chulak of the* Imperial Warbird Raon. *You are encroaching on space that has been formally annexed by the Romulan Star Empire. You will withdraw immediately."*

"Commander, this is Captain Jonathan Archer of the *Starship Enterprise.*" Archer infused his voice with as much duranium as he could muster. "Even if Earth or the Coalition of Planets recognized your claim, your vessel is in no condition to enforce it. I advise *you* to withdraw."

He sat in silence, awaiting the vainglorious reply he'd come to expect after so many similar audio-only encounters.

"I read a buildup of power in the warbird's impulse engines," Malcolm Reed said, prompting Archer to grip the arms of his chair tightly.

A moment later, the *Warbird Raon* fell away from the backdrop of Galorndon Core's limb and began dwindling swiftly into the dark reaches of the system.

Archer released his grip on his chair. He turned toward Malcolm, who was watching his tactical board closely. "I'll be damned, Malcolm. Those new high-yield photonic torpedoes must have hit him harder than I thought."

"Perhaps," Malcolm said with his usual conservatism. "Or else Chulak would like us to believe that."

"Either way, he's given us the opening we need," Archer said. "Stay alert, in case that warbird comes back. Or reinforcements somehow manage to sneak up on us."

"Aye, sir."

"Give Major Kimura the signal to send down his ground team."

Galorndon Core

Pressing his face against the port, MACO Private Owen Salazar-Tucker admired the planet that slowly turned hundreds of klicks beneath the belly of the descending shuttlepod. This world's rapidly expanding vista looked even bluer than the waters off of Ireland's Iveragh Peninsula, where he had spent so much of his childhood. It was an achingly beautiful planet, and it filled him nearly to bursting with thoughts of home.

A hard but familiar voice spoke up directly behind Owen's head. "Stay focused, Private. We're here to rescue two research scientists. We haven't come to admire the scenery."

Good-natured laughter and jeers from the rest of the assault team reverberated throughout the auxiliary craft's snug personnel compartment, which now accommodated a dozen tense and beaked-up MACOs. Startled by the abrupt onslaught, Owen turned in his seat and found himself face to face with Selma Guitierrez, the most senior noncom currently serving aboard *Enterprise*.

"Yes, sir," Owen said. "I'm focused on this mission like a laser, sir."

She sat in the row behind him and started arranging the multiple straps of her crash harness. "Glad to hear it, kid. Just make sure you're not so focused that you forget to strap in before this bad boy hits the atmosphere. These fast landings are designed to inflict kidney damage."

Owen suppressed an embarrassed gasp as he scrambled to follow Guitierrez's example by untangling his restraints.

"I think it's all about a lack of restraint," Albert Tucker said while Miguel Salazar, Dad's husband, scowled in silence.

Owen had no idea what his father was talking about. He did, however, have a pretty good grasp of why both his parents had reacted with such reflexive negativity to his announcement that he intended to join the MACO. He could only hope that they'd rise above their protective impulses in order to see the bigger picture.

"I *have* to do this, Dad," Owen said, careful to keep any hint of pleading out of his voice. "People are dying every day. The Romulans are on their way, and they're bulldozing everything in their path. I can't just *ignore* that."

"You're overstating things," Dad said.

"I agree," said Miguel.

"And you're both burying your heads in the sand." Owen crossed his arms truculently to show his folks that he wouldn't be dissuaded from doing his duty.

"I know what *my* parents would say to this," Dad said, shaking his head. "This family has sacrificed more than enough already to threats from outer space. Didn't this family earn a pass after those Xindi horror shows vaporized your Aunt Lizzie? Or when those space pirates murdered my brother, your Uncle Trip?"

"I really can't see what Aunt Lizzie and Uncle Trip have to do with this," Owen said. "And I don't need Grandma and Grandpa Tucker's permission any more than I need yours. But I *was* hoping for your blessing."

"Owen, you're only sixteen!" said Dad, his tone and manner almost begging. Owen was finally beginning to understand why most adults found the whining and wheedling of children so irritating.

The shuttlepod struck the upper troposphere with the force of an asteroid collision, interrupting Private Salazar-Tucker's retrospective musings.

He prayed silently that everything that was inside his body would remain there, at least until after he and his fellow MACOs had debarked on the bright blue world that now completely filled the port.

The ground rushed swiftly upward to greet the shuttlepod, which completed its descent moments before Owen's breakfast could begin the ascent it was threatening to make. He unharnessed in tandem with the rest of the assault team and rose unsteadily to his feet. His stomach slowly backed away from the slippery edge of reverse peristalsis. Like everyone else, he gathered his pack and phase rifle, letting his training put his body on autopilot.

"I'm only seventeen," he said before he even realized his mouth was moving.

"If you want to get any older, stay alert and stay frosty," said a gear-encumbered Sergeant Guitierrez as she led the way out of the shuttlepod and into the field of lush greenery beyond.

"The MACO is no place for a kid your age," Miguel said, backing up Dad completely. "Sixteen is nowhere near old enough to make this kind of life-or-death decision."

"Sixteen is as old as I *have* to be," Owen said. "Go look it up."

Owen suddenly became aware of the tree-lined canopy outside the shuttlepod. Standing beneath that dazzling backdrop, Sergeant Guitierrez was shouting—and shouting at *him* specifically. "Let's see a little more of that laser focus, Private," Guitierrez yelled, her irritation plain. Owen heard more scattered laughter from the ranks, which the sergeant dispatched instantly by flashing a withering look across the rest of the assault team.

Maybe the folks back home were right, he thought as the team fell in and began crossing the indeterminately wide grassy span that separated the landing site from the endangered science lab. *Maybe I* wasn't *really ready to join the MACO after all.*

Realizing he could not afford the luxury of misgivings, Owen Salazar-Tucker clutched his weapon and marched forward, matching the pace of the rest of the team.

Romulan *Imperial Warbird Raon*

Silence reigned on the soot-streaked command deck, though the eyes of the junior officers displayed fear and accusation. Commander Chulak studiously avoided looking at them. The viewscreen images of the *hevam* starship and the world it appeared to have stolen from the Romulan Star Empire quickly shrank until the blackness of the infinite swallowed them both. No one dared to speak.

No one save Subcommander Taith, Chulak's second in command. "We cannot just . . . retreat from the *hevam*," Taith said in icy tones that reverberated starkly throughout the otherwise silent command deck. "No matter how badly outgunned we may be."

Chulak smiled at his exec. "Do not worry, Subcommander."

"But, Commander, we still have personnel on the planet's surface. We cannot recover them by running."

Chulak's tone grew stern. "I have no intention of running. It will be enough to misdirect the *hevam* into believing that we have done so."

"Commander?" Taith said, looking surprised. Had she expected to have cause to draw her Honor Blade and slay him? If she had, Chulak realized, he had just disappointed her.

Leaning forward in his chair, Chulak said, "Helm, take us to the comet field at the system's periphery. Maximum warp."

"Yes, Commander," said Yienek, immediately busying himself at the helm.

Turning back toward Taith, Chulak said, "Fortunately, the *hevam* vessel did not do significant damage to our stardrive."

Taith frowned. "Commander, we would be fortunate to

attain warp factor four in our current condition. I believe that qualifies as 'significant.'"

"Warp four will more than suffice for our purposes, Subcommander," Chulak said.

"What are you planning, Commander?" Taith said, her eyes narrowing with evident suspicion.

Chulak said nothing until Yienek reported the *Raon*'s arrival in the system's cometary zone.

"Full stop," Chulak said. "Helm, set a course for Galorn'don Cor. Warp four."

"Yes, Commander."

Chulak felt the slight shuddering of the deck plates, confirming that the *Raon* had gone back to warp *avaihn mne*, four times light speed, cubed.

"Commander?" Taith said in undisguised perplexity. Or perhaps disbelief.

Chulak faced Taith squarely. "Subcommander, are you familiar with a world known as Cor'i'dan?"

Enterprise **NX-01**

"Sensors are picking up a subspace wake," Malcolm shouted from the tactical console. "An incoming vessel."

"It's the *Warbird Raon*," confirmed T'Pol, who was hunched over the hooded viewer that was built into the science station. "Approaching the inner system at approximately warp four point one six."

This was the other shoe Archer had been waiting for; he had never believed that the *Raon*'s commander had run away. *Not when* Enterprise *and that warbird are so evenly matched,* the captain thought as he rose from his command chair in a single fluid motion.

"Pinpoint her angle of approach, Malcolm," Archer said. "Ensign Leydon, prepare to execute an intercept course from Commander Reed's scans. T'Pol, keep an eye out for reinforcements. The *Raon* might have brought along a few friends this time."

"I'm reading only one ship's warp signature," said Malcolm, shaking his head in frustration as he scowled into his readouts. "But the *Raon*'s still approaching at high warp, even though she's already come pretty far in-system."

Archer considered his opponent's tactics. "Commander Chulak will do whatever he can to keep us from aiming our first salvo accurately. So he'll come out of warp right on top of us, just to keep us off balance."

"I'll be ready for him, Captain," Malcolm said.

"Captain," said T'Pol. Archer turned in time to see an uncharacteristic flicker of apprehension disrupt her Vulcan impassivity. "If Chulak is returning to Galorndon Core without the benefit of reinforcements, then it is entirely possible that he has no intention of coming out of warp at all."

An all-too-familiar queasiness seized Archer's guts.

"T'Pol, get me a fix on Shuttlepod One," he said. "Hoshi, recall the rescue team. We have to get them back to *Enterprise*—*immediately*."

Galorndon Core

The rescue was at first uneventful, so much so that Owen doubted he'd remember very much about it other than the blue of the sky, the green of the grass, the stolid weight of his pack and phase rifle, and the stark bone white of the science station's handful of small, modular structures. His intense apprehension seemed to etch these aspects of his first real MACO operation indelibly into his memory.

But it was the men in the black body armor, their featureless silver helmets gleaming enigmatically in the afternoon sun, that Owen thought he'd remember for the rest of his life.

"Who the hell *are* these guys?" Owen shouted over the

weapons fire. He had dived behind the scant cover of a small berm and noticed that Corporal Costa was there as well.

"Who the hell do you think?" Ogilvy shouted back as she returned the enemy's fire, which flashed uncomfortably close just overhead.

Romulans, Owen thought as his MACO training grappled with millions of years of endocrine-ruled fight-or-flight reactions.

Owen couldn't say how long the back-and-forth salvos went on. Then the word had gone out that *Enterprise* had recalled them. He remembered seeing a pair of gray-haired humans, terrified though otherwise none the worse for wear, being escorted aboard the shuttlepod.

He remembered staring at the outside of the shuttlepod for an eternity, apparently long after most everyone else, MACO or civilian, had already gone aboard. He recalled the sound of the thrusters firing, though the craft remained on the ground despite somebody's continued urgent demand that she take off without delay. He remembered looking down and seeing silver-helmeted bodies on the ground and wanting to remove one of those helmets to see what a Romulan actually looked like. But there was no time for that: The greenery beckoned, and Owen ran headlong into it.

Then someone was shouting at him, and the shouts seemed to come from somewhere very close, as though they were being delivered directly into his ear. His arms ached, and his back felt strained; his movements were sluggish, his body meeting resistance, as though pushing through water, or gelatin.

Then the shuttlepod reappeared. It was now a couple of meters off the ground, hovering.

More shouting. "I told you to *leave* me, Private!"

Confusion. He realized only then that Sergeant Guitierrez was in his arms, bloodied and grimy. But alive.

"We don't have time for heroics!" Guitierrez yelled. "*Enterprise* has given us an emergency recall order! The Romulans——"

Her voice broke up, disintegrated by a fit of coughing that brought a bloody foam to her lips. Owen thought he might have told her something about MACOs never leaving anybody behind. But he wasn't sure.

From somewhere far behind the tree line, a brilliant light flashed, forcing him to close his eyes momentarily.

He focused on the shuttlepod as it settled back to the ground. The starboard hatch opened, and strong arms relieved him of his burden. When Guitierrez was safely aboard, some of those same arms seized him with surprising gentleness.

The next thing he remembered was staring out the shuttlepod window at the spreading, all-consuming fire that was rolling in from the eastern horizon. In the distance, thunder rumbled, sounding like the combined rage of all the gods of every civilization in the galaxy.

Enterprise NX-01

"Galorndon Core is already no longer a *Minshara*-class world, Captain," T'Pol said.

Archer stood before the main viewer, arms at his sides, clenching and unclenching his fists. On the screen, an entire world was aflame. What had once been a cradle of life was rapidly becoming a planet-sized crematorium. A volcanic fissure was opening right before Archer's eyes, spewing magma skyward for tens of kilometers. According to T'Pol's initial report, the multiwarp impact that Galorndon Core had just endured was even creating havoc with the planet's magnetic field, unleashing all manner of unpredictable and potentially lethal atmospheric effects. Even the oceans appeared to be igniting.

And there's nothing I can do to stop any of it, he thought. Recalling T'Pol's earlier report about magnetic-field anomalies, he said, "What's the status of Shuttlepod One?"

Pressing a small white receiver to her ear, Hoshi turned her seat toward him. "She's just cleared the planet's atmosphere and is preparing to make her approach. The MACOs accomplished their mission."

In the proverbial nick, Archer thought. "Thanks, Hoshi. Ensign Leydon, take us back to our regular patrol route once the shuttlepod's secure in the launch bay."

"Aye, Captain." The helmswoman began adjusting the settings on her board.

"I can't believe that the *Raon* just . . . rammed the planet at better than warp four," Malcolm said, his tone tinged with shock. "Why would anyone do that?"

"I can believe it," Archer said. "I think the Romulans have done this before."

"Where?" Ensign Leydon said. She sounded just as shell-shocked as Malcolm had.

"Coridan Prime," Archer said. "Two and a half years ago."

Like Coridan, Galorndon Core's crust was widely believed to contain countless large deposits of high-grade dilithium ore—enough to create a lengthy and catastrophic conflagration under certain circumstances, such as the abrupt release of warp-engine levels of kinetic and thermal energy.

"What a waste of biodiversity," Hoshi said.

"Illogical," T'Pol observed.

Coridan's burning sea, an inferno of dilithium, had the potential to continue blazing for centuries. The prosperity the Coridanites enjoyed prior to the catastrophe would remain forever out of their reach, unless and until they could find a way to capitalize on what remained of their underground dilithium supply.

"There was so much here that either side could have

used, from medicine to warp-flight to weaponry," Malcolm said. "It's hard to believe that anyone could be so callous as to destroy a whole world, just to deny us access to it."

"That's because you're not as paranoid as the Romulans," T'Pol said.

To Archer's surprise, a snatch of half-remembered John Milton sprang to his lips: "'The mind is its own place, and in itself can make a heaven of hell, a hell of heaven.'"

Malcolm smiled wryly. *"Paradise Lost."*

Archer met his tactical officer's gaze. "I wonder how many more paradises Earth can afford to lose."

FOURTEEN

Hoshi Sato felt thoroughly numb as she completed her tasks at the comm station. The medical and damage-control teams had all been dispatched, both aboard *Enterprise* and among the Starfleet task force's handful of surviving vessels. The captain had just silenced the Tactical Alert klaxons.

Except for the dull background noise generated by the automated systems, the bridge sounded, at least to Sato's sensitive ears, as still as a tomb. She found that simile appropriate, since the vista through the main viewer was essentially a graveyard—a quietly cooling remnant of a killing field through which countless starship hulls, or fragments thereof, tumbled in a weird billiard-ballet of angular momentum, inertia, and chaos. Some of the debris shards moved uncannily fast, their motions set to crazed intensities by whatever weapon had shredded them in the first place; others appeared to move much more slowly, wandering and drifting as the laws of physics decreed.

The intense fireworks had begun precisely thirty-six minutes earlier. Weaponry encompassing everything from phase cannons and photonic torpedoes to disruptor tubes and old-style atomic warheads had done a thorough job of converting three dozen ships into countless hundreds, or perhaps even thousands, of fragments. Many of the drifting pieces were so small, burned, or twisted that she could scarcely tell which had come from members of the Starfleet task force and which were formerly Romulan warbird components.

In the end, does it really even matter? Sato thought.

Very gradually, Sato became aware that not all life in the universe had been extinguished by the battle *Enterprise* had just survived. T'Pol calmly recited an inventory of Starfleet's losses.

Losses, she thought, her breathing suddenly inhibited by a chest-crushing sensation of futility. *And we won this one. I think.*

For some unmeasurable interval, the bridge once again went quiet.

Then she noticed with a jolt of surprise that Commander T'Pol and the captain were standing beside her seat. A moment later she became aware that every eye on the bridge was now focused on her. *Great.*

"Lieutenant, I hardly think laughter is an appropriate reaction," the Vulcan XO said, her words underscored by her slight frown and a noticeably disapproving tone. "Even for a human."

Sato could only blink mutely as she tried to contain her surprise. Finally, she said, "I . . . I'm not sure what you're talking about."

"You started *laughing,* Hoshi," Captain Archer said quietly, lines of concern etched into his craggy face. It occurred to Sato only then how the war seemed to be aging him. "Are you all right?"

She couldn't remember laughing. Tears felt more likely, but her eyes remained stubbornly dry. She tried to draw a deep, cleansing breath and found she couldn't quite fill her lungs. Something close to panic rose within her.

"I don't know, Captain," she said. She shook her head and released a small, self-deprecating smile. "Maybe it's battle nerves."

"I want you to go down to sickbay," said the captain, softening his words with a gentle smile. "Have Phlox check you out."

Though she knew he was probably right, she hated the idea of being the only member of the entire bridge crew to fold under pressure. "But, Captain, I don't thi—"

"That's an order, Lieutenant," he said, speaking more sharply this time.

With a sigh and a nod, Sato rose unsteadily to her feet.

Evading the glances of all of her fellow bridge officers except for Ensign Leydon, she stepped into the turbolift. *I wonder if there's anything in Phlox's little menagerie that can cure war.*

T'Pol was surprised to hear her door chime ring so late in the ship's night.

She was even more surprised by the identity of her visitor.

"What can I do for you, Lieutenant?" she said as she rose from the mat she had set beside her burning meditation candle.

"I'm sorry to bother you so late in the evening, Commander," Hoshi Sato said, her nervousness evident in that she continually shifted her weight from foot to foot as she stood on the threshold.

"It's no bother," T'Pol said as she increased the illumination to half the daytime level. She gestured toward the spartan interior of her quarters. "Come in, Lieutenant."

"I'd prefer it if you'd just call me Hoshi, Commander," the human woman said as she stepped into the room and let the hatch hiss closed behind her. She stood just inside the room, wringing her hands.

"Are you all right, Lieutenant?" T'Pol said. After a slight hesitation, she added, "Hoshi?"

T'Pol's use of the lieutenant's first name appeared to put the human woman at ease, at least somewhat. "I don't know.

Doctor Phlox seems to think so. He couldn't find anything wrong with me, so he chalked up my little . . . performance on the bridge this morning to post-traumatic stress."

T'Pol nodded. That sounded reasonable. She said, "Humans are prone to emotional repercussions following highly stressful situations. And ship-to-ship combat is unquestionably stressful."

The lieutenant shrugged and displayed a dissatisfied scowl. "It's not as though I actually got injured, Commander."

"That is entirely beside the point. You need not experience a physical injury to be traumatized emotionally. Witnessing such occurrences can suffice as the cause." T'Pol had spent the last two hours in meditation in an effort to purge her subconscious of the terrible spectacle she had seen earlier today—the horrendous tableau of decompressing, burning, disintegrating spacecraft that otherwise might follow her into her dreams.

But such things were entirely too personal to share, even among her fellow Vulcans.

"Maybe you're right," Lieutenant Sato said. "Phlox ordered me to spend the rest of the day trying to relax."

"Did you succeed?"

The human released a brief laugh, creating small facial lines that T'Pol had never noticed before. "Do I *look* relaxed to you? I haven't been able to sleep very well at night for weeks now, let alone take naps during the middle of the day. But I've *never* folded up like that on the bridge before."

T'Pol thought she was beginning to understand the source of the lieutenant's distress. "You believe you have somehow demonstrated weakness."

"I survived having my brain infested by Xindi reptilian parasites." Sato's eyes shone with unshed tears. "I suppose turning out to be weaker than I thought I was is part of the problem."

The intensity of Sato's emotions was beginning to make

T'Pol uncomfortable. "Then perhaps you should discuss this with Major Kimura. I know that the two of you have grown close over the past year."

Sato's round face flushed. "Have we been that obvious?"

"*Enterprise* is a small ship, Lieutenant. Such relationships may be unwise, but they violate no regulation of which I am aware. Regardless, they can be difficult even for Vulcans to avoid noticing."

Judging from Sato's breathing and complexion, the human appeared to be regaining a measure of her self-control. "I don't feel quite right about talking to Takashi about this. I know he likes to come off as the quiet, deep MACO warrior-philosopher, but I don't think even he can get his head around what's really bothering me."

T'Pol's curiosity suddenly began wrestling with her reluctance to involve herself in the personal matters of a subordinate. In spite of herself, her right eyebrow went aloft.

"And you believe that I would understand your problem better than the major could?" she asked.

Sato nodded. "Of everybody on board, you may be the *only* one who can."

Several seconds passed in silence as T'Pol considered Sato's request. The moment stretched until her curiosity and a desire to help a colleague overcame her natural Vulcan reticence.

She gestured toward the mats on the floor of the small but adequate central living area. "Make yourself comfortable, Lieutenant."

"Hoshi," the lieutenant said as she nimbly lowered herself to one of the mats and sat there, cross-legged, near T'Pol's meditation candle. T'Pol adopted a similar posture, her back to the port and the star-flecked infinity that lay beyond it.

"Hoshi," T'Pol said, correcting herself. Apart from Trip,

and on rare occasions Captain Archer, being on a first-name basis with a human colleague felt awkward.

After a lengthy pause, Sato said, "You're a Vulcan."

Again, one of T'Pol's eyebrows rose. Sato's remark reminded her of how a *V'tosh ka'tur*—a so-called Vulcan without logic she had met during her tenure as a V'Shar agent—had responded to the very same words uttered by an Andorian soldier. *"What was it that gave me away?"* the *V'tosh ka'tur* had asked the Andorian. *"The ears? Or the way I snort when I laugh?"*

"Whatever you may believe to be wrong with you, Hoshi," T'Pol said, "your grasp of the obvious remains unimpaired." It occurred to her that even among the strictest Syrrannite orders on her homeworld, there might be no such thing as a *V'tosh rik'ortal*—a Vulcan without sarcasm.

Flushing again, the human said, "What I meant was, you're a student of the philosophy of Surak."

"I am," T'Pol said softly, nodding. "It is a lifelong pursuit."

"I've read Skon's translation of *The Teachings of Surak,*" Sato continued. "I've even read it in the original Vulcan."

T'Pol could not help but be impressed. While Skon's volume was a relatively common sight on the bookshelves and coffee tables of humans from Earth to Alpha Centauri to the Altair system, humans willing expend the energy to read Surak in *Vulcan* were rare indeed.

T'Pol experienced a sudden pang of deep regret for her earlier sarcasm.

"And you have questions."

Sato nodded. "More than I had before I started. And *way* more since the war got under way."

"And you wish to understand how a Syrrannite—a follower of Surak, bred to the ways of peace—can take part in such destruction and bloodshed."

Sato answered with a nod and a small, sad smile. "Yes."

I wish I had a simple answer for you, Hoshi, T'Pol thought.

The Vulcan paused to consider all the killing she had abetted since the war had begun. Did the lives her actions had arguably helped save truly balance the scales? Did the fact that *Enterprise* and the rest of the Starfleet task force had succeeded in stopping the Romulan advance here at Prantares, preventing an aggressive empire from annexing the worlds of the Pi 3 Orionis system and thereby folding their abundant resources into its war effort mean anything in the end?

Perhaps T'Pau had been right all along. Maybe there really was no way back onto the path of peace for any Vulcan who succumbed to the temptation to pick up the sword. Could she ever embrace Surak's teachings, or would they always elude her?

And her participation in the war wasn't the only issue. In addition, she had become psychically bonded to a human mate. Did she even still deserve to call herself a Vulcan?

T'Pol knew that she wouldn't settle the matter anytime soon. At least not so long as she remained aboard *Enterprise*. *And certainly not,* she thought, *until I can return to Vulcan and climb the steps at Mount Seleya.*

A pang of regret and homesickness sharper than any blade pierced her guts. *The place where Surak's essence was forever taken from us.*

She rose, crossed to the environmental controls on the wall, and lowered the lights back to meditation-chamber levels.

"Commander?" said Sato, still seated cross-legged on the mat.

T'Pol sat, resuming her contemplative posture. "I'm afraid I can furnish no easy solutions," she said, "for either of us."

"I was afraid you were going to say that," Sato said and started to rise.

T'Pol held up a hand, and the lieutenant settled nimbly back into her cross-legged, seated position. "I did not, however, say there were no answers. I would encourage you to remain for a while."

"You'll let me meditate with you?" Sato said, her gratitude clearly audible.

T'Pol began trying to focus her attention upon the flame that burned atop the candle between them. "If there *are* answers for either of us," she said with a nod, "perhaps we can find them more quickly if we seek them together."

FIFTEEN

STANDING ALONE on the darkened observation deck of the *Warbird Pontilus*, Admiral Valdore ignored the trio of battered, broken spacecraft that drifted across his visual field. He tried not to notice the steady, insistent approach of the *Bird-of-Prey Nel Trenco*, which had arrived right on schedule. Instead, he focused his attention on what remained of the former province-cum-protectorate that had been such a thorn in the side of Praetor Karzan's last two predecessors.

Even from low orbit, he could discern precious little detail on Haakona's dayside surface other than a few indistinct blotches that might be columns of smoke. It was only beyond the boundary of the terminator, the edge of the shadow of Haakonan night, that the really telling signs lay. Rather than the brightly illuminated, straight-line geometries that characterized an advanced world, the lights that punctuated the darkness were scattered and chaotic. The artful, alternating curves and straight edges of vehicular thoroughfares and cities had been supplanted by the randomness and disorder of fires burning hither and yon, untended and out of control.

In slightly less than four complete turns of this planet on its axis, Haakona's civilization had been eradicated. It appeared that it would never again represent a threat to the Romulan Star Empire, or to anything else.

Valdore was now free to concentrate the entire war-making apparatus of the Romulan Star Empire upon the urgent task of bringing the *hevam* homeworld of Earth to its knees, along with its remaining allies.

He heard the hiss of a hatch opening directly behind him. A familiar, confident voice followed. "Admiral Valdore, the *Nel Trenco* is docking with us."

"Thank you, Subcommander Terix," Valdore said without lifting his gaze from the desolate vista that lay beyond the panoramic window.

"Admiral Dagarth and Colonel Talok are aboard. The colonel says they have orders to report to you in person, immediately."

"That is correct, Subcommander."

"Shall I conduct them to your office?"

Valdore turned away from the port and shook his head at the subcommander. "Bring them here. I will wait."

The younger man's heels clicked as he delivered a textbook elbow-over-the-heart salute before turning and exiting.

After pausing to straighten the Honor Blade that dangled from his belt, Valdore resumed staring at the vast, quiescent planetscape that slowly turned below him. A small, scorched native spacecraft tumbled past, apparently merely one of the hundreds of such vessels whose operators had proved too inept to get clear of the planet and into deep space. Others had no doubt escaped Haakona, perhaps even making it out of the system entirely, compelled by mutagenic demons toward a destination that probably had never existed in the first place.

He wondered how many remained alive but stranded on the planet's surface—hagridden by the same delusion yet unable to flee the planet in order to act upon it.

Uncounted moments later, the hatch behind him opened again. He turned in time to see Admiral Dagarth and Colonel Talok enter the observation deck. The two officers approached, then abruptly stopped to deliver crisp salutes to Valdore in unison.

Valdore turned away from his officers and set his gaze back upon the planet below. "Sit-rep on Haakona, Admiral," he said. Though Dagarth and Valdore nominally shared the same rank, she occupied a lower echelon of the admiralty; while she was a *Khre'rior*, or vice-admiral, he was supreme commander of the fleet, with seniority that far and away outstripped hers.

Dagarth's reply dripped with pride. "As you can see, Admiral Valdore, Haakona has been completely neutralized, per your orders."

Valdore scowled as he surveyed the dying planet. "Your orders, Dagarth, were to present me with a *plan* for the neutralization of Haakona. Not to implement one without my prior authorization."

"I understand, sir," she said, still sounding infuriatingly confident. "Unfortunately, it proved necessary to take pre-emptive action."

He turned back in Dagarth's direction and approached her almost closely enough for their noses to touch. To his surprise, she stood her ground.

"It proved *necessary* to defy my orders?" he shouted.

She answered without hesitating and without raising her voice. "The viral material my men released into Haakona's atmosphere was the product of paid specialists from B'Saari II and Adigeon Prime," she said. "The bioscience expertise available on those worlds is far in advance of ours."

"Or so says the Yridian I'm told sold you the material. Your virus should have been thoroughly tested by our own technologists before you deployed it here. It might have unforeseen long-term residual effects on *us*." The thought of virus-infected Romulan soldiers suddenly abandoning their posts in legionary numbers chilled him to the marrow.

"The research team guaranteed that the viral agent would affect only the genome we provided," Dagarth said. "That of the Haakonans. My science officers confirmed it."

"I should have been consulted," Valdore repeated. "My science specialists may have found something that yours missed."

"The material had an extremely limited shelf life, Admiral," Dagarth said, galloping on as though her transgression had been a mere breach of utensil protocol at a formal consular dinner. "I also had to consider the low likelihood of obtaining more of the material later, given the protests the B'Saari scientists made."

"I've already heard about that," Valdore said, nodding toward Talok, who had furnished the information. Turning his ire fully upon Dagarth, he said, "You led them to believe that they were participating in a project that would restore a dead civilization to life. Not extinguish a living one."

Dagarth looked straight ahead, apparently expending real effort to avoid Valdore's angry gaze. "Like the accelerated deployment of the viral agent, deceiving the B'Saari was an unfortunate necessity." Only now was she beginning to sound defensive, if not properly chastened.

"'An unfortunate necessity,'" Valdore repeated, turning away from Dagarth and back toward the sprawling panorama of death and chaos that she had created.

This is really my fault, he thought. *I failed to impress upon her the danger of overweening ambition.*

Instead, Valdore had recognized and rewarded that ambition, thus encouraging the current potential debacle. While serving as captain of a ship of the line, Dagarth had distinguished herself during the crucial testing phase of the *arrenhe'hwiua* telecapture system. With the Coalition worlds having blunted their vulnerabilities to that weapon—and with a workable *avaihh lli vastam* warp-seven stardrive still lying out of Valdore's reach—it should have come as no surprise that Dagarth would seek to distinguish herself in other ways.

I placed her in the admiralty, he thought as a deep sadness settled across his soul. *Therefore I should not be surprised that she would seek to climb its hierarchy boldly and quickly.* It was axiomatic that the ascent to power and authority was neither a pursuit for the timid nor one that would tolerate half measures.

Valdore also understood that the same could be said about the *defense* of power and authority.

Drawing his *dathe'anofv-sen*—his razor-keen Honor Blade—Valdore turned and lunged.

The blade pierced Dagarth's heart before she could either move or utter a sound. She slumped to the deck plates, her eyes wide, her face frozen in a rictus of surprise that matched Colonel Talok's expression almost perfectly.

Valdore knelt beside Dagarth, withdrew his blade, and wiped her verdant heartblood on her sleeve. A great green pool was forming beneath her body.

"Your orders, Admiral?" Talok said, adopting a parade-ground posture. He appeared to be expending a great deal of effort not to make direct eye contact.

Valdore rose to his feet and sheathed his Honor Blade. "Get somebody in here to clean this place up. And say a prayer to T'Vet that Dagarth was right."

Talok looked at him then, apparently confused. "*Right,* Admiral?"

The chill he had felt earlier returned. "About that virus being incapable of doing to *us* what it did to the Haakonans."

SIXTEEN

Tuesday, February 14, 2158
Romulan *Scout Ship Kilhra'en*
Carraya sector, Romulan space

GAZING THROUGH ONE of the windows in the little vessel's cramped galley, Trip Tucker searched in vain for the star of his homeworld.

Home usually wasn't far from his mind, but on this day of all days—Valentine's Day marked not only the fourth anniversary of the successful resolution of the Xindi crisis, but also the passage of three years since his "death" aboard *Enterprise*—he was particularly aware of the immense gulf that separated him from everything and everyone he'd ever cared about.

T'Luadh, Trip's "minder" from the Tal Shiar, took a seat on the opposite side of the galley table at which Trip was seated, abruptly scattering his train of thought. He suppressed a reflexive frown, deciding that he didn't mind the intrusion.

T'Luadh touch-activated the viewer embedded into the flat tabletop. A two-dimensional map of local space obediently appeared, and T'Luadh placed one of her long index fingers against the screen's surface. "It is there, in the Carraya system," she said, her voice and manner all but bursting with a confidence that bordered on arrogance. "And we are fortunate, this time. At this vessel's maximum speed, that's slightly more than four *eisae* away from our present position."

Nearly five Earth days. Trip was relieved that this destination didn't lie months away. It would be nice to have a real, planned-out destination, especially after having spent the better part of the last two weeks engaged in a more or less random search for the quarry that had already eluded them for more than half a year now: the new *Ejhoi Ormiin* shipbuilding facility, a high-tech complex that the upper echelons of the Tal Shiar, the Romulan Senate, and the Romulan military all feared might have already secretly completed a number of highly advanced, warp-seven-capable warships.

Even a relative handful of such vessels had the potential to bring down the Romulan Star Empire's civilian government as well as its military, both of which were the *Ejhoi Ormiin's* goals. More important, at least to Trip, was the terrible exacerbation of Earth's disadvantage in the Romulan conflict that would result should Admiral Valdore succeed in capturing, rather than destroying, the *Ejhoi Ormiin's* alleged creations.

Yes, it would be good to have a definable, concrete destination once again. Unless, of course, the prize at the end of this particular rainbow turned out to be yet another pot of fool's gold.

Staring down at T'Luadh's star chart, Trip wondered whether the Tal Shiar agent's confidence was warranted this time.

"Why are you so sure we'll find the *Ejoi Ormiin's* shipbuilding complex in the Carraya system?" he said, folding his arms before him.

T'Luadh's left eyebrow rose almost imperceptibly, which Trip recognized as a sign of defensiveness. "The Tal Shiar has taken great pains to verify its findings, Mister Sodok."

Shrugging, Trip said, "Oh, as opposed to all the *other* times your people have given us unreliable intel since this mission began." After having already spent nearly nine months cooped up with her in this little scout vessel, he was wary of committing to yet another wild-goose chase, even one whose endpoint was so close, relatively speaking.

But he also was reluctant to wrap up their ongoing arrangement. Whether the search for the *Ejhoi Ormiin* and their illicit high technology finished in success or failure, he knew that the mission's conclusion would mark the end of his usefulness, both to Admiral Valdore and to Colonel T'Luadh of the Tal Shiar.

Despite the uneasy trust that had grown between them during their collaborations over the past few months, Trip was willing to bet money that the moment that happened she'd waste little time slipping a blade between his ribs.

"It is difficult to maintain current intelligence on an adversary as clever, as secretive, and as committed as the *Ejhoi Ormiin*," T'Luadh said with a scowl. "You of all people, Mister Sodok, should understand that."

"I probably understand it better than just about anybody working in your spook bureau," Trip said. Memories sprang to mind of the friends and colleagues who had perished because of the *Ejhoi Ormiin*'s machinations: Trip's first Section 31 part-ner in the field, Tinh Hoc Phuong, whom a Romulan double agent named Ch'uivh—aka Sopek of Vulcan—had reduced to smoking meat with a pitiless blast of disruptor fire; and Dr. Ehrehin, the kindly old warp-theory genius who had died in the never-ending crossfire between the *Ejhoi Ormiin* radicals and the Romulan military.

The hard but handsome Romulan woman stared at him in silence for the length of several dozen heartbeats before she spoke. "That is arguably true, Mister Sodok. In fact, your extensive espionage experience was what prompted me to draft you on this mission after Terix captured you."

And I hope you don't think for a minute that I'm not grateful for the change of scenery, he thought, though he had always recognized T'Luadh's intervention as less a pardon than a temporary stay of execution. Not for the first time, Trip wondered if she had drafted him because she knew more than she was letting on about his "extensive espionage experience."

"Guess it pays to keep the résumé up to date," he said. Over her perplexed frown, he added, "What makes the Tal Shiar so sure we'll find the shipyard in the Carraya system?"

"Our intelligence analysts have noted a pattern in recent pirate attacks on civilian shipping convoys. In almost every case, much of the materials stolen have relevance to starship construction. And the general pattern of the raids converges upon the Carraya system."

Trip scratched his jaw and discovered that he needed to shave. "But why Carraya? I thought the system's only habitable planet had no intelligent life, no civilization, and was covered nearly from pole to pole in tropical jungle."

"The fourth planet," she said with a solemn nod. "Correct."

"But there wouldn't be any industrial infrastructure there for the *Ejhoi Ormiin* to exploit."

"Correct again, Mister Sodok. Evidently the radicals perceived the need for remoteness and secrecy to trump the need for efficiency and speed. As you say, the planet can provide the radicals with little in the way of refined resources. The jungle canopy, however, possesses biosensor-scattering properties, thus providing the *Ejhoi Ormiin* a good deal of cover."

"So how do we know they're there?"

"Romulan military vessels supervised by Tal Shiar field agents conducted both long- and medium-range scans of all the worlds of the Carraya system very recently. They yielded sensor profiles indicating quantities and concentrations of polyalloys, duranium, and other refined materials consistent with a large-scale shipbuilding operation."

Trip had to admit that the information sounded compelling. Whatever those scans had picked up on Carraya

IV sure as hell wasn't just a bunch of beavers building a dam.

"You said that the Tal Shiar think the radicals might have finished building some of these high-warp vessels," he said. "Have they found any sign they've deployed the ships?"

She shook her head. "Not definitively. But we cannot afford to wait for proof, which could come with whole worlds abruptly set ablaze. Like Cor'i'dan, or Galorn'don Cor."

It didn't escape Trip's notice that the Romulan military and the Romulan government, not the *Ejhoi Ormiin* radicals, were the parties responsible for the destructive energies released in those two places. But he decided there was nothing to be gained by pointing that out.

"So what's the plan?" he asked instead.

T'Luadh favored him with a look of long-suffering patience, as though he were a defective child. "Except, perhaps, for specific tactics, our plan remains unchanged. We will make a stealth approach to Carraya IV and find the *Ejhoi Ormiin* shipyard complex. Then, before the radicals have an opportunity to flee the system, we will seize it— along with their *avaihh lli vastam* warp-seven technology."

"Or at least destroy it all to keep it out of the wrong hands," Trip ventured.

Her eyes narrowed as she regarded him with unconcealed suspicion. Trip had seen this same expression on numerous prior occasions, so it no longer bothered him. Clearly, she had reservations about his loyalty, either to the mission, the Romulan Star Empire, or both.

The smart money's on both, Trip thought, well aware that she was no fool.

"We will exercise *that* option," she said icily, "only as a last resort."

His face and neck flushed under the intensity of her

glare, and the sudden warmth made him grateful for
his hidden supply of the sulfatriptan compound that
maintained the green coloration of his blood.

Like T'Luadh, Trip couldn't afford to allow the radicals to escape Carraya IV with their high-warp technology intact. Neither could he afford to allow T'Luadh to
capture it.

It came to him then that all the advances and reversals
in the ongoing cat-and-mouse games that he and T'Luadh
had played with the *Ejhoi Ormiin* would finally come to a
head within a week, or even sooner. Despite the surprisingly
easy working relationship that he had forged with T'Luadh,
he might soon have no choice other than to kill her. And
he didn't doubt that she had the very same imperative
regarding him.

Pushing aside these unpleasant thoughts, Trip stared down
at the tabletop viewer. T'Luadh had replaced the star map with
a half-meter-wide image of a preternaturally green planet. Except for a single kidney-shaped ocean, a smattering of large
inland seas, and a pair of anemic-looking polar ice caps, the
place was essentially one vast planet-girdling tropical rain forest. Trip sighed as he contemplated the prospect of searching
such a place for such a determinedly hidden adversary as the
Ejhoi Ormiin. Though he'd spent a fair proportion of his life
in sunny, humid Florida, he doubted that had prepared him
adequately for the ordeal that was to come.

Resigning himself to the inevitable, he decided that the
best way to deal with the mission ahead was to get as much
sleep as possible before the *Kilhra'en*'s arrival at Carraya IV.
He hoped that the planet had some unexpected positives to
balance out its many apparent negatives.

As Trip rose from the table, headed for his sleeping
quarters, he asked, "Does the Tal Shiar know if Carraya
IV's ocean has anything in it like a Terran catfish?"

*   *   *

Secure in the aft sleeping compartment, Trip slumbered.

And dreamed.

But in the midst of the dreaming, he entered a decidedly different state, a mode of consciousness far more vivid and real than the realm of dreams. Like an ancient film negative, the universe transformed itself into an infinitude of brilliant whiteness right before Trip's eyes. As always, the suddenness of the effect startled him.

He'd come many times before to the all-white expanse in which he now stood, though the frequency of these . . . spells? . . . episodes? . . . had declined steadily the more deeply he ventured into Romulan territory.

He saw a slender, upright shape in the distance, indistinct yet nonetheless familiar. His booted feet somehow gaining purchase on the insubstantial white nothingness beneath them, he jogged toward the approaching figure.

He grinned as he recognized her. *T'Pol.*

Her voice answered inside his mind, no doubt being transmitted via the insubstantial, gossamer psi connection that still tethered them together in spite of the gulf of light-years that separated them.

Trip.

Even before she drew close enough to give him a clear look at her olive-toned face, he could sense that something wasn't right. She was in emotional turmoil, though he knew she'd be loath to admit it.

What's wrong? his inner voice asked her.

She continued to approach him until she was nearly close enough to touch. *These . . . psionic assignations of ours*, she said silently.

It took him a moment to realize that she was referring to their more-than-occasional meetings in the Bright White Place. He reached toward her, but she seemed to recoil from him slightly, just enough to stay beyond his reach. *What about 'em, T'Pol?*

Perhaps we should try to further reduce their frequency, she said.
Why?

She closed her eyes. He saw a tear on her cheek. He reached out to brush it away, but she remained just centimeters too distant.

My emotions, she said, her breathing labored. *They have become increasingly difficult to control.*

It doesn't exactly surprise me, T'Pol, Trip said. *You've been through a lot over the past few years. Losing your mother, and baby Elizabeth. And then that business with Surak on Vulcan.*

I should be able to manage those traumas, she said. Tears now ran down both her cheeks. *Were I truly Vulcan, that might be the case. But I fear I am becoming something other than Vulcan.*

Trip's now human forehead crumpled into a concerned frown. *You are Vulcan, T'Pol. What the hell are you talking about?*

I have mind-linked with a human, Trip. No Vulcan has ever done such a thing before. I must return.

To Vulcan? he asked, his confusion escalating. *Now? In case you hadn't noticed, T'Pol, there's still a war on, a war that Vulcan has decided to sit out.*

She nodded sadly. *I know. And I regret it deeply.*

You have a responsibility to Captain Archer, he said.

And I will honor that responsibility in my own way, just as you do. But I have responsibilities on Vulcan as well. Two of my oldest friends, Denak and Ych'a, remain under suspicion for the destruction of Surak's katra. They are still in detention, even now. I need to help them clear their names. . . She trailed off into silence.

For an instant, Trip wondered absurdly whether the bountiful garden at T'Pol's house had gone completely to seed since his departure from Vulcan; after all, T'Pol, Denak, and Ych'a were in no position to pitch in with the chores these days.

Pushing that matter aside, he lunged forward in an effort to close the distance between himself and T'Pol, but to no avail. He acknowledged with some shame that he was being selfish; he had allowed the loneliness of his current plight to win out over any consideration of T'Pol's feelings. He was dozens of light-years away from anything and everything familiar, and T'Pol was his lifeline. The prospect of her cutting him loose while he lay asleep and defenseless in a cramped scout ship, alone but for the company of a Romulan spy who must surely kill him within a matter of days, was simply too much to bear.

The Bright White Place suddenly began to rock and shake, as though some huge creature were hurling boulders at it from the outside. No sooner had the first shock subsided than a second, even stronger one knocked his boots out from under him—

"What the hell?" Trip shouted as he rolled out of the aft sleeping compartment.

The lighting was dim and green, the Romulan color of emergency and danger. His footing was unsteady on the deck plating, which rattled as though from a massive collision. He realized immediately from the feel of the deck that the *Kilhra'en* had dropped back into normal space.

It came to him suddenly that the *Ejhoi Ormiin* must have somehow detected their approach, even though Carraya IV still lay days away at maximum warp.

At least my lungs aren't sucking vacuum yet, he thought as he stumbled into the forward compartment, where T'Luadh was furiously entering commands into the cockpit console. *Maybe there's still time to get us out of this.*

"We're under attack," T'Luadh said, stating the obvious with a businesslike calm that T'Pol might have envied.

He took the right chair, directly beside hers, and began accessing the tactical systems. "By whom?"

"One ship. It's a small civilian vessel, armed with at least one disruptor cannon. The configuration matches that of a private Haakonan transport ship."

Trip didn't bother trying to conceal his surprise. "What would Haakonans be doing all the way out here?"

T'Luadh remained focused on her console, but her words took on an impatient timbre. "Firing on *us*, evidently."

That much was obvious. But the situation made no sense. Dead, defeated Haakona, a former annex of Romulan space against which Admiral Valdore's forces had fought fiercely until the end of Praetor D'deridex's reign, lay more than a thousand light-years away. Relative to Earth, Haakona was located in the Romulan Star Empire's opposite frontier, about as far away from the Earth-Romulan conflict as one could get. A Haakonan commander would have to have a compelling reason to venture so very far from his homeworld—and as far as Trip knew, the Haakonans had never exhibited much interest in exploration for its own sake.

"Are you *sure* these people are Haakonans?" Trip asked.

"At the moment, Mister Sodok, I'm not entirely sure of anything," she said as she tried to route additional power to the *Kilhra'en*'s polarized forward hull plating. "Except for the fact that these were the strangest-looking Haakonans I've ever seen. Little better than wild animals, from what I observed."

"You hailed them?" Trip asked.

The *Kilhra'en* rocked and jounced brutally under another disruptor fusillade. T'Luadh grabbed the edge of her console to steady herself. "I did. And they appear to have disliked the way I answered their question so much that they felt obligated to melt our comm system."

And with the comm system down, Trip thought, *they've switched over to the universal language of mindless violence.*

The hostile vessel's bulbous, tubular shape came about again and approached, its forward guns blazing. Trip tried to lock the *Kilhra'en*'s pulse cannon on what appeared to be an external ramscoop intake, but the targeting system wouldn't maintain contact. Switching to manual, he opened fire as the two vessels crossed paths, apparently passing nearly close enough to trade paint jobs. It looked to Trip that the Haakonan ship couldn't be much more than twice the *Kilhra'en*'s size.

"What did they ask you?" Trip said as orange and blue flames rushed out of the hostile's intake vent. Long fingers of orange lightning crackled across the vessel's entire hull as adjacent systems surged with excess energy from the overloading ramscoops. With any luck, every major system aboard would soon fail as they succumbed to a cascade of power surges.

Apparently satisfied that the Haakonan ship had been neutralized, T'Luadh began tapping her remaining functional comm controls.

The telltale static hash of a downed subspace transceiver cleared from Trip's comm screen, replaced by what appeared to be an image recorded from T'Luadh's earlier conversation with the Haakonans.

Trip hadn't had any direct encounters with Haakonans, though he had seen pictures. Those images looked nothing like the blue-eyed, vaguely reptilian forms that stared out of his console.

Nor were they half as familiar looking.

"They demanded to know the location of a planet," T'Luadh said. "One I'd never heard of."

"What planet?" Trip said. He resumed watching the Haakonan ship as it tumbled away, its hull glowing intermittently before fading out until it was nearly as black as space itself. Even the external running lights were extinguished.

"Urquat," T'Luadh said.

The familiar name unlocked a memory that the image of the hostile crew had summoned.

Urquat wasn't a planet. Looking down at the image T'Luadh had sent to his comm panel, Trip said, "Urquat is a city. Or at least it *was* a city. A long, long time ago."

During a past age, Urquat had been the ancestral home of a race native to the former Delphic Expanse, an extinct people known as the Loque'eque. About five years ago, the crew of *Enterprise* had discovered a mutagenic virus on the Loque'eque's homeworld, a DNA-altering pathogen that had temporarily remolded Jonathan Archer, Malcolm Reed, and Hoshi Sato into Loque'eque. After Dr. Phlox had neutralized the virus and reversed the transformation, Captain Archer had instructed Phlox to preserve a single vial of the virus. It was all that remained of an entire civilization, encompassing both its biology and its culture.

Either that vial had fallen into the wrong hands, or another supply existed—a supply that had somehow made its way to Haakona. *If somebody can smuggle Vulcan weapons all the way to Haakona,* Trip thought, recalling Terix's boasts about such things during his interminable interrogation sessions, *then why couldn't a few milliliters of viral bugs get there the same way?*

Trip raised his eyes from the comm screen. Looking forward, he saw the Haakonan ship reappear momentarily as a distant but bright cloud of expanding gases; the molecular fires and lightning on the hull had metamorphosed into internal explosions and venting atmosphere.

Trip suddenly became conscious of T'Luadh staring at him. The green emergency lighting cast the planes and hollows of her long, angular face into sharp relief. "Interesting, Mister Sodok. Who built this ruined city of Urquat?"

"A race of people who died out centuries ago."

"Where was their homeworld?"

He made a noncommittal shrug. "At least as far from here as Haakona."

Trip realized only then that he might already have

said entirely too much about a subject that no one in the Romulan Star Empire, including even the Tal Shiar, was likely to know much about. The last thing he needed was to make her suspect that he might be anything other than the Vulcan he appeared to be.

A horrific notion all but froze his breath in his throat: The Romulans might already possess the Loque'eque virus. *What if they've weaponized it and deployed it? That would sure as hell explain why everything's been so quiet lately along the Haakonan front.*

An entire civilization could have been made to vanish nearly overnight, its citizens transformed into billions of determined Loque'eque pilgrims prepared to do anything to gain passage to dead, ruined Urquat.

Fortunately, T'Luadh seemed too focused on their mission to waste any more time pursuing the matter.

"Mister Sodok, do you detect any other hostile vessels in the vicinity?"

He touched his console and checked the readouts. "Not so far. But the only sensors that are operating at the moment are the passive ones. That Haakonan ship hit us pretty hard."

"How hard?"

Trip scrolled through the damage-control inventory. "Subspace transceiver is out. We can forget about calling Admiral Valdore for help."

"At least until we can get it repaired."

Trip shook his head. "I'm not sure it *can* be repaired. At least, not outside a fully equipped drydock facility."

T'Luadh flashed a humorless grin. "Well, we were already headed for just such a place, were we not?"

"I'd prefer reaching a base staffed with friendlies. But it's not as though it'll matter."

Her eyes narrowed. "What do you mean?"

"I mean we won't be getting there anytime soon. The warp drive is fried. We still have impulse power, but that won't do any better than accelerate us to a high *tahll* velocity."

"How high?" T'Luadh asked.

"Ninety percent of light speed, if what's left of the equipment cooperates," Trip said. "Maybe a bit more if we're lucky. Either way, those last few *eisae* of our journey to Carraya IV could end up taking as many *fvheisn*." Start with a vast cosmos, stir in a little unexpected engine damage, and days suddenly begin stretching out into years.

"And I suppose you've taken into account the effects of the *ahhaid'rawn*," she said with a frown.

He nodded. Unfortunately, there was no getting around the effects of time dilation when one's vessel was restricted to the highest possible sublight speeds. In fact, it was only when traveling at a very high percentage of *c* that starfarers needed to factor in such disconcerting temporal distortions.

"On the bright side, only a few weeks would have passed for us while we were crossing the rest of the distance between here and Carraya IV," he said.

"But outside this ship, orders of magnitude more time will have passed before we arrive," T'Luadh said, her gaze unfocused, as though she were recalling facts she learned long ago but had rarely considered since. She suddenly looked very drawn and haggard as she paused to breathe a low curse. "The *Ejhoi Ormiin* could have time to build and launch an unstoppable fleet in the interim."

"Admiral Valdore must have other options," Trip said, citing a fact he didn't much like thinking about. "We can't be the only set of eyes he's sent to search out the *Ejhoi Ormiin* shipyard."

"True enough. Perhaps that also means some of those eyes will find us before the radicals make much more progress," said T'Luadh.

Trip shrugged. He was all for maintaining an upbeat attitude, but he couldn't avoid acknowledging reality. The

Kilhra'en was a very small ship, moving at a relative crawl across an immense cosmos without generating a telltale warp signature. Although Valdore was aware that she was en route to Carraya, he hadn't been advised of the scout ship's specific trajectory, which T'Luadh had chosen to make the little vessel harder for the *Ejhoi Ormiin*, and incidentally the Romulan Fleet, to detect.

"At least there's an upside to the *ahhaid'rawn*," Trip said, looking elsewhere for sources of encouragement. "We probably won't run out of provisions before we get where we're going."

T'Luadh appeared to draw new strength from some hidden reserve. "Resume our course for Carraya IV, Mister Sodok. And do everything possible to get the warp drive back online as quickly as possible."

With that, she rose and retreated aft, perhaps to return to her own sleeping compartment.

After he'd finished putting the *Kilhra'en* back on course at high impulse, Trip remained in the right chair and continued using his console to further assess the damage the propulsion system had sustained. He still wasn't convinced that the warp drive was fixable under the present circumstances.

This provided a sense of relief rather than frustration.

At least T'Luadh probably won't kill me before I get this bird back up to warp, he thought, grateful for whatever cold comfort the universe might permit him. *I guess there's something to be said for job security.*

SEVENTEEN

Early in the Month of *T'keKhuti*, YS 8767
Wednesday, July 17, 2158
Central ShiKahr, Vulcan

YCH'A FELT A STRONG TEMPTATION to conclude that Silok's interrogation sessions, which had been incessant during the early days of her confinement by the Vulcan Security Directorate, had finally come to an end.

And yet she and Denak remained in detention, both due process and interaction with the outside world denied them. The days passed slowly, piling into deep drifts of uneventful tendays that gradually accumulated into months, and finally into two entire Vulcan years. Fortunately, meditation and *Suus Mahna* exercises made the tedium of inactivity bearable, as did the reassuring presence of her mate in the adjoining detention cell; Silok had not been so cruel as to deny her that. Illogically, it buoyed her spirit immeasurably to see how Denak had recovered from the mental trauma that he had suffered on the day of the Mount Seleya bombing.

Ych'a understood that this situation could not continue indefinitely. Despite the fact that Denak was nearly as accomplished as she was in the Syrannite mental disciplines that the V'Shar cultivated in all its operatives, he was both older and frailer than she was. Inevitably, he would fall into an irreversible physical decline if this open-ended incarceration continued. In part because of that realization, she was finding it increasingly difficult to keep at bay her feelings of incipient despair; that emotion lurked just out of sight like a hungry desert *sehlat*, all coiled-steel muscle and ravening appetite.

We have not allowed Silok to break us, she told herself, as she had done on countless previous occasions. *Not yet.*

A cluster of low-volume sounds startled her out of her contemplation. Somewhere an ancient iron door creaked, then bumped gently against a stone wall. She heard footfalls from somewhere in the corridor just beyond her line of sight.

Ych'a turned her gaze upward from where she sat in the middle of her cell's cold stone floor and observed a pair of slight, dark-robed figures entering the cell block, each one accompanied by a uniformed, helmeted guard. The faces of both robed figures were obscured by loose, billowing hoods.

She felt despair's sharp claws in her back. "Interrogators," Ych'a said, wondering what more they could possibly want to ask her. And why their dread master, Security Minister Silok, wasn't with them this time.

"We are not interrogators," said one of the robed figures, pulling back the hood to expose a surprisingly familiar face.

Ych'a sprang to her feet. "T'Pol! I thought you were aboard *Enterprise.* Helping the humans fight off the Romulans."

T'Pol approached the ancient iron bars, as did the guards. "I *was* aboard *Enterprise.*"

Ych'a lofted an eyebrow. "Does that mean the war is over?"

"I wish that were so," T'Pol said with an almost melancholy shake of her head. One of the guards opened the door to Ych'a's cell while the other did likewise for Denak.

"Then why have you come, T'Pol?" Denak said from the adjoining cell.

The younger woman seemed ill prepared for the question. "I have . . . unfinished business on Vulcan," she said at length.

Ych'a watched with near incredulity as her door swung open. Was this really happening? Or had prolonged imprisonment caused her sanity to unravel?

She stepped through the open door, as though performing an empirical scientific experiment. Brushing past the guards, she walked into Denak's open cell and offered him her arm as he made an unsteady exit into the corridor. As though responding to a signal Ych'a hadn't noticed, the guards turned as one and left the cell block.

Steadying her husband with her arm, Ych'a now stood face to face with T'Pol and the second hooded figure.

"What now?" Ych'a said.

"I will have you taken to my home," T'Pol said. "You may stay there as long as you like."

"Under house arrest?" Ych'a asked.

Both of T'Pol's eyebrows rose steeply. "Of course not."

"We can't stay at your home, T'Pol," Denak said. "That's the first place Silok will look for us. Or weren't you aware that his people first arrested us there?"

"I believe you are laboring under a misapprehension," T'Pol said.

Denak raised a hand, the one that had only three fingers. "I may not be in optimal condition at the moment, but I believe I can still recognize what the humans call a 'jail break' when I see one."

The second robed, hooded figure finally spoke. "No one will come looking for you, regardless of where you go. The V'Shar is in a state of disarray."

"Why?" Ych'a asked.

"Security Minister Silok has resigned. Members of his senior staff have been implicated as Romulan operatives."

The hood fell away, revealing a face nearly as familiar as that of T'Pol—not to mention a good deal more famous.

"Administrator T'Pau," Ych'a said as she grabbed at the cell bars to steady both herself and Denak.

"Silok's bureau has become a nest of traitors?" Denak said with undisguised astonishment.

T'Pau nodded. "Spies charged with disrupting a plan by my deputy, Minister Kuvak, to provide covert assistance to the Haakonans in their struggle against the Romulan Star Empire."

T'Pol approached Denak and gently placed a hand on his shoulder. "Their other task was to coordinate the terror attack at Mount Seleya."

As incredible as it all sounded initially, Ych'a now could see how the pieces of the puzzle might fit together. She received the news, and the insight that accompanied it, with a great rush of relief. *Whatever gaps may exist in my memory or in Denak's from the day of Surak's assassination,* she thought, *we're no longer considered the prime suspects.*

But part of it still made little sense to her. "Why would the Romulans seek to antagonize us, especially after Vulcan has officially removed itself from the fight?"

"They've evidently discovered Vulcan's *un*official collaboration with Haakona," said T'Pau.

"From the Romulan perspective," T'Pol said, "Vulcan's formal withdrawal from the conflict provided them no assurance that we would not pursue informal channels. They sought to discourage this by demoralizing Vulcan."

By destroying the katra *of Surak,* Ych'a thought. *Perhaps the Romulans have seriously overreached themselves.* It would be ironic indeed if the destruction of Surak ended up awakening the proverbial sleeping tracehound, thereby ensuring that the Romulans generated the exact opposite of their desired outcome.

Meeting T'Pau's gaze squarely, Ych'a said, "The commander must have come to try again to persuade you to bring Vulcan directly into the Romulan War."

"Among other things," T'Pol said, then nodded toward her two oldest friends.

Noticing for the first time the premature lines that marred T'Pau's otherwise flawless, youthful face, Ych'a said, "And what have you decided, Administrator?"

"My original determination on the matter remains unchanged," T'Pau said. "War is not logical."

"Neither is dying," Ych'a said.

"Illogical," T'Pau said. "You raise a false dichotomy. Entering this fight poses an unacceptable risk of leading our people away from the path of Surak and toward the way of the raptor."

T'Pol spoke with ill-concealed bitterness. "How can you continue to say that in light of recent developments?"

"To which developments do you refer?" Ych'a asked, frowning at both of her interlocutors.

"The commander refers primarily to something terrible that occurred more than half a year ago," T'Pau said. "On the Romulans' Haakonan front."

Ych'a's interest was now fully piqued. Prior to her arrest and imprisonment, Haakona had been her main area of concentration.

"*What* occurred?" she said.

"Our intelligence is still somewhat fragmentary," T'Pau said, "but we have gleaned enough information to determine that the Romulans have used a biogenic weapon against Haakona."

Haakona. The world to which she had helped Minister Kuvak funnel weaponry and other matériel to be used against the Romulans. Haakona, a former Romulan possession that she had helped develop into a second battlefront calculated to distract the Romulan Star Empire from its aggressive ambitions against Earth and its Coalition of Planets allies.

T'Pau nodded, her expression grim. "A biogenic weapon that members of Minister Silok's staff may have secretly helped them acquire, in collaboration with third parties on Adigeon Prime and perhaps B'Saari II as well."

"Doctor Phlox has confirmed that the viral-weapon modality the Romulans used against Haakona is a modified variant of a mutagenic virus the crew of *Enterprise* encountered in the Delphic Expanse five standard years ago," T'Pol said.

Denak was shaking his head, clearly not convinced. "Historically, the Romulans haven't relied on biogenic weaponry," he said.

"Perhaps not," Ych'a said, "but they've always been a highly adaptable people."

"Indeed," T'Pol said as she cast a none-too-subtle glare at T'Pau.

If the administrator noticed the implied reprimand, she made no sign of it. Alternately facing Ych'a and Denak, she addressed them both, in the manner of a campaigning politician. "I only recently became aware of Minister Kuvak's covert plan to assist Haakona in its fight against the Romulans—as well as your involvement in carrying out that plan."

"A plan that ultimately led to Silok placing us in indefinite detention," Ych'a said.

An intense emotional presence seemed to come over T'Pau as her gaze continued to move between Ych'a and Denak. "Regardless, I offer both of you my gratitude for your participation in Kuvak's plan, rather than any further punishment or opprobrium."

"Why?" Ych'a said, frowning.

"Because your assistance to Haakona has provided Vulcan with a valuable object lesson."

Once again, Denak held up his maimed hand. "Wait, please. Since the Romulan biogenic attack, what is the condition of the Haakonan civilization?"

T'Pau's dark eyes opened into deep pools of grief. "The Haakonan civilization no longer exists."

A wave of vertigo swept over Ych'a, forcing her to tighten her grip on the bars beside her.

"Administrator," T'Pol said, a barely restrained anger audible in her voice, "no one could have foreseen the Haakonan disaster. You cannot blame Denak and Ych'a for a choice that the Romulans ultimately made."

"No?" the administrator said, her eyes flashing.

"Before you took charge of the government, *you* were prepared to sacrifice a man's life for what you considered a higher purpose."

Thanks to her relationship with T'Pol, Ych'a was familiar with the incident. Following the untimely death of Syrran, Captain Jonathan Archer temporarily became the storage vessel for the *katra* of Surak. T'Pau had insisted that Archer undergo a potentially lethal extraction procedure in order to move the *katra* into a more compatible Vulcan brain. Archer had submitted willingly, but T'Pau would have forced it upon him had he refused, regardless of the risk.

T'Pau cast her eyes downward. "I have since recognized that to have been a mistake," she said. "An ethical lapse that Surak himself never would have countenanced. Like entering the current war."

"Perhaps you're right," said T'Pol. "Or perhaps you are merely committing the logical fallacy of the false analogy."

"I am trained in the Syrrannite disciplines, Commander. Do not presume to lecture me about logic," T'Pau replied calmly.

"The choices Surak faced during his time are not the same as those you must deal with now. You cannot claim to know how Surak would respond to them."

"I cannot make that claim now," T'Pau said, raising her hands to her temples. "But there was a time when I could have told you precisely what Surak thought about any given matter."

T'Pol nodded. "The time when you served as the keeper of Surak's *katra* has passed."

"The time for *anyone* to touch Surak's living spirit is

gone." Though T'Pau's voice remained level, it carried an overtone of sadness that Ych'a had only rarely heard a fellow Vulcan express outside of the ancient chants.

What she was hearing, what she was feeling, Ych'a realized, was the collective grief of her world.

"That is true, Administrator," T'Pol said. "However, it is not logical to dwell in the past. Nor is it logical to allow reticence and fear to drive one's decisions."

"You believe I am doing these things?" T'Pau asked.

T'Pol nodded. "Excellency, you cannot deny that your reticence has aided in the destruction of an entire civilization."

"I *do* deny it," T'Pau said, the slope of her eyebrows forming an extremely acute angle above the bridge of her nose. "That was Kuvak's doing. I had no knowledge of his providing assistance to Haakona until it was too late to avert the consequences."

"Irrelevant. Kuvak has answered to you since you assumed Vulcan's highest office, T'Pau. You are therefore responsible for his actions."

The younger woman's mouth opened and closed for several heartbeats, without emitting any sound. At length, T'Pau nodded and dropped her gaze, a gesture Ych'a could interpret only as one of grim acknowledgment.

"The blood of Haakona is on my hands," T'Pau said. "I can never change that. But I need not compound my errors by sanctioning *more* destruction."

T'Pol's angular face seemed to lengthen in disappointment. "Then I have failed again," she said. "Your mind remains unchanged. Earth will continue to stand essentially alone against the Romulans, even if the result is humanity's extinction."

T'Pau met T'Pol's beseeching gaze, as though attempting to offer succor. "When I first took office, humanity's leaders all agreed that the time had come for 'Earth to stand on its own two feet.' Those were Captain Jonathan Archer's words."

"Much has changed since then, Administrator," T'Pol said.

T'Pau nodded. "Granted, Commander. But I have faith in the resourcefulness of the human species."

"As do I, Administrator," T'Pol said. "But this isn't about faith. It's about fulfilling our obligations to our closest ally."

Her expression growing suddenly stern, T'Pau said, "The Haakona disaster has proved that the stakes are now far too high for Vulcan to risk meddling any further in this conflict."

Both women lapsed into silence, watching each other and waiting. It seemed to Ych'a an opportune moment to speak.

"Administrator, I have been out of circulation for the last two years. However, I can think of at least *one* other Vulcan operative who is almost certainly still interfering in the Romulan conflict as we speak—regardless of any decisions you have made."

EIGHTEEN

Day Six, Romulan Month of *Tasmeen*, 1183 YD'E
Tuesday, June 24, 2159
Gasko II

THE BREVITY OF THE FIGHT for control of the shipbuilding complex had come as no surprise to Subcommander Terix; with a few notable exceptions, the *Ejhoii Ormiin* radicals weren't known for their combat prowess. Terix's men, by contrast, were all drawn from elite units attached to Valdore's Fifth Legion. They had completed every phase of today's assault, from the surprise landing to the securing of the dissident base's perimeter, in less time than it took an enlisted uhlan to consume a meal in the crew mess.

What *had* surprised Terix was the identity of the man in charge of the small group of dissidents his strike force had captured today. His black paramilitary garb reduced to charred rags, his cheek and brow a mottled, livid green mass of second-degree burns, there could be no mistaking him for anyone else.

"Ch'uivh," Terix said, allowing more of his incredulity to show than he had intended. "Or would you prefer I call you Captain Sopek?"

The traitor's words came in short, rasping gasps, as though the very act of breathing pained him. "You seem . . . surprised . . . to see me."

Terix leaned against the heavy obsidian-surfaced desk in what remained of the traitor's disruptor-seared office. He was tempted to dismiss the pair of guards that he'd posted just inside the blast-charred doorway but decided that doing so would be imprudent.

"The Tal Shiar reported that they'd killed you," Terix said.

The traitor chuckled, then groaned in pain. "You can't believe . . . everything . . . the Tal Shiar tells you."

Terix shrugged. The Tal Shiar had been reliable enough in obtaining the coordinates of this planet and relaying that information to Terix's logistics unit. When it came to information about Ch'uivh/Sopek, the spy bureau may have had a different agenda. Perhaps the bureau had its own designs on the man and thus preferred that anyone who wished to detain him believe instead that searching for him would be an exercise in futility.

Ah, the twisted life of a spy, Terix thought. He rejoiced that he had answered the call of the soldier.

Moving at a brisk clip, Centurion Sitav—a young male officer dressed in a combat-distressed uniform—entered the office, a padd clutched in his hand.

"Report," Terix said as he accepted the padd from the centurion. After all the setbacks—not least of them the radicals' sudden abandonment of their facility on Carraya IV and the disappearance of the reconnaissance mission—Admiral Valdore was going to expect good news for a change.

"We've counted seven completed vessels in the *Ejhoi Ormiin* manufacturing and storage complex, Subcommander," Sitav said.

"Warp-seven-capable vessels, Centurion?" Terix allowed himself a slender reed of hope that Dr. Ehrehin's elusive dream of *avaihh lli vastam* not only might have come to fruition, but had also fallen right into his lap.

"Apparently so, Subcommander."

Terix grinned. "Have you found evidence that the radicals might have launched any of their new vessels prior to our arrival?"

"No, Subcommander." Sitav shook his head. "We appear to have caught them in the midst of their final preparations."

Terix nodded. "What about the vessels the radicals stole from us—our original *avaihh lli vastam* prototype and the Vulcan cruiser they took from our base near Achernar?

"We can find no sign of either vessel, Subcommander," Sitav said. "However, our chance of tracking them down will greatly increase once the engineering teams determine exactly how to operate the seven new high-warp vessels we captured today."

Terix hoped that was so. Those missing ships had doubtless served as templates for the construction of the *Ejhoi Ormiin*'s new vessels. The Romulan military could not afford to allow that situation to continue.

Still, Terix thought, *space is large. And scouring it from end to end for two ships can take a great deal of time.*

"Tell the engineering team that Admiral Valdore is going to expect results very soon," Terix said.

"At once, Subcommander," Sitav said, reprising his salute. Then he turned smartly on his heel.

And nearly collided with Decurion Ahrrek, the assault team's principal engineering specialist, as he entered the office.

Terix found nothing encouraging in the engineer's demeanor or appearance. The younger officer sounded slightly out of breath and his uniform was askew, as though he'd come all the way from the hangar complex at a dead run.

Terix displayed an impatient scowl, hoping to encourage the nervous young decurion to explain himself. "Well?"

"Subcommander," Ahrrek said, his tone infuriatingly tentative and cautious, "the engineering team has encountered something of a problem . . ."

*   *   *

The Hall of State, Dartha City, Romulus

Admiral Valdore momentarily turned away from the holodisplay above the massive sherawood desk in his office. *"Kllhe'mnhe,"* he said, muttering the ancient scatological curse under his breath.

Raising his voice back into the audible range, he faced Terix's image and said, "What *kind* of problem are you talking about, Subcommander?"

To his credit, the younger officer did not flinch at Valdore's steely tone. *"None of the new ships we seized are flyable yet, Admiral."*

Though he knew he might have placed too much trust in the optimistic nature of the assault force's initial sit-rep, Valdore experienced a palpable sense of disappointment. He could no longer count on quickly committing the captured fruits of the *Ejhoi Ormiin's avaihh lli vastam* technology specialists to the struggle against the expansionist *hevam* and their allies.

"Can you pilot the vessels out of the hangar?" Valdore asked.

Terix nodded. *"We can do that much, Admiral. We may even be able to fly the craft safely under impulse power, or even possibly at the low end of the warp scale."*

Valdore scowled. "Then your engineers should have no difficulty throttling the engines all the way up from there."

"Decurion Ahrrek advises very strongly against making the attempt," Terix said.

"Explain."

"All seven of the new ships appear to lack a handful of crucial command-and-control components and programming. They appear to have been present during a recent battery of static tests and then removed afterward. We've found no trace of them so far, but we're still searching."

"The *Ejhoi Ormiin* must have hidden them deliberately to prevent our using the ships against them."

"I agree, Admiral. Unless they took the components off the planet entirely before we arrived. Regardless, if we try to bring any of the engines up to full capacity without first taking the time to reverse-engineer the missing pieces, a runaway reactor breach is a virtual certainty. I wish I had better news to report, Admiral."

As do I, Valdore thought, pondering his options. For the first time since his Honor Blade had feasted upon the blood of the *Ejhoi Ormiin* traitor Nijil, the admiral experienced a small yet sharp pang of regret for having sent the *tam'a'katr* of his chief technologist down to cold Areinnye and into the chill grasp of Bettatan'ru and Erebus.

But the admiral had a war to win. He could spare no time for self-recrimination or second-guessing.

"Instruct Decurion Ahrrek to make the replacement of the missing components and protocols his top priority," Valdore said. "I expect his crews to work around the clock."

"It shall be done, Admiral," Terix said.

"And continue the search for the original pieces. That is *your* top priority, Subcommander. Use any means necessary to recover what's missing and get it into Ahrrek's capable hands as quickly as possible."

"The search is already ongoing, Admiral." Terix's face took on the calculating smile of a raptor. "In the meantime, I will interrogate the captured Ejhoi Ormiin personnel myself, starting with their leader, Ch'uivh. One way or another, we will get these ships flying up their full capability." He saluted smartly. "Jolan'tru, Admiral."

"Jolan'tru." Valdore returned the salute unsmilingly, then shut down the connection.

Taking stock of the day's events so far, Valdore decided to regard the assault on Gasko II as a qualified success, his inability to use the radicals' new ships notwithstanding. At least he had prevented the *Ejhoi Ormiin* from using their new vessels to undermine the power of the Romulan military or the Praetorate itself. He considered the destruction of Haakona, ill-advised though it had been when the late Admiral Dagarth had carried it out more than a year ago. Thanks to the multilayered inefficiencies that were built into the vast bureaucracies that distributed men and matériel across the Romulan Star Empire, the war resources that had been committed to the Haakonan front were only now making a difference in the war that raged all along the Empire's *hevam* front.

The war against the upstart colonizers from the Sol system, those who would push the Romulan Star Empire off the map's edge, could at long last get properly under way.

Imagine the terror of the humans and their increasingly reticent allies, he thought, exulting, *after we discover how to bring the war into their very backyard at warp speeds that they now can scarcely imagine.*

NINETEEN

Friday, November 21, 2159
Enterprise NX-01
Vorkado system

DURING THE WAR'S EARLIEST engagements, Jonathan Archer wondered about the limits the Romulans placed on the number of ships they deployed at the tip of their spear. In many instances, if the enemy had equipped each invasion squadron with even a few additional ships, several battles that had become costly stalemates might have ended in victory for the Romulans. It made no sense that such tenacious fighters would be so reticent about doing what was necessary to win decisively. After all, the Romulan Star Empire had been plying deep interstellar space longer than Earth had; it was hard to believe that humanity's most determined enemies had reached the limits of their galactic infrastructure or their war-production capacity. There had to be another reason behind this fortuitous parity.

Archer had heard stories about the enemy being distracted by a different conflict, along a second line—a wide band of space that faced a frontier region on the far side of Romulan space, relative to Earth and the Coalition worlds. However, he had begun to hear fresh rumors that the Romulans had recently *won* this second campaign. Commander T'Pol had been able to corroborate these stories, to some extent, based on information she had gleaned during her most recent trip to Vulcan. If true, the intensity of the Romulan war effort would increase markedly, perhaps by at least a factor of two. What remained unknown was how many additional ships and troops the Romulans would bring to bear along the forward edge of Earth's war effort, and how soon.

Not to mention, Archer thought, *how much farther back the Romulans might force us.* Prime Minister Samuels's plan to limit the combat front to the radius of the notoriously unreliable Vulcan warp-field detection grid that marked the effective boundaries of the Sol system might be about to become a self-fulfilling prophecy.

Archer was relieved to have an excuse to put such grim matters aside—once Malcolm Reed confirmed that the Romulan warbird the *Starship Intrepid* had discovered entering the Vorkado system seemed to have arrived there alone and unescorted.

Perched on the edge of his command chair, Archer watched the hostile vessel gradually swell in the bridge viewer until it filled nearly the entire image area. Because of the arthropod character of the dozen or so weapons tubes that bristled from its green, battle-scarred ventral hull, Archer thought the small but powerful ship more closely resembled some crablike ancient sea predator than a bird.

"Have they noticed us yet, Malcolm?" Archer asked, his gaze still riveted to the screen.

"They've shown no sign of it so far, Captain," the tactical officer said in his clipped, businesslike Leicester accent. "They've obviously seen some action recently. Maybe their sensors are damaged and they haven't yet had the opportunity to make repairs."

Archer nodded, acknowledging the possibility, though he wasn't convinced. "And they might be playing possum—trying to draw us away from our convoy to give other ships we haven't detected yet a chance to get close enough to pounce."

That was an outcome Archer couldn't permit. The new starbases at Calder II and Beta Virginis V—in reality they were hastily constructed forward operating bases, or military FOBs, rather than the fully appointed starbases Starfleet had originally planned to establish during more peaceful times—couldn't wait any longer for the supplies the convoy carried. The supply problem had become so critical that Starfleet Command had seen fit to divert *Enterprise* to the task of helping the *Intrepid* and the *Republic* shepherd the convoy through the final legs of its vitally important journey.

T'Pol looked up from her science console. "I must point out that leaving the Romulan ship unmolested will do nothing to ensure the convoy's safety later on."

"Good point," Archer said, rubbing his bristling jaw.

"I wonder what Captain Ramirez and Captain Jennings are planning," said Lieutenant Sato.

"I don't want to break subspace silence to find out," Archer said.

"Evidently neither does Ramirez," Reed said, intent on the new data his console was displaying. "*Intrepid* has just broken formation with the convoy and is now on an intercept course for the Romulan vessel."

"*Republic* is now executing a similar maneuver," T'Pol said.

"Her trajectory is a mirror image of *Intrepid*'s," said Reed. "It's an extremely well-coordinated maneuver. They'll converge on the Romulan vessel, entering weapons range from her port and starboard sides in thirty-two seconds."

A classic pincers attack, Archer thought.

Ensign Elrene Leydon, the young helmswoman, turned her chair so that she faced Archer. Her eyebrows were raised, forming mirror-image question marks.

"Maintain position, Lieutenant," Archer said, suppressing his impulse to charge into the fray despite the battle plan that he, Captain Ramirez, and Captain Jennings had already agreed upon; whatever might become of either *Intrepid* or *Republic*, Earth could not afford to lose *Enterprise*, any more than Starfleet's struggling forward operating bases could afford to lose the contents of those convoy vessels. "We have a convoy to protect."

As he slowly counted down the seconds, Archer breathed a silent prayer that his fellow captains weren't flying their vessels right into the teeth of a Romulan trap.

Imperial Warbird Aoi'fvienn

"Two of the vessels are closing on us quickly, Captain Khazara," said Uhlan Rhadak from the sensor station. "Approaching from opposing lateral trajectories."

Like a pair of airborne mogai *hunting on the wing,* Captain Khazara thought.

Ever since the *Aoi'fvienn* had suffered damage during the recent attack by a surprisingly well-armed convoy of Andorsu— a species that had always taken pains to avoid altercations with the Romulan Star Empire—Khazara had prayed to Akraana that his vessel would succeed in limping to a friendly repair facility before any *hevam* vessels got in his way.

Abandoning his thronelike command chair, he rose to his feet. "What kind of vessels?"

Rhadak looked up from his scanner, his forehead a road map of concern. "*Hevam* vessels, Captain. Their forward tubes read hot."

"Both vessels are opening fire," said Decurion T'Linaek, who was running the tactical board.

"Full Alert!" Khazara shouted, just as the lights dimmed and the deck rocked sharply, sending him sprawling.

Enterprise NX-01

Archer watched the battle on the viewer unfold. The sleek, mantalike shape of *Intrepid* unleashed salvo after salvo from her forward phase cannons, stitching the Romulan's unprotected port side as the bulbous, clumsier-looking *Republic* mounted a similar effort on the Romulan's starboard side.

"Her main power is failing, and she's taking heavy damage," Malcolm said.

Archer returned to his chair, though he merely perched on its edge. Despite the battle tension he felt, with each passing moment the captain was more confident that the *Intrepid*-class and *Daedalus*-class vessels were up to the task of taking down this lone Romulan warbird.

"Hail the Romulan, Hoshi," he said. "Tell them we'll do what we can to assist their survivors if they'll stand down."

Hoshi looked at him askance for a moment before she carried out his orders.

I know, he thought. *In all the years since this damned war started, I've never seen a Romulan commander let an enemy take any of his people alive.*

But he also knew that if he failed to extend the offer, he'd be no better than the worst Romulan he'd ever encountered.

Warbird Aoi'fvienn

"Principal power circuits are down!" Rhadak cried. "Shields are nonfunctional."

Lovely, Khazara thought. Speaking loudly enough to drown out the alarm klaxon, he said, "Switch to backups!"

"I think I can have the shields powered up on the secondary circuits soon," T'Linaek said, the dull green emergency lighting giving the planes and angles of her lean, long face a decidedly eerie cast. She rubbed her cheek to disperse the soot that had landed there after an adjacent console had exploded in a shower of fire and sparks.

"Do it!" Khazara barked as more incoming fire rocked the command deck. He grabbed at the sides of his chair to prevent his being knocked to the deck again.

T'Linaek nodded as she commenced tapping commands into the nearest undamaged console. "It is done."

"What's our shield strength?" Khazara asked.

"About sixty percent, sir."

Khazara nodded. "Engine status?"

"Impulse only. We just lost whatever minimal warp capability we retained following the Andorsu attack."

"Kllhe'mnhe," he muttered. "I suppose what little we have will have to do."

Erebus's balls, he thought. A new plan had just taken shape in his mind, but he had no idea whether the *Aoi'fvienn* could still generate sufficient power to enable him to carry it out.

Khazara decided it didn't matter. "'Complete victory or utter destruction,'" he said, repeating one of his favorite quotes from the *Axioms* of the great Commander Amarcan. "'For a warrior, there can be no middle path.'"

Every eye on the command deck was upon him. He saw faith in those eyes, but also fear and even puzzlement. They needed him now more than ever before.

Leaning forward in his command chair, he said, "Listen carefully. You especially, Decurion T'Linaek . . ."

Enterprise NX-01

"The Romulan's internal power readings are changing, Captain," Malcolm said. "As though he's tapping into resources we didn't know he had."

Archer turned away from tactical, facing the main science station. "T'Pol?"

"Confirmed, Captain. The Romulan vessel has raised its shields, though only to about half strength."

Malcolm spoke up, sounding puzzled. "He's doing more than just *raising* his shields, Captain. He's extending their boundaries. Expanding the reach of his shields by a factor of two. No, four, or perhaps higher."

"Why would the Romulans do that?" Hoshi said.

"Won't they end up attenuating the strength of their shields until they're so porous they become useless?"

"Correct, Lieutenant," T'Pol said. "All deflector shield systems with which I am familiar are subject to the inverse square law."

Which meant that shield intensity diminished geometrically rather than in a linear manner, just like luminosity, gravimetric forces, and tidal effects. If a shield generator extended a shield's radius by a factor of two, its intensity would fall off by a factor of four; a fourfold increase in shield radius would dilute shield strength sixteenfold. Obviously, a ship's deflector shields didn't have to extend very far to make them all but useless for defensive purposes.

So defense must not be what the Romulan has in mind, Archer thought.

"The Romulan vessel seems to be venting something," T'Pol said, concern evident in her voice.

"Malcolm, put a tactical plot up on the screen," Archer said, chilled by a dawning realization. "I need to see the Romulan ship and its shield boundary in relation to the *Republic* and the *Intrepid*."

"Aye, sir." Malcolm hastened to enter several commands into his console.

A scant couple of heartbeats later, a stylized wireframe representation of the Romulan vessel appeared on the main viewer. Surrounding it was a slowly expanding ellipse whose limits were portrayed as a dotted line.

One *Intrepid*-class-shaped blip approached the Romulan from its port side, while an icon that resembled a *Daedalus*-class vessel approached from starboard.

Both Starfleet vessels had just crossed into the faint yet expanding boundaries of the Romulan vessel's deflector shields.

"Hoshi, warn Ramirez and Jennings," Archer said. "They have to withdraw, *now!*"

But Archer could see that there was nothing he could do; it was already too late.

Imperial *Warbird Aoi'fvienn*

"Ignite the warp plasma," Khazara said. "Then activate the impulse engines."

"But the detonation will have already occurred *within* our shield boundaries by the time the engines engage," T'Linaek said. "We'll all be killed."

"Unless you carry out my orders, Decurion," Khazara said, "that fate awaits us all. After, of course, you lead the way to cold Erebus for the rest of us." He placed his hand on the pommel of his Honor Blade for emphasis.

Spurred by the gesture, T'Linaek immediately busied herself at her console.

Enterprise NX-01

"The *Republic* and the *Intrepid* have both taken heavy damage, Captain," Malcolm said. "They're adrift near the fifth planet now."

Archer turned toward Hoshi. "Can you raise either ship?"

Hoshi shook her head, clearly frustrated. "Negative, Captain. Their comm systems must both be down."

"Keep trying." Archer approached the tactical station. "Malcolm, what exactly did the Romulan ship do to them?"

Archer heard both anger and grudging admiration in the armory officer's voice. "He evidently crippled them both by using his shield generators and some vented warp plasma to create an improvised photonic shock wave. As weak as the deflector shield was extended like that, it retained enough strength to focus the photons being given off by the burning warp plasma into a coherent weapon."

"Is there any chance that this little trick blew up the Romulans?" Archer asked.

Malcolm shook his head. "I'm afraid not, sir. The Romulan vessel fell off my screen the moment the warp plasma detonated. But it reappeared moments ago, on the long-range scanners."

"Confirmed," T'Pol said from the science station. "The vessel appears to be withdrawing, on a heading for Romulan space at high impulse."

"Any sign of Romulan reinforcements?" Archer asked, addressing no one in particular.

"Not so far, sir," said Malcolm. "But that could change in the proverbial shake of a jackal mastiff's tail."

"Are we going to pursue the Romulan, Captain?" said Ensign Leydon. "His warp drive has taken damage from the shock wave. There's no way he can outrun us."

At that moment, what Archer wanted more than anything else in all the universe was to order her to do just that. But the fate of one damaged Romulan ship was inconsequential; he had more immediate responsibilities.

Shaking his head, he said, "We still have a convoy to babysit, Ensign. There could be wounded aboard the *Republic* and the *Intrepid*, and there's the damage to both ships to consider."

"I recommend sending shuttlepods to both vessels to assess the situation," T'Pol said.

"See to it, T'Pol," the captain said as he made his way to the hatchway leading to his ready room. "I want a complete status report as soon as possible."

Malcolm Reed activated the door chime. When the ready room hatchway failed to open after a slow, silent count to five, he raised his hand to touch the button again.

"Perhaps the captain is in his quarters," Commander T'Pol said.

Reed shook his head. "Hoshi says he hasn't left his

ready room for nearly four hours. Ever since we took the shuttlepods out to *Intrepid* and *Republic*."

"Perhaps he didn't hear the chime," T'Pol said, despite the implausibility of the idea.

Something's wrong, Reed thought as he brought his hand back into contact with the button.

The hatchway slid open. "Come in," Archer called from within, sounding none too pleased. The ready room's interior illumination was turned down.

Reed made an *after you* gesture to T'Pol, who preceded him through the hatchway.

A supremely weary-looking Jonathan Archer sat at his desk. The cabin's dim light emphasized the hollows of the captain's craggy face, as well as the brilliance of the starscape visible through his port.

"Report," he said, his voice sounding like a gravel-strewn rural road.

T'Pol extended a padd. When the captain made no move to take it, she set it on his desk, whose surface was already cluttered with numerous padds and printed dataflimsies.

"Casualties aboard *Intrepid* and *Republic* were relatively light," she said. "Six fatalities and fourteen injuries, only four of which were serious. "

"I see. Ship status?"

"Comm systems and propulsion are expected to be back online aboard both *Intrepid* and *Republic* within the hour," T'Pol said. "The convoy is ready and waiting to get back under way. As is *Enterprise*."

Archer nodded. With a haggard, downcast expression that belied his words, he said, "Good. Very good."

Though he hated the idea of adding to his captain's obvious misery, Reed forced himself to say what was on his mind. "Travis Mayweather is among the injured aboard *Republic*."

"Travis." Archer looked up for the first time since Reed and T'Pol had entered the room. Pouches of dark, orange-peel flesh ringed his eyes. "How seriously was he hurt?"

Reed swallowed hard. "Quite seriously, sir. But the surgeon aboard *Republic* has high hopes for him. And Travis has always been a fighter."

Archer sat in silence, apparently digesting the news. Reed wondered if he was kicking himself for not having tried harder to talk Travis out of transferring off *Enterprise*.

"Yes," the captain said at length, "Travis is a fighter. But then, so is Carlos—so *was* Carlos . . ."

Reed nodded bleakly. "I know that you and Captain Ramirez were friends, sir. I'm sorry."

Archer rose from his chair, as though he'd suddenly become aware of how glum he appeared. A smile spread across his face, but to Reed's eye it appeared forced.

The captain placed a hand on Reed's shoulder. "Don't apologize, Malcolm. It's not your fault. It's the damned Romulans."

"Aye, sir," Reed said with a nod. Sparing a glance at T'Pol, he said, "And speaking of the Romulans, I would like to point out that we can still catch up to the warbird that caused the current situation."

T'Pol shook her head. "The warbird is no longer moving at impulse."

"She's moving at very low warp," said Reed. "Under warp two, and she's leaving a trail of hard radiation that's pretty hard to miss. That tells me she's made some ad hoc repairs on the fly and probably *can't* go any faster. If we go after her now at warp five, we can intercept her in a matter of hours, before she can make it back to the Romulan lines."

Archer walked toward the port. He leaned forward, as though trying to catch a better glimpse of the infinite. It was obvious to Reed that the captain was considering the matter carefully, and in the most classical sense of the word; thanks to the Latin component of Reed's British boarding school trivium, he recalled that "to consider" meant "to be with the stars."

After an uncomfortable and lengthy silence, Archer turned back to face Reed and T'Pol. The captain looked pale and drawn.

"No," he said.

Reed struggled to maintain his British equanimity but failed to prevent a look of confusion from striating his brow.

"We're not going after that ship," Archer said, frowning.

"I don't understand, sir," Reed said. A surge of anger at the havoc the Romulans had wrought strained against his control.

"We still have a convoy to protect, Commander," T'Pol said, her tone faintly chiding.

"I should think *Republic* and *Intrepid* can manage until we're finished with the Romulan," Reed said. "Surely, after what they did to Captain Ramirez—"

"Enough," Archer snapped. "This is no time for pursuing vendettas."

"I agree, sir. It's time to pursue this *war*." Reed noticed belatedly that he had raised his voice.

"Commander," T'Pol said, her eyebrows sloping into a steep attitude of warning.

Archer held up a hand. Speaking softly, he said, "I just spoke with Admiral Gardner. It seems that the Romulans have finally dropped the proverbial other shoe."

Reed's anger and frustration receded, displaced by puzzlement. "Other shoe, sir?"

"You must have heard the stories about the Romulans' other war, Malcolm—a war they're said to have recently won."

"Of course, sir," Reed said.

"Gardner has received word that the Romulans have retaken the Altair VI colony," Archer said. "Using the resources they no longer have to commit to a second front."

For a moment Reed feared that the gravity plating had malfunctioned. He reached for the bulkhead to support himself. The prospect of abruptly losing all the progress they had ever made in this war was intensely demoralizing.

"Starfleet chased the bastards out of that system four years ago," Reed said at length.

Archer shook his head. With a wry but humorless expression, he said, "No, Malcolm. The *Coalition* chased the bastards out of that system four years ago."

Reed finally understood the captain's attitude toward the fleeing Romulan vessel. Compared to the loss of Altair, the fate of a single enemy ship now seemed a vanishingly small thing.

Forcing himself into a posture of attention, Reed asked, "May I assume that we'll be heading straight for Altair?"

Archer nodded, and T'Pol responded by excusing herself from the ready room, presumably to relay the captain's intentions to Ensign Leydon at the helm. Reed turned to follow her.

"Wait, Malcolm."

"Sir?"

"It's possible we won't go straight to Altair."

Malcolm suspected he wasn't going to like what the captain was about to tell him. "Are you planning a detour?"

"That depends on where our task force assembles," Archer said. "And that will depend, at least partly, on what the Romulans do next. They have a large contingent of ships en route to Deneva right now."

"Deneva again. Damn."

Deneva. Another colony that the Romulans had taken from humanity, which later rallied and won its freedom back—only to face losing it again.

How much more of this can we take? Reed wondered, not daring to voice his cascade of questions. *Now that we have the bastards' full attention, how much longer will it be before they have Earth surrounded? How long will we have to wait for the end, then? A year perhaps? A few months?*

Only one thing was certain: The coming year would be a red one.

PART III

2160

TWENTY

Wednesday, February 18, 2160
Enterprise NX-01
Earth Station McKinley

SURROUNDED BY AN APPARENTLY limitless universe of pure white light, T'Pol sat cross-legged on the floor, both sets of eyelids open to the all-encompassing ambient illumination. For the first time since she had begun coming to this neutral interior space—a realm unencumbered by anything that might divert her from the disciplined suppression of conscious thought that was the hallmark of Vulcan meditation—she found herself wondering idly why an infinite realm should have a floor upon which it was possible to sit.

Or concepts such as "up" or "down," for that matter.

The persistent trickle of thought suddenly made her aware that she was thinking, and therefore no longer meditating. Something was distracting her, though she couldn't yet identify the cause. She closed her eyes in an effort to regain her focus.

It was only then that she sensed a presence, both familiar and welcome.

She opened her eyes and noted with a barely restrained start that a figure stood over her, still as a statue. Though his eyes were directed down toward her, his gaze appeared unfocused, as though he was looking *through* her rather than *at* her.

"Trip?"

This wasn't the first time he had appeared to her during a meditation session via the mind-link they evidently still shared even now. Far from it. But it was the first time she had seen him in his present state. He replied to her query with an unnaturally deep sound that seemed to issue from far inside his strangely motionless form. The low growl reminded her of the ancient 2-D Terran horror films with which he had always been so inexplicably enamored— particularly those in which slow-moving, cannibalistic, reanimated corpses had driven the story.

Discomfited as though exposed to the horrifying imagery associated with the Vulcan *tarul-etek* ritual, T'Pol wasted no time executing the defensive *Suus Mahna* martial arts maneuver known as the *Naworkot*, and rolled swiftly to her feet. She came up in a crouch slightly behind Trip and to his right.

Her first impression was that he had remained utterly motionless, although he continued to make the guttural, growllike moaning sound. But after several seconds had passed, his body slowly turned in her direction, as though he were struggling to move through a viscous medium that for some unknown reason affected only him.

T'Pol approached Trip and studied his face. She was relieved to note that his expression was one of benign concern and bore none of the savagery that the undead had demonstrated in those all-but-unwatchable Earth films.

"Trip, why have you come here?" T'Pol said. He answered with another low moan, though the fact that the sound had overlapped slightly with her question made her suspect that he might not be able to hear her.

It was almost as though something was interfering with the psionic bond they shared, the way a comm signal could be jammed by a complementary transmission occupying the same part of the subspace band.

"Trip, is something wrong?" T'Pol said. *"Is there anything I can do?"*

She reached toward his face, placing her fingers at his temple. Although she had never taken the training required to reliably initiate a mind-meld, she had experienced melds on several occasions.

"My mind to your mind," she said.

He moaned, and the sound made a bizarre upward glissando that terminated in something that resembled a bosun's whistle. The white space that enfolded them both grew suddenly brighter, prompting her outer and inner eyelids to close.

When she opened her eyes again, she found herself back in her quarters on B Deck, and alone. Her now-extinguished meditation candle was upended and on its side, and it had left scorch marks on the supposedly fire-resistant carpet. She knelt beside the mess, recovered the candle, and began cleaning up the debris that surrounded its crash site.

"Commander T'Pol, respond, please." It took her a moment to recognize Captain Archer's voice, though she heard immediately the note of concern that it carried.

Leaving the wreckage of her meditation area where it lay, she moved quickly to the companel on the wall. "I apologize, Captain. I was momentarily . . . preoccupied."

"Please meet me in the observation gallery," the captain said. *"I've just received some news. You need to be briefed on it right away."*

Judging from Archer's grave tone, she decided that asking whether the news was favorable would be illogical. "I'm on my way, Captain."

Jonathan Archer stood before the observation gallery's wide viewport, which presented a view of the aft portion of *Enterprise*'s primary hull as well as most of the length of both warp nacelles. The bright blue-and-white expanse of Earth, which turned serenely some four hundred kilometers below, served as the backdrop. The latticework of struts and armatures that composed Earth Station McKinley, which now bore the burden of nursing the flagship of Starfleet and United Earth back to health, obstructed his vision in places.

Archer noted with relief that the various support gantries and umbilicals obscured his view of some of the vessel's most severe war wounds.

The door chime sounded, right on schedule. "Come," Archer said without averting his gaze from either his injured vessel or the planet he was sworn to protect.

The entry hatch hissed open, then closed a moment later. T'Pol spoke from almost directly behind him. "Captain."

"Commander," he said. A tiny workpod caught his eye as it maneuvered, mosquitolike, between *Enterprise*'s warp nacelles; on the open cargo bed behind it lay a pair of bulky generators whose purpose was to power the deflector-shield system that was due to be installed next week. For a fleeting moment he wished he could change places with the little vehicle's pilot; as extensive as *Enterprise*'s damage-repair and retrofit schedule was, the many weeks of drydock work she was enduring would be simplicity itself compared to the task that lay before him now.

"You said that I needed to be briefed," T'Pol said.

He nodded as the door chime sounded again. "Come," he repeated.

Once more, the hatch opened and closed. Archer turned away from the window and saw that T'Pol had been joined by Malcolm Reed and Dr. Phlox.

"Captain," the new arrivals said, speaking in a near unison as they stood in uneasy anticipation.

"I assume there has been a significant new development in the war since *Enterprise* went into drydock," T'Pol said, her bearing military-straight.

Archer nodded. "You might say that. But I suppose that depends on your point of view."

"Captain, at the risk of seeming hopelessly overoptimistic," Phlox said, his somber expression belying his overtly lighthearted tone, "I'm still holding out some hope that you've called us here to deliver a bit of *good* news. Something like, say, an announcement that Vulcan has reconsidered its decision to sit out this war."

The only reaction that Archer could see in T'Pol to Phlox's doubtless innocent comment was a slight deepening of the coloration of her skin. Although Administrator T'Pau continued to keep Vulcan on the sidelines, no one aboard *Enterprise* had worked harder to change that fact than Commander T'Pol.

Focusing back upon Phlox, Archer could suppress neither a wry smile nor a humorless chuckle. "Doctor, I'd do just about anything to justify your optimism." His smile fell away. "Unfortunately, I can't."

"Don't tell me the Romulans have just chased Starfleet out of yet another major forward operating base," Malcolm said.

Archer really couldn't blame the phlegmatic Englishman for his bleak expectations, given that it was the tactical officer's job to anticipate worst-case scenarios—and especially given all that had been happening lately. During the three months since the inconclusive Battle of Vorkado, Archer had all but lost count of the engagements that had ended with the Romulans on top—and with Starfleet continually being forced to move the war's scrimmage line ever closer to Sol. After Starfleet's reversals at Altair and Deneva—battles in which Starfleet had been overmatched by the Romulans' sheer numbers—the entire war effort seemed to have devolved into a slow pageant of inevitable, incremental retreat. Since before the New Year, the war had become an unbroken streak of large and small failures and fallbacks that girdled the sky from Beta Virginis to Delta Pavonis.

Despite Earth's having achieved some spectacular, if costly, victories during earlier years, Archer could no longer escape the truth: Earth's war fortunes were very grim indeed.

Shaking his head, Archer said, "No, Malcolm."

Archer noticed T'Pol's eyes suddenly widening, as though she had just come to a realization. "This is about Trip . . . Commander Tucker."

Archer nodded. "How did you know?"

She turned momentarily to look at Malcolm and Phlox before focusing her gaze back on Archer. "Captain, everyone in this room knows that the death of Commander Charles Tucker five years ago was merely an official fiction designed to cover up his ongoing activities behind the Romulan lines."

"That's right," Archer said. "All of you know that Trip's death was faked. As far as I know, the four of us are the *only* ones who are aware of that, at least besides whoever Trip's been working for ever since . . ." He trailed off.

"Captain?" Malcolm prodded.

Archer took a deep breath as he steeled himself. "I just received a message from Harris."

"Harris?" Phlox said, bewildered.

"My former section leader," Malcolm said with a scowl, no doubt precipitated by unpleasant memories. "Back when I worked in intelligence. Before I came aboard *Enterprise*."

"Trip went to work for Harris's bureau after he . . . left us," Archer said.

"And what did this Harris have to say?" Phlox asked.

Archer could avoid the inevitable no longer. "He called to tell me that his people haven't heard anything from Trip in more than two years. So they've declared him dead."

"I assume you mean for real, this time," Malcolm said quietly.

Archer nodded. His breath caught in his throat. "I'm afraid so, Malcolm. Killed in action, according to Harris. He thought I . . . ought to know."

"Quite magnanimous of him," Malcolm said, his craggy face becoming a mask of grief and anger. "Harris uses people—sometimes he uses them up entirely—and then the man gives everyone they knew his most oh-so-sincere condolences."

Archer had no strong feelings about Harris, despite the many complications he had created; after all, both Malcolm and Trip had made conscious decisions to work for the spymaster.

"Trip knew the job was dangerous when he took it," Archer said. "He did his duty. Just as you did when you cooperated with Harris during the Terra Prime crisis."

Malcolm nodded, his gaze downcast.

"I just thought all of you should know," Archer said. "I didn't want to hide the truth from any of you."

Malcolm and Phlox both looked funereal as they muttered their desultory thanks.

"Dismissed," Archer said quietly.

Then he turned and resumed gazing out the broad observation port at the machinery that tended his injured ship. The hatchway behind him once again hissed open and closed.

Although the captain had just issued a general dismissal order, T'Pol's feet remained motionless, as though rooted in place. A few moments after the hatch had closed behind Commander Reed and Dr. Phlox, she gently cleared her throat to let Archer know she hadn't exited with the others. "Captain, perhaps everything is not so grim as you believe."

"You'd have a hard time convincing me of that right now, Commander," he said, still facing the port.

"Perhaps you should take the Draylaxians into account," she said. "They dispatched a sizable contingent of ships to the engagement at Tenebia two weeks ago."

"After making us jump through bureaucratic hoops

for years. But Tenebia is in Draylax's backyard. And the Draylaxians took such a terrible beating at Tenebia that I'm hearing that they might scale back their involvement—particularly when it comes to battles that are a lot farther afield from home."

"That would be contrary to the mutual-defense provisions of the Coalition Compact," T'Pol said.

He chuckled, shaking his head. "Which we've already seen aren't worth a damn."

Her face burned with shame. Administrator T'Pau's intransigent insistence that Vulcan sit out the conflict doubtless lay at the core of Captain Archer's bitter sentiment.

He turned to face her. "Was there something else, Commander?"

"Only one other item," T'Pol said as a rush of conflicting emotions threatened to overwhelm her. "I'm . . . troubled by what Harris told you."

"You and me both. But I guess I don't have any choice other than accepting it."

"I'm not certain that's true, Captain."

"I know how much this hurts, T'Pol," Archer said, his tone mild yet insistent. "But denial doesn't strike me as very logical."

Her back stiffened. "I am not in denial."

He approached her and laid his hands gently on her shoulders. "I know how much he meant to you. Trip was my best friend, too. Losing him—again—is almost too much. And with the Romulans ramping up so much that it's only a matter of time before they overwhelm us, I've lost more than a friend—I've lost any hope that Trip might turn out to be the wild card that lets us pull off a last-minute victory."

She wavered for a moment, assailed by doubts. Was she simply denying reality to provide herself a temporary respite from her pain? She pushed the matter aside. Something more was happening here.

"Perhaps losing that hope is premature," she said.

"Why?"

"Because I don't believe Harris."

"Do you think he's lying?" He frowned quizzically as his arms fell to his sides.

"I don't know, Captain." She shook her head. "Perhaps he is merely mistaken."

"Do you know something he doesn't?" Archer asked. "Something *I* don't?"

The Vulcan debated how much she ought to tell him. Though she trusted him implicitly, he was still an outworlder. In spite of the fact that Archer had once briefly served as the keeper of Surak's *katra*, she still felt an ingrained Vulcan reticence about discussing very intimate matters.

Such as the nature of the strangely attenuated mind-link that she and Trip shared.

It was clear to her that something was amiss with Trip. But it seemed just as obvious that the problem wasn't death—at least, not death per se.

"I don't know," she said at length. "But I *am* certain of one thing."

"And what's that?"

"Charles Tucker is still alive."

TWENTY-ONE

Monday, April 19, 2160
Scout Ship Kilhra'en
Carraya sector, Romulan space

ONCE AGAIN, HE FOUND himself standing, all at once and unaccountably, in a featureless white space that seemed to stretch out into infinity all around him in every direction.

Or am I just dreaming again? Charles Tucker thought as he turned in a circle, his boots somehow finding purchase against the apparent insubstantiality of this place that actually wasn't a real place at all. *I might even be day*dreaming, he thought, hoping that he hadn't been in the midst of some hazardous, mission-critical task when the daydream had seized him.

After pausing to examine the up and down dimensions— which appeared no more or less infinite than any other direction in which he had looked—Trip decided that what he was experiencing was no mere hallucination, fantasy, or dream. As in all the many other occasions when his mind had been drawn here, the blankness of this place seemed as brilliantly vivid as reality itself.

It's just too bad that this mindspace T'Pol creates when she meditates is so damned homogeneous, he thought. Not for the first time, he wished she had generated a more interesting backdrop for her contemplations—like the fiery caldera of Vulcan's Mount Tarhana, or maybe the Dantean red-and-ocher beauty of the Forge.

A nice dip in the Voroth Sea would be even better, he thought.

Since the seas and lakes of Carraya IV still lay frustratingly distant from the *Kilhra'en*'s present position, Trip wondered idly whether any of Vulcan's few small bodies of water produced anything that resembled either marlin or catfish.

Despite the mind-link he still shared with T'Pol, Trip doubted he would hear an answer to that question today. The link had manifested itself many times over the years since his errands of espionage in Romulan space had begun, but ever since the damaged scout ship had been limited to high sub-*c* velocities, his encounters with T'Pol had changed in a disturbing way.

Something seemed to buzz past his ear, accompanied by a brief, high-pitched insectlike whine. He saw something out of the corner of his eye, a flash of motion that felt somehow familiar except for its extreme speed. When he turned toward whatever had sped past him, it was either gone or had become indistinguishable from the featureless whiteness all around him.

He thought he understood what was happening, though he still had no way to prove or disprove the notion.

"T'Pol!" he cried. "*It might look like we're having some trouble with the mind-link. Like maybe distance is screwing up the connection, or putting a crimp in the bandwidth to keep us from communicating on this channel of our brains.*" He winced, pausing momentarily as he heard how ridiculous he sounded.

"*You're still here with me, aren't you, T'Pol?*" he said, pressing on despite the clumsiness of his words. "*The problem isn't the distance between us, is it? We've been farther apart before and still could reach across——*"

The rush of motion in his peripheral vision interrupted him again, followed by a strange, rippling distortion that hovered directly in front of him for the span of several heartbeats, a wavering blue zone that dissipated almost as quickly as it had formed. A high, buglike buzzing whine accompanied the visual effects, as though a swarm of invisible insects had suddenly dive-bombed his head, then just as suddenly flown away.

"*This problem is as old as Einstein, isn't it?*" Trip said. "*What's happening to us is all about relativity. You're still trying to talk to me, T'Pol. But the flow of time here and the flow of time where you are aren't compatible. You and I are out of sync by a factor of seven or better. That's like squeezing two whole years into a little more than three months. The ship I'm on is stuck at more than ninety-eight percent of warp one, so time has slowed way down for me. From my frame of reference, time dilation has turned you into a gnat. And from yours, it's probably turned me into a marble sculpture.*"

The whine returned, accompanied by an abrupt intensification of the whiteness that surrounded him. Reflexively, he closed his eyes and raised his hands to his face.

Trip heard T'Luadh calling out to him. "Sodok! Are you all right?"

He brought his hands down from before his eyes and discovered that the all-white universe was gone, replaced in a twinkling by the *Kilbra'en*'s small but equipment-crammed cockpit. He was strapped into the starboard flight seat, while T'Luadh piloted the little scout vessel from behind the portside flight console.

The ship rocked and shook.

"You went away for a while," she said as she put the ship through what his gut interpreted as a quick succession of evasive maneuvers. "I was starting to think that you were having a seizure."

Trip shook his head. "Forget about that. What's going on?"

"A ship just came out of warp. It's trying to grab us with a tractor beam."

Damn, Trip thought. "More Orion slavers?" he asked.

"I can't tell. Maybe if you'd managed to get the sensor

grid back up, or the comm system, we'd be able to find out."

Sure, Trip thought. *But if I'd accomplished either of those things, then maybe you'd have arranged for the Romulan fleet to pick us up by now. And there's a good chance I'd already be sucking vacuum.*

He smiled sheepishly as the ship bounced and rocked again. "Sorry, T'Luadh. I thought keeping the impulse drive going at speeds that maximize the *ahhaid'rawn* was a higher priority. Slowing down subjective time by a factor of seven might keep us from starving."

The phenomenon of *ahhaid'rawn*—time dilation—wasn't an issue with which the Romulan Star Empire's mature starfaring culture had to cope. The Romulans had possessed warp-drive technology for centuries and therefore had no contemporary experience with the temporal distortions inherent in star travel via high sublight speeds.

T'Luadh continued entering commands into her console at a frantic pace. "Stretching out the rations won't do us much good if whoever's out there blows us to pieces."

Trip accessed the tactical systems on the console before him. "Guess I'm more of a theoretician than a practical, tool-using guy," he said.

A quickly intensifying hum interrupted T'Luadh's response. Before the sound crescendoed, a curtain of light impeded Trip's vision.

Transporter, he thought as he felt a sensation roughly akin to countless insects crawling on his skin. He couldn't help recalling how an Orion slaver had once spirited away nine of his *Enterprise* shipmates in the same manner.

The light faded, and Trip found himself deposited unceremoniously on his hindquarters on a three-meter-wide stage that resembled a scaled-up version of *Enterprise*'s transporter. It filled most of a square, metal-floored chamber that couldn't have measured more than five meters on a side. Trip noted immediately that T'Luadh, her pride similarly wounded, sat across the stage from him.

A deep, familiar voice boomed from Trip's left. "Allow me to apologize for my abruptness, Agent T'Luadh. But you weren't answering our hails. Welcome aboard the *Imperial Warbird Dabhae*."

Trip struggled to get his feet under him and succeeded at the task a moment after T'Luadh did. He turned toward the voice and saw the familiar face from which it had originated. That face bore a triumphant smile.

"Admiral Valdore," T'Luadh said. "Thank you for your timely intervention. We've been having some . . . technical problems."

"I see," Valdore said with a nod. He fixed his gaze upon Trip, as did the pair of armed, uniformed uhlanu who flanked the admiral. Valdore's eyes narrowed slightly but perceptibly as he spoke. "But I assume you would have had any such difficulties tamed sooner or later, Mister Cunaehr."

"That's pretty much all I've been doing lately, Admiral," Trip said, bowing his head forward slightly to show respect. Though his guts seemed to be about to leap into his mouth, he hoped the admiral wouldn't notice that anything was amiss. "After all, we still have to reconnoiter that *Ejhoi Ormiin* shipyard in the Carraya system."

Valdore shook his head. "Not anymore."

T'Luadh looked more than slightly bewildered. "Admiral?"

Valdore spread his large hands in a beneficent gesture. "We read the chronometer aboard your vessel remotely. So we know that a great deal more time has passed outside your vessel since its voyage to Carraya began than has passed within it."

Trip's eyebrows rose like the windshield wipers on an old-style internal-combustion automobile. "Sir?"

"The radicals have relocated their base to the second planet in the Gasko system. We have already seized the base there along with its entire complement of *avaihh lli vastam* starships."

Trip's insides abruptly went into freefall. If Valdore's forces had seized the *Ejhoi Ormiin* shipbuilding facility, complete with the fruits of its labors, then his usefulness to Valdore had come to an abrupt end.

Judging from the intensity of the admiral's stare, Trip decided that Valdore might well be thinking the very same thing.

"Agent T'Luadh," Valdore said, his gaze still locked with Trip's. "I want you to report to the ship's infirmary immediately. Once Doctor Tivarh has cleared you, you will report to my office for a thorough debriefing before you're returned to Romulus."

T'Luadh hesitated momentarily, as though discomfited by the prospect of visiting the doctor. At length, she said, "Yes, Admiral," and made the traditional Romulan salute. After favoring Trip with a final expressionless glance, she dismounted from the transporter stage and exited the room.

"I have somewhat different plans for you, Mister Cunaehr," Valdore said.

No kidding, Trip thought, visions of airlocks and the deep dark of space dancing through his head. Of course, being excused from the scrutiny of Valdore's medical staff wasn't an altogether bad thing. If a body scan revealed him to be a red-blooded human, Trip had no doubt that his inevitable execution would be preceded by a lengthy and painful interrogation session.

"I have sent a team aboard your vessel," said the admiral. "They are at present securing it in preparation for bringing it aboard the *Dabhae* for inspection and repairs."

"Thanks," Trip muttered.

"Once your ship is aboard," Valdore said, "the *Dabhae* will proceed to Gasko II."

Trip wondered why the admiral was sharing this information with him after implying that he wasn't likely to live much longer. *Maybe his plan is to monologue me to death.*

"Gasko II," Trip repeated. "The location of the *Ejhoi Ormiin* starship factory you say you just captured."

Valdore nodded. "The same."

"And once we get there?"

"When we arrive, Mister Cunaehr, you will help us ascertain exactly how to operate the seven *avaihh lli vastam* starships we have seized from the radicals."

Trip's confusion only deepened. "I'm afraid I don't understand, Admiral."

"The vessels we took weren't flight ready when we found them, Mister Cunaehr. Certain critical command-and-control hardware and software components were missing."

Of course, Trip thought. *If the people who built those ships had them completely ready to go before Valdore's raid, then each one of 'em would have made its own individual beeline out of the Gasko system. At warp seven.*

"You want me to figure out what's missing and replace it," Trip said.

And, in essence, arm Valdore with a blade capable of slitting humanity's throat. The acquisition of a warp-seven-capable fleet could enable the Romulan Star Empire to annex most of the key worlds in Coalition space in very little time.

"You are the late Doctor Ehrehin's protégé, Mister Cunaehr," Valdore said. "I can think of no mind better suited to solving this problem."

"What about Chief Technologist Nijil?" Trip asked. "His qualifications are light-years ahead of mine. Why don't you talk to him about this?"

Baring his large, white teeth, Valdore said, "To do that, I would have to consult with a spiritual medium, or some other type of mystic. Unfortunately, I have never placed much stock in such things."

"Nijil is dead?" Trip kept forgetting how long he had been out of circulation, thanks to the effects of the time dilation he had experienced over the past hundred or so days of subjective time.

Trip shook his head, raising his hands in a warding-off gesture. "You might be expecting a little too much of me, Admiral. Doctor Ehrehin was always the brains behind the *avaihh lli vastam* program. I was a glorified apprentice."

Valdore's visage hardened, as did his stare. "False modesty is ill-advised. Particularly in *your* case, Mister Cunaehr."

Trip studied the bigger man in silence and saw no indication that he was anything other than sincere and resolute. *He thinks I'm a Vulcan spy*, he reminded himself. *Even if he believes I'm not fit to carry Ehrehin's padd, he might be assuming that I'm privy to a lot of knowledge of Vulcan warp technology.*

"No, Admiral," Trip said after a seeming eternity. "I will sit this one out. I respectfully decline."

Valdore nodded to the vigilant troopers who still bookended him. The two uhlanu drew their weapons and stepped menacingly toward Trip.

"You will reconsider," the admiral said as his men grabbed and pinned his arms at his sides, then none too gently frog-marched him out of the room.

The next several hours passed in a haze of rage and pain.

Trip awakened, very slowly, in a tiny, overly illuminated detention cell that seemed to have been molded out of a single block of gleaming stainless steel. A hard bench, an equally unyielding cot, a sink, and a malodorous squat toilet built into the cell's slightly slanted floor were the room's only amenities.

"Not exactly five-star accommodations," Trip said, eyeing the place in groggy disgust from the vantage point of the cot.

With a start, he caught a glimpse of himself in one of the room's many reflective surfaces. He rolled painfully off the cot and moved closer to the wall to get a better look at his injuries.

Both temples bore livid green welts. Something had dug into the flesh there in multiple places, ripping and tearing, probably worsening as his interrogation delirium had deepened and his struggles had intensified. His head throbbed as he recalled what little he could of the interrogation he had just endured, which was next to nothing.

Mind probes, he thought, chilled to the marrow. He remembered having seen this very same pattern of laceration on Ehrehin, whom the *Ejhoi Ormiin* had subjected to endless rounds of merciless questioning in their own quest to break the warp-seven barrier.

An almost inaudible electronic hum sounded, distracting Trip from his musings. A heavy metal hatch less than a meter away swung open. Knowing he was in no condition to put up a physical fight, Trip backed away and tried to appear as nonthreatening as possible.

T'Luadh stepped into the cell as a pair of armed uhlanu watched her back from out in the corridor.

"You may close it until I call for you," T'Luadh said, facing Trip as she spoke over her shoulder to the guards.

One of them answered her with undisguised trepidation. "I don't think that—"

"I didn't *order* you to think," T'Luadh snapped. "Close it!"

Trip heard a sigh in the corridor, then a muttered curse, before the heavy door moved back into place with a resounding metallic slam.

"Let me guess, T'Luadh," Trip said, rubbing the scabs at his right temple. "You've come to start my next interrogation session."

After a few moments' apparent hesitation, she said, "I am not here to question you further. I have, however, persuaded Admiral Valdore to place me in charge of you for the duration."

Which means until the goddamned mind probes finally kill me, he thought. With an incongruous smile spreading across his artificially Vulcan features, he said, "T'Luadh! I didn't know you cared."

She favored him with a frosty scowl. "You still sound delirious. I hope Valdore's people did not damage you severely."

Trip shrugged. "I have to admit, I've felt better. And frankly, I've *looked* better, too. Were you there when Valdore's people interrogated me?"

She nodded. "I was present during your . . . debriefing."

"So that's what they're calling it these days." He pointed at his skull. "I thought it didn't count as a debriefing if it left a mark."

"Semantics."

"Pretty damned painful semantics," he said. "So, what did I tell 'em?"

"Surprisingly little."

Trip hoped he could take her at her word. Nevertheless, he felt an enormous sense of relief, which he did his best to conceal.

"If that surprises you, T'Luadh," he said, "then you must have assumed that I know a little bit more than I've been letting on."

She raised an eyebrow. "You'd almost have to."

Trip wasn't sure he'd heard her right. "That was uncalled for. Brutal interrogations are one thing, but gratuitous insults? Seems beneath you."

Ignoring his comment, she continued. "Throughout your . . . questioning, you kept refusing to perform the work required to make the *Ejhoi Ormiin* ships operational. Why?"

He shrugged, and his temples throbbed painfully in response. With a wince, he said, "Because I'm not the right man for the job."

"*Seikkea kllhe,*" T'Luadh said, employing a bit of scatological Romulan vernacular. "You're the best man for the task—in ways that Valdore probably doesn't even expect."

Trip frowned. "What are you talking about?"

"Sit down," she said.

He took a seat on the edge of the cot as she withdrew a small, round metal device from a pocket inside her uniform jacket.

He recognized it immediately. "That's a mind probe! I thought you said you weren't here to interrogate me!" He tried to stand, but she grabbed his shoulder and pushed him back down.

Before he could do anything about it, she had the mind probe pressed against his right temple. Her right hand supported the left side of his skull, her fingers splayed in a spiderlike fashion.

"I know that you aren't precisely who you seem to be," she said.

Her voice made a strange transition, as though her words were now passing through some medium other than the air on their way to his ears and brain.

I know who you really are.

Recalling the many "white room" encounters he had shared with T'Pol, he realized that she was speaking directly inside his mind. Maybe she was using the probe as a way to conceal their conversation from any listening devices Valdore's crew had hidden in the cell.

I know that the Romulan warp scientist named Cunaehr is a fictitious identity, she continued. *He existed once, but years ago became a casualty of Doctor Cunaehr's pursuit of the* avaihh lli vastam *program. Your alternate persona of Sodok of Vulcan evidently has a similar history.*

Trip was impressed in spite of himself. *How do you know this?*

I am a colonel in the Tal Shiar, Mister Cunaehr. It is my business to know such things. Just as it is my business to know that you are really neither Romulan nor Vulcan—and that your real name is Tucker.

Trip felt as though he'd just been gut-punched, hard. The jig, as it were, was finally up. Had he somehow given himself away? Or had she come into possession of recordings of the brief audio exchanges he and Malcolm Reed had shared with Valdore before the Romulan War began, on that remote-piloted drone vessel that had nearly set Andoria and Tellar at each other's throats?

It didn't matter, he decided. His cover was blown, and knowing exactly how the cat had got out of the bag couldn't do him any good now.

If you knew my real name, he thought to her, *then you didn't need to ask me why I can't fix those ships for Valdore. He'd just use 'em to slaughter my people.*

I know, Mister Tucker. Which is why I want you to tell Valdore that I have persuaded you to get started working on the problem immediately. I want you to tell him that you will give it your most diligent effort, even if it takes the rest of the war to make those vessels operational.

He reached up to his right temple and felt for the smooth edges of the mind probe. Ignoring the pain of tearing skin, he dug his fingernails under it and ripped the thing loose.

"Why would I agree to do that, T'Luadh?" he said aloud. He threw the probe hard, and it smashed against one of the walls in an impressive shower of broken circuitry.

Inexplicably, T'Luadh's voice continued speaking in his mind, despite the disruption to the probe.

Because he will kill you if you continue to refuse, she said. *And because appearing to acquiesce to the admiral's demands may be the only way to buy enough time to enable both our worlds to survive what is to come.*

TWENTY-TWO

Day Forty-Three, Romulan Month of *Khuti*, 1184 YD'E
Saturday, May 1, 2160
Bird-of-Prey Terrh'Dhael
Outside the Draylax system

COMMANDER T'MET LOOKED ANXIOUSLY at the command deck's wide forward viewer, which displayed an indistinct blue-green crescent that seemed to be no bigger than the palm of her hand.

"Such a waste," she muttered, not bothering to conceal her feelings about today's mission from her executive officer, Subcommander Genorex.

Genorex shrugged but otherwise maintained his customary impassive mien. "Admiral Valdore has conveyed Praetor Karzan's warnings to the Dray'laxu," he said. "Repeatedly. We are therefore without any option gentler than the one we must employ presently."

T'Met nodded. "Of course we are. I am merely surprised that the Dray'laxu failed to choose the wiser part of valor over sheer obstinacy."

"They are renowned for being slow to make substantive decisions," said Genorex, "as well as for living up to the smallest letter of their agreements, regardless of the consequences."

"That is truly regrettable," T'Met said. "It is as though they have no memory of the damage that Commander Chulak inflicted upon Galorn'don Cor. Or what became of the Cor'i'danu homeworld prior to that."

Genorex shrugged again. "We all must live with the choices we make. Or die with them."

"But to throw away so many lives, Genorex." She shook her head in both sadness and disgust. "How do their leaders live with themselves?"

"I surmise that many of them will not have such worries for much longer, Commander. They have, after all, opted for suicide."

"But suicide is a waste unless the deed can be made to serve a higher purpose, Subcommander."

A flashing light on a nearby operations console caught T'Met's attention, as well as that of Genorex, who moved closer to the display in order to study it.

"Centurion Khazara reports that his scout ship is ready for launch," Genorex said, his voice uninflected by irony—as though any conversation undertaken moments before Khazara's last flight wasn't automatically freighted with irony.

There had been a time when Khazara had been one of Admiral Valdore's most favored officers, as well as one of T'Met's lovers. There were many, T'Met herself included, who had thought him destined to become Valdore's replacement.

But the Battle of Vor'ka'do had radically changed his fortunes. Khazara had held the rank of captain prior to that engagement, during which he had managed to disable two *hevam* warships, despite the severely damaged condition of his own vessel.

But he had failed to capture either of those ships, and a military tribunal subsequently decided that victory should have been well within his grasp.

If not for my consanguinity with the current praetor, T'Met thought, *I might suffer just such a fate.* She was uncomfortably aware that praetors came and went, as did political favor. Regardless of how secure she might feel now, no one could guarantee that she wouldn't someday share Khazara's misfortune—being busted down to the rank of centurion and then forced, either literally or figuratively, to fall upon her Honor Blade. She could only hope that Khazara's sacrifice would rehabilitate him in the eyes of history, thereby allowing some measure of prestige and honor to accrue to the family he was about to leave behind. Such things weren't all that uncommon, as was attested by the recent prominence of the family of the late Commander Chulak, who had defied imminent defeat at the Battle of Galorn'don Cor by sacrificing not only his own life but also the lives of his subordinates.

"Thank you, Subcommander," T'Met said. "Acknowledge Khazara's message. Let's send him on his way."

Though she knew it amounted to little more than primitive superstition, T'Met felt certain that no good could come from speaking with Khazara, even to the extent of merely saying farewell, or wishing him *Jolan'tru*. She decided it was best to treat him as though he were already dead.

Her executive officer paused, as if to study her. Keeping her face blank, she silently wondered how much he knew about her personal relationship with the doomed centurion.

Genorex tapped several commands into his console. "Khazara has initiated launch countdown."

"Lock onto his telemetry and display it," T'Met said. If she was to be a party to the Dray'laxu's mass suicide, then the least she could do was watch as death descended upon its hapless victims.

Genorex counted down. *"Rhi. Mne. Sei. Kre.*

"Hwi."

The command deck shuddered slightly as a bright streak lanced across the forward viewer, arcing in a long ellipse toward the still-distant blue crescent. T'Met knew that Khazara's little vessel was still moving at subluminal speed in order to avoid setting off whatever active warp-field sensors the Dray'laxu had planted about the periphery of their system.

The image of far-off Dray'lax, generated by the *Terrh'Dhael*'s long-range passive sensors, wavered and vanished, replaced by the imagery that was streaming in over the subspace bands via the telemetry link with Khazara's scout vessel.

Because the scout needed to fly subluminally to minimize the chance of detection and interception, the image of Dray'lax remained stubbornly tiny for a seeming eternity. T'Met decided this was no matter. She would sit in her command chair, patiently awaiting the fall of the hammer of death, for as long as it took.

To his credit, Genorex, who continued working the ops console throughout Khazara's flight down the Dray'lax system's deep gravity well, appeared to be doing likewise.

Ever so slowly, T'Met's patience was rewarded. The crescent grew steadily until it was recognizable as a disk, and finally a far-off semishadowed blue sphere. She glanced at the telemetry readout on the arm of her chair, and the figures that scrolled across it confirmed that Khazara was nearing his optimal range for switching to superluminal flight. According to the mission profile, his chances of being intercepted or interdicted at that distance were essentially nil.

"Khazara has signaled his readiness to cross the *vastam* threshold," Genorex said.

"Acknowledged," T'Met said, nodding.

The image on the main viewer showed the last thing Khazara would ever see. Once he brought his craft up to full speed, the little vessel would cross the remaining distance between it and Dray'lax in the space of a few heartbeats. Though the ship crashing into that world would be small—its mass negligible in comparison with that of the planet—the amount of energy released by the impact would be almost unimaginable, even without factoring in the violence that the ship's ruptured antimatter pods would unleash.

T'Met leaned forward expectantly. Dray'lax seemed to distort slightly, as though she was viewing it through a weirdly curved lens. Then the planet rushed toward her, vanishing into an oceanic hash of static as Khazara's ship rammed it at a maximum speed of *avaihh mne*, or approximately sixty-four times the speed of light.

The static on the screen dispersed as the viewer resumed its earlier mode, displaying the imagery yielded by the long-range sensors. A tiny blue-green crescent remained stubbornly in place, as though Khazara's vessel had never left the *Terrh'Dhael*'s hangar bay. But despite the evidence of her eyes, T'Met knew that Dray'lax was already experiencing destruction on a planetary scale. She decided to wait until the light generated by those fiery death agonies reached the system's edge, where her vessel waited quietly for the end of Dray'lax, and of Khazara.

Jolan'tru, *Khazara*, T'Met thought. *My love.*

She settled back into her chair and resumed her vigil.

TWENTY-THREE

Sunday, May 2, 2160
Sol 49 of Martian Month of Libra/Sol 209
   of Year 107 Z.C. (Zubrin Calendar)
Outside New Chicago, Mars

AFTER STOPPING TO CHECK the indicators on the glove of her environment suit, Gannet Brooks prepared to enjoy a spectacle that she could never see back home on Earth. Thanks to the nearness of the horizon, the city lights and those of the nearby ground vehicles and hovercars that had brought everyone out here would provide no serious competition for the pyrotechnics that soon were to illuminate the star-bedecked Martian night sky. She was part of a sparse, thinly spread crowd of perhaps a hundred—a claustrophobic multitude by local standards. She looked upward at the distant stars of other worlds, several of which she had once seen from a much closer vantage.

Years ago. When she'd still been allowed to cover the war. *Before Nash McEvoy clipped my reportorial wings,* she thought.

She watched the slow, celestial pageant. Brooks understood the futility of dwelling on her bitter resentment of having been summarily pulled back from the Earth-Romulan War's front lines. But under the current circumstances—which amounted to a paradoxical yet very real sense of isolation in the presence of so many others—she found she could do little else. Though the wound was years old, it still felt far too fresh.

Maybe I'll feel better once the fireworks start, she thought.

Redoubling her efforts to focus on her comparatively mundane current assignment, Brooks planted her feet widely in an effort to stave off the vertigo that the sky and the weak Martian gravity sometimes conspired to engender in nonnatives. Once she felt reasonably certain she wasn't about to topple onto her back, she set her eyeballs to the task of searching the heavens for any sign of anomalous motion. Initially she saw only the stars she expected to see, as apparently immobile as chunks of white chocolate baked into a tray of brownies. The stars were arranged in the familiar groupings her father had taught her during her childhood: Cygnus and Cassiopeia both slowly pinwheeled almost directly overhead, near Aquila, which lay in the northeastern sky, while Ophiuchus looked on from the west and the Big Dipper drifted lazily above the southern horizon.

She was grateful that Epsilon Indi lay below the horizon and thus out of her sight. That fact, of course, did nothing to ameliorate the shocking knowledge of what the Romulans had done to that system's sole inhabited planet. Draylax had lost a billion or more people in minutes, and the death toll continued to mount as the fires and volcanism spread. The Draylaxian civilization might never recover. It was Coridan all over again.

The starscape before her differed hardly at all from those fondly remembered evenings of stargazing, a fact that was glaringly evident despite the visual impediment of her helmet visor. In fact, she felt some surprise that the starscape didn't look any brighter or sharper than it did through the still relatively tenuous, if steadily thickening, Martian atmosphere. The clarity of the Martian night was something she had expected to wax poetic about in the piece Nash McEvoy, her editor at *Newstime*, had sent her here to research. Instead, she was already all but certain that after another century or two of sustained terraforming, the only difference between watching the sky from here and from, say, Scottsdale, Arizona, would be the heft of the local gravity.

Then Brooks saw a flicker of motion in the western sky. She turned her head toward it, and it immediately vanished. She was about to give up when the apparent movement just as suddenly reappeared. This time the motion was connected to a clearly visible object.

A point of light, a single pinprick among countless others, had separated itself from the distant backdrop of westerly fixed stars. She wondered if she'd caught a glimpse of either Phobos or Deimos, the two moons of Mars. She decided it couldn't be Deimos, the outer moon, because that body always rose in the east. And she dismissed the inner moon Phobos as a possibility when she noted that the point of light seemed to be growing steadily, as though it were approaching the planet. But she still couldn't be absolutely sure that this was the leading edge of the spectacle the crowd had come to see.

It might be a passing ship, Brooks thought. *Enterprise is supposed to be in the neighborhood, shoring up the local defenses now that the Romulans can attack us from their forward base on Tau Ceti.* Recalling that fact triggered a bittersweet cascade of memories of Travis Mayweather. How long had it been since she had seen him in person, or at least spoken with him across the gulf of light-years that nearly always separated them? Too long, she supposed. Or perhaps not nearly long enough. She knew that he had transferred off *Enterprise* years ago, though she wasn't sure where he was supposed to be serving at the moment. For all she knew, Travis might have joined the war's ever-expanding list of casualties.

The approaching object morphed into what could only be described as an incoming missile. Brooks kept imagining the Romulans using the Martian terraforming program as a means of concealing a sneak attack. After all, what better Trojan horse could one ask for than a kilometer-long, potato-shaped collection of ice and dust that originated in the depths of the Sol system's dark and frigid Kuiper belt?

Putting aside that unsettling—and arguably paranoid—notion, she decided that she was observing precisely what she and everyone else who had gathered here this evening had come to see: the making of Martian climatological history. Its terminal disintegration abetted by a tracery of ruby fire from the ground-based verteron array near Sagan Station in the northern lowlands, the plummeting comet fragment left a superheated, ionized wake across the southeastern horizon as the Martian atmosphere converted much of the object's kinetic energy into heat. The brightly glowing mass descended quickly out of sight before exploding in a nimbus of golden-orange brilliance that momentarily drove even bright Spica, Beta Virginis, and Porrima from view. Fortunately, the horizon itself protected the impact's audience from the violence of this energetic exchange.

Though she couldn't safely get close enough to see the process in detail, Brooks knew that the core constituents of the comet fragment—primarily water and various organic compounds, such as carbon and nitrogen—had already appreciably increased Mars's global supply of much-needed volatiles. At the same time, the impact, and those that were soon to follow, would release large quantities of the surface and subsurface volatiles that already lay frozen in the planet's uninhabited and forbidding south polar region. As she stood watching, a great column of particulate and gaseous ejecta rose into the sky, glowing with the heat of the impact that created it and from the sunlit regions beyond the horizon. Time passed with great elasticity, but she noticed it only after she felt the rumbling vibrations beneath her boots; the planet's cold and ancient crust was reverberating gently in response to the distant collision.

Brooks noticed a new sound beyond the hiss of her breathing and the faint whirr of her suit's internal ventilation fans. After a few breathless heartbeats, she identified it as the applause of the crowd of which she was a part. She joined in, smiling at this confirmation that what she'd just seen was in fact *not* a Romulan attack, but rather a spectacular baby step in the ongoing process of transforming a world that had endured untold eons of utter desolation into another green and lush Earth—a scaled-down, low-gravity Earth located right next door to the original.

"We have plenty more where that one came from," said a suit-muffled voice that suddenly began speaking directly behind her.

Brooks jumped, then cursed herself for her skittishness; such sudden moves on the part of those reared on Earth tended to become exaggerated—often comically so—in Mars's one-third-*g* environment. In spite of the care she had taken earlier to avoid experiencing vertigo and its unfortunate consequences, she found herself being drawn inexorably into a slow-motion backward pratfall.

Her fall suddenly arrested itself. Strong arms were holding her up. As her boot treads dug into the regolith, she saw another suited figure, standing close enough to her that she could see his blue eyes clearly through his visor. A fortyish man with a strong aquiline face, framed in dark brown hair.

"*Excusez-moi,*" said the man. His accent, Brooks noted, very much matched his apology. "I didn't mean to startle you."

"I'm not startled," Brooks said as she tested her footing. Now that she was no longer trying to stare straight up into the sky, she felt reasonably confident that she wasn't about to tip over again. "You can let go of me now."

"Pardon," he said as he released her. He took a careful step backward, evidently pausing only to satisfy himself that she wasn't about to fall again. "I don't usually grab strange women this way."

She took a moment to appraise him. He was of medium height. Apart from the pleasant smile, he seemed unremarkable. Then she noticed the twin insignia patches on his right arm. The DYTALLIX-BREMCO logo was emblazoned on one; BLUE HORIZON, framing an artist's image of a warmer, wetter version of the Red Planet, adorned the other.

Before she could open her mouth to speak, another streak of fire cast a few more moments of brilliance across the great star-flecked canopy overhead.

Still smiling, the man spoke again. "As I said, there are plenty more where that one came from."

"I suppose you ought to know," she said, pointing at his patches. "You seem to have some expertise in the field."

His smile broadened. "Very observant of you. Of course, I should expect no less from a *Newstime* reporter." He pointed at the press pass, emblazoned with the distinctive angular logo of the Solarcorp News Service, that was attached with a lanyard to her right sleeve.

"You're not so bad at the fine art of noticing things yourself, Mister . . ." She trailed off, by way of prompting him.

"Forgive me. My name is Picard. Alexandre Robert Picard. I work as an engineering consultant for the Dytallix-Barsoom Resource Extraction and Mining Corporation, as well as for the ongoing Mars terraforming operations that the Martian Colonies government runs out of Sagan Station." He extended his gloved right hand.

"Gannet Brooks." She shook the proffered hand.

His eyes widened. "I *thought* you looked familiar. I followed your war reportage religiously. It's a pity we haven't received more of it over the past few years."

Don't get me started, please, she thought, not wanting to rehash the ignominious end of her war correspondent work. She said, "I'm covering the home front for the most part these days. Specifically the big environmental remediation projects of the inner system—particularly the ones that depend on hauling volatiles down from Kuiper belt, like the Green Sahara project—"

"And Blue Horizon," Picard said, nodding. "Well, I suppose this is destiny."

Brooks suppressed a chuckle. "I wish I had a UE credit for every time I've heard *that* line."

A look of horror crossed his face, and she couldn't quite make up her mind about his sincerity. "Oh, I wasn't using a line, I promise you. I was merely thinking . . ." He trailed off, as though woolgathering.

"Thinking what?" she said, curious in spite of herself. He seemed almost to be blushing.

Picard shifted awkwardly from foot to foot. "How differently the Green Sahara people must have to handle the inbound comet fragments than we do here. I mean, we can just drop them on the south pole because we have no large settlements there yet."

You silver-tongued devil, Brooks thought. She said, "You're right. Africa is a good deal more crowded than that, even in the Sahara. I imagine the Green Sahara people have to be a little more careful getting their, ah, deliveries down to the ground. Come to think of it, I wonder how they manage it."

Picard shrugged. "I suppose they attach impulse boosters and guidance packages to the comet fragments to bring each one in for a 'soft landing.' But that end of things isn't my main area of expertise. These days, I spend most of my time on the other end of the supply chain, as it were."

"Meaning?"

"The source of the comet fragments that we occasionally send in for 'hard landings' in the south polar region," he said. "In fact, I'm taking a shuttle out above the ice line tomorrow."

"Ice line?"

"Sorry. That's engineerspeak for the cold outer edges of the Sol system. I'm headed out tomorrow to visit a platform that's orbiting in the Kuiper belt. I'm consulting with a team there that's in charge of redirecting volatile-rich objects intended for use in the inner system—specifically Green Sahara on Earth and Blue Horizon here on Mars. We make the bulk of our Mars deliveries this time of year, during the relatively calm months that immediately precede the global dust storm season."

Brooks grinned. "Do you think you might have room to bring a passenger along tomorrow?"

"Certainly," Picard said, his earlier warm smile returning as they began programming their suits to exchange personal contact information.

Then they watched, from a safe distance, as seven more comet fragments slammed into the Martian polar hinterlands, each one tossing up its own great plume of glowing gas while shaking the small, rapidly changing red world beneath their feet.

New Chicago, Mars

Brooks wasn't naïve enough to believe that Alexandre Picard's interest in her was purely professional, and he confirmed her suspicion by insisting on walking her back to her rented hovercar once the cometary "fireworks display" had ended. She decided she'd give him the benefit of the doubt and consider him a chivalrous gentleman— particularly after he'd helped her get into the small cockpit and finished bidding her a warm adieu.

"Until tomorrow," he said, then turned and walked away, his boots leaving deep tracks in the powdery regolith.

Guided by the car's onboard GPS system, it took Brooks only ten minutes to make the trip back to the New Chicago dome. Inside, her helmet and cockpit both open to the dome's brisk shirtsleeve environment, it took nearly twice that long to reach the central core, where her hotel was located.

Brooks decided to stop at the nearly deserted hotel bar before turning in for the evening. She quietly nursed a glass of cherry mash whiskey mixed with carbonated water pumped from Margaritifer Terra. A dozen or so other hotel guests—many of whom also appeared to have just returned from the terraforming fireworks—slowly drifted away to their rooms in the lower levels.

It wasn't until the place was almost entirely empty of other patrons that she noticed the dark, muscular man quietly staring at her from across the bar. She nearly sprayed her drink on the barmaid, and the man grinned. Brooks had no doubt that her expression was a dopey one. How long had he been watching her, his presence camouflaged by an uncharacteristic civilian suit?

"Travis?"

He rose from his stool and strode toward her, taking the seat next to hers. Setting the pint of amber beer he was carrying down on the bartop, he said, "Gannet. It's good to see you again."

"It's been too long," she said, admiring the stylish cut of his brown linen jacket. "Did you come to Mars on official Starfleet business?"

He shook his head. "My sister Rebecca and her husband both have planetology professorships at Endurance University. This is the first time I've seen either of them in years."

She smiled, knowing how important family was to space boomers—especially to those who had experienced the loss of nearly every immediate family member, as Travis Mayweather had after the mysterious disappearance of the *E.C.S. Horizon* more than five years ago.

"Were you out watching the fireworks display with the rest of the tourists?" Brooks said, eager to steer the conversation toward less sensitive matters.

He nodded. "Wouldn't have missed it. But why are *you* here? I thought you were mostly covering the Earthside beat these days."

She didn't feel much like exploring that topic either. With a shrug, she said, "Stories of my grounding have been greatly exaggerated. I still get out to the Great Red Wilderness every once in a while. Besides, isn't it weirder to find you this close to Earth?"

Travis's smile fell in on itself. "Well, lately Starfleet seems to have developed some funny ideas about whether it's better to fight 'em out there or back here, near the home fires. Ours is not to reason why."

"Strange that I missed seeing you out there at the fireworks display," Brooks said. "Must be losing my touch."

"I'm going to be here on shore leave for the next three days, so I thought it'd be best just to blend in with the tourists and the locals."

"I understand." She nodded. There was little point in reminding every random stranger of the ever-tightening noose that the Romulans seemed to have placed around humanity's home system during recent months.

She decided to avoid doing the same thing to Travis by asking an innocuous question. "The last time I checked, you were convalescing aboard the *Republic*," she said. "*Intrepid* class. NCC-415."

He looked impressed and paused to sip his beer before replying. "That's some pretty detailed research. But it's a little out of date now. For the past couple of months I've been serving on the *Roosevelt*. *Daedalus* class. NCC-217." As he set the beer glass down, a wistful sadness crossed his face. "But it looks like that tour will be finished soon."

She hadn't expected to hear that. "Are you staying in Starfleet?"

"For the duration," he said. It took her a moment to realize that he was talking about the war. "I wouldn't want to be anywhere else, especially now. And even if I wanted to leave, where would I go?"

She nodded, unable to think what to say to that. "I understand," she said at length, awkwardly finding her voice.

"What brought you to Mars, Gannet?" he said.

"I'm covering the terraforming project. In fact, I have an appointment tomorrow to fly out to the place tonight's fireworks display came from. It's part of my research."

"Damn. The *Lovell* will be picking me up to take me back to the *Roosevelt* when my shore leave here is finished. I thought for a minute we might have more time than just this evening to catch up with each other."

The very same thought had just crossed her mind. Then she considered the prospect of sharing a potentially lengthy and unchaperoned shuttle ride with a certain suave francophone named Alexandre Robert Picard.

It would be awkward, to say the least, if he were to reveal an ulterior motive while cooped up with her in a small Kuiper belt–bound spacecraft.

"Maybe we *can* arrange to spend a little extra time together," she said.

Leaning toward him, she began laying out an ad hoc itinerary for tomorrow morning.

Monday, May 3, 2160
Sol 50 of Martian Month of Libra/Sol 210, 107 Z.C.
Bradbury Spaceport, Mars

"Damn," Brooks said, glancing again at the chronometer on her wrist. "I hope we won't have to suit up before we get aboard Picard's shuttle."

She led the way off the pressurized tube train, and Travis fell into step alongside her, moving at a leisurely pace, apparently in no particular hurry. They crossed the pressed-regolith surface of the train platform, which was host to a noticeably sparse population of both arrivals and departures. As they moved past the platform to the broad spaceport transit lounge, Brooks decided that there was nothing particularly remarkable about this; the omnipresent threat of a Romulan attack on the home front had evidently made interplanetary travel a low priority.

Through the transparent aluminum windows on the lounge's far end, Brooks spied a small, squat, well-used spacecraft that conformed to her notion of what a Dytallix-Bremco shuttle ought to look like.

Then she caught sight of one Alexandre Robert Picard, who was sitting in the transit lounge's carpeted waiting area and seemed to be studying his boots intently. Why wasn't he in his ship now, going over his preflight checklists, or performing whatever other rituals pilots always undertook just before setting out on a long interplanetary flight?

Picard looked up and waved as she and Travis approached him. "Mister Picard," she said, shaking his hand.

"Please. Call me Alexandre." As Picard turned to shake hands with Travis, she noted a look of disappointment in the francophone's blue eyes.

"This is Travis Mayweather," she said. "He's an old friend."

The two men exchanged murmured greetings. Travis smiled, but Picard maintained a stony, pensive expression. He was obviously preoccupied by something. *What's the matter, Alexandre?* she thought. *Afraid of a little competition?*

"I hope my bringing Travis along on this little junket won't pose a problem, Alexandre," she said.

Picard seemed to jolt slightly, as though he had just come to realize what his discomfiture looked like. "No, of course not. But a problem of a different nature has arisen."

"What kind of problem?" Brooks asked.

"I can't raise Iceberg Fourteen on any of the subspace channels," he said.

"I take it that's the name of the Kuiper belt comet-processing station we're visiting today," Brooks said.

Picard nodded. "My shuttle is loaded with a cargo of technical equipment bound for Iceberg Fourteen today."

"What's the equipment for?" Travis asked.

"To enable the crew to make the final adjustments to the impulse thruster packs they've attached to a series of large, icy comet fragments. The engineering team is getting ready to alter the trajectories of the fragments so that we can move them 'downhill' through the solar gravity well and get them safely to their destinations at the Martian polar caps and Earth's Sahara Desert."

"Strange," Travis said. "Having the comm go dead just as they're getting ready to bring down multiple heavy inner-system-bound payloads."

"Exactly, Mister Mayweather," Picard said. "I just hope that everyone is safe up there—and that whatever has gone wrong won't create significant further delays."

"What about the other Iceberg stations out in the Kuiper belt?" Brooks asked, her curiosity roused slightly more than her fear. "Have any of them fallen off the grid besides number fourteen?"

Picard shook his head. "Not so far. But none of them has succeeded in raising Iceberg Fourteen either."

Brooks sighed in frustration. "So what do we do?"

"Until I can ascertain exactly what has gone wrong," Picard said, spreading his hands in a gesture of helplessness, "I'm afraid I must cancel our trip up to Iceberg Fourteen. Or at least postpone it."

Only now did Brooks understand the source of Picard's disappointment. But she had a tougher time understanding his failure to act.

"Why don't we get your shuttle under way, Alexandre?" she said. "Why not find out for ourselves what's going on up at Icebeg Fourteen?"

Picard shook his head, a move that catapulted a few strands of his wavy brown hair forward. "The company rules are very explicit, as are the governing regulations and laws. We must wait until we receive official clearance from both the United Earth Bureau of Extraterrestrial Resource Extraction and from the Martian Colonies' Terraforming Authority."

Brooks muttered a pungent curse. "Of course," she said. "It makes perfect sense. Red planet, red tape."

Brooks noticed then that Travis had withdrawn a small device from his jacket pocket. Although he wasn't in uniform, he had evidently brought at least some of his Starfleet equipment with him.

With a practiced flip of his wrist, the communicator's antenna grid opened. A birdlike electronic chirp signaled that it was operational and ready to receive and transmit.

"I just might know somebody who can cut through some of that red tape," he said.

Enterprise NX-01
Kuiper belt

"There's still no answer to our hails, Captain," Hoshi said from the comm station.

Archer watched as the image on the viewer slowly increased in apparent size. Flanked by a pair of enormous-looking comet fragments and shrouded in the Sol system's outer darkness, Iceberg Fourteen reminded him of one of the forbidding-looking iron platforms whose sole purpose was to pump petroleum out of the ground on Earth during the twentieth and twenty-first centuries.

It also reminded him, absurdly, of a haunted house. An

abandoned structure that might contain some frightening secrets.

"Strange," he said. "Silence on all the comm bands. No power readings, right down to life support. Even the exterior running lights are down. T'Pol, have you found any life signs yet?"

"Negative, Captain. However, it is possible that some of the comet materials in the station's processing facilities are obscuring our sensors. I will continue scanning."

"Malcolm," Archer said, "this facility is way off the beaten track, at least in terms of the local neighborhood. In my book, that makes it more vulnerable than most targets to a Romulan peripheral sneak attack."

"Not only that, Captain," Malcolm said. "All of the Iceberg stations are in the business of catapulting heavy things sunward. Which could make any and all of them a potential weapon the Romulans could use against us."

It was a grim thought, and Archer couldn't deny its validity. The Romulans had yet to try this tactic in the Sol system. But elsewhere—including Draylax, Galorndon Core, and Coridan—they had already demonstrated a marked affinity for pounding their adversaries with superballistic missiles.

"What kind of security does Iceberg Fourteen have in place?" Archer asked, addressing no one in particular.

"Two squads of MACOs," Malcolm said. "That's a total of sixteen troopers. And all nineteen of the Iceberg stations throughout the Kuiper belt receive regular patrol visits from one of the ships in Starfleet's *Daedalus*-class fleet—the *Franklin Delano Roosevelt*."

The Roosevelt, Archer thought. *Travis's ship, at least for the moment.* Archer had reluctantly granted his erstwhile helmsman's transfer request shortly after the *Kobayashi Maru* debacle; however, he had kept abreast of Lieutenant Mayweather's career since then.

"Captain, I have widened my scanning radius," T'Pol said. "I'm now picking up debris."

"The remains of a ship?"

"Confirmed. The wreckage is consistent with a *Daedalus*-class configuration."

"I'm picking up escape pod beacons," Hoshi reported.

Almost as though some ship that's hiding deep in the Kuiper belt had been jamming their signals, Archer thought. *Until just now.*

"Ensign Leydon, intercept those escape pods," he said.

"Aye, Captain."

The deck plating shifted slightly but noticeably under Archer's boots as the ship responded. Iceberg Fourteen dropped away into the void, and in a matter of minutes Ensign Leydon reported that *Enterprise* was coming within grappler range of the nearest of the *Roosevelt's* escape pods.

"Bring 'em aboard, Ensign," Archer told the helmswoman.

"Aye, Captain."

Turning his chair toward the comm station, Archer said, "Hoshi, can you raise any of the escape pods?"

The comm officer entered several commands, then shook her head.

"I'm not certain this is such a good idea," said Malcolm. "I'm picking up some strange readings from that escape pod."

Archer approached the tactical station. "Life signs?"

"I'm not sure, Captain. It's all a jumble. As though someone is deliberately trying to jam—"

"Launching grapplers," Leydon interrupted.

Grappler One was a clean miss, but the second found its target and held it tightly in its magnetic grasp. Archer watched the image of the tethered escape pod's battered surface as the grappler cable drew it inexorably toward *Enterprise's* launch bays.

"I'm picking up a sharply rising energy curve coming from inside the escape pod!" Malcolm said. "It may be a Romulan nuclear device."

"Confirmed," T'Pol said. "And I have just noticed a similar reading coming from Iceberg Fourteen."

"Malcolm, polarize the hull plating, " Archer said.

"My console has picked it up, too," Leydon said. "Iceberg Fourteen has just launched two large objects, both moving at high impulse speed on steep downsystem trajectories."

"Those inbound comet fragments," Archer said, suddenly fully cognizant of the trap that was springing shut all around him—and Earth. "Ensign Leydon, release that escape pod and put some distance between it and us."

Leydon wasted no time executing the commands. The pod and grappler cable both vanished from the screen as the vibration pattern in the deck plating shifted subtly, indicating a change in velocity.

That same instant, the viewer emitted a momentary blinding flash and went abruptly dead. The shock wave arrived a split second later, upending Archer's vestibular system as the ship's grav plating and inertial dampers struggled to null out the rolling and bucking of the deck. Darkness engulfed the bridge momentarily, replaced several heartbeats later by the dull red glow of the emergency lighting.

"Romulan atomic warhead, Captain," Malcolm said.

Archer nodded. He wiped something wet from the corner of his mouth with the back of his hand. It appeared to be blood, and a twinge of pain confirmed that he'd bitten his tongue during the explosion.

"Report."

"We seem to have surfed on the shock wave instead of being vaporized by it. Looks like we managed to put maybe fifty klicks between us and the device before it detonated," Malcolm said.

"Unfortunately," Leydon said, "the warp drive is down. The impulse engines took a beating as well."

"And we still have to catch up to those comet fragments," Archer said.

"We'll have to make at least one-quarter impulse to have a chance of doing that," Leydon said.

"Then do it," Archer said. "If the Romulans have booby-trapped them like that escape pod . . ." He trailed off, the implications of his thought being more than clear.

"I would call that a safe assumption, Captain," said T'Pol.

Archer nodded. "Then we can't afford to let them get any closer to Earth, or to the Martian Colonies. Intercept course, Ensign Leydon."

Now all I have to do is figure out what we're going to do, he thought, *if and when we do catch up to those giant ice balls.*

New Chicago, Mars

The great curvature of the city's transparent aluminum outer dome caught the rays of the setting sun. Though the orange orb looked attenuated by Earth standards, the atmosphere stretched and pulled its light into multicolored taffy. Between the dome and the sun, a narrow ribbon of chondritic debris, metallic fragments, and water vapor drifted lazily in the upper atmosphere, forming an elliptical ring that by now probably circled the entire planet.

Thanks to the combined efforts of *Enterprise* and the ground-based verteron array, that ribbon of rubble was all that remained of the Romulan assault against Mars.

"I hope what happened today will wake up Prime Minister Samuels once and for all," Gannet Brooks said as she watched the lingering light show. "Earth can't expect to defeat the Romulans over the long haul without taking a few risks."

"I'll keep my fingers crossed," said Travis, who stood beside her, his gaze locked on the vista that was all that remained of the closest call Mars had survived since humans had begun thinking of it as a second homeworld. "But I don't think I'm going to hold my breath."

"It's incredible," she said, still looking out at the debris-dappled horizon in undisguised wonder.

"Incredible that the Romulans finally managed to sneak a squadron of their sublight fighter ships right into our backyard? Or that we survived it?"

"Both, I guess." She turned and faced him. "But I think the main reason we survived it was because you got the warning out in time."

His expression grew serious, tense. "That was mostly luck."

"You're way too modest, Travis. You weren't content to sit and wait for official instructions from Alexandre's bosses. So you took charge. How'd you figure out that the Romulans would try to use comet fragments as cover to sneak a couple of sublight attack squadrons all the way down into the inner system?"

He grinned. "I sneaked an assault team to Mars once by using an inbound comet for cover. It seemed natural enough to assume that the Romulans might try the same tactic."

"Maybe they'll think twice next time, considering how badly it turned out for them today." She returned his grin, with interest.

A look of sadness suddenly occluded his smile. "Or else they'll learn to be more careful the next time they try it. One of those two comet fragments made it all the way to Earth, where the Romulans focused the brunt of their attack. And Earth wasn't quite as lucky as Mars."

Brooks responded with an unhappy nod. Judging from the earliest news reports, Madrid and Tunis had learned the hard way that each of the Romulan fighters had carried at least one medium-yield nuclear warhead, in addition to its complement of disruptors and other armaments.

"Still," she said, "if you'd been doing what most people assume sailors do during a shore leave, Earth and Mars both would have been devastated."

His eyes narrowed in undisguised suspicion. "I hope

you're not thinking about writing another one of those 'war hero' pieces about me."

She counterfeited a wounded expression. "It never crossed my mind," she lied.

"Good. Because that kind of press is the stuff reputations are made of. A buildup like that can be damned hard to live up to. Besides, Captain Archer and about a dozen other starship captains had a hell of a lot more to do with stopping the Romulans than I did."

It occurred to her that Captain Archer would know a thing or two about how the media can make or break reputations. The *Kobayashi Maru* incident was half a decade old, yet more than a few could neither forgive nor forget it.

Travis, she knew, had long numbered himself among them.

"I thought you were no longer a member of the Jonathan Archer fan club," she said quietly.

He shrugged, and his broad shoulders took on an uncharacteristic slope. "Maybe I haven't been fair to Captain Archer. Maybe I needed to blame somebody for the *Horizon*'s disappearance so badly that I turned him into a convenient target. Maybe all he's really guilty of is not being superhuman."

"Or just somebody who's subject to the same random luck that everybody else is," she said, placing a hand on his shoulder. "Even Travis Mayweather."

His posture straightened. "I guess I owe the captain a long-overdue apology."

"And when do you plan to do that?"

"When *Enterprise* makes its stopover at Utopia Planitia tomorrow morning. Right before I give him an answer to the offer he made me a couple of hours ago. This is off the record, by the way."

Her eyebrows rose. "Of course. What offer?"

Travis's familiar carefree smile returned at full wattage. "He wants me to take the helm again aboard *Enterprise.*"

TWENTY-FOUR

Wednesday, May 5, 2160
Vulcan Diplomatic Compound, Sausalito, Earth

IN THE QUIET QUARTERS Foreign Minister Soval had procured for her during her post-battle shore-leave interval, T'Pol sat alone in a field of infinite white brilliance, meditating with her eyes closed.

Until she sensed that she was alone no longer.

She opened her eyes and saw that Trip stood before her. As during similar encounters over the past several days, his face bore the appearance of a Vulcan, from his upswept eyebrows to his aristocratically pointed ears.

"The Romulans are massing for a final assault," he said, skipping the usual banter and pleasantries. His directness surprised her, and the urgency of his tone provoked a frisson of worry.

"A final assault," she repeated. "Against Earth?"

He nodded. *"That's right. But first, Admiral Valdore is going to gather just about everything he's got at Cheron. That'll be his staging post for hitting Earth. Vulcan, Andoria, and Tellar will probably come next, one by one."*

She frowned. *"Charon? That makes no sense from a tactical standpoint. Starfleet would almost certainly detect a massing of forces that close to Earth."*

He scowled and made a waving-off gesture with both hands. *"No, not Charon. That's the co-orbital companion of the dwarf planet Pluto. I'm talking about* Cheron——*the fifth planet of 83 Leonis B."*

Cheron, she thought, trying to place the nomenclature. She knew she'd have to look the planet up in the Vulcan database to be certain, but if she recalled correctly, Cheron was located near the galactic southern hemisphere's farthest reaches, within the bounds of what the Terrans called the galaxy's Beta Quadrant.

That world was certainly remote enough from the farthest-flung Coalition world to prevent its being easily discovered as the rallying point for a large-scale Romulan assault against Earth. But it was also arguably *too* far away to make an effective beachhead.

"Trip, where did you get this information?" she asked.

He blinked and regarded her in silence for several moments. She wasn't certain, but she thought she saw a look of confusion cross his face.

"From a source I've learned to trust, T'Pol," he said at length. He approached closely and sat down beside her. Looking into her eyes, he said, *"I know we can feel each other's thoughts and emotions. That's what this mind-link of ours is made of, when you get right down to it."*

"Indeed," she said. Somehow, discussing the link felt more awkward than simply experiencing it.

"So feel my thoughts now, T'Pol. Feel how certain I am."

She reached toward him, touching his temple with her splayed fingers. A link within a link developed, deepening the bond they already shared.

In an instant that might have been an eternity, she understood. Then the whiteness abruptly vanished, along with Trip. Her spartan quarters sprang back into existence just as quickly, complete with the mat beneath her and the meditation candle that burned silently before her.

She rose in a single smooth motion and retrieved her communicator from the corner table. She flipped open the antenna grid.

"Commander T'Pol to *Enterprise*," she said.

"*Enterprise*," replied a familiar voice. *"Lieutenant Sato here."*

T'Pol spoke with an adamantine certainty that mirrored that of Trip. "Please get me the captain, Lieutenant. I need to speak with him immediately."

Starfleet Headquarters, San Francisco, Earth

Jonathan Archer was perched on a low, leather-upholstered sofa, watching in anxious silence as Admiral Samuel William Gardner sat quietly behind his massive desk, stroking his short, iron-gray beard. Despite the admiral's furrowed brow, he appeared to be doing his best to look patient as he considered Archer's recommendation.

"Cheron," Gardner said at length. "Planet Five in the Eighty-three Leonis B system. That seems pretty far afield to make an effective staging post for a mass invasion of Earth."

"I realize that," Archer said. "And I'm sure that's a big part of the reason why the Romulans chose it. You know better than to take appearances at face value when it comes to the Romulans."

Gardner answered with a curt nod. "You're right about that, Jon. I saw what the bastards did to Tunis and Madrid."

Archer suppressed a wince; he, too, had seen the mushroom clouds over Europe and North Africa, when *Enterprise* had come streaking through the troposphere in hot pursuit of that final Romulan attack craft, after Earth's defenses had finished dispatching its brethren.

Enterprise had arrived moments too late.

"Admiral, it still seems to me that Starfleet Command's intel squares with what my own sources out in the field are telling me," Archer said.

Gardner scowled. "If by that you mean that your field sources tell you that the Romulans are planning a large assault against Earth sometime in the next few weeks, then

I have to agree with you. But there's no getting around the fact that your interpretation of some of the specifics strikes Starfleet Command, the MACO, and Prime Minister Samuels as somewhat reckless."

"Starfleet Command, the MACO, and the prime minister aren't in possession of all the facts," Archer said.

"No one ever is, Captain," said Gardner, his gray eyebrows gathering in the middle of his forehead like distant thunderheads. "Especially during wartime. But what information, specifically, do you think we haven't been properly read into?"

"The composition of the Romulan fleet, Admiral. You're aware that they've been trying to create a workable warp-seven-capable engine for years now."

"As have we. We've been racing against them for the past five years. Unfortunately, it appears that the Romulans have just won that race. Starfleet Intelligence has a high degree of confidence that the Romulans are ready to deploy at least half a dozen warp-seven-capable warships."

"Do the intel people have proof?" Archer asked. "My sources tell me that the Romulan military's warp-seven program has never gotten any farther than ours. They're deploying propaganda, not high-warp technology."

"Strange that Starfleet Intelligence disagrees with you," Gardner said, his eyes narrowing.

Archer met his suspicious gaze without flinching. "It wouldn't be the first time an intel bureau let itself get fooled."

"No, it wouldn't," said Gardner. "Where did you find this particular nugget of information?"

Archer wasn't certain how best to answer that question. He knew that the sudden revelation that his late chief engineer, Charles Tucker, was actually still alive and working as a deep-cover spy behind enemy lines would very likely be bad for his credibility. A confession that he had been one of those responsible for keeping that fact obscured for the past half decade might get an even worse reception.

Not to mention the fact that Trip had delivered this crucial bit of intel to him across parsecs of interstellar space via Commander T'Pol, who had received it by means of a peculiar and poorly understood outgrowth of Vulcan mysticism known as a telepathic mating bond.

"You know my orders, sir. *Enterprise* has done a lot of good deeds all along the Romulan front," Archer said at length. "We've quietly assembled a deep-space intel network that has a longer reach than Starfleet Intelligence. What that network tells me about the current state of the Romulan warp-seven program is that it's still confined to the lab. But that won't stop them from launching a massive invasion force soon—a force that comprises the bulk of the regular Romulan fleet and is gathering right now at Cheron.

"Starfleet Command has decided to divide Earth's forward forces among Yadalla, Sirius, Iota Horologii, Barradas, Gamma Equulei, and Eighty-two Eridani."

Gardner nodded. "It's a prudent arrangement."

No longer able to contain his nervous energy, Archer rose from the sofa. "Only if you're expecting to encounter Romulan warbirds that clock at warp seven, Admiral. Our fastest ships are still limited to warp five. Without help from the Vulcans or the Andorians, our current deployment plan will leave us far too spread out to cope with the fleet that's already massing at Cheron. What happened at Madrid and Tunis was just a taste of what's coming unless we deploy our forces properly, starting *right now*."

The admiral shook his head. "Madrid and Tunis happened because the Romulans caught us with our pants down. That's *not* going to happen again."

The captain leaned forward across the admiral's desk, his hands gripping its oaken sides. "With respect, Admiral, the Romulans did what they did *without* the benefit of their alleged warp-seven fleet. There'll be no stopping the Romulans unless we make up our minds right now to hit 'em hard with everything we can at Cheron."

Archer let his words hang in the air and gave Gardner time to consider them. He had genuine respect for the admiral, who had once captained a starship. About a decade ago, when they had both held the rank of captain, Gardner had been on the short list of candidates for the job of CO of *Enterprise,* Earth's first warp-five starship. Fortunately, Ambassador Soval's recommendation that Gardner be awarded that job failed to get traction, and the posting had gone to Archer at the insistence of Admiral Forrest.

Archer wondered if he would be sitting on the other side of the desk now had that decision gone the other way. *Would Captain Gardner sound any less crazy to me if he had just given me the very same speech?*

Gardner was always hard to read, but Archer thought he saw doubt creasing the older man's forehead. "If Starfleet Command is correct about the Romulans incorporating warp-seven-capable ships into their invasion fleet, then our forces are already optimally placed," he said.

"And if *my* intel is right," Archer said, straightening as he backed away from the desk, "then when the big Romulan attack comes, Starfleet will be out of position."

And you and the rest of the brass hats will have left Earth wide open for conquest.

TWENTY-FIVE

Early in the Month of *Z'at*, YS 8771
Saturday, May 8, 2160
Central ShiKahr, Vulcan

T'PAU LOOKED OUT over her homeworld's capital city from the administration building's highest observation tower. Aside from the constant low whine of aerial and street-level vehicular traffic, the stone streets and spires of ShiKahr's government district comprised a study in order, efficiency, and peace. The surrounding commercial and residential districts, all appearing similarly placid from this lofty, *sha'vokh*'s-eye perch, spread away toward the ruddy desert horizon beneath the watchful eyes of distant, fiery Nevasa and cold, nearby T'Rukh.

Would, she thought as the observation chamber's door slid open behind her unbidden, *that the world remained this way forever.*

She turned toward the sound. Her deputy, Minister Kuvak, and Foreign Minister Soval stood on the threshold. A glance at the dour countenences of both gray eminences told her immediately that her wish was not to be.

"My apologies, Administrator," said Koval. "I told the foreign minister that you had asked to be left in solitude here."

T'Pau nodded expressionlessly. "That was the reason I left my telecommunications devices in my office."

"I understand," Kuvak said. "However, he was insistent about speaking with you at once."

When T'Pau failed to respond right away, Kuvak appeared to be preparing to move Soval bodily away from the door.

"*Kroykah,*" T'Pau said, raising her right hand for emphasis. "Please allow the foreign minister to remain here with me."

Kuvak appeared surprised but quickly recovered his composure. "As you wish, Excellency," he said. "If you will excuse me, I have duties to perform."

T'Pau dismissed him with a nod, and Kuvak wasted no time disappearing.

"Thank you for agreeing to speak with me, Administrator," Soval said, stepping into the room. The door slid shut behind him, ensuring their privacy.

"It appeared to be a matter of some urgency," T'Pau said.

He nodded. "It is, though it is a matter we have already spoken about on a number of previous occasions."

"You speak of the Terrans," T'Pau said, steepling her fingers before her as she turned and looked out again across the expanse of ShiKahr and the Forge that lay beyond. "And the war our Romulan cousins continue to wage against them."

"Yes, Administrator. That war is about to enter a crucial phase. Perhaps the *final* phase."

"My opinion remains unchanged. As Captain Archer has said himself, 'Earth must stand on its own.'"

Soval shook his head. Taking a sidewise glance away from the cityscape, she saw how tired and haggard he appeared as he stepped into the natural light of red Nevasa.

"Left to stand on their own," he said, "the humans will fall. The forces arrayed against them are simply too great."

She turned in his direction and raised an eyebrow, putting her suspicions plainly on display. "You are certain of this?"

He nodded. "I have sources that operate inside Romulan space. Some of these have inside access to the Tal Shiar, the Romulan Star Empire's intelligence service. Some may be unknown even to Minister Silok and our own V'Shar bureau."

"Very well. I accept that whatever information you wish to impart might carry a compelling pedigree. So speak plainly."

"The Romulans are at present massing at Cheron for a large-scale assault on Earth," he said, dispensing with any further preamble. "Soon, perhaps a matter of one or two tendays, it will be too late to aid the Terrans should you decide to do so. If I am to change your mind about Vulcan's nonparticipation in the conflict, I must do so *now*—while some chance of victory remains."

T'Pau turned back to face the city, and the peace and order that it represented. It looked like a great model that stretched out to infinity, or some beautifully realized *Kal-toh* game structure.

"Soval, I know that you, like the rest of Vulcan, still grieve the loss of Surak," she said. "You mourn that you will never know him through his *katra* the way that I and a handful of others have been privileged to do."

"I cannot dispute that, Administrator," Soval said. "Although grief is a particularly intense emotion, no living Vulcan who is aware of Surak's destruction can claim an immunity to it."

"I was the penultimate keeper of Surak's *katra*," T'Pau said. "Speaking as one who knew Surak intimately, I must insist that he would oppose entering this war. Surak's destruction has overtaxed the emotional control of every Vulcan."

"Perhaps," said Soval.

"Becoming party to a war could only worsen the collective damage. We would risk becoming atavisms, returning to the primal, bloodthirsty ways of our ancestors."

"Perhaps."

"We would risk becoming the very Romulans you insist that we fight, Soval."

"Administrator, we can avoid that risk only by condemning an entire world to death, or whatever might be worse than death."

T'Pau turned to face him again. "Surak has taught us that peace sometimes comes at great cost." She moved toward the exit, signaling her wish to end the discussion.

"I do not dispute that, Administrator," Soval said as she walked past him to open the door. "But allow me to pose a final question, if I may."

She paused on the threshold and looked back at the senior diplomat. "Very well."

"Should Earth fall before the coming invasion," Soval said, "which world do you believe our Romulan cousins will go after next?"

T'Pau left the room without answering the question.

TWENTY-SIX

Day Seven, Romulan Month of *ta'Krat*, 1184 YD'E
Monday, May 10, 2160
The Hall of State, Dartha City, Romulus

THE MAN KNOWN AS Cunaehr and Sodok sagged between
the grasp of the two uhlanu who half carried, half dragged
him into Valdore's office. The admiral studied the vacant
expression on the engineer's face with some trepidation.
Then he turned toward the paramilitary-garbed young
woman who stood at rigid attention beside his sherawood
desk.

"If you've lobotomized him by overusing those damned
mind probes, Agent T'Luadh, I promise I will spit you on
my Honor Blade," he said, speaking in a low growl.

"A Tal Shiar physician has certified that he is essentially
unharmed," she said, apparently unfazed by Valdore's
bluster. "No permanent damage has been done. I believe he
may be coming around now."

The engineer's head lolled limply as the two guards
continued holding him upright. Then his neck stiffened and
he raised his head, blinking repeatedly in the harsh, orange-
tinted light of Valdore's office. Valdore doubted he even
knew where he was.

"Mister Cunaehr," the admiral said, approaching the
engineer very closely. "I have been told you are making
steady progress preparing the *avaihh lli vastam* fleet for
maximum warp."

He blinked again, and a look of recognition crossed

his face. "That's right, Admiral. I still need to . . . make some settling-in adjustments to the command-and-control interfaces. But those ships you found at Gasko II will be ready to deploy alongside the main invasion force, right on schedule."

"I hope for your own sake that you're correct about that," Valdore said, recalling the many occasions when the late Nijil had disappointed him with unfulfilled promises.

"I have . . . faith in my work, Admiral," said the engineer.

"Then surely the other members of your engineering team can handle the remaining details," T'Luadh said, placing a hand on the disruptor pistol she kept holstered at her hip. "Admiral, I would be happy to dispose of him for you."

Valdore held up a hand. "Not yet, T'Luadh. As Mister Cunaehr has already indicated, we may have further need of his technical expertise as our invasion plans near fruition.

"You will take charge of him aboard the *Warbird Dabhae* tomorrow, when we begin the voyage to Cheron."

TWENTY-SEVEN

Early in the Month of *Z'at*, YS 8771
Monday, May 10, 2160
Vulcan's Forge, Vulcan

LOST IN HER MEDITATIONS, T'Pau sat cross-legged on the wind-carved top of Surak's Peak. She had left her robe's hood down, since the slowly lengthening shadow of T'Klass's Pillar provided more than adequate shielding from the rays of brilliant red Nevasa, which illuminated a wide, crescent-shaped swath of T'Rukh, the Watcher that dominated the entire hemisphere's vermilion sky. The thin but not uncomfortably warm desert air caressed her hair and the tips of her ears, which picked up the long, echoing shrieks of the scavenging *sha'vokh* birds that wheeled vigilantly somewhere overhead.

Before her and far, far below lay a wide span of flat, blistering, red hardpan, a forbidding stretch of inhospitable desert that spread out in all directions from the ancient mountain's foothills. Beyond lay the distant expanse of ShiKahr, Vulcan's venerable capital, whose outer agricultural fields, roads, dwellings, and delicate central stone spires rippled thanks to the heat distortions of the desert air.

The cries of the carrion-eaters gave way to a gravel-crunching footfall behind her. T'Pau's spine stiffened; she had ordered Kuvak to have this space cleared for her exclusive use.

She turned her head and saw a tall, slender man in a dark traveler's robe approaching her. Moving with the grace of a *Suus Mahna* master, he dropped gently to the stony ground near her and adopted T'Pau's cross-legged posture.

"Forgive me, Administrator," he said, his robe's baggy hood still obscuring his face.

"Who are you?" T'Pau demanded.

"Do not be concerned," the man answered. "I am not actually here."

She scowled. "You are speaking blatant illogic."

"That would be ironic if it were so. Allow me to offer you proof." He raised his hands to his head and doffed his hood.

T'Pau recognized the man's long, angular, gray-topped face immediately. "Surak," she said. "This isn't possible. You can't be here. You can't be *anywhere*."

"You are correct, in essence. However, no process can be one hundred percent efficient. Whenever a Vulcan's immortal *katra* is extracted and moved—be it from permanent interment within one of the *vre'katra*, or *katric* arcs, that the Vulcan Masters maintain deep within Mount Seleya, or from the mind of an individual *katra* keeper such as yourself—a small residue is left behind. An echo, if you will."

T'Pau had never seen any empirical research into this topic, yet the argument presented by this . . . apparition? . . . echo? . . . of Surak struck her as logical.

"If what you say is true, then this conversation must be taking place entirely inside my mind."

The man who resembled Surak nodded. "Indeed. But this fact alone cannot invalidate the truth of anything you and I may discuss. After all, what is the entire universe, at least as you perceive it, other than a construct of your mind?"

Her senses reeled momentarily. Perhaps she had been working too hard. With all the weighty matters that burdened her at the moment, the last thing she wanted was to debate epistemology with a likely hallucination.

"What do you wish to discuss?" she asked the Surak simulacrum.

"Many things are now vying for your attention," he said. "For one, you aren't certain you are pursuing the correct course of action."

T'Pau controlled an impulse to reply. Given everything that had happened during the years since she had transitioned from revolutionary leader to politician, how could she be certain of anything?

"Your reticence is only logical, T'Pau," Surak's image said softly. "You worry that you lead out of vanity. You have a world to govern, day to day and hour to hour. Ceaseless responsibility that allows no time for misgivings."

A world to govern, she thought with bitterness. During the years she had spent opposing Administrator V'Las's warmongering, she had never envisioned taking V'Las's place. Even after the reactionary administrator's ouster, she'd assumed that Kuvak, the veteran minister who had proved instrumental in thwarting V'Las's plan to start an Andorian-Vulcan war, was the most logical choice. Kuvak had probably harbored the same assumption, though he never spoke to her of such things.

Three tendays after V'Las's fall, a special planetary plebiscite was called. The results had taught her two important things immediately: that the Confederacy of Vulcan's highest leadership post was hers, and the wisdom of doubting her hitherto unquestioned trust in the logic that guided the Vulcan electorate.

"I believe I understand what troubles you, T'Pau," Surak's image said. "You are experiencing second thoughts about having accepted the mantle of leadership."

"Perhaps."

"Do not underestimate yourself, T'Pau. You have much to offer Vulcan."

"No. *Syrran* had much to offer Vulcan." Her eyes stung at the thought of her late colleague, a fellow peaceful revolutionary and student of Surak, and the man after whom the Syrrannite sect had been named. "*You* had much to offer Vulcan, Surak."

"As you have noted, I no longer exist, even as a discorporate *katra*. Whatever I have to offer Vulcan is already available to all through the *Kir'Shara*. Finding the wisdom to interpret those offerings for the benefit of all of Vulcan is up to you."

Hearing the words of Surak delivered in mild tones but with such authority was gratifying. Illogically, her doubts remained. "My skill set has made me a successful revolutionary," she said, "but it has also made me a poor choice for the task of governing *after* the revolution, at least so far." *A logical electorate would have understood that,* she thought, *and chosen Kuvak over me.*

Surak's lips curled into something that looked suspiciously like a small smile. "Assuming that your dismal assessment of our people's logic is correct," he said, "then who better to correct this deficiency than a Syrrannite leader?"

"Perhaps." T'Pau could not deny the logic of his words, having already concluded that the best way to navigate the paradoxes of war and peace was to follow the strict discipline of logic as laid out in the path of the *Kolinahr.*

"But there is another subject that you need to discuss," the residue of Surak continued. "I speak of the war that our Romulan cousins are prosecuting, and the fate of the Terrans. I know you have had a change of heart regarding Vulcan's involvement in that war."

T'Pau understood why her mind had conjured this image of Surak. He represented the repressed guilt she felt over her tentative decision to violate the great man's central teaching of pacifism.

"T'Pol is right, Surak," she said at length. "So are Kuvak and Archer, and every one of Vulcan's allies."

Surak's image raised an eyebrow. "Right?"

"About Vulcan not being able to afford pacifism during this time of crisis. Before the Romulan threat to the entire Coalition is neutralized, and Earth is back on a path to long life and prosperity."

Surak's countenance remained neutral, but T'Pau sensed a profound sadness. "You are aware, of course, that this . . . reversal puts at risk your vision of a reformed Vulcan."

She nodded. "I understand that. I have come to accept that the risk is an acceptable one. It would be logical for me to step aside and allow Kuvak to take charge. He understands that staying out of the conflict may be riskier than entering it."

"Kuvak is a fair-minded public servant," said Surak. "But he isn't a Syrrannite. He lacks a long-term vision for Vulcan."

"Perhaps. But his leadership may be crucial in securing Vulcan's short-term survival. His analysis of the conflict has always been sound."

Surak's gray eyebrows gathered together. "Has it? Does Kuvak recognize that a decision to fight in this war will turn Vulcan entirely away from the philosophy contained within the *Kir'Shara*? Does he understand that the war could transform Vulcan into a second Romulus?"

T'Pau noticed that Surak was staring at her. She met his gaze squarely.

This is my own mind, she cautioned herself. *I argue with myself, not with Surak.*

"Vulcan will embrace the *Kir'Shara.* It will take time. It will be a lengthy process. But as you say, no process can be one hundred percent efficient."

"You believe it better to sanction *some* violence than to risk an entire civilization being destroyed," the shadow of Surak said, speaking in tones both accusatory and disappointed. "How do you reconcile that with your Syrrannite beliefs?"

Weary of the counsel of her conscience, T'Pau brought her knees together and stood. "I no longer find it logical to try," she said.

Without sparing a backward glance at the spirit that had climbed the mountain to haunt her, she began making her descent to the Forge.

When T'Pau reached the hot, rocky flatland, she was gratified to discover that she had arrived there alone.

Fourthmoon, Fesoan Lor'veln Year 471
Northern Wastes, Andoria

Anishtalla zh'Dhaven stood on the ice plain, her sighted eyes trained upon the ringed gas giant that Andoria endlessly circled. The little girl's intense feelings of fear reverberated through the mind of her mother, Thirijhamel zh'Dhaven, causing an almost palpable sensation of pain.

Thirijhamel—known to her bondmates and fellow Aenar simply as Jhamel—was as blind as any Aenar. Nevertheless, her antennae formed a nonvisual map of her daughter's small, delicate features as the girl's antennae turned upward in an inquisitive yet cautious posture. The tears that had gathered in the child's eyes and on her cheeks crystallized in the harsh wind.

Jhamel's only non-Aenar bondmate, Hravishran th'Zoarhi— his three *shelthreth* mates called him Shran—had often spoken wonderingly about the unique blend of Andorian and Aenar-Andorian traits that their daughter, the first and only product of their quadrogenetic union, had so far exhibited. For example, Shran had described the little girl's facial skin tone as greenish blue, beneath a full head of hair as white as the face of the fairest Aenar.

Not for the first time, Jhamel wished that she could see her daughter, her precious *zhei*, through the sighted eyes of Shran, the little girl's *thaan*-father.

The child spoke aloud, as had been her habit since she'd attained her initial fluency in Old Common Andorian three winters earlier.

"Where has Father *Thavan* gone?"

Jhamel smiled at Talla's use of a childish endearment to refer to Shran. But her smile faded as she considered her daughter's almost plaintive question. She did not wish to frighten the girl unduly, but she also had no desire to mislead her. Speaking wordlessly directly into Talla's brain, Jhamel said, *"Your thavan had to leave Andoria for a while, my heart."*

"What is he doing?" Talla said, still speaking aloud. If she had inherited any psi potential from her Aenar parents, it had yet to manifest itself as telepathic ability.

"He's . . ." Jhamel paused, trying to decide how much to reveal. *"He had to help some friends who are in trouble."*

"Why?"

"Because that's what friends do, Talla. Because that's who your father is." She'd seen how hard Shran had worked to fit in among the Aenar, who had over the centuries built a pacifist society. Shran had tried to adopt the ways of peace, and Jhamel felt confident that he would continue to try, no matter what impediments the outside world threw into his path.

"When is he coming home?"

Jhamel paused momentarily to compose herself before replying. *"Soon, I hope, Talla. Soon."*

"*Is* he coming home?"

Jhamel silently cursed herself; she had allowed too much of her own fear to show. Now she couldn't muster another telepathic answer without revealing even more of her anxieties about the call Shran had found impossible to ignore. She could only hope that her other two bondmates, Lahvishri sh'Ralaavazh and Onalishenar ch'Sorichas—Vishri and Shenar—would do a better job than she had of allaying Talla's worries once they concluded the day's business and returned home for the evening.

In the meantime, Jhamel replied by shedding tears of her own.

TWENTY-EIGHT

Tuesday, July 29, 2160
Enterprise NX-01
Near 83 Leonis B

THE STAR FRAMED almost dead center on the bridge viewer glowed a dull orange, conjuring incongruous images of peaceful citrus orchards in Archer's mind. *It's weird where your imagination can wander when you're looking right down the cannon's throat,* he thought as he leaned forward in his chair.

"Any sign yet of the Romulan fleet?" Archer asked.

"No sensor contact with vessels of any kind as yet, Commodore," T'Pol said as she squinted into the hooded viewer that extended toward her face from the main science console. "Aside from the other twenty-three vessels in our task force, we appear to be alone in this system."

"Navigation beams confirm Commander T'Pol's sensor scans," said Lieutenant Travis Mayweather, who briefly turned his chair toward Archer.

Archer favored his alpha-watch helmsman with a small smile. It was good to have him back—especially under the present dire circumstances. Elrene Leydon was an able pilot, but Travis Mayweather was the best in the fleet.

"Bring us to a full stop and keep station here, Travis," the captain said. "Hoshi, relay that order to the rest of the task force."

Lieutenants Mayweather and Sato answered with simultaneous "Ayes" as they set about their business. A few moments later, a subtle shift in the vibrations that passed from the deck plates to his boots told Archer that his order had been carried out.

"Task force reports all stop, Commodore," Hoshi said. "Keeping station just outside the fifth planet's orbit."

"Starfleet Intelligence reports that the Romulans have a small garrison on that planet, Commodore," Lieutenant Commander Malcolm Reed said from behind the tactical console.

Here's hoping we won't have to land MACOs on the planet's surface this time, Archer thought.

"Any sign of activity on the ground, or in nearby space?" Archer asked T'Pol.

"No. Perhaps the Romulans haven't noticed us," said T'Pol.

"Or maybe they *have* seen us," Malcolm said, "and they're just hunkering down because their outpost here isn't provisioned well enough to stand against us."

"They could just be waiting for an incoming Romulan fleet to take us down," Commander D. O. O'Neill said from the secondary tactical station.

Malcolm nodded. "With the possible exception of the Romulan troops already on Cheron's surface, it appears that we're the first guests to arrive at the party."

"Let's hope we aren't the only ones, Malcolm," Archer said. "I'd hate to think the Romulan fleet has decided to stand us up."

Archer deliberately kept his tone light. He had finally convinced Admiral Gardner to devote the lion's share of Starfleet's resources to the Cheron operation. If he turned out to be wrong, two dozen critically needed Starfleet vessels might have traveled seventy-five days to reach a system fifty-eight light-years from Earth only to discover that they had been deployed to the wrong location.

No, Archer told himself. *The information I acted on came from Trip, so it's solid. It has to be.*

Archer stepped onto the bridge's upper level and came

to a stop halfway between T'Pol and Malcolm. "We know the Romulans are big on stealth."

"How could I forget?" Malcolm said with a wry grin. "Thanks to that incident in the minefield, my leg still aches whenever it rains."

T'Pol raised an eyebrow. "The mines were obscured with cloaking technology."

"Exactly," Archer said, nodding. "Do you think the Romulans could have adapted that same technology to the purpose of concealing entire ships? Maybe even a whole fleet?"

"That has been a distinct possibility for the past several years," T'Pol said. "Given the facility the Romulans have demonstrated in the field of holography, cloaking entire fleets of warbirds could be within their ability."

"Frankly, I have serious doubts about that," Malcolm said, shaking his head.

"Why?" Archer wanted to know.

"A cloaking device capable of concealing a ship—as opposed to small things, like ordnance—would suck up a tremendous amount of power," said the armory officer. "A power-consumption curve that steep would put strict limits on anything else the cloaked ship might need to do—like fire its weapons."

T'Pol nodded. "That is a valid point. In addition, power utilization on the order we are discussing might, in itself, be difficult to conceal. No matter how well shielded such a vessel was, a telltale power signature might be detectable when the cloak is active."

Archer's eyebrows rose. "Well," he said, returning to his chair, "we'd better keep a sharp eye out for anything like that. Hoshi, pass that along to the fleet."

Time passed slowly as the bridge crew maintained its vigil.

T'Pol looked up from her scanner. "Commodore, it

occurs to me that the Romulans may not need cloaking technology to conceal their presence from us."

"Don't keep me in suspense, Commander," Archer said, frowning as he moved back up to T'Pol's station.

"Approximately half the stars in this galaxy are part of multistar systems," she said as she continued working her console. "On the star charts of both Vulcan and Earth, the local star is considered part of a binary system."

Archer nodded. He already knew the system's basic astronomical catalog boilerplate data: 83 Leonis B, the sun that the Starfleet task force presently circled, was an orange dwarf star that massed a little less than eighty percent of Earth's sun, a difference that made it considerably cooler and duller than Sol. The nearly circular orbits of its family of six planets were spaced more closely than were their counterparts in the Sol system, an arrangement that helped Cheron qualify for the Vulcan habitable designation of *Minshara*-class.

Eighty-three Leonis A was an orange subgiant star with a planetary brood of its own. The critical difference was that A had started off with more mass, and therefore was hotter. As a consequence, A had already exhausted its supply of hydrogen fuel, which limited its internal fusion processes to helium and heavier elements. A was therefore actively transforming into a bloated red giant. This was bad news for any humanoid-type life-forms that might have arisen in the A system. B's planets, which included Cheron, were more fortunate, since A lay a considerable distance from its stellar sibling—about 80 billion kilometers, or more than five hundred times the average distance between Earth and Sol.

Archer watched the displays on his science officer's console as T'Pol summoned up both text and images. A schematic representation of two orange stars appeared, one slightly larger than the other. Lines that emanated from the poles of each star looped out and crossed one another at a point nearly equidistant from both bodies.

"The lines represent the boundaries of each star with respect to interstellar space," T'Pol explained. "The point at which the particle density of the interstellar medium exceeds that created by the solar flux."

"You're talking about the distance where the solar winds peter out," Archer said. "The heliopause."

"Exactly." T'Pol placed her long index finger at a point between the A and B stars and traced a long downward arc to show where the heliopauses of both bodies either touched or overlapped. "The complex interheliopause particle interactions I've identified here could cause a great deal of sensor confusion."

Archer brightened. "Enough to hide a Romulan fleet?"

"Unknown," she said.

Grinning, Archer walked over to Hoshi's station. "Lieutenant Sato, place the fleet on High Tactical Alert. And open up a hailing frequency."

Day Fifteen, Romulan Month of *et'Khior*, 1184 YD'E
Tuesday, July 29, 2160
Imperial Warbird Dabhae
Extreme edge of the Cheron system

"The *hevam* fleet continues to simply *sit* there, Admiral," said Subcenturion T'Velekh, who operated the primary sensor network of the flagship of the Fifth Legion of the Romulan Star Empire's Imperial Navy.

Valdore smiled. The only thing more satisfying than slaying a deadly enemy was doing so before one's target even glimpsed the Honor Blade that streaked toward his unprotected neck.

"Alert the fleet," he told the female centurion who was running the communications hub. "Prepare to move all eighty ships from concealment. On my order, we will bring all the cold fury of Bettatan'ru and Erebus upon the heads of the *hevam* before they understand what is happening to them."

"Immediately, Admiral." The comm officer began tapping commands into her console.

The entry hatch slid open, and Colonel T'Luadh of the Tal Shiar entered. The woman strode forward and came to a stop beside his chair, where she stood at rigid attention. "I have come to relay a request from Mister Cunaehr," she said.

"What does he want?"

"He wishes to assist you in winning the coming battle."

Valdore chuckled. Although the man's engineering talent appeared so far to be extensive, it was also beyond question that he was a spy for the *Ejhoi Ormiin* radicals. Did Cunaehr think him a fool?

"Tell Mister Cunaehr that if the engines of our new *avaihh lli vastam* vessels perform as well as he has promised during the S'ol system invasion, then he will have contributed enough assistance for two lifetimes."

T'Luadh nodded, then performed a perfect salute. "I will convey your words, Admiral."

She turned toward the hatch, but he stopped her by placing a hand on her shoulder. "More importantly, I want you to maintain constant vigilance over him."

She nodded, saluted again, then exited the command deck.

"I am receiving an incoming message, Admiral," the comm officer said. Valdore turned in time to see her suppress a bemused frown.

"A message?" Valdore said, scowling. "From whom?"

The young officer turned toward him, her face a study in surprise. "It's from the *hevam* flagship—from *En'ter'priz.*"

Captain Archer, Valdore thought, his heart pounding with martial eagerness. "What does it say, Centurion?"

"There's a great deal of interference, Admiral. I am attempting to clean it up, translate the initial message, and put it on audio."

Tension-filled heartbeat after heartbeat passed. Just as Valdore was about to admonish the centurion, a burst of tinny sound emerged from the command deck audio system.

"—*athan Archer. There's no need to be coy, Admiral. Come out, come out, wherever you are.*"

Valdore growled, intensely angry at whatever unjust force was responsible for robbing him of the element of surprise at the very last moment.

"Helmsman!" he roared, sitting back in the thronelike chair that dominated the command deck. "Do not keep the *hevam* waiting any longer!"

"What's the word, T'Luadh?" Trip asked after letting his Tal Shiar "minder" back into the quarters Valdore had issued him.

She stepped inside the small but functional suite of rooms and fixed him with a sober stare. "I'm afraid he doesn't trust you enough to give you the run of the ship, Mister Tucker."

Trip winced at the mention of his real name here aboard the Romulan flagship. If T'Luadh had spoken that name to Valdore . . . if she had ratted him out as a human spy, he'd be inhaling vacuum.

"Well, thanks for asking," he said, trying to reveal none of his anxieties. "I should have figured that the admiral wasn't the trusting type after he refused to let me stay aboard any of the new warp-seven ships."

"I'm sure that's just until the present battle concludes," T'Luadh said.

"I hope so. Because being stuck on the flagship makes it pretty damned difficult for me to make those new vessels fly the way Valdore wants 'em to fly."

T'Luadh chuckled and adopted a rueful expression. "For reasons I'm sure you understand very well, the admiral has great difficulty trusting you at the moment. One of the great Commander Amarcan's sayings from his *Axioms* expresses it best—"

"'Keep your friends close and your enemies closer,'" Trip interrupted.

T'Luadh's eyebrows rose. "I had no idea you were so well read outside the disciplines of engineering and espionage, Mister Tucker." With that, she excused herself.

Trip examined the comm terminal that T'Luadh had graciously allowed him to use to pass the time during much of the long voyage to Cheron. As he had already done several times, he paid close attention to the delicate connectors that accessed both the *Warbird Dabhae's* electroplasma system and its data network.

Whatever "contribution" I end up making to Valdore's war effort, he thought, *I guess I'll have to make it from right here.*

Enterprise NX-01

"Romulan vessels, Commodore!" Malcolm cried. "They're coming out of the overlapping heliopause zones."

Archer sprang from his chair. "How many ships?"

"Twenty so far," Malcolm said, his fingers making frantic gyrations across his console. His rough-hewn face was turning pale. "And they're still coming."

T'Pol consulted the displays at her station with similar, if more graceful, urgency. "Confirmed. I have picked up the subspace wakes of approximately sixty Romulan vessels. And that number is steadily increasing."

Sixty-plus against twenty-four, Archer thought. He tried to use his incredulity as a shield but found that offered scant protection. "How fast are they approaching?"

"They're moving toward us as a unit," Malcolm said. "At a uniform speed of warp four point six."

At least nobody's coming in at warp seven, Archer thought, returning to his chair. He studied the main viewscreen. It displayed a tactical rendering of the two fleets, which had arranged themselves into opposing spear-point shapes. Only the Romulan vessels, rendered in red to distinguish them from Starfleet's blue icons, appeared to be moving, and the gap between the red and blue shapes was steadily decreasing. *Trip's intel about their high-warp program not being ready yet is accurate.*

For now.

"No more vessels are emerging from the high particle-flux region," said T'Pol, leaning over her scanner's hooded visor. "I now read a total of eighty-one ships in the Romulan contingent."

Archer braced himself, his hands clutching hard at the arms of his command chair. Very little time remained before immovable object and irresistible force were to collide in the war's biggest engagement to date. Crossing the 515-AU-wide gulf that separated the two fleets would have taken Zefram Cochrane's prototype warship nearly three days. Moving nearly at *Enterprise*'s top safe speed, the Romulan force would close that gap in considerably less time.

"What's the Romulan fleet's ETA?" Archer asked.

T'Pol answered with her usual alacrity. "At present speed, twenty-six point two minutes."

Archer nodded. "Hoshi, are the emergency subspace frequencies clear?"

"Yes, sir. The Romulans haven't gotten close enough yet to jam them. But I expect they'll do it the first moment they can."

"Inform Starfleet Command that we are about to engage the enemy. Then aim a second transmission at every world we've asked to join us in this fight so far. Tell them that the war's most decisive battle is about to start."

"Aye, sir," Hoshi said, immediately beginning to tap the appropriate commands into her console.

Archer noticed only then that T'Pol had approached his chair and was standing to his immediate left. "I'm curious. What do you think that second message will accomplish?"

"'Grave men, near death, who see with blinding sight.'"

"Sir?"

"It'll warn the Romulans' next victims."

T'Pol regarded him quietly, then returned to her science console.

"Interesting that the Romulans didn't appear right on top of us," Malcolm said.

"They would have if they could have," Archer said.

"Perhaps the Romulans have simply decided that their numerical superiority obviates any need for the element of surprise," T'Pol said.

"Maybe." Archer stroked his unshaven chin. "Or maybe their commander just can't take a good taunting and jumped the gun on his attack."

T'Pol did not appear satisfied with that. "Commodore, our fleet is *seriously* outnumbered. Starfleet has erred, deploying too many of its resources at Iota Horologii, Eighty-two Eridani, and elsewhere. Therefore it is likely that the Romulans will succeed."

Archer's jaw hardened. "The Romulans won't win their victory easily. If we go down, then I swear we'll take more than half of them with us. Starfleet's other ships will regroup from their positions at Iota Horologii, Eighty-two Eridani, and Gamma Equulei. They'll catch up with the rest of the Romulan fleet before they get to Earth or Vulcan."

"Perhaps," she said. "Regardless, we could employ a different option while the time still remains to do so."

Anger flared from some deep place within him. "Are you suggesting we run away, Commander?"

Her eyebrows rose, and she looked genuinely hurt. "No, sir. Only *Enterprise* and three retrofitted *Daedalus*-class vessels have warp-five capability. The remaining twenty ships in our contingent would be unable to outrun the Romulans. We would be abandoning them to certain death or capture."

"Then what do you have in mind?"

An alarmed-sounding Hoshi Sato interrupted the discussion. "Commodore, I'm picking up incoming subspace signals from the Romulan fleet."

"Are they hailing us?" Archer asked

"No, sir." said Hoshi. "It looks like the Romulans are recycling one of their older tricks—they're trying to hijack the helm consoles of *Enterprise* and the rest of the fleet remotely."

Fear and outrage warred within Archer's belly, and outrage won. "They must have been revising this technology the entire time we've been working on countering it."

"It appears they haven't revised it nearly enough," said Malcolm as he ran some quick diagnostics. "The most recent antihijacking computer protocols we received from the Cochrane Institute team are neutralizing the new Romulan code as fast as it comes in. I'm already purging the bad code from the system."

"Good work, Malcolm," Archer said. "Ready weapons. Hoshi, screen all incoming signals for Trojan horses. The Romulans could still get lucky."

Archer glanced down at the chronometer on the arm of his chair. A little less than twenty-three minutes remained.

He turned his attention back to T'Pol. "Commander, you were about to explain a tactical option I hadn't considered yet. Go ahead."

The Vulcan outlined the details. To Archer's surprise, the notion left him grinning.

He wasted no time giving the orders. "Hoshi, open a secure channel to the entire fleet. This is going to take quite a bit of ship-to-ship coordination . . ."

Warbird Dabbae

"We have dropped back into normal space, Admiral," Subcenturion T'Velekh reported from the sensor station.

"Receiving confirmation from the fleet," said the comm officer.

Valdore looked intently at the image on the command deck's forward viewer. He saw only empty space, the distant, wan disk of the daystar that dominated the Cheron outpost's skies, the faint crescent of Cheron itself, and the myriad of tiny points of light that filled the infinity that lay beyond it all.

"What happened to the *hevam* ships, Subcenturion?" Valdore rumbled. "Where is *En'ter'priz?*"

"The enemy fleet appears to have, ah, changed location," T'Velekh said, his voice unsteady.

"That much I could have told you already," Valdore said. "What I fail to understand is how they could have 'changed location' without your having noticed it."

Subcommander Threl rose from behind the main tactical panel, inclining his silver-helmeted head toward Valdore as he executed the time-honored elbow-over-heart military salute. "I believe I may be able to explain what happened."

"Speak," Valdore said, scowling. He hoped his tone made clear that he wasn't fishing for excuses or apologies.

"Whenever our ships drop out of superluminal mode and reenter normal space," Threl said, "there is a very brief delay between the time when our superluminal sensors disengage and the sublight sensors become active."

Valdore did not enjoy hearing such things. During his entire tenure in the military, and even during his Senate career before that, he'd had little patience for the vicissitudes of high technology—to say nothing of those who seemed to be apologists for its frequent shortcomings. Fair or not, his suspicions were roused.

"How much of a delay?" he asked, his eyes narrowed.

"It is extremely small," Threl said. "A couple of heartbeats. No more than a small fraction of an *ewa*."

"And the *hevam* somehow managed to time their

departure to the precise moment of our sensor transition?" Valdore said.

"Apparently," said Threl. "As you have said yourself many times, Admiral, it does not pay to underestimate the *hevam*."

"Other than, perhaps, their courage," Valdore said.

Threl favored his commander with a martial, predatory smile. "Do not be concerned, Admiral. They won't get far."

As if on cue, T'Velekh spoke up. "Sensors reveal multiple warp trails."

"Follow those trails," Valdore said. "Did the *hevam* flee the system?"

"No, Admiral. They've gone to Cheron."

The outpost, thought the admiral, his heart and spine suddenly as cold as space. He imagined the *hevam* savages picking the flesh from the charred bones of loyal soldiers of the Empire.

"Redirect the fleet accordingly," he said.

Enterprise NX-01

Robust though the planet's ionosphere was, Archer knew that it wouldn't conceal the fleet for very long. Malcolm's shouted report, therefore, came as no surprise.

"The Romulan vessels are entering the atmosphere, Commodore."

"Don't keep 'em waiting, Malcolm. Give us some altitude and fire at will. Hoshi, advise the rest of the fleet to do likewise."

The next several minutes both crawled and sprinted, forming a blur composed entirely of shouted orders, the rumbling and moans of strained hull plating, and the smell of fear, blood, fire, and ozone.

Enterprise took a terrific pounding but somehow remained both operational and spaceworthy as the scrum of battle spread through all three dimensions, encompassing both the blue of Cheron's sky and the blackness of the space that lay beyond its slender layers of atmosphere. One particularly vicious disruptor strike caused T'Pol's station to erupt into a shower of sparks and smoke, knocking her to the deck. Private Davis, a MACO corpsman, offered his arm to steady her. T'Pol shook it off and moved back to her charred and darkened console and began trying to reactivate it.

Archer saw that her right temple had received a nasty-looking burn. Green blood was dripping down the side of her soot-smeared face, tracing the outline of a cut she had received from the explosion, presumably from a piece of flying shrapnel from her station.

"Get down to sickbay, Commander," Archer said.

"We're in combat," she said. "I don't have time for medical attention at the moment. And my injuries aren't that extensive."

Under the present circumstances, he found he couldn't argue with her.

Instead, Archer immersed himself in the all-consuming task of directing the fight, which spiraled upward into ever-higher orbits above the Romulan outpost world. As the battle spread out and unfolded, he pushed aside his emotional reaction to the wanton destruction. Large, charred hull fragments from Starfleet vessels burned as they tumbled in low, decaying orbits, cracked open like so many eggshells. Vacuum-asphyxiated bodies tumbled along with them. The Starships *San Antonio, Iroquois, Argus,* and *Hermes* had been reduced to scrap during the initial exchanges of fire. Perhaps half of the Starfleet force remained functional. Seeing the occasional explosion among the Romulan lines, Archer could only hope that his task force had given as good as it had gotten.

But at the rate things were going, there could be only one outcome. Though the battle had reduced it considerably, the Romulan force was still too large to overcome. Archer was gradually coming to fatalistic terms with a harsh but increasingly unavoidable reality.

Humanity had lost the Battle of Cheron.

"I'm picking up new warp signatures," Malcolm said.

"Incoming ships confirmed," T'Pol said. "At least twenty warp signatures."

Archer decided there was no harm in allowing himself a kernel of hope. "Ours?" he asked.

Malcolm's tone and expression were as somber as a cenotaph. "I don't think so, sir."

Warbird Dabhae

"The enemy is at our mercy, Admiral," Threl reported. "Their fleet is reduced by more than half, and the remainder are so badly damaged as to be effectively neutralized."

"And yet they fight on," Valdore said, astonished as he watched the relentless exchanges of fire on the central tactical viewer. Cheron, now relatively safe from *hevam* incursion, fell away into the distance. "Though they are beaten, they continue to fight."

Through the *hevam* were nowhere near as physically repulsive as the warrior race known in the decadent circles of "polite" Romulan society as the *kll'inghann*—Valdore preferred to use the pejorative designation *klivam*—the two species had to be closely related. Both races lacked the capacity to recognize an existential superior and could not admit to having been defeated by same.

"A number of ships are dropping out of superluminal mode," said T'Velekh.

Valdore's brow contorted in puzzlement. "If they're reinforcements, they have arrived well ahead of schedule."

T'Velekh blanched, his olive complexion transforming to a fish-belly white before Valdore's eyes. "Admiral! The incoming vessels aren't Romulan!"

Yikh ships, Valdore noted with no small amount of surprise. Alien vessels of unknown origin—at least so far. "Identify them."

"They're opening fire, Admiral," Threl said.

"On whom?" Valdore asked.

"On *us!*"

Valdore performed a quick count and realized to his horror that the combined opposition now narrowly outnumbered his own forces. The *Dabhae*'s hull groaned and shuddered as one of the newcomers' weapons found its target, and he muttered a heady curse. He needed time to regroup, to reassess the suddenly altered situation.

"Bring the fleet about," he barked to Subcommander Threl. "Fire all aft tubes as we turn. I want to put some distance between us, the *hevam*, and their allies—at least for the moment."

Enterprise NX-01

Archer was delighted at the prospect of the cavalry coming over the hill in the proverbial nick of time. As the battle continued to rage all about *Enterprise*, the viewer caught it only in slices, and the constant tumbling motion of the new combatants as they evaded and returned salvo after salvo of Romulan disruptor fire made it difficult to examine the particulars of each ship's configuration.

Then, astonishingly, the Romulan line began falling back in response to the surprise entrance of so many armed defenders; nearly every remaining warbird opened fire from aft in an obvious bid to discourage pursuit.

Loath to tempt fate any more than necessary, Archer ordered the fleet to cease firing and hold its present position as the Romulan remnants withdrew. The main viewer showed the newcomers as they ceased firing and took up what Archer hoped were protective positions around the eleven surviving Starfleet ships.

"The Romulans have come to a relative stop," Malcolm said, keeping a weather eye on his tactical displays. "Thirty-eight vessels, keeping station at about one point five AU."

"Sensors confirm a distance of approximately 225 million kilometers," T'Pol added.

"They could come back within weapons range in a matter of seconds," Malcolm said.

"I doubt they'll do that before they've taken a good, long look at the new arrivals," Archer said. "But keep a close eye on them just the same, Malcolm."

"Aye, sir."

"T'Pol, how many ships have just dropped in on us?" Archer asked.

"A total of thirty-one," she said. "Their weapons remain active, but none of them is directing any sign of aggression toward us."

"Allies," Malcolm said. "Well, better late than never."

"The more the merrier," Archer said with a nod, wondering if he might summon another appropriate cliché or two. The image of an unfamiliar ship, apparently a beat-up freighter of some kind, was moving slowly across the main viewer.

Archer frowned as he studied it. "Do we have any idea where these ships came from?"

"It is an extremely heterogeneous group of vessels," said T'Pol, staring into her scanner. "All, apparently, have recently received significant weapons upgrades. In addition to a number of configurations that do not appear in the Vulcan ship database, I'm reading several obsolete military vessels of Klingon and Andorian manufacture, both large and small. As well as a number of Klingon and Andorian cargo ships."

Klingon, Archer thought as a grin spread slowly across his face. *Andorian.*

"Commodore, I'm receiving two simultaneous hails," Hoshi said.

"Put them both on the screen, Hoshi," Archer said. "Conference mode."

A moment later, the image of black space dappled by spacecraft and stars vanished, replaced by a pair of humanoids who were separated from one another by a vertical graphical border. A gaunt, gray-haired Klingon male in civilian clothes scowled from the screen's left side. A hard-eyed, blue-skinned Andorian male in formfitting paramilitary garb—sans any Imperial Guard insignia, Archer noticed—glowered from the right.

"Advocate Kolos," Archer said. "And General Shran. This is quite a surprise."

Kolos, the Klingon defense attorney to whom Archer owed his life, spoke in a tone deeper and richer than his aged body appeared capable of generating. *"Captain Archer,"* he said with a snaggletoothed grin. *"I did caution you not to expect any official Klingon help. The assemblage of Klingon freebooters, military outcasts, and escaped but penitent criminals that I have gathered may be as far from official as one can possibly get. Regardless, we Klingons are creatures of duty, any lack of imprimatur from the chancellor or the High Council notwithstanding."*

"Thank you," Archer said, his voice catching slightly in his throat. "You and your people have taken a hell of a risk on our behalf."

The convolutions of Kolos's brow deepened noticeably. *"By venturing out to your Romulan front? Or by defying the High Council's decision to leave Starfleet to fend for itself?"*

"Both," Archer said.

Kolos chuckled as he raised and lowered his broad but bony shoulders in an apparent shrug. *"Both risks are preferable to the alternative of embracing the High Council's dishonor, which would have cost all of us the privilege of entering Sto-Vo-Kor. If you ever reach my advanced age, Captain, you will come to understand the importance of such considerations."*

His antennae moving in slowly accelerating circles that

Archer interpreted as mounting impatience, Shran cut in. *"My people are all likewise displeased with Andoria's decision to abandon Earth to the Romulan cutthroats."*

Archer nodded, keeping his expression otherwise neutral. "I understand, Shran. Which is why I will direct my gratitude toward you and your people, rather than to your government. Besides, I don't want to get you into any trouble back home."

"For helping you? Or for caravanning with Klingon pirates?"

Archer smiled. "Take your pick. Or you could just say I don't want to give Andorian Foreign Minister Thoris an opportunity to deny that you were ever here."

A smile split Shran's cerulean features, revealing his even white teeth. His antennae probed gently forward. *"It's more likely Thoris would attempt to take credit for routing the Romulans."*

Archer's smile fell in on itself. "Let's not get ahead of ourselves, General. I wouldn't exactly describe the Romulans as 'routed.'"

"Perhaps not yet," Shran said, his expression suddenly as cold as the grave.

"There's another incoming message, Commodore," Hoshi said, interrupting.

"Please excuse me," Archer said to both men on the screen. Almost in unison, Kolos and Shran nodded, and their images abruptly vanished, replaced by the stars, portions of the combined Starfleet-Klingon-Andorian force, and the great black emptiness that enfolded both.

Moving to the comm station, Archer said, "Who's contacting us?"

"It's a subspace burst with an ID marker I've seen only a couple of times before," Hoshi said, looking puzzled. "It's already stopped."

"Damn," Archer whispered.

"But I managed to capture most of it."

"Most of it?"

"The transmission definitely came from the Romulan flagship. Because of that, our latest communications security protocols shunted the message into a special memory buffer designed to screen out incoming Romulan malware. The transmission was in the process of being purged from the buffer when I noticed the name attached to the message header: Lazarus, a name I've seen only twice before. I assume it belongs to the author."

Lazarus. That name froze time in its tracks. It belonged to a dear friend who, like his namesake, had cheated death. Twice before, Charles Tucker III had used that alias to bring important information to Archer's attention.

Trip's on the Romulan flagship? Archer thought. *But why? How?*

He said, "There must be more to this message than the name."

Hoshi nodded and began tapping commands into her console with the speed and grace of a concert pianist. "There is. Whoever sent this embedded several strings of code sequences into the message. Not all of it survived our security 'watchdog's bite,' but I unscrambled the remainder using a standard Starfleet decryption key."

"Interesting," T'Pol said. Archer's exec had approached Hoshi's station only moments after he had. As she watched the strings of numerals and other characters parade across the primary linguistics display, she added, "The text appears to be a string of computer commands. Raw machine code."

"This still could be just another Romulan attempt to take control of our systems remotely," Hoshi said. "In fact, I'm not sure what else it *could* be, since there don't seem to be any instructions embedded inside it."

"I'd probably think it's a trap," Archer said, "except for the name that's attached to the message."

"'Lazarus,'" Hoshi repeated, nodding. "I'm assuming that's the name of some sort of double agent, or deep-cover spy."

"I'm afraid I can't tell you, Hoshi," Archer said.

The comm officer held up a hand. "I don't want to know," she deadpanned. "It's never good to stumble onto anything that's above your security clearance."

"Send the message to my ready room, Hoshi," Archer said, then turned to face the tactical station. "Malcolm, you have the bridge. Coordinate repair efforts aboard *Enterprise* and throughout the fleet. And alert me if the Romulans so much as sneeze in the meantime."

"Aye, sir."

Archer strode toward the situation room located just aft of the bridge. "T'Pol, you're with me. We're going to figure out what the hell this information is supposed to do. And if it really came from Lazarus."

"I am confident that it did," T'Pol said from a few paces behind.

Archer heard a thump and turned in time to see T'Pol staggering away from a railing she appeared to have just collided with. He rushed toward her, catching her as she pitched forward, limp and unconscious.

Damn you Vulcans, he thought, *and your delusions of invulnerability.*

"Hoshi, call Phlox. T'Pol needs medical attention, *now.*"

Warbird Dhhae

"Taken together, the *hevam* and their new allies now outnumber us," Subcommander Threl said. He gestured toward the image of the cluster of enemy vessels depicted three-dimensionally in the small holo-imager atop Valdore's desk. "Perhaps we should consider waiting for our reinforcements to arrive before renewing the offensive, lest we sustain even more serious losses. Otherwise we may not be able to continue to ensure the safety of all seven of the *avaihh lli vastam* vessels."

Seated behind the bulky desk in his private office, Valdore wasn't convinced. Nor was he eager any longer to protect the high-warp vessels as though they were so many fragile *mogai* eggs. Despite the constant efforts of his technologists, including Mr. Cunaehr, none of the vessels had yet reached the speeds of which they were supposedly capable.

"Waiting for reinforcements would take up more than a dayturn." Valdore said. "S'Task would not have sanctioned such timidity."

"Perhaps, Admiral. But I would be remiss in my duty were I not to point out that we have only thirty-eight spaceworthy ships now, to their forty-two.

Valdore waved his large right hand dismissively. "Many of the *hevam*-allied vessels are far smaller and less well-armed than our warbirds. There is no reason to delay—"

The door buzzer sounded, interrupting Valdore's argument. He tapped a button on his desk, and the entrance hatch hissed open.

Subcenturion T'Velekh stepped into the chamber, saluted, and stared straight ahead. "Admiral, we have traced the unauthorized transmission to its source."

Valdore nodded, though he did not attempt to conceal his displeasure at the lengthy span of time the task had taken.

"And?"

"It originated from Mister Cunaehr's secure quarters. Unfortunately, the information he transmitted was encrypted, so we have yet to determine the signal's content. But it was clearly aimed at the *hevam* fleet. Specifically at *En'ter'priz.*"

Valdore was sorely tempted to draw his Honor Blade. Instead, he dismissed the subcenturion. When he was once again alone with Threl, he said, "Those quarters must have been something other than secure."

Threl looked stricken. "Mister Cunaehr may have discovered a hitherto unknown method of gaining access to the communications grid, Admiral. He is, after all, quite a clever engineer."

Yes, the admiral thought. *So clever that he might have been directly responsible for some of the losses we just sustained in battle.* He wondered whether his fleet would have suffered a more than fifty percent reduction had Cunaehr not been aboard, plying his evil trade.

"Not for much longer, Threl." Leaning forward, Valdore punched a button, opening up a comm channel.

"Colonel T'Luadh here, Admiral," said the voice on the channel's other end.

"Your charge has just proved himself a thoroughgoing traitor, T'Laudh," Valdore said in a quiet growl. "Kill him."

There was a pause on the comm, and he wondered if that, too, might be attributable to Cunaehr's cursed tampering.

"But he has not yet completed his work bringing the new ships up to full speed," T'Luadh replied.

Had Cunaehr ever had any intention of making the *Ejhoi Ormiin's* seven high-warp prototype ships fully operational? Valdore bared his teeth as he decided that this no longer mattered to him.

"No one is indispensable, Colonel. Cunaehr tried to communicate with our enemies, and he will pay the price for that crime. Do you understand?"

"It will be done, Admiral. At once. T'Luadh out."

Valdore rose and faced Threl, meeting his gaze squarely. "Back to the business at hand. We will grind *En'ter'priz,* Starfleet, and their ragtag allies beneath our heels. By the time our reinforcements arrive, we will be ready to sweep across the Coalition and lay waste to the *hevam* homeworld itself.

"Advise me the moment you are ready to renew the attack."

TWENTY-NINE

Enterprise NX-01

ARCHER WATCHED THE FIGURES that Hoshi Sato and Donna O'Neill were running through their paces across the many monitor screens that festooned the situation room. "It's definitely software," Hoshi said as she worked. "An executable computer program."

"I'm not sure that was ever seriously in doubt," O'Neill said. "What *I'd* like to know is this: If this . . . program really did come to us from a secret ally aboard the Romulan flagship, and if it really is capable of sabotaging their fleet, then why didn't this mysterious 'Lazarus' simply put it to use himself instead of handing it off to us?"

Archer spread his hands. "There could be any number of reasons. Maybe he can't do it without rousing suspicion. Sending a quick burst transmission to us—and trusting us to figure out the rest—might have been his only real option."

"Or maybe this 'Lazarus' isn't actually the friendly we're assuming him to be," O'Neill said. "Sir."

"So far, I'm satisfied that Lazarus is playing on the same team we are," Archer said. "I'm much more interested at the moment in figuring out exactly what all this code is supposed to *do*."

"*That* question might be even tougher to answer," O'Neill said. "The software didn't come with a user's manual. And with Commander T'Pol injured . . ." She trailed off, looking embarrassed.

"It's all right, D.O.," Archer said, placing a reassuring hand on her shoulder. "T'Pol would be up here with us if she could. But I have faith that you two will have this mystery cracked before she wakes up and Phlox declares her fit."

O'Neill's lamentation about T'Pol's absence was more trenchant than she knew. If T'Pol were conscious and working with the team on the current problem, then the mind-link she shared with Trip probably already would have restored any data that *Enterprise*'s security protocols had deleted from the transmission. And it doubtless also would have provided Trip's own expert technical guidance in putting the information to its best and highest use.

Until T'Pol was back among them, they were on their own.

"Is it possible that this is a Romulan security key?" Archer asked, addressing nobody in particular. "Maybe it's their equivalent to our new prefix-code system."

"Makes sense to me," O'Neill said. "After all, burglars always buy the best locks."

"I've been thinking along the same lines," Hoshi said, her eyes never leaving the fast-moving parade of machine code on the large monitor before her.

Archer found a ray of hope in that. "We already have a piece of Romulan-compatible command-and-control technology at our disposal, thanks to our run-ins with their drone ships before the war. As far as I know, it's still hooked into the communications grid. Maybe we can use that in conjunction with this software."

Hoshi paused the data and looked over her shoulder at him. "You mean to send our own commands to *their* ships' control consoles?"

"Why not?" Archer said with a grin. "It would serve them right if they got bitten by their own snake."

"It's a great idea," O'Neill said. "But I'll be damned if I can think of a way to test it."

"I know one way," Hoshi said. She returned to her figures, which resumed their quick scrolling in response to her ministrations over the console. "I'll show you in five minutes."

"All right," Hoshi said, visibly crestfallen. "I guess that idea worked better on paper."

Archer sat in silence, watching the image of what remained of the Romulan fleet—still a considerable force, roughly on par with the Starfleet-allied fleet that kept station near Cheron—as it hung in space, each vessel seeming to maintain a predator's hungry vigil.

"Where's the *kaboom*?" Travis asked. "Shouldn't the Romulans be powering up their weapons and firing on each other by now?"

"That *was* the plan," Archer said with a sigh.

"I was really looking forward to using the Romulans' own tactical systems against them," Malcolm said. "Have you noticed those seven ships they've kept to the rear throughout this entire engagement? They appear to be of an entirely new configuration, and the Romulans seem to be going to considerable cost to make certain none of them receives so much as a scratch."

In fact, Archer *had* noticed that, almost right from the beginning.

Seven ships, he thought, pondering the strange numerical coincidence. He said, "I wonder if those are the seven ships Starfleet thinks have warp-seven engines."

"I think we can't afford to dismiss the possibility, Commodore," Malcolm said. "I recommend we make them priority targets, preferably for capture."

Archer nodded. "It doesn't seem likely that we're going to get our hands on them anytime soon."

"Because we've evidently misinterpreted something about this software that Lazarus sent us," Malcolm said. "Perhaps it isn't designed to affect command-and-control systems at all. Perhaps it's really an elaborate weapon aimed at *us*."

"I don't think so," Hoshi said. "It's still not showing any sign of trying to migrate into other systems aboard *Enterprise*. Maybe we just haven't sent it the right commands yet."

"We've ordered them to lower their deflector shields and open fire on one another," Malcolm said. "Starting with their flagship."

A vertical line on the main viewer split the image area into two large squares. On the left was the static image of the Romulan front line provided through subspace by the long-range sensors. On the right was an incomplete wireframe rendering of the fierce, horseshoe crab–shaped hull of the vessel Malcolm had identified as the central coordinator of the Romulans' forces. Text callouts and lines pointed out the specific locations of the vessel's various components—each datum acquired at tremendous cost to both Starfleet and the MACO.

Whatever advantage Archer had hoped would emerge from Lazarus's unexpected gift seemed to evaporate before his eyes. Without a miracle, frankly, given the battered and depleted condition of his fleet and the long odds against Starfleet's thinly spread forces arriving soon and in significant numbers, even the reinforcements that Shran and Kolos had provided were unlikely to make much difference in the coming battle.

"Long-range sensors show the Romulan fleet's weapons heating up," O'Neill reported from the science station.

"Maybe our little gambit is finally working," Hoshi said. "Thank you, Mister Lazarus, whoever you are."

"Perhaps the command codes needed a little time to work their magic," Malcolm said.

O'Neill let out a whoop. "If we were right about this, then we should see some lovely fireworks soon." But the grin on her face collapsed only a few moments later. "Oh, crap."

Like O'Neill, Malcolm's expression abruptly turned grim. "They're not firing. They're *accelerating*. Going to warp."

"Speed?" Archer said.

"A little better than warp two," Malcolm said. "They'll be on top of us in approximately eighty seconds. And their weapons will be hot when they arrive."

"Alert the fleet, as well as Kolos and Shran," Archer ordered as he turned from Hoshi. "Tactical Alert. Power up shields and polarize hull plating. Lock and load all batteries."

As his crew and those on the other ships carried out his orders, Archer sat back in his command chair and continued studying the warbird's schematic. As his eyes moved from system to system, finally coming to the antimatter-containment component, an idea occurred to him.

Leaning forward, Archer turned toward Malcolm. "So far we've been concentrating on ordering the Romulan systems to *do* things."

"Well, that *was* the general idea, sir," said the armory officer with a bemused frown. "What alternative is there?"

"Since we still have a few seconds before the Romulans get here," Archer said. "Let's send an order *not* to do something."

Warbird Dabhae

Approximately a heartbeat after the *Dabhae* went to warp, an alarm klaxon began shrieking.

Valdore turned his command chair so that it faced the tactical station behind which Subcommander Threl was working frantically.

Threl had gone pale. But at least he'd managed to mute the klaxon before it awakened the dead.

"What's wrong?" Valdore barked. This was a most inopportune time for alarm malfunctions, or for hysterics among the senior staff.

Threl looked up from his console, and Valdore saw a light of fear shining in his eyes. "Our antimatter containment system is failing, Admiral. Destruction is nearly upon us."

"That's not possible," Valdore growled.

"Look for yourself, Admiral." Threl gestured at the console before him.

Valdore approached the console and swore when he saw the displays.

"I want you to track down the source of the fault," Valdore said. "Repair it."

"Admiral!" Threl said, desperation coloring his tone. "We have very little time before the engine core breaches explosively. We should abandon ship."

"Abandon ship? So that our enemies can swoop in and pick off our escape pods like so many lobe-finned *in'hhui* along the northern Apnex shore?"

Threl made a subtle adjustment to the small receiver that dangled from his right ear. "I have begun receiving calls from other ships in the fleet. We aren't the only vessel to experience this . . . difficulty."

Valdore realized that this could be no mere malfunction or accident. Someone was responsible. The culprit had to be Cunaehr. Or *En'ter'priz*. Or perhaps both.

"Drop us out of warp," Valdore shouted. "Order the rest of the fleet to do likewise."

And if we cannot resolve our engine trouble immediately thereafter, he thought, *then I will make certain this vessel takes Archer with us on the voyage to cold Erebus.*

The hefty disruptor pistol that T'Luadh was aiming at his head made it more than a little difficult for Trip to concentrate on what she was saying.

"Before you do anything I might regret," Trip said, "don't you think we ought to find out what that alarm was all about?"

"Forgive me," she said, "but this will take only a moment. If I fail to carry out Valdore's order, suspicion will fall upon *me*."

"I get it. This is just business. Nothing personal. But—"

"I am deeply sorry for what I must do now," she said, interrupting him as she raised the gray metal weapon higher and tightened her grip on its handle.

He raised his hands reflexively to remind her that he was no threat, especially here in what amounted to a glorified Romulan brig. "You're *sorry*, T'Luadh? Why is that? Could it be because you're actually a Vulcan operative working under deep cover?"

Her eyebrows both went aloft in surprise, but her gun hand never wavered. "Why would you say that?"

"Come on. Did you really think I didn't notice that mind-meld you sneaked on me a few months back, when we were working together in the Carraya sector? I've never met a Romulan who knew that trick."

She nodded. "I see."

Oh, crap, he thought. *I didn't give her a reason to spare me. I gave her an entirely new reason to pull the trigger on that hog leg and incinerate me with it.*

At that moment he felt a subtle change in the vibrations beneath his booted feet. A distant alarm blared.

"Wait a second," he said.

She frowned, puzzled, or perhaps merely annoyed. "What?"

"You feel that? We've dropped back out of warp. And we only went to warp maybe a minute ago."

She shrugged. "Valdore must have his reasons."

"It's an opportunity for you, T'Luadh. You don't have to regret anything if you put me in an escape pod now. You can't launch 'em at warp, you know."

She shook her head sadly. "Valdore might discover the deception. In that event, my life would be less than worthless."

"Trust me, Valdore has his hands full at the moment," Trip said. Judging from the alarm klaxon, and the short duration of the *Dabhae*'s most recent warp flight, the admiral should be preoccupied trying to discover why every warp core in the fleet just went into an unexplained state of antimatter-containment failure, only just as mysteriously to return to normal after returning to subwarp speed.

He suppressed a triumphant grin as he digested another implication of the emergency warp shutdown. It meant that he and Captain Archer were on the same page. His subspace burst to *Enterprise* had been received and understood.

"You would say anything to stay alive, Mister Tucker," she said, still aiming the weapon squarely at his head. Only a meter or so separated them, but there was no question that she would get off a fatal shot if he made any aggressive moves.

"Damned straight I would," he said. "But the fact remains: You don't have to do this. You can tell Valdore that you vaporized me. Hell, you don't even have to admit that I was right about your Vulcan pedigree. You can chalk the whole thing up to some sealed, secret Tal Shiar order that you're not authorized to discuss, even with Valdore."

Her eyes narrowed into a squint. Trip kept his hands up but closed his eyes tightly; if he'd misjudged her, he didn't want the last thing he saw to be the disruptor beam that cooked him alive.

"All right," he heard her say. He opened his eyes and dropped his hands when he saw that she had lowered her weapon. "Come with me, Mister Tucker. Quickly."

"I wish you'd stop using that name," he stage whispered as he followed her out into the corridor.

Enterprise **NX-01**

"The Romulan fleet is coming out of warp," Malcolm said, looking up from behind his tactical displays. "All thirty-eight vessels have dropped back into normal space, approximately two light-minutes from our current position. They're still closing, but only at one-quarter impulse. They'll enter weapons range in about eight minutes."

Archer stared appraisingly at the central viewer, which at the moment was using wireframe icons to show the relative positions of both fleets with respect to Cheron.

"Something tells me they put on the brakes a little ahead of schedule," Travis said.

"Based on the Romulans' usual tactics," Malcolm said, "I'd bet real money on that."

But Archer knew from experience never to underestimate a Romulan commander.

"Look sharp, everybody," he said. "It looks like we've just gained some time before the fireworks start up again. But I'm sure the Romulans are busy right now looking for ways to use that time against us. You never know what tricks they might still have up their sleeves."

As if on cue, three of the incoming Romulan warbird icons on the viewer began flashing rapidly, creating a strobing effect reminiscent of a pulsar.

"What the hell?" Archer wanted to know. "Show me what's going on out there."

The tactical wireframes wavered and vanished, replaced a split second later by real-time imagery received via the subspace band by the long-range sensors. The image settled down just in time for Archer to see a Romulan warbird explode. Two of its adjacent sister ships did likewise almost immediately, bringing to mind strings of firecrackers going off, each detonation setting off the next. All three vessels had evidently just finished launching large numbers of escape pods, which were spreading out in a cone-shaped pattern, like seeds blown from a dandelion. A pair of battle-scarred but apparently still intact warbirds broke from the rest of the fleet to begin the doubtless time-consuming task of using tractor beams to gather up the pods, one by one.

"Let's hope they pull a few more tricks like *that* one out of their sleeves," Travis said, gesturing toward the screen. Three clouds of metal fragments and flash-frozen atmosphere slowly expanded as inertia carried them forward with the rest of the Romulan fleet, forcing its formation to loosen for safety's sake.

"I wouldn't count on it," Malcolm said. "My guess is that the ships that just exploded were among the most damaged in their fleet. The Lazarus protocols we transmitted did them in, but only indirectly."

"Meaning that their antimatter-containment systems weren't up to standing down from 'imminent warp-core breach' status," said Travis.

"Which begs the question: How many more of their ships are in nearly as bad shape as those three?" Malcolm said.

O'Neill spoke up a moment later. "And *that* question begs another one: Should we launch an immediate all-out attack? We *do* have about a twenty percent edge over them now, sir."

Archer continued staring at the menacing phalanx of horseshoe crab–shaped vessels and considered his options.

"It might look as though we have a numerical advantage at the moment, D.O.," he said at length, "but that's only in terms of raw numbers of ships. The Romulans probably still have us outgunned, Shran's irregulars and Kolos's freebooters notwithstanding.

"Let's sit tight, stay ready, and see what the Romulans do next."

And hope like hell for another cavalry charge.

Warbird Dabhae

Standing uneasily in the empty causeway, Trip wasn't entirely sure of the sincerity of T'Luadh's change of heart until she used the wall-mounted keypad to open the hatch. Moving cautiously, he peered inside to satisfy himself that the interior of an escape pod, rather than that of an empty airlock, lay on the other side of the aperture.

"So I *was* right about you," he said as he moved onto the escape pod's threshold and turned back to look at her. "You've got to be working for the Vulcans. Otherwise you'd never have agreed to let me go."

Her neutral expression darkened into a glower as she holstered her disruptor pistol. "Hurry, Commander Tucker. Neither of us wants anyone to observe your departure."

He grinned. "You're still denying your connection to Vulcan? After rescuing me? After the mind-meld you performed?"

"Never make assumptions." She suddenly became a blur of motion. With one hand, she removed a small object from a pouch attached to the belt of her black paramilitary uniform. With the other hand, she pushed Trip hard in the chest, sending him reeling backward to get him clear of the hatchway. With a sibilant pneumatic hiss, the hatch began to close.

Trip fell awkwardly to the escape pod's hard deck. As he rose, he realized that something had tumbled inside with him. Belatedly he recognized it as the object T'Luadh had pulled from her belt. Suspicious of the thing he now held in his hand, he faced the hatchway. It was sealed, and T'Luadh was no longer visible through the narrow porthole.

Next he heard a loud *bang*, then fell against the hatch as the escape pod launched and the forces of acceleration made the pod rock and shimmy, pinning him in place. Somehow, he never lost his grip on the object that T'Luadh had tossed into the pod.

It must be a beacon, he thought, trying to calm his mounting anxiety. *Probably set to a Vulcan frequency. I bet all I have to do is find the switch that activates it.*

The object was a gray metallic ovoid roughly twice the size of an egg, and a recessed panel opened in response to a push from his thumb, which almost immediately fell upon a small internal button.

Let's see what frequency this baby broadcasts on, he thought as he pushed the button and brought the device near his face to take a look at its digital display.

Instead of the flowing, musiclike Vulcan script he'd expected, he saw a slow succession of numerals.

Romulan numerals, changing at a rate of roughly one per second as they counted down inexorably. It was clear to him immediately that he didn't want to be anywhere near this object when it ticked down to the Romulan equivalent of zero. But there seemed to be no way to chuck the thing overboard without depressurizing the pod and dying of asphyxia.

"Shit," Trip muttered. "I *hate* when this happens."

An instant later, a blinding white light flooded the universe.

THIRTY

Enterprise NX-01

THE SHOUT FROM THE BIOBED behind him startled Phlox, nearly making him drop the container he had been filling with Regulan bloodworms.

"Trip!" T'Pol shrieked, pulling the restraints so taut that Phlox feared she might injure herself. Her eyes were open wide, her tone one of terror. "He's out there!"

Phlox knew that the Vulcan healing process usually passed through a critical stage during which the body concentrated all of its prodigious energies on repairing injured tissues. At this time, the patient faced the very real danger of forever losing the ability to return to full consciousness. Though he had always found it counterintuitive, Phlox knew that all it usually took was a few well-timed, open-handed blows to the face to shepherd most Vulcans through this crisis.

What he *hadn't* expected was that T'Pol would reach the crisis portion of her recovery so soon.

"Trip!" she cried again, still straining against the biobed straps. "We have to find his escape pod."

Phlox quickly released her restraints, grabbed her arm, and pulled her up into a sitting position so that her legs dangled over the edge of the biobed. He drew his right hand back.

"Forgive me, Commander," he said before releasing a

vicious slap across her face. He gave her another with the back of his hand, then repeated the process, forehand, backhand, forehand, backhand. All the while, she continued speaking about Commander Tucker, insisting that he was in danger, that he was in an escape pod, that *Enterprise* had to find him.

As he prepared to initiate another slap, T'Pol reached out and caught his arm, immobilizing it in an iron grip.

"Thank you, Doctor," she said. Her eyes focused, and an appearance of calm and rationality returned to her. He urged her to lie back on the biobed while he examined her, and she complied with what seemed to Phlox to be the greatest reluctance. Though the burns on her face were scarcely noticeable now thanks to the treatment he had administered, both with dermal regeneration gel and his osmotic eel, he wanted to check for any lingering internal injuries.

"You might not remember any of this, Commander," he said as he ran his scanner over her head and chest and checked the readings. "But in your, ah, delirium, you mentioned Commander Tucker several times."

She sat up abruptly, as though he had just reminded her of an important task she'd forgotten. "That's because I know where he is."

"That seems unlikely, Commander," Phlox said. "You've sustained a serious trauma, and such injuries can distort the normal operation of sense and memory."

"I know where Trip is," she repeated as she got to her feet. He reflexively reached out to steady her, but she shook him off. "Where is my uniform?"

"I don't think—"

Her brows folded downward, casting sinister shadows across her face. Beneath the brows, her eyes were twin flames.

"My uniform, Phlox. I'm needed on the bridge. Otherwise Commander Tucker may not have much longer to live."

✿   ✿   ✿

"I'm afraid she insisted, Captain," Phlox said, the comm speaker built into the arm of Archer's chair conveying the doctor's intense concern. *"She's become convinced that a certain . . . mutual friend has left the Romulan flagship in an escape pod. And that this individual is in imminent danger if we fail to intervene on his behalf."*

Trip? Archer thought. "Understood, Doctor. Thanks for the heads-up."

At that moment, the turbolift hatchway hissed open and a surprisingly well-poised T'Pol stepped onto the bridge. Without pausing to acknowledge the presence of either her captain or crewmates, she made a beeline to the science console. Commander O'Neill stepped away from the station, and T'Pol immediately began running the scanners without saying so much as a word.

Archer quietly approached his exec, concerned. "T'Pol, are you all right?"

"Lazarus is out there," she said. "In an escape pod."

He leaned in close to her and matched both her tone and her volume. "You've probably noticed by now that the Romulans have launched a whole bunch of escape pods, and they've already gotten busy with recovery operations. Finding a particular pod in a hurry might be a real challenge. Besides, what do you intend to do if you find it?"

"We'll use the transporter. We'll beam him aboard."

"T'Pol, you're not being . . . logical," Archer whispered, shaking his head. "We're nowhere near within transporter range."

She turned from the scanner display and faced him. Jabbing at a specific dot on her screen, she said, "That's the one. I'm certain of it. We have t—"

A shout from Malcolm interrupted her. "The Romulan fleet has just entered weapons range, Commodore. They're powering up their forward tubes."

"The fleet reports ready at Tactical Alert," Hoshi reported from the comm station. "Hull plating polarized. Shields engaged. Weapons locked and loaded."

Archer straightened and nodded to Malcolm. "Fire at will." Turning to Hoshi, he said, "And direct the fleet to do the same."

"Incoming fire, Commodore," Malcolm said an instant before the lights cut out and the deck pitched abruptly forward.

Warbird Dhabhae

As his fleet began slicing through the forward ranks of the *hevam* and their allies, Valdore felt the approving breath of the *haein* upon him.

How could it be otherwise? The gods of his ancestors had to smile upon any venture that purged the Romulan Star Empire's Outmarches of the mongrel, marginally sentient races who would surely try to annex them.

"The enemy force has been cut in half yet again, Admiral," Subcommander Threl reported.

"Our losses?" Valdore asked.

"A total of six warbirds thus far. The *avaihh lli vastam* vessels remain safely in the rear as we continue driving the enemy toward the system's periphery and away from Cheron's orbit."

It was a triumph. Except for one thing. And its image mocked him from the command deck's central viewer.

"*En'ter'priz* remains in one piece, Subcommander," Valdore growled. "Once you remedy that situation, the residue of the enemy force will lose whatever remains of its will to fight."

Threl bowed his helmeted head as he saluted. "It will be done, Admiral."

"Target her bridge," Valdore said.

Subcenturion T'Velekh spoke up from the sensor station. "I'm reading a large number of incoming warp signatures, Admiral."

"The reinforcements," Valdore said, his spirits rising. "Hail them."

Enterprise NX-01

His nostrils assaulted by the stench of fire and ozone, Archer found it nothing short of miraculous that nobody on the bridge was dead. But he knew death would come soon enough.

In the ruddy semidarkness of the bridge's emergency lights, he sat on the half of his command chair that the falling ceiling beam hadn't clipped. Having only one armrest felt extraordinarily awkward. The main viewscreen flickered and filled with momentary bursts of static as they conveyed a stark real-time portrait of what was going on all around *Enterprise*.

A pair of *Daedalus*-class ships, the *Armstrong* and the *A. G. Robinson*, completed their death throes in the viewer's foreground. Both vessels yielded almost simultaneously to the structural stresses caused by cascades of internal systems failures, a result of the pitiless impacts of countless pieces of Romulan ordnance. In the distance, a nuclear explosion flared; Archer could see fragments of at least four other *Daedalus*-class vessels tumbling away from the expanding orange sphere of the conflagration.

It struck him then just how calm and emotionally disconnected he had become as he contemplated the end that was surely coming for everyone aboard *Enterprise*, not to mention the remainder of the fleet. His crew needed him. He owed them all the dignity of staying busy, fighting until the end.

"T'Pol, status?" Archer said.

"Twelve ships remain in our combined force," she said. "Shran's vessel is intact but has been disabled. Kolos's ship was destroyed, and much of his force has been scattered or disabled."

Archer nodded. "And the Romulans?"

"They outnumber us more than two to one, sir," Malcolm said, his soot-smeared face the epitome of British stoicism. "And most of their ships have taken less damage than we have."

We're done, Archer thought. *I might as well order anybody still capable of going to warp to withdraw.*

He opened his mouth to give the order.

He found he couldn't get it out.

"The Romulan flagship is closing on us, Commodore," Malcolm shouted. "Targeting the bridge!"

"Evasive, Travis!" Archer cried, and grabbed his chair's right armrest as the hull groaned and the slight delay in the overstrained inertial dampers kept his stomach a few critical milliseconds behind the rest of his body. The bridge rocked and shuddered again as the lights dimmed and something struck the primary hull with unbridled savagery.

"Hull breaches on Decks B through D," T'Pol said. "Engines are offline."

Under circumstances such as these, Archer knew that once the warp drive failed, the impulse engines wouldn't be far behind. Still, it felt surreal to hear that that had happened.

"Life support is now on tertiary backup," O'Neill reported. "Battery power only."

"Helm's gone dead, too," Travis said.

"Same with the hull plating, shields, and most of the tactical system," Malcolm said. "Sensors are still working, at least for the moment. I'm reading a number of incoming warp signatures. More than thirty vessels."

"Starfleet?" Archer said, though he no longer held out any real hope.

"I'm afraid not, sir," Malcolm said, his tone and manner funereal.

Of course, the captain thought. *On the plus side, at least I won't have to put up with this "Commodore" business for much longer.*

"T'Pol, I need a positive ID on those ships," Archer said.

"Sensor resolution is less than optimal at the moment," T'Pol said. "It may be attributable to battle damage. However, I have determined that the incoming vessels have begun coming out of warp. They are still on an approach vector, at high impulse."

"Hoshi, hail them," Archer said.

"I just tried, sir," said the communications officer. "It's no good. The comm system can't deliver much power at the moment. And the Romulans appear to be jamming us."

"Can we get a look at the incoming ships?" Archer said, gesturing at the main viewscreen. At the moment, it displayed only a chaotic hash of static.

Malcolm said, "I think so." He began entering commands into his console, and the big screen slowly and grudgingly yielded an expansive image of ship debris, scorched Romulan vessels, and the star-bejeweled blackness beyond.

One of the warbirds was making a leisurely, looping turn. Archer recognized it as the flagship that had done so much damage with its previous salvo. Very soon, she would come about and, presumably, deliver the coup de grâce.

Archer suddenly became aware that every eye on the bridge was now fixed squarely upon him.

They understand that we're all about to die, he thought. *And they need me to either summon a miracle or say something to make the end a little less terrifying.*

Turning slowly in a full circle, he looked around the ruined bridge, fixing in his mind the image of each crew member.

"It's truly been an honor serving with you all," he said at length. The acrid air filled with murmurs of agreement.

Most remarkable, he thought, was the almost complete absence of any overt signs of fear—even from Hoshi, who had from time to time expressed diffidence about facing the unknown. It occurred to him only then just how far they all had come over the past decade.

"I see *something* on the viewer," Travis said, pointing.

"The incoming vessels," Malcolm said. "Boosting the magnification to maximum."

Archer could see the approaching ships only indistinctly. As the swelling multitude of craft steadily grew before his eyes, his first impression was of streamlined cylinders.

Dozens and dozens of cylinders unevenly bisected by

the circular propulsion assemblies that ringed their cigarlike aft sections.

Archer could scarcely believe what he was seeing. *Dozens and dozens of—*

"Vulcans, sir!" Malcolm cried, completing Archer's thought as a great whoop went up across the dark and smoking bridge.

The phalanx of Vulcan ships had been accompanied by other vessels whose designs Archer quickly recognized. The long, dual-nacelled lines of Andorian heavy cruisers, ships whose sleek forward sections reminded him of the business end of a terrestrial Venus flytrap, blended in with their Vulcan counterparts with remarkable grace, as did—surprisingly—the rounder and more bulbous shapes of at least ten Tellarite frigates.

The bridge watched in silence as the combined Vulcan-Andorian-Tellarite assemblage took up positions that cut off all immediate avenues of escape for the Romulans save those trajectories that made for easy navigation back to Romulan space.

The newcomers wasted no time opening fire. The Romulan vessels that had survived the earlier phases of this engagement put up a perfunctory fight, but Archer could see right away that their hearts weren't in it.

"The Romulans are withdrawing," Malcolm said. "Those that still *can* withdraw, at any rate."

A nuclear fireball erupted near one of the far edges of the spreading ship-to-ship melee, annihilating no fewer than four of the alleged warp-seven ships that the Romulans had taken such pains to protect. Moments later, three other apparently crippled Romulan vessels initiated the same maneuver, vanishing in globular clouds of orange, fission-generated brilliance as their still-mobile sister ships abruptly brought themselves about before exercising the better part of valor.

Those self-immolations spoke volumes to Archer about the Romulan attitude toward war. This was an adversary that obviously preferred death to the indignity of capture.

Good riddance, you bastards.

He wondered whether Lazarus—Trip—had managed yet again to cheat death while hiding among the enemy.

Crossing to T'Pol's station, he leaned close to her and whispered, "See if you can find Lazarus out there again."

Her eyes seemed to be brimming with unshed tears. "His escape pod . . . exploded."

Archer felt as though he'd been stabbed in the gut. "Was he inside the pod?"

"The sensors have been unreliable, so I found the pod by tracing its previous trajectory," T'Pol said. "When the detonation occurred, I could not tell for certain whether he was in the pod or not."

"Commodore," Malcolm said as he gestured toward the forward viewer.

Archer watched one of the Vulcan ships, a long, flat, ring-tailed *D'Kyr*-class military vessel, spin off from the main group and approach *Enterprise.*

The viewer abruptly went dead, joining the many other systems that had given up. Archer cursed under his breath.

"Captain T'Pak of the Vulcan *Defense Force Cruiser Sepok* wishes to speak with you, sir," Hoshi said. "He asks if we require any assistance."

Archer chuckled, and the sound rolled, snowball-like, until it became a belly laugh. To his relief, he saw that Hoshi, Malcolm, Travis, and D.O. had all joined in, while T'Pol sat at the science console in a silent display of put-upon, long-suffering patience.

Who says that Vulcans don't have a sense of humor? he thought.

After he'd regained some measure of control over himself, Archer said, "Hoshi, please ask Captain T'Pak what gave him the idea that we needed any help."

THIRTY-ONE

Early in the Month of *T'keKhuti,* **YS 8771**
Wednesday, July 30, 2160
Central ShiKahr, Vulcan

"*THANK YOU FOR AGREEING to speak with me, Excellency,*"
Commander T'Pol said from the wide oblong screen that
dominated the subspace transceiver located near the center
of the Administration Tower's top level.

"Not at all, Commander," T'Pau said, noting how tired
and gaunt the blue-uniformed woman on the other end of
the subspace connection appeared. "Are you still aboard
Enterprise?"

"*I am, though there will be little for me to do here until the Sepok
finishes towing us to Earth so that* Enterprise *can be properly
decommissioned.*"

"Will you remain in Starfleet after that, Commander?"
T'Pau asked.

The commander looked almost wistful. "*I haven't decided
yet. Some matters of a personal nature must be resolved first.*"

T'Pau could wait; the commander would doubtless
furnish details if she felt the need to do so.

"I understand, Commander," T'Pau said. "If there
is anything I can do . . ." She trailed off, the end of the
sentence being an obvious rhetorical superfluity.

"*Perhaps there is,*" the younger woman said. "*I have reason to
believe that a close . . . colleague of mine was carrying out a mission of
espionage on the Romulan flagship during the Battle of Cheron. You know
him as Sodok.*"

Despite her well-known emotional control, both of T'Pau's eyebrows rose almost with a volition of their own; Starfleet's only Vulcan officer seemed to be an inexhaustible font of surprises.

"Indeed," T'Pau said, recovering her composure. "It would be gratifying to know that Mister Sodok somehow succeeded in avoiding the fate that befell so many others at Cheron."

"I concur. He appears to have debarked in an escape pod. But it exploded a short time after its launch. I haven't been able to determine whether he was in the pod at the time."

"I will order the Vulcan Defense Directorate to undertake a thorough investigation," T'Pau said. "And I will offer your friends Denak and Ych'a prominent roles in the proceedings."

"Thank you, Administrator," T'Pol said. T'Pau thought for a moment that the commander might be about to weep.

"I have been told that Mister Sodok was . . . *is* your mate," T'Pau said.

It was T'Pol's turn to raise her eyebrows. *"That is true, Administrator."*

"Then may I assume that the two of you were linked in the Syrrannite manner?"

T'Pol nodded. *"We shared a psionic bonding, yes."*

"Does your link persist?" T'Pau knew she didn't need to mention the fact that the death of a mate would immediately break any telepathic marriage bond.

"I am finding it difficult to tell," said T'Pol. *"I suffered some neural trauma during the Cheron engagement. And the other neurological difficulties I experienced years prior to that seem to have compounded the problem."*

"Problem?" T'Pau asked, recalling the *Pa'nar* Syndrome that she had helped the commander overcome several years earlier during the waning hours of the V'Las regime.

"I cannot tell my impressions of the link from mere wishful thinking," T'Pol said. *"It is . . . a most frustrating experience."*

"Do you have reason to believe that anyone—on either side—might have recovered him prior to the pod's explosion?"

"*Not specifically, Excellency,*" T'Pol said, her dark eyes glistening brightly. "*I have only hope.*"

Hope, T'Pau thought, marveling at the commander's unconscious, unrepentant show of emotion. *She has dwelled almost exclusively among humans for far too long.*

She said, "Now that our adversaries are suing for peace, Commander, a visit to your homeworld may be in order. After all, you have earned the thanks of all of Vulcan."

"*Perhaps, Administrator,*" said T'Pol. "*But I am not the one most deserving of gratitude. As you say, the enemy now sues for peace. That is a direct consequence of the breaking of much of the Romulan fleet at Cheron yesterday, both their primary invasion force and their reinforcements. And all of that is a direct result of your decision to commit the Vulcan Defense Force to the conflict.*"

T'Pau had little faith that the Romulan desire for peace was genuine; she knew only too well that they preferred to play a centuries-long game of treachery, conflict, and conquest. They would negotiate a treaty while refusing to show their faces. That made the current Romulan peace overture little more than an insincere bid to buy time, in increments of years or decades, during which they would revert to type by breaking their pledges and going back on the offensive.

"As you have pointed out on numerous occasions," T'Pau said, "it was the only logical decision possible, given the complete dearth of better options. Had the Romulans not been stopped at Cheron, their forces might already be headed for both Vulcan and Earth. Whatever the risks, I could not afford to allow that to happen. I could not allow the Romulans to deny Vulcan its future by denying humanity theirs."

"*I understand.*" T'Pol tipped her head slightly to one side in evident curiosity. *"But I can see that the decision continues to trouble you, even now."*

T'Pau nodded. "Yes. It remains freighted with grave implications. Whether history ultimately judges it a necessity or an indulgence, my decision may yet prove inimical to the Syrannite cause over the long term. Rather than accept accolades uncritically, I must face the possible repercussions honestly."

"I'm sure that Syrran would have told you that regrets are illogical," T'Pol said. *"As would Surak, for that matter."*

"I shall learn to live with my decision," T'Pau said. *Or at least I shall find a way to atone for it.*

"If you will forgive my boldness, Excellency, allow me to suggest that your fears might be unwarranted."

Once again, T'Pau raised both eyebrows. "My *fears,* Commander?"

"Forgive me, Excellency. I chose my words poorly. I merely meant to suggest that your . . . concerns about warfare causing our species to lapse into an earlier, less-evolved condition may be groundless. We aren't Romulans and will never emulate them, either by accident or by design."

"You seem very confident of that." T'Pau experienced a pang of fervid longing for such certainty.

"I am, Administrator. Because unlike the Romulans, who lack the guidance of the Kir'Shara, Vulcan will select its own future, using logic and deliberation to navigate there. Unfortunately, there will be instances when the road to that future requires brief detours."

"Perhaps," T'Pau said with a nod. "But I . . . hope that your observation proves incorrect."

Regardless, T'Pau thought, suddenly feeling more determined than ever before, *the Battle of Cheron is the final act of violence I will ever sanction on Vulcan's behalf.*

THIRTY-TWO

Day Forty-Three, Romulan Month of *T'Ke'Tas*,
   1184 YD'E
Tuesday, September 13, 2160
The Hall of State, Dartha City, Romulus

TERIX KEPT HIS EXPRESSION carefully neutral as he stepped
into the foyer to greet the admiral's visitor.

"I see you have risen steeply in rank since our previous
encounter," First Consul T'Leikha said. She eyed the
new plumage on his collar and then dipped her head in
an imperfect counterfeit of respect. "Congratulations,
Commander. The new rank suits you."

"Such are the vicissitudes of war, First Consul," Terix
said curtly, returning the politician's nod. In truth, Terix
took little pride in his rapid rise through the ranks during
the past few wartime *fvheisn*; the deaths of far too many
good officers, some of his closest friends numbering among
them, had been responsible for a good deal of it.

"Ah, yes," said the First Consul. "The very thing I've
come to see Admiral Valdore about."

Terix nodded. He turned and led the way through a
high archway, his clacking boot heels echoing through the
ancient cavernous building, into an outer vestibule, and
then finally into the personal office of Admiral Valdore.

Still healing from the burns he had sustained at Cheron,
Valdore remained seated behind his huge sherawood desk.
He acknowledged the First Consul's entrance only with his
eyes.

"Admiral," said T'Leikha, visibly annoyed by Valdore's

casual greeting. Terix suppressed a smile, quietly enjoying her discomfiture.

"To what do I owe the pleasure of this visit, First Consul?" Valdore said.

"This isn't a social call, Admiral. I have come to discuss the treaty that the Praetorate is at present allowing the *hevam* to dictate to us."

Since he hadn't been formally dismissed, Terix merely stood at parade rest near the door, quietly watching the exchange.

"The praetor is hardly allowing the Earthmen to dictate terms," Valdore said, still seated because it would have caused him a great deal of pain to stand. Having seen the admiral's wounds, Terix understood how much healing and therapy still lay ahead before Valdore could be considered fully recovered.

T'Leikha began pacing the ancient stone floor that fronted Valdore's desk. "That is not how it appears to many of us on the Continuing Committee of the Senate. First, the cowards have refused to consent to face-to-face negotiations. Not only do they insist that the entire agreement be conducted via the subspace channels, they're restricting us to audio. Our negotiators cannot even look into their eyes as they bargain for the future."

Valdore scowled. "Don't start believing your own party's propaganda, T'Leikha. We're negotiating via the audio subspace channels because the glorious Praetor Karzan insisted upon it. He believes that if the *hevam* ever discover our distant relationship with our *thaessu* brothers—the Vulcans—then they will come to believe that we share their obvious weaknesses."

"Weaknesses that snatched victory from our grasp at Cheron," the First Consul scoffed. "You evacuated Cheron when we could have held it. You have done damage to the fleet that has set our military posture back half a century or more."

"That's ridiculous," Valdore said, visibly angry. "All it really takes to do *that* is a succession of warmongering civilian regimes, such as those that preceded Karzan's."

T'Leikha pointed one of her long, delicate fingers at him as though it were a disruptor pistol. "You go too far, Admiral!"

"*Kllhe'mnhe*," he swore, using language more commonly heard among enlisted uhlanu than among those who wielded the levers of power. "How many of you august members of the Continuing Committee have ever been in uniform, First Consul? How many of you have carried arms in the Empire's service? How many of you have shed your blood securing the Outmarches?"

T'Leikha averted her eyes, looking downward and thereby proving the admiral's point. "It is true what they say about you, then," she said at length. Now Terix heard more sorrow than anger in her tone. "You really *do* lack the heart to defend and expand the Empire."

"Nonsense, First Consul." Valdore's anger appeared to have receded as well, at least somewhat. "But after having spent so much of my career planning and executing the Empire's military adventures, I can see the benefit of putting up a treaty-defined border, with a corresponding demilitarized region."

"The so-called Neutral Zone," T'Leika spat.

"Yes. Karzan appreciates the positive aspects of this as well, First Consul. I find it strange that you do not. Were you not one of the strongest supporters of his ascension to the Praetorate?"

"Perhaps I made my choice too hastily, Admiral. I can see now that Senator Vrax would have been a better candidate."

Terix recognized T'Leikha's words as nothing less than treason. But Valdore chuckled, dismissing her words as though they were merely the gripes of enlisted legionaries.

"Vrax is a foul-tempered old man with a sadly limited imagination," Valdore said. "He would fail to use the Neutral Zone, and the coming interval of peace, to our advantage. On the other hand, Praetor Karzan will make the Neutral Zone an impenetrable curtain, behind which we will work to rebuild everything we have lost to the *hevam*, their Coalition, and Haakona."

"And you will trust the *hevam* and their allies not to go right on expanding their presence, with or without this 'Neutral Zone.'"

Valdore smiled slightly as he shook his head. "It isn't a matter of trust, First Consul. It is a matter of constant vigilance. We will watch them well from our side of the Neutral Zone."

She nodded, and a look of extreme sadness creased her otherwise unlined face. "Just as you are watching me now."

Terix didn't much like the sound of that, so he began moving toward Valdore's desk.

But not in time to prevent her from drawing a forearm-long blade from her sleeve. Almost before Terix realized what was happening, she had thrown the knife with all the skill and grace of a professional assassin. The blade's elegant bone haft protruded from the right side of Valdore's upper abdomen, where it very likely had pierced his heart. The admiral slumped forward across his desk, his face frozen in a rictus of surprise.

"That was for the Empire," she said, glaring at the admiral's bleeding body. "For our humiliation at Cheron, and for the all the future humiliations that you, Praetor Karzan, and the *hevam* would heap upon us all. And for Nijil."

Judging that little could be done for admiral, especially while his killer had yet to be dealt with, Terix drew his Honor Blade.

Then T'Leikha, first consul of the Romulan Senate, turned away from her victim and faced Terix.

"Where do *you* stand, Commander?" she asked, her eyes agleam with a fervor that Terix could interpret only as madness. "With the past or the future?"

Idly wondering whether his next action would gain him yet another promotion or summary execution, he raised his sacred, ritually sharpened *dathe'anofv-sen*—the Honor Blade of his ancestors—in a two-handed grip.

Deciding to let the gods of ancient ch'Rihan sort past from future, he lunged forward.

"I stand," he said as the weapon's lethal downward arc neatly cleaved the first consul's head from her shoulders, "with the Romulan Star Empire."

THIRTY-THREE

Wednesday, November 9, 2160
Earth Outpost 1

FOR UNCOUNTED BILLIONS of years, the battered potato-shaped asteroid had tumbled through the cold depths of interstellar space between yellow Iota Virginis and yellow-white Gamma Tucanae. Today, thanks to the half-decade-old foresight of both the United Earth government and the United Earth Space Probe Agency, as well as the Starfleet Corps of Engineers' diligent application of controlled fusion blasts and high-intensity mining lasers over the past four years, the ancient five-kilometer-long body's nickel-iron interior now boasted a two-kilometer-wide hollow space.

Roughly spherical in shape, this internal lacuna—protected from external attack by approximately one and a half kilometers of nickel-iron in every direction—now supported a permanent crew of upwards of sixty civilian technical specialists, Starfleet officers, and MACO personnel, all living and working in a honeycomb of observation facilities, work areas, and residential space. From its inception during the first year of the Earth-Romulan War, Earth Outpost 1, along with the nearby Earth Outpost 2, had been dedicated to keeping a vigilant eye on the Romulan fleet.

Now, in the war's long-overdue aftermath, Outpost 1 still functioned like a well-oiled machine, and Commander Richard C. Stiles, the outpost's Starfleet CO, wouldn't have had it any other way.

Especially today, when the prospect of conducting regular daily business had to overcome a new and significant challenge: the arrival of the Vulcan *Diplomatic Vessel Maymora* and the pair of VIP guests she was carrying.

After delegating his responsibilities for the rest of the afternoon to key members of his senior staff, Stiles returned to his quarters to change out of his rumpled blue duty jumpsuit and into his meticulously pressed dress uniform.

He was still adjusting his tie minutes after the maglev had deposited him at the docking bay built into the asteroid's surface. He continued fiddling with it nervously as he waited for the indicator light on the airlock door to turn from red to green. After a seeming eternity, the hatchway rolled open with a pneumatic hiss, and a man and a woman emerged onto the maglev platform a moment later. A pair of civilian-garbed bodyguards, a human female and a Vulcan male, stood discreetly behind them.

Stiles's mouth fell open, and he had to make a conscious effort to close it again. Before this moment, he hadn't realized just how much "I" the term "VIP" was capable of carrying.

Though apparently quite young for one who wielded so much influence, the woman was dour faced, slight of stature, and wore a loose, flowing robe that brought to mind images of abstemious monks and dawn prayers. She raised her right hand in a split-fingered gesture of greeting as distinctive as the delicate upward taper of her ears, which her long, dark hair nearly concealed from view.

"Administrator T'Pau of the Confederacy of Vulcan," she said. "We come to serve."

The man beside her wore a blue standard-duty Starfleet jumpsuit with captain's bars on the collar, and stood a full head taller than the woman. There was no mistaking his identity as he smiled and extended his right hand. Numb with surprise, Stiles took Archer's hand, gripped it firmly, and shook.

"Welcome to Earth Outpost I, Commodore Archer," he said. "Commander Richard Stiles."

Archer made a face. "'Captain' will do, Commander. I'm not in command of fleets these days. Hell, since *Enterprise* was mothballed, I haven't put even a single sheet to the wind. So instead of 'Commodore Archer,' try to think of me as a celebrity hitchhiker who's just dropped in for a quick autograph signing."

Stiles chuckled at Archer's description of the purpose for his visit to Earth Outpost I. Flip though it was, it was accurate enough. Once Stiles conducted Archer to the subspace transceiver room in his office suite, the captain's participation in the formal signing of the Neutral Zone Treaty between Earth and the Romulan Star Empire would consist of little more than a biometric identity confirmation, an electronic endorsement of the treaty's complex and manifold provisions, and the pressing of a button marked SEND on a technician's console.

Stiles led the way to the maglev that would carry his guests and their chaperones down into the outpost's nickel-iron bowels.

That ride, Stiles realized, represented a once-in-a-lifetime opportunity to ask a few burning questions—and, perhaps, to get a better take on the unfolding of history than the first draft that media venues such as *Newstime* provided.

"I'm curious, Captain," Stiles said once everyone was settled and the maglev car began to move, its acceleration scarcely noticeable thanks to the new grav plating. "Why hold the formal treaty signing way out here in the sticks? It's all being transacted through subspace. You could have done it in San Francisco."

"True," Archer said, "but I've never visited Outpost I or 2 before. And San Francisco's full of reporters."

That made sense to Stiles. But he still had plenty of other questions. "Some of us out here on the edge were surprised that Starfleet and the Vulcan Defense Force didn't show any interest in pressing on into Romulan space," he said. "Captain, shouldn't we have taken the fight right to the Romulan homeworld itself?"

Archer nodded, a grimly thoughtful expression on his face. "You're not the first to bring that up. Some within Starfleet had a similar take on the war. Fortunately, cooler heads prevailed."

Stiles couldn't help but frown. "You don't think we'd have been better off beating 'em down a little more thoroughly than we did?"

"No."

Stiles was having trouble believing what he was hearing. "Well, at least we managed to hang on to the Eighty-three Leonis system. We didn't let 'em drag *that* onto their side of the Neutral Zone."

"True," Archer said. "And if we'd tried to go any farther than that we could have undone the entire treaty effort."

"I'm not sure I see how, Captain. We won. They lost. End of story."

Archer shook his head. "You have to consider the history of World War One, Commander—how the terms of the Treaty of Versailles crushed Germany after the Allies won the war. If we'd done the same thing to the Romulans, we might have just given their next generation a damned fine reason to make war on us again."

"Respectfully, sir, the Romulans aren't Germans," Stiles said, scowling. "They aren't even *human*."

T'Pau cleared her throat and raised an eyebrow in his direction.

Stiles reddened. "Sorry. I must have sounded just like one of those Terra Prime knuckle draggers. I didn't mean to offend you."

"I am incapable of being offended, Commander," T'Pau sniffed.

It's a good thing I don't know when to shut the hell up, Stiles thought. "What I meant was, nobody even knows what the Romulans look like, let alone how they think. As far as anybody knows, there's no reason to assume we can trust them to stick to any peace agreement."

Archer shrugged. "I'll grant that all of that is arguable, Commander, especially from your perspective—after all, it's your job to stand on the ramparts and keep a watch on whatever the Romulans might be up to from day to day. But even on Earth we know how aggressive and paranoid and territorial the Romulans are. We know we might have to cross swords with them again someday."

"Let's hope that day is a long way off," Stiles said.

"From your lips to the Great Bird's ears," Archer said. "But even if the treaty *does* hold for years, or even generations, there's no guarantee that it'll last forever. Still, less than a generation ago humans and Vulcans had misgivings about one another, just as we do today with the Romulans. Andorians and Tellarites could barely stand being in the same room with each other only a few *years* ago. Now, all four species are on the verge of formalizing a permanent multispecies partnership."

"I hope you're right about that, Captain. But I'll believe it when I see it."

Archer smiled in the manner of an indulgent parent. "*I* believe it, Commander. I've seen it already."

Stiles was about to ask Archer what he meant by that when he noticed that T'Pau seemed to be studying him closely, almost dissecting him with her sharp, dark gaze. He found it quite distracting.

"Please don't take this the wrong way, Administrator T'Pau," he said, "but why is Vulcan involved in this treaty signing at all? I mean, until the very end, the war was strictly between Earth and the Romulans."

To Stiles's relief, neither T'Pau nor Archer appeared to take offense at his blunt query. "Our involvement in the war may have been brief," she said, "but our participation in the consequent peace will be both intensive and open-ended. Vulcan, Earth, and all of our mutual allies will benefit from the labors of our most experienced diplomats, such as Foreign Minister Soval, Ambassador L'Nel, and Minister T'Maran."

"Forgive me, Administrator," Stiles said, "but if my experience out here on the ragged edge of Here There Be Dragons territory has taught me anything, it's that we're going to need a lot more than diplomacy to make the Romulans toe the line."

To his immense surprise, she said, "I agree. That is why the number of outposts like this one needs to be increased greatly."

"I wasn't aware that was in the cards," Stiles said. "I thought the end of the war might have been the prelude to the end of my job."

"I imagine it will be quite the opposite," T'Pau said. "Vulcan will be instrumental in expediting the process of building more Earth outposts, which will enjoy the support of the bulk of the Vulcan Defense Force fleet. Meanwhile, Earth and Alpha Centauri will continue to provide most of the required personnel."

"This stuff is all in the back of the treaty, Commander," Archer said, leaning toward Stiles as he stage whispered from behind a raised hand. "Next time, give it a read before you criticize."

Stiles's face flushed red with embarrassment. "Of course, sir. You're quite right. I should have familiarized—"

Archer interrupted, chuckling. "The document has about a thousand pages, Commander. Relax."

The maglev reached its destination, another platform

that was essentially identical to the one at the asteroid's surface. The walk from there to Stiles's office took only minutes.

As he stood before the computer-festooned desk that had been specially set up to convey Captain Archer's electronic signature to his mysterious counterpart deep inside Romulan space, Stiles turned toward T'Pau to ask a final, nagging question.

"Administrator, you mentioned something about supporting our new Earth outposts with most of the Vulcan fleet."

"I did," she said.

"Don't you worry . . . Let me rephrase that. Aren't you concerned that the Romulans might panic and attack if they see that kind of military buildup just outside the Neutral Zone? I mean, they'll no doubt be watching *us* at least as closely as we'll be watching *them.*"

"Indeed they will," said Vulcan's highest official. "And they should be reassured by it."

"I don't understand," Stiles said, blinking.

"Because they will witness with their own eyes Vulcan's commitment to interstellar peace. The new Earth outposts, you see, are to be constructed on asteroids similar to this one. But this new construction will incorporate the hulls and power-generation systems of many of Vulcan's most potent military vessels."

"What?" Stiles exclaimed, horrified.

Archer, who had just finished having his retina scanned, turned away from the desk so that he faced both Stiles and T'Pau.

"When it comes to peace, Commander, the Vulcans aren't just talking the talk," said Archer. "But they know better than most that the work of maintaining peace can be a lot harder than making war." With that, Archer turned back toward the desk.

I hope to hell the Romulans believe in this treaty as much as Archer does, Stiles thought, his chest filled nearly to bursting with both exhilaration and fear.

As only Stiles, T'Pau, and the two bodyguards looked on, Jonathan B. Archer pressed the button that transmitted the official imprimatur of United Earth's highest officials and brought humanity's bloodiest war since the Xindi crisis to its formal conclusion.

At least for the moment.

PART IV
2161

THIRTY-FOUR

THE IMMENSITY of the enclosed auditorium gave Jonathan Archer a distinct sensation of déjà vu. He had seen this time and place before, or had at least glimpsed it, thanks to the machinations of the time traveler he had known only as Crewman Daniels.

A crowd of at least fifty thousand, a few of whom were the former crew of the mothballed *Starship Enterprise*, watched him from the galleries that towered over him in every direction. Seemingly light-years away from the audience, Archer stood on a red carpet that bisected a wide circular stage in a centuries-old former sports arena. The San Francisco Giants had once called this place home, long before professional baseball itself had passed into cultural oblivion. Here, during earlier centuries, the San Francisco 49ers had played football—the kind that had involved helmets, rudimentary body armor, and tackling. Nearly two centuries ago, the Beatles gave their last concert here, perhaps on the very spot where Archer now stood, just another tiny figure on a stage that he shared with dignitaries he considered far more notable than himself.

However, today's spectacle was much more than mere entertainment or a sporting event. The murmuring throng that had assembled here today had come to witness history.

Straightening his blue civilian blazer, Archer tried

to avoid looking at the crowd, its uppermost extent in particular. He knew that at this moment a younger, angrier version of himself was standing behind the railings alongside Daniels, looking out over today's proceedings. Daniels had begged him then to reconsider his decision to carry out a risky operation during the Xindi crisis. In those dark days, Archer's only priority had been preventing the Xindi from completing the weapon with which they planned to annihilate the entire planet Earth.

Archer would have gladly accepted death then if doing so could have accomplished his objective. But that eventuality wouldn't have allowed him to be here now, years later, playing his own small part in launching this nascent multicivilization partnership, this fledgling United Federation of Planets. The UFP's symbol, a white-on-blue star-map-and-laurel-leaf insignia, was emblazoned across the wall that overlooked the red-carpeted ramp that led to this very stage. Had he died trying to neutralize the Xindi threat, he would have missed this rare opportunity to stand behind the enormous boomerang-shaped table alongside the distinguished representatives of all five founding members of the new Federation.

Now that the last of the seemingly interminable round of speeches was finished, each of these luminaries took a turn approaching the table, upon which multiple actual paper copies of the Federation Charter lay, alongside large numbers of old-style pens and countless modern padds, each of the latter containing an electronic version of the printed document.

The United Earth contingent went first, signing the paper documents before thumbing a padd, beginning with Lydia Littlejohn, the recently elected UE president, and Prime Minister Nathan Samuels. Archer signed after Interior Minister Haroun al-Rashid, Environment Minister Thomas Vanderbilt, and Coalition of Planets Ambassador Sarahd had finished.

Archer moved awkwardly along the carpet, following

Sarahd, until the Earth contingent stood facing the crowd. The audience applauded, evidently aware that the work of Earth's representatives was done for the day.

The line of dignitaries that had yet to sign paused while the crowd settled down, then resumed shortly as Ambassador Jie Cong Li of Alpha Centauri III reached the table, followed by a couple of dozen others, including Special Representative Qaletaqu of the Martian Colonies, Vulcan's Administrator T'Pau, Foreign Minister Soval, Ambassador L'Nel, Peace Minister T'Maran, Ambassador Solkar, Tellar's Foreign Minister Gora bim Gral, Andoria's Foreign Minister Thoris, retired Imperial Guard General Shran, and Special Aenar Representative Jhamel.

Archer found the sight of Shran and Gral standing shoulder to shoulder inspiring yet somehow surreal. As the entire assemblage, Archer included, bowed as one before the cheering crowd, like the cast of a play making a curtain call, he thought, *We put on a pretty good show on opening night.*

I wonder how long it's going to run.

"I'd be shocked if the straw vote is anything other than unanimous on the issue," Samuels said afterward in the secure hospitality room, once he finally saw the chance to speak to T'Pau alone.

Samuels was even more surprised, however, by the administrator's reaction to the idea. "Thank you, Prime Minister. But no. Vulcan's first seat on the Federation Council must go to another."

Not altogether certain he had heard her correctly, Samuels very nearly spilled his champagne. "But you're the natural choice for the job. You're not only the woman who overthrew a corrupt regime on your homeworld, you're also the one who decided the outcome of the Romulan War."

She shook her head. "Only by abandoning the most fundamental teachings of Surak. I must rededicate myself to those teachings. Approach T'Maran instead."

"I don't know T'Maran," Samuels said. "Besides, she's even younger than *you* are. Inexperienced, I mean."

"After this war, Mister Prime Minister, few of us qualify as truly 'young' anymore. But youth and inexperience are not necessarily liabilities. Building the Federation may be a craft best suited for the young. Or you could pursue the alternative of offering the seat to Soval. Or to Solkar."

"There's no point in doing that," Samuels said, swirling what remained of his champagne in the bottom of the glass. "They've both already made it clear that they don't want to leave Vulcan's diplomatic service."

"Indeed," T'Pau said. Samuels couldn't tell whether the news about her colleagues surprised her or not. "Have you considered Minister Kuvak?"

"Bad idea, Administrator. I don't doubt that he's a fine leader—you trust him, after all—but he still carries baggage from the V'Las era. The Andorians and the Tellarites wouldn't be happy with him because of that."

"I will grant that the war may have aged me, Prime Minister, but I believe that T'Maran is older than I am. I have come to realize that my skill set is that of a revolutionary. It is ill suited to the task of governance. Which is why I'll be supporting Kuvak's candidacy for the office of administrator in Vulcan's next planetary plebiscite."

With that, Administrator T'Pau, the most powerful person on all of Vulcan, bid Samuels adieu and vanished from the cocktail party throng of dignitaries.

Samuels drained his champagne glass, found another on a nearby tray, and began searching the room for a Vulcan woman named T'Maran. It occurred to him then that he was on a quest for the future. And the future of this new Federation was bound to be fraught with surprises of all sorts.

I hope T'Maran can surprise me at least as much as T'Pau just did, he thought.

PART V
2186

EPILOGUE

Friday, August 11, 2186
Late in the Month of *T'Kuhati*, YS 8805
Outer ShiKahr, Vulcan

AFTER THE EXPRESSIONLESS hovercar driver handed the FNS credit chit back to her, Rachel McCullers stepped out onto the red flagstone walkway that ran along the front of the house. As the vehicle began to hum and then rose back into the salmon-and-peach sky, a hot breeze brought her the sweet-pungent scent of exotic fruit. Though the smell was decidedly alien, it was also unexpectedly pleasant.

Well, what did you expect? she asked herself. *Pools of fire and brimstone? The caldera of Mount Tarhana, the catacombs of Jia'anKahr City, the Vuldi Gorge fogs of the Lyr T'aya region, or the Fire Plains of Raal don't represent all of Vulcan, any more than Yosemite, the Atacama Desert in Chile, the Eyjafjallajökull volcano in Iceland, or the McMurdo Dry Valleys in Antarctica represent all of Earth.*

Hoping that the directions she'd been given were accurate, she walked up a gravel path that led toward the house's front door.

"Can I help you?" said a male voice that seemed to come from almost directly above her head. Rachel froze in her tracks, looking upward but failing to locate the source of the voice. All she saw were the tops of the tall trees—the Vulcan version of pines, from the look of them—that towered over the roof from behind the house.

"Hello?" she said.

The face, shoulders, and hands of a man appeared just

over the edge of the terra-cotta roof. He looked to be in his early sixties, had the weathered complexion of a man who had spent a good many of those years exposed to Vulcan's harsh elements, and was clad in a lightweight T-shirt and gardening gloves.

"Sorry," the man said with a disarming and decidedly non-Vulcan smile. "Didn't mean to make you jump like that."

"No problem," Rachel said. "I didn't mean to jump. My name is Rachel McCullers."

He grinned and held out his gloved hand, but pulled it back when it became apparent that he couldn't shake her hand from the roof's edge. "Hello, Rachel McCullers. I'm Michael Kenmore. But you can call me Mike. I tend the garden, trim the trees, and generally keep the orchard at bay for the lady of the house."

"Ambassador T'Pol?"

Kenmore nodded. "You know her?"

"Only by reputation," Rachel said with a small shake of her head. "But I'm hoping to get a little bit better acquainted. I'm a journalist from the Federation News Service. Since this year marks the twenty-fifth anniversary of the founding of the Federation, I've spent the past several months tracking down and interviewing all the surviving senior officers of the pre-Federation Starfleet's first warp-five-capable starship: *Enterprise* NX-01."

"You mean you've interviewed *almost* all the surviving senior officers, don't you?" Kenmore said.

Rachel nodded. "You're right. I shouldn't count my stories before they're filed. Ambassador T'Pol is the last holdout on my list of people I want to interview before Federation Day Twenty-Five."

"You're a very determined woman, Miz McCullers. Unless I've miscounted, Federation Day Twenty-Five is tomorrow."

"Your calendar is correct, Mister Kenmore. You should see the preparations they've been making at Times Square. I'm surprised that the Vulcans aren't making a bigger deal about this."

Kenmore laughed. "Determination, beauty, and a sense of humor, too. The Vulcans aren't known for putting on fireworks displays or throwing ticker-tape parades."

"I don't know about the rest of it, Mister Kenmore, but I will plead guilty to being determined. I figure that since I've already discussed tomorrow's milestone with Doctor Sato at her home on Tarsus IV, and even landed a face-to-face interview with President Archer on the same subject—right in the Nathan Samuels Room of the Palais de la Concorde, no less—then I ought to be able persuade a Vulcan diplomat to let down her hair and reminisce a little bit about the past and speculate about the future. I still have nearly a whole day left to complete the set."

"Are you sure about that?" Kenmore rested his chin on his hands as he lay on his stomach near the roof's edge. "You've left one name off of that list of yours, haven't you?"

Rachel frowned. "I don't think so. Unless you're one of those conspiracy nuts who believe that Commander Tucker faked his death, went underground to work for a clandestine spy bureau that nobody can find any trace of today, and won the Earth-Romulan War single-handed while operating behind enemy lines."

The man perched on the rooftop seemed impressed by her logic. "When you put it that way, I guess it all does sound pretty silly. Everybody knows that Tucker died in a scuffle with pirates, right before they signed the Federation Charter. Or maybe it was the Coalition Compact. I forget which one." He paused and shook his head as though trying to dispel his internal confusion. "Anyway, I guess we 'conspiracy nuts' are a dying breed these days. And it's just as well, I suppose."

Rachel's neck was beginning to stiffen from having to crane her neck back so far in order to carry on this conversation. "Mister Kenmore, do you think the ambassador might spare a few moments of her time?"

He shrugged. "There's only one way to find out, Miz McCullers. Knock on the door and ask. Good luck." With that, he dropped out of sight, presumably to return to his arboreal labors.

After rolling the kinks out of her neck and shoulders, Rachel continued following the pathway that led to the front door. She gently touched the chime switch on the door's keypad.

The door opened a few moments later, and a young woman who couldn't have been any older than nineteen or twenty appeared. She was clad in a white semiformfitting civilian suit, her dark, lustrous hair arranged in the bowl-shaped style that was so typical on Vulcan. And although she had a Vulcan's characteristic upswept eyebrows and pointed ears, there was something exotic about her—something that seemed to be *other* than Vulcan—that Rachel couldn't quite identify.

"May I help you?" the young woman said.

Resisting an ingrained impulse to extend her hand, Rachel kept her arms at her sides and said, "I certainly hope so. I'm Rachel McCullers of the Federation News Service."

The young woman's eyes narrowed in evident suspicion. "Then you must be here to speak with my mother."

Rachel finally placed the young woman's face, though she hadn't seen any up-to-date images of it for the past several years, at least. The girl had the same delicate patrician features as her mother.

"You must be T'Mir, the ambassador's oldest child," Rachel said.

"I am Ambassador T'Pol's *elder* offspring," said the young woman, making a pedantic show of correcting Rachel's admittedly sloppy usage.

Rachel made a mental note then and there to revise T'Mir's estimated age downward from "nineteen or twenty" to "snotty teenager."

Another voice, this one male, spoke up from inside the house. "Who's at the door, T'Mir?"

"No one you know, Lorian," T'Mir said as she met Rachel's gaze squarely, still yielding no ground at the open door.

That's got to be her younger brother, Rachel thought. *He'd have to be about sixteen now.* Then she saw Lorian walk into view.

The pair couldn't have looked more unalike. Her hair was straight and dark brown, her skin was olive, and she was dressed in white. His blond hair was tousled, his complexion was fair, and he was dressed in black. Both had pointed ears, but Lorian's eyebrows lacked the distinctive Vulcan angularity.

The boy reminded Rachel rather forcefully of the conspiracy theories that Kenmore had broached. For many years she had made a second career out of lancing such cultural carbuncles and had often debunked the tale in which Charles Tucker not only survived his fatal encounter with the pirates but had also had secretly moved to Vulcan afterward to marry T'Pol. Today, only that particular conspiracy's few surviving true believers remained convinced that both of T'Pol's children were the hybrid products of this apocryphal union, rather than the result of the ambassador's eventual reconciliation with a former husband named Koss, years after Commander Tucker's death.

"Did you make an appointment to see my mother, Miz McCullers?" T'Mir asked as her brother vanished, evidently as easily bored as any human teenager.

Rachel shook her head. "No, but not for any lack of trying. I was passing through, so I thought I'd drop in to ask the ambassador if she wouldn't mind briefly sharing her reflections about the past and the future on the eve of such an auspicious occasion."

"Auspicious," T'Mir repeated. "A celebration of an arbitrary number of revolutions of a planet sixteen light-years away from here. A milestone that was calculated using a calendar that in no way meshes with that of Vulcan."

Rachel flashed what she hoped was her most persuasive smile. "Exactly, yes. Federation Day Twenty-Five. My readers would like to know how the past quarter century has affected the ambassador and what she expects the next twenty-five Federation Standard Years to bring."

T'Mir turned away for a moment, as though consulting someone else within the house who was out of Rachel's line of sight. The ambassador, presumably.

When T'Mir once again faced Rachel, she said, "As it has always been, my mother has nothing to say." The girl started to close the half-open door. As she pushed it, however, the bottom of the door evidently struck her foot and bounced off, momentarily widening the aperture.

For an instant, Rachel got a view of the dining room. Ambassador T'Pol sat at a table, her posture almost regal as she dined on a bowl of Vulcan berries of some sort. Opposite her was Lorian, who was in the process of sitting down before a meal that Rachel couldn't identify.

Between mother and son sat the human male who had spoken to Rachel from the roof, seated at the head of the table as though he were a typical Vulcan pater familias.

Then the door slammed shut.

Long-debunked conspiracy theories swirled once again through Rachel's head. *Wouldn't it be great,* she thought, *if one of those crazy stories turned out to have been true all along?*

"Happy Federation Day, Ambassador," she said quietly to the closed door. "And to you, too, Commander Tucker."

ACKNOWLEDGMENTS

With his newest outing in the *Star Trek: Enterprise* line, the author must once again recognize the contributions of the legions of others who enriched the contents of these pages: Andy Mangels, who collaborated with me on three earlier *Enterprise* volumes, as well as on numerous other tomes; my editors past and present (Marco Palmieri, Margaret Clark, Jaime Costas, Emilia Pisani, and Ed Schlesinger), and John Van Citters at CBS Consumer Products, for their unflagging support and assistance; the kind and indulgent folks at Northeast Portland, Oregon's New Deal Café (née the Daily Market and Café), where much of this volume was written and revised; and the entire *Star Trek* internet community and all the tireless compilers of indispensable wikis, whose multitudinous and serried ranks defy enumeration here.

For providing unending supplies of continuity Easter eggs and/or inspiration, thanks are also due to my fellow Pocket Books *Star Trek* fiction writers, including, but not limited to: Diane Carey (whose novel *Battlestations!* contributed the Vulcan place names Jia'anKahr and Lyr T'aya); Keith R. A. DeCandido (for creating T'Maran of Vulcan, among many other things); Diane Duane and Peter Morwood (whose novel *The Romulan Way* introduced the Romulan forebear S'Task and the Romulan underworld location Areinnye); David R. George III; Jeffrey Lang; David Mack (whose *Vanguard* novel *Harbinger* gave me Ambassador L'Nel of Vulcan); S. D. Perry; Judith and Garfield Reeves-Stevens (who deserve special recognition for their work on many fine fourth-season episodes of *Star Trek: Enterprise*, from which arose the continuity that led to the events of this novel and its four predecessors); Susan Shwartz and Josepha Sherman (creators of the eminently quotable Romulan Commander Amarcan, whose *Axioms* were cited in *Vulcan's Heart* before they popped up here); Dayton Ward and Kevin Dilmore; Christopher L. Bennett (whose *U.S.S. Titan* novel *Orion's Hounds* introduced the term "cosmozoa" to the *Star Trek* literary universe); S. D. Perry (again) and Robert Simpson (whose story "Allegro Ouroboros in D Minor" in *The Lives of Dax* anthology debuted the *syn lara*, or "Trill piano"); Jeanne Kalogridis, aka J. M. Dillard (whose *Star Trek V: The Final Frontier* novelization set the standard for *katra* storage and debuted the ancient Vulcan warrior-goddess Akraana, whose name appears more than once in these pages); Anne Crispin, whose novel *Sarek* originated Vulcan's *lanka-gar* bird; Jean Lorrah (whose novel *The Vulcan Academy Murders* introduced the ancient Vulcan warrior-goddess T'Vet, who is still known on twenty-second-century Romulus); Michael Jan Friedman (whose serialized novel *Starfleet: Year One* introduced United Earth President Lydia Littlejohn); John Takis (for introducing Skon's future wife T'Rama in his short story "A Girl for Every Star" [*Strange New Worlds V*]); and Della Van Hise (whose 1985 novel *Killing Time* debuted the Romulan underworld deity Bettatan'ru).

Recognition should also go to John Winston Ono Lennon (1940–1980), whose song "Beautiful Boy (Darling Boy)" contained the line that inspired T'Pol's advice to Jonathan Archer in Chapter One; Dylan Thomas (1914–1953), whose poem "Do Not Go Gentle into That Good Night" helped keep Captain Archer's morale up during this novel's climactic battle; John A. Theisen, author of FASA's TOS role-playing game module, *The Starfleet Intelligence Manual: Agent's Orientation Sourcebook*; L. Ross Babcock III and John A. Theisen (again), authors of FASA's *The Romulan War* RPG module (both modules reference the Battle of Prantares); Tammy Moore, for suggesting the distinguished name *U.S.S. Cowpens* for one of Starfleet's ships of the line; C. S. Forester (1899–1966), whose 1962 novel *Hornblower and the "Hotspur"* inspired one of Archer's major wartime strategic directives; Kenneth Hite, Ross A. Isaacs, Evan Jamieson, Steven S. Long, Christian Moore, Ree Soesbee, Gareth Michael Skarka, John Snead, and John Wick, for creating the name of the Confederacy of Vulcan, the Vulcan place name Han-shir, and the namesake of my Romulan "Year of D'Era" calendar, in the Last Unicorn Games RPG module *The Way of Kolinahr*; Geoffrey Mandel, for his ever-useful *Star Trek Star Charts*, which kept me from getting lost in the galactic hinterlands on countless occasions; Michael and Denise Okuda, whose *Star Trek Encyclopedia: A Reference Guide to the Future* (1999 edition) remains indispensable even in this modern age of ubiquitous wikis; and Mike Burch of Expert Auto Repair, whose skillful maintenance of Andy Mangels's car earned him a billet as *Enterprise*'s current chief engineer.

Copious gratitude accrues as well to: writer-producer Mike Sussman, whose name inspired the Vulcan martial art known as *Suus Mahna* and who created the biographical information, seen peripherally in "In a Mirror, Darkly," that forever entangled the destinies of Hoshi Sato and her future husband, MACO Major Takashi Kimura; Eric A. Stillwell, whose name became attached to a fictional Starfleet captain in the *Enterprise* series finale, a tradition that continues in this volume; Original Series scenarist Dorothy (D. C.) Fontana, who created the Vulcan death-god Shariel that Trip mentioned in Chapter Twelve; the entire cast of

Star Trek: Enterprise, with special attention to Scott Bakula (for leaping into not one, but two, of science fiction's most compelling and conflicted heroic roles) as well as Connor Trinneer and Jolene Blalock, whose portrayal, respectively, of Charles Anthony "Trip" Tucker III and T'Pol created a classic portrait of truly star-crossed lovers; Gene Roddenberry (1921–1991), for originating the universe in which I get to spend so much time playing; all the readers and fans who have stuck with me throughout Trip's long, strange, um, trip; and lastly, though never leastly, my wife, Jenny, and our sons, James and William, for their long-suffering patience and unending inspiration.

ABOUT THE AUTHOR

Michael A. Martin's short fiction has appeared in *The Magazine of Fantasy & Science Fiction,* and he is the author of *Star Trek: Typhon Pact—Seize the Fire, Star Trek Online: The Needs of the Many,* and *Star Trek: Enterprise: The Romulan War—Beneath the Raptor's Wing.* He has also coauthored (with Andy Mangels) several *Star Trek* comics for Marvel and Wildstorm as well as numerous other works of *Star Trek* prose fiction, including: *Star Trek: Enterprise—Kobayashi Maru; Star Trek: Excelsior—Forged in Fire; Star Trek: Enterprise—The Good That Men Do;* the *USA Today* bestseller *Star Trek: Titan—Taking Wing; Star Trek: Titan—The Red King; Star Trek: Enterprise—Last Full Measure;* the Sy Fy Genre Award–winning *Star Trek: Worlds of Deep Space 9 Volume Two: Trill—Unjoined; Star Trek: The Lost Era 2298—The Sundered; Star Trek: Deep Space 9 Mission: Gamma Book Three—Cathedral; Star Trek: The Next Generation: Section 31—Rogue; Star Trek: Starfleet Corps of Engineers #30 and #31* ("Ishtar Rising" Books 1 and 2, re-presented in *Aftermath,* the eighth volume of the *Star Trek: S.C.E.* paperback series); stories in the *Star Trek: Prophecy and Change, Star Trek: Tales of the Dominion War,* and *Star Trek: Tales from the Captain's Table* anthologies; and three novels based on the *Roswell* television series. Other publishers of Martin's work include Atlas Editions (producers of the

Star Trek Universe subscription card series), Gareth Stevens, Grolier Books, Moonstone Books, the *Oregonian*, Sharpe Reference, Facts On File, *Star Trek* magazine, and Visible Ink Press. He lives with his wife, Jenny, and their sons, James and William, in Portland, Oregon.